RAIN
DAYS

R. E. BRADSHAW

Titles from R. E. Bradshaw Books

Rainey Bell Thriller Series:
The Rainey Season (2013)
"Rainey's Christmas Miracle" (2011) (Short Story-eBook)
Rainey Nights (2011) 24th Lambda Literary Awards Finalist
Rainey Days (2010)

The Adventures of Decky and Charlie Series:
Out on the Panhandle (2012)
Out on the Sound (2010)

Molly: House on Fire (2012)
25th Lambda Literary Awards Finalist

Before It Stains (2011)

Waking Up Gray (2011)

Sweet Carolina Girls (2010)

The Girl Back Home (2010)

RAINEY
DAYS

A Rainey Bell Thriller

R. E. Bradshaw

Published by
R. E. BRADSHAW BOOKS

USA

●R.E.B.BOOKS●

Rainey Days

R. E. Bradshaw

© 2010 & 2013 by R. E. Bradshaw. All Rights Reserved.

R. E. Bradshaw Books/Sept. 2010 – April 2013

ISBN-13: 978-0-9883520-7-0

Website and Blog: http://www.rebradshawbooks.com
Facebook: https://www.facebook.com/rebradshawbooks
Twitter @rebradshawbooks
For information contact rebradshawbooks@gmail.com

Acknowledgments

I sit here two years after this book was first published, thankful that readers gave a fledgling writer a chance. Thank you for your encouragement and pushing me to become a better writer.

As always, friends and family, thank you for your support. And Deb, I'm blessed to be able to spend all my rainy days with you.

REB

About the book…

Rainey Days is the first novel in the Rainey Bell Thriller Series. After its first publication in 2010, the second in the series followed, Rainey Nights, a 2011 Lambda Literary Award Finalist.

This is the second edition of Rainey Days. No major changes to the story were undertaken, but an editor did go through and clean it up a bit.

Special Agent Rainey Bell is on medical leave and has been for over a year, after a horrific attack left her scarred both inside and out. She drinks too much and hasn't had a good night's sleep in months. On a hung-over morning, in June, a request for help from an old friend plunges Rainey back into the world of stalkers, rapist, and serial killers. The next thirteen days will change Rainey's life forever, if she survives. On top of all that, the woman she is supposed to protect brings out feelings Rainey didn't know she had. Thrown together, by a bizarre series of events, they learn to depend on each other for survival.

REB

"There is neither happiness nor misery in the world; there is only the comparison of one state to another, nothing more. He who has felt the deepest grief is best able to experience supreme happiness. We must have felt what it is to die, that we may appreciate the enjoyments of life."

Alexandre Dumas

CHAPTER ONE

Rainey heard the key turning in the ancient lock, the bolt finally receding with the familiar clacking sound, after much key jangling. The old front door creaked open and closed again, reaching a higher pitch on the return. She heard the sound of the Open/Closed sign hanging in the front window, as it was flipped over and slapped against the glass. Small feet, in heels, clicked across the concrete slab floor. Rainey continued to lie face down on the old leather couch, her back turned to the new occupant of the room. Instead of rolling over, she took several deep breaths, taking in the scent of her father's cologne still lingering in the worn leather.

The aroma of fresh brewing coffee roused Rainey from her morning haze. She rolled over, blinking against the sunbeams streaming through the east windows, casting rays through the small dust particles dancing in front of her. She groped for the sunglasses she left on the coffee table in the wee hours of the morning. Once found, the black Ray Bans were hurriedly placed over the area where she was sure her eyes used to be, before the hot stinging coals, located there now, replaced them. Sitting up, she tried to focus her blood-shot green eyes on the small gray-haired woman standing by the coffee pot. That was her first mistake of the day. Once eye contact had been made, Rainey became a target.

"It seems the good Lord did not see fit to delay the sunrise today, so that means the office is open at its regular time," the older woman drawled. "Of course, if you had gone to sleep in your own bed, in that adorable cottage next door, this would not be a problem. But, since you chose to crash on the office couch in your clothes again, it appears you are here and ready to go to work."

Ernestine Womble had been behind the front desk of the office as long as Rainey could remember, and showed no signs of retiring anytime soon. Known affectionately as Ernie, she came to work for Rainey's father before Rainey even knew his name. At sixty-seven, Ernie had not lost a step or her looks. Her once free-flowing blond hair was now pulled back tightly into a gray bun, but her petite figure had never changed. She dressed that figure immaculately, rain or shine, and her makeup always appeared professionally done. Today, she was wearing her favorite lavender power-suit with the mood to match. Ernie was one of those women who just got better with age, even though her attitude was a little less than pleasant this morning.

Rainey only grunted in reply. Her vocal chords were not ready to go to work yet and her head felt like it would burst any minute. She slowly untwined her five-foot-ten-inch lanky body and stood on shaky legs. Standing may not have been the thing to do, because it added to the pounding in her head. She placed her hands on both sides of her skull, pressing hard against her chestnut waves in case the contents did decide to explode.

"Good Lord, child. Sit down before you fall down," Ernie said, placing a hand on Rainey's elbow and easing her back down on the couch. "I'll get you some coffee. You just sit there." Ernie's heels clicked across the floor while she muttered under her breath, "She's going to kill herself if this keeps up. She is a grown woman acting like a petulant child. If her daddy were alive, he'd straighten her out, no doubt about it."

Rainey heard Ernie's comments, as she was meant to. Ernie was not trying to conceal her disappointment. Rainey had to admit Ernie might have a point about self-destructive behavior, because at the moment, she felt as though she might die any second. Too much tequila and not enough sleep were taking their toll on her recently turned forty-year-old body. She felt her stomach roll over as Ernie approached with the coffee. Rainey was up from the couch and out the front door in a flash. She rounded the corner of the building before the contents of her stomach abruptly left her. She bent over, hands on her knees, retching, and then the dry heaves set in.

Rainey did not move when gentle hands pulled her hair back. She had not heard Ernie approach, but knew it must be her. She was startled when the deep voice spoke behind her.

"Go on, get it out. You'll feel better."

"Damn Mackie, you scared the shit out of me," Rainey said, standing and wiping her mouth with the back of her hand.

The extremely large, very dark, black man produced a handkerchief from the front pocket of his Hawaiian print shirt. Mackie had an immense collection of Hawaiian shirts that took the place of the ever-present black leather trench coat he wore in the cooler months. He handed the soft white cloth to Rainey, as he spoke, "I see you had another rough night. You got to get a handle on your demons, Rainey. You can't go on like this."

Rainey retched again then wiped her mouth with the handkerchief and stared up at the large man. She knew he understood demons. He had his own. Miles Cecil McKinney, or Mackie as his friends knew him, had served with her father in Vietnam. His demons came from deep in a far off jungle.

Mackie was a giant of a man. At six-feet-six-inches, he was built like a defensive end, which he had been for the NFL, before he got in a little trouble and had to join the Army. He made the mistake of sleeping with a white man's wife. He ended up in Special Forces, where he met Rainey's father and they became lifelong best friends. Mackie worked with her father until he died a little over a year ago. Her father left Mackie forty-nine percent of the business and he stayed on to help Rainey run the place, as her partner.

"I don't need a lecture right now, Mackie," Rainey said, as she walked past the big man and headed back into the office.

3

Mackie shook his head and followed Rainey. "You are as stubborn as your old man," he said, as he entered.

"Amen to that," Ernie called out from behind her desk.

"And I'd rather you two didn't gang up on me either," Rainey countered. "I need a Coke. Are there any cold ones in the fridge?"

"If you didn't use them all for mixers last night, there should be," Ernie replied.

Rainey did not bother to tell Ernie she did not chase tequila with Coke and went to the back room to find one, but she could still hear Mackie and Ernie talking.

"Mackie, you've got to help that girl. She can't go on like this. It's been getting worse lately," Ernie said, with real concern in her voice.

"I'll talk to her, but you know this is something she's got to deal with on her own," Mackie tried to whisper, but his deep voice carried anyway. "She's got to come to terms with all that's happened. It won't do any good to fuss at her."

"Come to terms with it," Rainey said to herself. She had been trying to do that for a year now and it only seemed to be getting worse. Most of the time, she could handle it, but when the nightmares came back recently, she had begun to spiral downward, as she had right after it happened. The drinking kept the dreams away, but left her in her current state, hung-over and dead tired.

Rainey leaned back on the refrigerator. She was downing her second Coke when she heard the front door open and close, cutting off the conversation in the other room. Ernie's chair scraped the floor as she stood up.

"Why Representative Wilson, what brings you to this part of the world?" Ernie was using her best Southern drawl, a sign that this was a "somebody."

"Good morning, all. It's just JW to the home folks. I was looking for Rainey. Is she around?"

Rainey stepped out of the back room to see JW Wilson, a high school friend who had become a State Representative, and was rumored to be moving up the political ladder at rocket speed.

4

JW was always good looking, but Rainey never thought he would grow into such a handsome man. He had the looks and the old money background to make it big. He seemed to be on his way, from what Rainey read in the papers.

"Well, JW Wilson, as I live and breathe," Rainey said, as she crossed to him with her hand extended in greeting. "It's been fifteen years, at least, since I last saw you."

"Rainey Day, you look as good as ever," JW said, as he shook her hand.

"Wow, nobody's called me that in years. It's good to see you." Rainey smiled, even though her head continued to pound.

"I spoke to your mother last week." JW continued, "She's the one who told me you were out of the FBI and had taken over your father's business."

"I've been back almost a year now," Rainey said, as she noticed Ernie and Mackie staring at them. "I'm sorry; let me introduce you to Ernestine Womble, our office manager and M. C. McKinney or Mackie, my partner and my father's oldest friend."

JW went into politician mode right away. Rainey observed him as he shook both of her office mates' hands vigorously, looking deep into their eyes as he spoke, "It's so nice to meet you both."

The true politician, like Bill Clinton, could always make you think you were the only one in the room. JW had studied at the feet of the masters and was, from all accounts, a very good student. Rainey could see how he was able to woo his public. She smiled at him as he turned back to her.

"Rainey, is there somewhere we could talk privately?"

"Absolutely, let's step in here," Rainey said, leading JW to the adjoining room.

Rainey opened the wooden door that divided the rest of the building from the main office. The two old friends entered what Rainey called home base. In the far corner stood an old spindle-leg, wooden table that served as her desk. All of the furniture looked as old as the building itself. Rainey's computer, monitor, and printer occupied another smaller wooden table beside the

5

desk. In front of the desk were two worn leather chairs, matching the couch in the other room.

Rainey's office was on the backside of the building, facing the lake. All along the waterfront wall were large, screened-in windows with wooden shutters propped open to reveal a boat dock and canal that led out to Jordan Lake. Along the opposite wall were wooden shelves, painted an antique pale green, and a short, stainless steel topped counter. The counter had been a holdover from when the building was a bait shop and small grocery. On the shelves, Rainey had placed pictures of her father; some in combat uniforms from his war days, but mostly pictures of Rainey and her father throughout the years, fishing or visiting some far off place.

Her father's combat medals and the triangle shaped case containing his burial flag hung prominently in the center of the wall, over a walnut stained wooden box containing his ashes. Rainey liked to shake the box, to hear the small pieces of shrapnel that still remained in his body from a long ago war. When she did, she heard his voice telling her the old war stories of how each scar made its mark. On the wall, to the right of the door they had entered, hung two dry erase boards with pictures of fugitives taped above their information, hand-written underneath in various colors.

JW looked around the office, stopping to stare at the boards containing the fugitives' pictures. He turned to Rainey after a few minutes and she offered him one of the old leather chairs.

"Have a seat," she said, rounding the counter and digging into the old cooler that remained from the bait shop. "Can I offer you a Coke or coffee?"

"Coke's fine," JW said, perching on the edge of the old leather chair. "I was sorry to hear about your father's murder. Billy Bell was a great man."

"Yes, he was," Rainey answered quietly.

"I'm glad they caught the guy. I understand you had a hand in that."

"No, that was all Mackie. He's very good at hunting people down and he was extra motivated, because he loved my father,"

Rainey said, finally retrieving the Cokes and wiping the cans off with a towel.

"So you've taken over your father's bail bondsman business. I guess bounty hunting isn't too far from what you did at the FBI."

"The training has been useful, I must admit." Rainey sat in the other chair and handed him his Coke. "When dad died, I was already thinking about leaving the bureau, so opportunity knocked and now I am the proprietor of Billy Bell's Bail and Bait. We don't sell much bait, but dad was an avid fisherman and always kept the bait box full, so the name stuck."

"It looks like business is booming," JW said, indicating the fugitive pictures.

"I thought life would slow down after leaving the Bureau, but we keep pretty busy, and I get to sleep in my own bed every night," Rainey answered, trying to remember the last time she actually slept in her bed. She took another swig of Coke. Her brain was starting to make a comeback from hung-over land. She began to wonder what would bring JW to her door after all these years.

"Now, what can I do for you?" Rainey asked. "I know you didn't come all the way out here for a social call."

JW shifted uncomfortably in his seat before he answered, "I'm in a delicate situation and I need someone I can trust to handle it."

Rainey laughed. "I guess if you can trust me not to go to the media about some of the crazy, and might I add illegal, things we did in high school, you can trust me with just about anything."

"That's why I came to you," JW said, laughing along with her. "You've kept my secrets all these years, you and a few others, I might add."

They laughed for a moment then JW turned serious. "I have been trying to deal with this on my own, but when your mother told me you were here and what you were doing, I thought it was a God send."

Rainey was intrigued. "I hope I can help."

"I do too," JW said, looking away at the water before he spoke again. "It's my wife. Someone is stalking her."

"Have you been to the police?" Rainey sat up taller in the chair, becoming more attentive.

"Yes, I went to the police when it first started. You know they can't do anything, until we know who it is and catch him doing something illegal. So far, he has only sent pictures and notes. I have copies with me, if you'd like to see them."

"Yes, I would," Rainey said, reaching for the envelope JW took out of his inside jacket pocket. She began looking through the envelope, while JW continued his story.

"This all started six months ago, right after we had the accident and lost the baby."

Rainey looked up from the pictures. "I'm sorry for your loss." She said that so many times in the past fifteen years, it had become automatic.

JW took a deep breath and continued, "Thank you, we had been trying so long. We thought we were finally going to succeed. Anyway, a week after Katie came home from the hospital, that's my wife's name, Katie, we received the first picture. The dates are on the back," he indicated the pictures in Rainey's hands.

Rainey flipped the pictures over, examining the dates, and then studied the pictures again. "Your wife is very beautiful," she said, still looking at the woman in the photos. The pictures showed a blond woman involved in daily activities. Some were close ups, obviously taken with a telephoto lens, showing her big blue eyes and stunning smile. She was a natural beauty, thin and tanned. The perfect wife for a good-looking politician, Rainey surmised.

Rainey looked up from the pictures. "I agree. You do have a problem, one that usually doesn't go away on its own."

JW stood up and began to pace while he spoke, "That's what worries me. I tried to take steps to keep Katie safe. I hired a bodyguard to pick her up and take her wherever she needed to go. She hated it and refused to cooperate."

"Sounds like she doesn't want to let this guy interrupt her everyday life. Can she take care of herself?" Rainey asked.

"She thinks she can, but I'm not so sure. There's no telling what this guy will do," JW said, pacing even faster.

Rainey put the photos back in the envelope, as she said, "Well, as long as she's careful, she should be safe until the stalker makes his move and you can identify him. Then it's just a matter of following up with the court proceedings."

JW stopped pacing and stared down at her. "I want this guy caught, before he makes his move. I can't take the chance that he gets to her."

Rainey could see he was desperate. "I understand your anxiety, but I'm not sure what it is you want me to do."

JW sat down again. "Follow her, stalk her yourself. See who else is following her. Whatever it takes to find this guy."

Rainey stood up and crossed behind her desk. "JW, I'm not really set up to handle a full time surveillance job and my plate is a little full right now, but I can recommend a good—"

JW cut her off, "No, it has to be someone I can trust. This can't get out to the media."

Rainey was surprised. "Why? You've done nothing wrong."

"I'm a public figure. I am about to run for Senator. If the media gets wind of this, it will be front-page news. It could send the guy over the edge," JW gushed out.

"If you went to the police, there's already a public record," Rainey said. "Any good reporter could dig this up."

JW looked sheepish. "I didn't exactly go to the police. I had one of the State Troopers, at the capital, run the photos and envelopes for prints, but no prints were found, except mine. I can't go to the local police, because I don't want strangers poking around in our private lives, not during a Senate campaign."

Rainey sat down behind the desk. "So, no one is working this case?"

"No." JW paused before pleading, "I really need your help, Rainey."

"I'm a bounty hunter. You need a private investigator," Rainey explained.

9

JW countered, "Then I'll pay you a bounty for catching this guy. How about twenty thousand dollars plus expenses?"

She looked across the desk at her old friend. They were buddies long ago and kept each other's childhood secrets. She really wanted to help him, but something told her he was not being completely honest with her. Maybe it was the fact he was a politician that made her not trust him. Whatever it was, he did need help and his wife could be in danger. The money did not hurt either. Rainey sighed and picked up a pad and pencil, handing it across the desk to JW.

"Okay, I'll help you. I need you to write down some information."

JW visibly relaxed. He took the pad, prepared to write. "What do you need to know?"

Rainey went immediately into agent mode. "I need Katie's full name and your home address. Does she work?"

JW nodded his head yes.

Rainey continued, leaning back in her chair. "Work address and any other places she frequents. Also a description of her vehicle and tag number, names of her closest friends and associates, anything you think could be relevant to the investigation."

JW began to write vigorously, as Rainey went on, "I'll need to see the original photos and the envelopes they came in. Didn't you say there were notes? I didn't see them in the with the pictures."

JW answered without looking up, "They're at my office. I'll get them to you this afternoon."

"Will your wife be aware that I'm following her?" Rainey asked.

JW stopped writing and looked up. "I think it's best if she doesn't. She might act differently and tip him off."

"Okay, that's fine. She won't know I'm there," Rainey assured him. "Of course, you know I have to tell Ernie and Mackie what's going on, but since I trust them both with my life, you'll have to trust them too."

"Yes, of course. I'm sure you'll need help anyway. Katie is a very busy person," JW said, before going back to his writing.

Rainey stopped asking questions and busied herself behind the desk. She checked her calendar and made notes to give to Mackie later. They had a full board of skippers this week, which was going to mean hiring extra help. Over the years, her father and Mackie had put together a small posse of part-time bondsmen they used when the job called for more work forces. Mackie would definitely need to contact them, because Rainey was not going to be around to help. She knew from experience surveillance jobs can eat up many hours.

Although she still had her doubts about JW's full disclosure of the facts, Rainey was glad to have an investigation to occupy her thoughts. Maybe this would keep the dreams away. It had to be better than drinking herself into a stupor every night. That plan was not working out so well. JW's voice brought her out of her thoughts.

"I put down everything I could think of," he said, standing and placing the pencil and pad back on the desk.

Rainey stood and crossed the floor to stand in front of JW. She handed him one of her business cards. "If you think of anything else, just email it."

"Rainey, I can't tell you how much this means to me. I feel better already." JW sighed in relief. "There's one more thing, though. I want you to call me, not the police, if you identify the person. I'll know if he's dangerous or not."

"What if you don't know him?" Rainey asked, a little hesitantly.

"Then I'll leave it up to you as to what to do with the information," JW answered.

"Okay, I'll call you first," Rainey agreed then shook his hand and began leading him to the door.

"I'll get started this afternoon. Do you know where your wife will be around three o'clock?"

"Katie is an elementary school teacher. She leaves school about four every day. I wrote the address down for you," JW was saying, as they entered the main office.

Once through the threshold, Rainey noticed an immediate difference in JW's persona. He visibly changed into the smiling politician, turning to her and shaking her hand again.

"Thank you again for visiting with me. We have to stay in touch more often," JW said, more as a cover for their real conversation than an actual invitation to strike up their old friendship. Before he left, he made sure to speak to Ernie and Mackie, leaving cards with them, should they ever need to discuss legislation.

Rainey marveled at the transformation he made into Representative Wilson, from the anxious husband to whom she was just speaking. She had to wonder if that was all an act as well. After all, she knew a teenage boy all those years ago, not the grown man who just walked out the door. Something began to nag at her, but she set it aside. Twenty thousand dollars plus expenses was a lot of money. She hoped it would be easy money. As soon as that thought crossed her mind, she heard her father's words echo in her head, "Rainey, nothing worthwhile ever comes easy."

CHAPTER TWO

Rainey was still standing in the doorway to her office staring after JW, when she noticed both Mackie and Ernie glaring at her with anticipation. She knew they were dying to know what JW wanted to talk to her about. Instead of telling them, she prolonged their agony by slowly walking across the room, where she adjusted the Venetian blinds with the tobacco smoke stained cords hanging beside the windows. She was unable to get the bottom even, making it worse with every adjustment, until Ernie could take it no longer.

Ernie strode over and took the cords from Rainey's hands. "For Lord's sake, leave that alone," she said, quickly making the blinds even, with a practiced hand, "and tell us what JW Wilson wanted to talk to you about, in private no less."

Mackie scratched the top of his salt and pepper gray head with his paw of a hand. "He probably just wants a donation. I heard he was running for Senator. I hope you told him we're Democrats around here," he said.

Ernie finished with the blinds and headed back to her desk. Cutting off Rainey before she could speak, she said, "Well, if money is what he wants then he'll have to come back another month. Too many skips out right now. You two need to produce some cash flow, or I'll have to park those fancy rides of yours and get you mopeds."

Mackie brought his considerable frame to its full height and stated emphatically, "I will not be a party to giving money to that redneck, tea bagging, Republican Party!"

Ernie countered, "Nobody is getting paid, if you two don't catch some crooks."

Rainey put her hands up and stepped between them. The two combatants gave way and quieted. Rainey cleared her throat and said, "JW did not want money. In fact, he has a job for us with a payday of twenty thousand, plus expenses."

"I hear a big 'but' in there somewhere," Mackie said, retaking his seat on the couch.

Rainey nodded her head. "The 'but' is, I have to do a surveillance job for him, a private matter."

"We're a skip trace business. Why would he come to you?" Ernie said. Then without taking a breath, added, "Oh, I bet he wants his wife followed to see if she's messing around, before he starts his Senate campaign."

Rainey laughed at her, saying, "Ernie, that's exactly how rumors get started."

Ernie was offended. "Well, what is it then?"

Rainey smiled at the older woman, and then started toward her office, waving her hand for them to follow. "Come in to the office and I'll fill you in."

When they were comfortably seated, Rainey went over the details she knew about JW's wife's stalker, and what she had been asked to do. All parties agreed the money was good and it should not take too long for Rainey to spot the guy if he was following Katie Wilson's every move. After an hour of rearranging schedules and contacting the extra bondsmen, Mackie was sure he could handle a week or two without Rainey.

Rainey could work the skips during school hours, when Mrs. Wilson would be safely locked away in the elementary school where she worked. Then Rainey would stay on her tail until school the next morning. It would be a rough job with fast food and little sleep. The little sleep she could live with. No dreams if she was awake. However, she would definitely have to pack some healthy foods in a cooler, so she would not be tempted to live off coffee and cheeseburgers. She was not looking forward to the extra workouts if she did eat that crap.

"All right then, I guess that's it," Rainey said, standing and stretching until her hip bones showed just above her button fly jeans. She yawned and shook her head.

Mackie stood up with her, putting his fedora back on his head. "I'm going to run down a lead on that Johnson boy before meeting up with the guys tonight. I'll be on my cell, so call if you need anything."

Ernie hung back as Mackie left. Rainey could tell she wanted to say something and was searching for the right words. Finally, she spoke, "Rainey, isn't JW the boy you got in trouble with in high school, the one your mother and stepfather wanted you away from when you were sent here to live with your father?"

"Yes, he is," Rainey said, chuckling at the memory. "My mother found pot in my room and assumed it was JW who put me up to it, but that wasn't the reason I came to live with dad."

Ernie's brow curved up in a questioning look, before she said, "I distinctly remember your mother marching you in here, at age fourteen, demanding that your father take responsibility for you."

Rainey smiled at the memory of her audaciousness. "My mother brought me here, because I said, 'If she could get pregnant in high school, then run off and get married after graduation, my smoking pot was a minor offense in the scheme of things.' She didn't think it was very funny."

Ernie was flabbergasted. "Were you high when you spoke to Constance Herndon that way? I'm surprised you lived."

"It was touch and go for awhile, but she finally decided to punish me by removing me from the grasp of my dope smoking friends. And that's how I wound up living here full time," Rainey finished.

"I never could picture prim and proper Constance and your father together. Billy was too much of a free spirit for a tight ass like your mother. No offense," Ernie added.

"None taken," Rainey said. "Dad always said she was different back then, before my grandmother sunk the hooks in so deep she couldn't get away."

15

Ernie waved a hand over her head. "Don't get me started on that…" she paused, then whispered, "bitch," as if someone might overhear her use a dirty word.

"I always wondered what my life would have been like, if my grandmother hadn't swooped down on my parents with threats to take me, and my mother had not left with her. My dad might not have gone to Vietnam. They may never have divorced. Dad said he would love 'his Connie' until the day he died. I guess he did," Rainey said, looking at a faded, wrinkled picture, on the shelf, of her mom and dad holding her at age three months.

"I know that's true. He carried that picture with him for nearly forty years," Ernie said.

With both of them fighting back tears, the two women stood silently until the moment passed. Then Ernie started in again, "I'm worried about you. The dreams are back aren't they?"

Rainey looked past Ernie, to the water and beyond, not answering at first, and then quietly said, "Yes, they are back—but they will be gone again soon. This job should help take my mind off of it, anyway."

Ernie would not be put off that easily. "Don't you worry that it could be the opposite? I mean, this could bring it all back."

Rainey did not want to talk about it. She dismissed Ernie with, "Yes, it could, but this is far from a serial killer case, believe me."

Rainey began to move toward the door. She would not let Ernie trap her into talking about him. Ernie stepped closer and gently grabbed Rainey's arm.

"I'm sorry. I just worry, that's all," Ernie said, and then added, "You know how much I love you, don't you?"

Rainey turned and hugged the little woman. "Yes, and I love you, too. I'll be all right and I'll lay off the booze, if that makes you feel better."

Ernie smiled up at her. "That would help," she said, slapping Rainey's butt as she turned to go, "and eat something good for you, and wash your hair. You look like something sent for that didn't come, as my momma used to say."

Rainey called back over her shoulder, "Yes, mother."

Rainey left the old building and made her way over to the cottage, built on stilts by her father many years ago. It was styled after the gray-shingled beach cottages that lined the shores in Nags Head, where her parents had gone when they ran away, and where she had been born. She and her father took many trips to the beaches of the Outer Banks over the years. It was one of his favorite things to do. He told her tales of when he was a crewmember on a fishing boat out of Wanchese, before he went to war. He loved to tell how she laughed and giggled at the waves, the first time he put her toes in the ocean. He was gone now and the once warm, inviting cottage seemed less welcoming these days. She hated sleeping here alone, after all those years of his comforting snore from the other room.

Now, she unlocked the door into silence and darkness, followed immediately by the alarm warning her to press in the code within twenty seconds, before the police would be dispatched. Due to her circumstances, the alarm company had been instructed to start the police to the residence before making a call to verify who had entered the property. A coded question was to be asked and depending on her answer, the proper procedures would be followed. She even had a code she could punch in, if she was being forced to do it, which would alert the alarm company that she was in immediate danger. Rainey had to be careful, at least until he was identified and caught, or preferably dead, as far as Rainey was concerned. She punched in the code and the beeping stopped.

She dead bolted the door behind her and reset the alarm. Rainey was fanatical about locking up when she left home, but even more so when she was home alone. Rainey kept the blinds pulled tightly down, which kept the sunlight from reaching into the corners of the rooms. She hated the thought of someone watching her from outside her home. She had to turn on the lights, even in daytime, to maneuver around the small cottage, so full of knickknacks and military memorabilia. Her father said it was in memory of those we left behind, so people would always remember. In some ways, he never left Vietnam. His fallen comrades were like pieces of him he left scattered across the

17

jungle floor. She had to do something with all this stuff, but she could never throw it out. She needed to find a museum to take it.

She was thinking, she should ask Mackie where to take her father's treasures, as she undressed in the master bathroom. Still unable to make the larger bedroom her own, she had started using the bathroom. It was much bigger than hers and it had a clubbed-foot, extra deep tub to soak out sore muscles, after a run or hard bike ride. Today, she would only shower, because she needed to start on the research for the new case. She had locations to plot out and she would have to make sure her camera equipment was ready. Her mind raced with all she needed to accomplish this afternoon. She felt refreshed by the water and steam and exhilarated by the new challenge. Find this guy, make some quick cash, and maybe get some juice on the hill if JW got elected.

Her thoughts came to a screeching halt when she caught a glimpse of her torso while toweling off. Her eyes followed the scar from her navel up to her breast where it split into a Y, mimicking the incision she had seen so often in autopsy rooms. It had been a year since the attack and the scar had finally turned white and begun to fade, but it would always be clearly visible no matter how much cream she applied. Most of the time, she avoided mirrors if her shirt was off, but preoccupied, she had let her eyes wander after the shower.

"Don't give him the satisfaction," she said aloud, moving her eyes away from the scar and quickly putting on a white tee shirt to cover it.

Rainey dressed in jeans and added another tee shirt over the thin white one she always wore, this one emblazoned with Carolina Tar Heels across the front. She did not need to wear a bra and only did when the outfit dictated it, because the bra rubbed and irritated the scar. She pulled her thick wavy hair back into a ponytail and chose a blue pair of Chuck Taylors from her rainbow collection of canvas tennis shoes. Putting on her shoulder holster, Rainey checked her nine-millimeter Glock, before snapping it safely into place. She added a lightweight running jacket to hide the gun from view.

She fed Freddie Krueger, her cat, and checked that his electronic collar to his miniature dog door was securely on his neck, so he could terrorize the wildlife and retreat inside when he grew too tired or hot. "No dead birds in my bed, Fred," she said, as the large black cat with the stubby tail rubbed against her legs and followed her onto the porch. She reached back inside the door and turned the timer on for the outside lights, set the alarm and locked the door behind her. Freddie meowed once and headed out to hunt while Rainey went down the steps after him, clutching her laptop case.

Rainey walked over to her pride and joy, a 2010 solid black Dodge Charger, custom outfitted with dark, bullet resistant glass and run flat tires. She opened the door and the hot air rushed out. Even parked in the shade under the cottage, the Carolina summer heat and humidity could not be escaped. She sat down, cranked the car, and rolled down the windows, turning the air conditioning on full blast. She removed the laptop from its case, set it in the station that made it easily accessible to the driver, and plugged it into the twenty-amp power supply she had installed.

Once the air began to cool, she rolled up the windows, popped the trunk, and got out, closing the door behind her. She stepped around to the back of the car. In the trunk, she grabbed her camera bag, checked its contents, and set the bag on the ground. She then pulled up the rug and checked the custom, foam-lined, gun case she had Mackie weld into the bottom of the car. Taking out the Mossberg 590DA, nine shot, slide action shotgun, she checked the load and replaced it in the case. She checked the nine-millimeter Berretta and Sig Sauer pistols, considered adding the other holster, so she could carry two weapons, and decided it was not necessary. Returning the pistols to their places, she took out the Taser instead, shut the lid on the case, pulled the rug back over it, and closed the trunk. Rainey picked up the camera case and set it on the passenger seat as she climbed in behind the wheel. She opened the case and plugged the charger for the camera into the power supply. The Taser went in the center console.

The cool air from the vents was a blessing as she drove the few feet from her cottage to the front door of the old building that housed the business. It still had the look of an old grocery store from the outside, including a faded Mountain Dew hillbilly advertisement painted on the side facing the road. They had painted the building several times over the years, but only put a clear protective coat over the Dew sign, because her dad thought it was cool. Over the main door, the aluminum sign read "Billy's Bail and Bait," painted in the same green as appeared in the Dew sign around the corner. The logo was not responsible for much business, being so far off the beaten path as they were. Located off Highway Sixty-Four, about twenty miles west of Raleigh, North Carolina, a person had to know where they were going to find it. Most of their business in the Research Triangle Park area, which included Raleigh, Chapel Hill, and Durham, came from the reputation her father and Mackie garnered for being fair and efficient.

She parked the car, leaving it running and went inside. Ernie was just coming out of the back room when Rainey shut the door behind her. Ernie was carrying a small cooler and a thermos.

"I took the liberty of making a few chicken salad sandwiches for you," Ernie said, setting the cooler on the edge of her desk. "There's water, a container of celery and carrot sticks and some sliced, fresh watermelon from Henry's farm in the cooler, and hot coffee in the thermos."

"Ernie, that husband of yours grows the sweetest melons in the county. Please tell Henry thank you. And thank you," Rainey added, pecking the older woman on the cheek. "What would I do without you?"

Ernie was quick with her answer, "Likely starve, wind up a homeless wino on the streets, any number of things, and don't you forget it."

Rainey laughed, and then said, "You are probably right." She headed for her office, calling back over her shoulder, "I need to grab a folder, and then I'm going to check out some of the addresses for good stakeout spots."

Ernie followed her. "Make sure you keep your cell charged. Will you be online later?" Ernie asked.

"My cell is charged and yes, I will be online," Rainey said, adding, "Don't worry so much."

Ernie ignored Rainey and continued, "I'll check on you later. I'll bring some more food if you need it. When can I expect to see you again?"

Rainey took the pad with JW's information from her desk, pocketed her cellphone, and started back out of her office, answering Ernie as she walked. "I'll see you in the morning, but I'll call you this afternoon. JW is sending something over and I'll need you to scan it and email it to me." She stopped talking and looked at Ernie's concerned face. "Really, stop worrying so much, it's not like I haven't done this for a living for the last fifteen years. I was an FBI agent," she patted her side where her pistol hung from its holster, "and they even let me carry a gun."

"Your father never went after anyone alone," Ernie snapped back at Rainey's sarcasm.

Rainey stopped at Ernie's desk to retrieve the cooler and thermos, and then turned to Ernie. "I promise, if I see the guy, I will call the police. I will not try to apprehend him alone. Cross my heart." She felt her finger prick across the still sensitive scar on her breast as she crossed her heart, remembering the promise she made to JW not to call them.

Ernie patted her on the shoulder, saying, "That's all I'm asking. Be careful," she added.

"Always," Rainey said as she backed out the front door and headed for her car.

She heard Ernie say, "Call me," just before the office door closed behind her.

Rainey smiled as she placed the cooler and thermos on the floor behind the passenger seat of the car. She teased Ernie about worrying so much, but deep down she really appreciated someone caring about her. Ernie loved her like her own daughter, which made having Constance for a mother more bearable. She climbed in the driver's side and quickly had the OnStar directions to the first location programmed into her radio, Rogers Elementary School, Chapel Hill.

"Let's go see where Katie Wilson works, shall we," Rainey said to no one.

She gunned the Charger into reverse, aimed it toward the road, and took off, letting her tires catch a little in the gravel. Just enough to have Ernie come out and wag her finger at Rainey, in the rearview mirror. Rainey laughed and mashed the throttle hard, roaring up the road and out of sight of the disapproving Ernie.

Rainey smiled. "God, I love my car."

CHAPTER THREE

Rainey ate one of the sandwiches on the way to the elementary school. She had not realized how hungry she was until the first bite and then she wolfed the remainder of the sandwich, as if it were her first meal in days. She drank two more bottles of water, trying to rehydrate from the alcohol last night. She had tracked a skip until one a.m. and then drank until she passed out just before dawn. The water caused the need for a restroom, so she pulled into a fast food restaurant where she used their facilities and bought a sweet tea. When she came out of the restaurant, there were five teenagers with gang tats and drooping pants checking out her ride.

The hoods started in on her the moment they saw her. The tallest stepped forward, taunting her with, "Bitch, you know that's my car, right?"

Rainey did not react at all. She learned years ago not to respond to the bravado these types of criminals used to intimidate would be prey. She simply smiled and unlocked the door with the remote entry on her key chain and sipped her tea through a straw. Rainey's non-reaction to his veiled threat upset the tall one.

He came closer, flapping his arms, saying, "What? What? You playin' me bitch?"

Rainey took the straw from her mouth, still smiling, as she stopped in front of the car. "I think you're mistaken. This appears to be my car. Do you have one just like it?"

Her calmness sent the group into belly laughs and they turned their taunts on the tall one. "Ooh, she dissin' you, man."

His fellow gangsters now egging him on, the tall one stepped an inch too close. Before he knew what was happening, Rainey's pistol was under his chin. She stepped into him and said quietly, "Nope, I really think you have the wrong car, don't you?"

The once angry gangster turned into the teenage boy that he was and answered her, dropping the "gangsta" persona, "Yes, ma'am, I believe I have the wrong car. Sorry to have bothered you."

Rainey returned the pistol to its holster, saying, "No problem. You have a nice day." With that, she got in the car and closed the door, locking herself inside. She could not hear what the others were saying to the young man as he walked back to the group. She could only see them laughing as the engine roared to life.

She rolled down the window and called to the boy, "Hey, come here a second."

The young man hesitated before walking cautiously back to the car window.

"What your name?" she asked.

He hesitated before answering, "Derrick."

Rainey reached out and stuck one of her bondsman cards in his hand, as she said, "Derrick, if you ever need this, don't hesitate to call." Then she drove away, knowing one day soon she would get a call from young Derrick, if he didn't find a new group of friends, or end up dead in some alley. At least she did not think he would be trying to steal another car tonight. She only hoped Derrick had not wet his pants. He would never hear the end of it from his friends.

Rainey turned off Old Oxford Road and onto Church Road just before noon. The school was just a little way down on the right. She located Katie Wilson's dark blue luxury sedan using the description and tag number JW gave her. Next door, she found an apartment complex with a parking lot facing the school.

She pulled into a shaded spot where she could clearly see Katie's car. She made a note on the pad to find out where Mrs. Wilson's classroom was located, so she could make sure the guy was not spying on her through the windows. Trees and shrubs surrounded the school, which provided Rainey great cover from which to watch, but also supplied the stalker with the same camouflage.

Rainey had four hours to kill before Mrs. Wilson would be leaving school. She decided to go by JW's home address. She was soon on her way to the exclusive Franklin-Rosemary Historic District, where the houses started at eight hundred thousand and were almost all built with old family money. JW Wilson belonged in "The District" with his family's millions from the meat packing business. Rainey did not need help from OnStar. She knew these streets better than a computer, having roamed them for the first eighteen years of her life.

Up until she was ten years old, Rainey happily lived her life as Caroline Marie Herndon, a rich daughter from an affluent family, living in a mansion in the famous historic district of Chapel Hill, North Carolina. Ancient homes occupied by families who could trace their roots back to before this land became a country lined the streets. Her father was a prominent heart surgeon, Dr. John Herndon, and her mother, Constance Lee Herndon, was a former debutante and direct descendent of the Virginia Lees, which seemed to be important in the South. Little Caroline went to the best schools and enjoyed the life of the privileged, but just after her tenth birthday she learned the truth about her own roots.

While hunting costumes in the back of her mother's closet, so she and her friends could play dress up, she stumbled on an old shoebox. In it, she found a picture of her mother and a tall young man, at the beach. Her mother looked like a teenager and she was holding a baby. The young man had his arm around her mother, smiling at the camera.

With the picture, she found a birth certificate for a baby girl named Rainey Blue Bell. How odd, she had thought, that she and the girl named Rainey shared the same birthday. There was also a letter addressed to her mother, but her name was different. The name on the little white envelope with the red and blue trim was Connie Lee Bell. It was in an airmail envelope from Vietnam. Young Caroline read the letter.

Dear Connie,
I don't have much time to write. Things are crazy here. I got the papers from your mother's lawyers asking me to give up any rights to our daughter. I guess I can't fight her from over here and if you won't fight her at home, I don't have much choice. So, I'm signing them and I hope that's what you want. I probably won't make it out of here alive anyway. Please take care of my little girl. I will always love her and you. Say a prayer for me. Goodbye Connie and thanks for the memories.
Love, Billy

Caroline read the letter over and over, trying to make sense of it all. She looked at the picture of the man, staring into green eyes that exactly mirrored her own. His wavy hair was the same ruddy chestnut color that thickly covered her head. Both John and Constance Herndon were blondes. She was a smart ten-year-old and soon she knew what it all meant. She tore down the stairs and accosted her mother and grandmother, evidence in hand.

She screamed, "Why did you make my father give me away?"

What followed was a night of tears and explanations. Her mother ran away at seventeen with William "Billy" Bell, her high school sweetheart. Connie was pregnant and afraid of what her mother, Martha Lee, would do. She hated Billy. He was not up to Martha's social standards, the son of hard working farmers from the county. Connie hid the pregnancy. She was having a small baby so it was easy at first, but by the end of the school year, she was having trouble hiding the round belly and weight gain. So, the day after graduation they got married and escaped to the Outer Banks. Billy became a fisherman to support his new wife and baby. Rainey was born in late June, just before Connie's mother found them.

Martha Lee was a very rich and powerful woman, who got what she wanted, and what she wanted was Billy out of their lives. She kidnapped Connie and the baby. She had rape charges filed against Billy, threatening that her good ol' boy network would hang him out to dry, if he did not disappear. Billy joined the army and shipped out, but that was not enough for Martha.

Martha had the marriage annulled, through some miracle, and had her lawyers demand Billy give up his rights as a father. She insisted on changing the baby's name, "Because civilized people have Christian names." Rainey Blue Bell became Caroline Marie, and her grandmother swore to excommunicate anyone who ever spoke her original name again. Shortly after receiving the letter from Billy, Connie gave in to her mother's wishes. She stopped being Connie and became Constance, a carbon copy of her mother. She married well to do Dr. John Herndon, who immediately adopted Caroline. Billy Bell was erased from their lives forever, or so they thought.

Little Caroline promptly demanded that she be called Rainey Blue Bell from that moment on. Despite threats of disownment from her grandmother, the new Rainey insisted on finding her father, which she did. When she found him living twenty minutes from her home, Billy told her how he had watched her grow up from a distance, since coming home from the war. He was fearful if he told her who he was, she would not want him to be her father, but she loved him fiercely from the first moment she saw him. Rainey immediately started spending time with Billy, finally coming to live with him at age fourteen, when her mother could no longer handle her. She still attended high school with her rich friends back in the city, but she never permanently lived at the big historic house in the District, ever again.

Her grandmother did not completely disown her, only because she was the lone surviving female heir, but the bulk of her estate was divided between Constance and her brother, with the remainder going to Rainey's two male cousins. The inheritance paid for Rainey's education at the University of Virginia, where she earned degrees in both Behavioral Science and Computer Forensics, which led to her recruitment by the FBI, and eventually to her dream job with the Behavioral Analysis Unit. She was a Special Agent in the unit for nine years when the bottom dropped out of her perfect world. She was technically still in the FBI, but officially, Rainey was on medical leave of an indeterminate duration. Now, coming full circle, she was back, prowling the old neighborhood, an intruder on her old turf.

She spotted the Wilson house set back from the street. A short rock and iron fence guarded the perimeter. A wrought iron gate opened onto a red brick walkway that curved up to the large white Gothic Revival home. The yard was abloom with bright red Crepe Myrtles and Pink Azaleas. Wild flowers, in multitudes of colors, were carefully groomed along the fence and in the small garden by the front door. The driveway cut into the lawn on the left side of the lot and disappeared around the corner of the house. Tall boxwood shrubs prevented viewing the back yard. They were also a perfect place to watch someone and not be seen. Rainey was sure at least one of the pictures she had received from JW, the one of Katie getting out of her car, had been taken from those very shrubs.

She pulled into the driveway, but did not follow it around the house. She made another note on the pad to ask if the Wilson's had an outdoor dog. If they did not, she would recommend they get a big one, with a loud, intimidating bark. That was usually enough to scare off all but the most serious kinds of criminals. The serious criminals knew how to get around the dog, the alarm, and most any other deterrents, because they were patient. Patient and cunning suspects were the most dangerous. They waited, planned, and struck at the optimum time of their choosing. She hoped the guy tracking JW's wife was not one of them, as she backed out of the driveway.

The next address was a Literacy Center near downtown Durham. JW noted that Katie spent most of her evenings at the Center, teaching reading. Rainey could not believe JW let his wife go alone to the run down area of Durham, where the Literacy Center was located. It took her about twenty minutes to get there from JW's house. When she pulled into the parking lot of the strip mall, she found the Center occupying an old furniture store on the end.

Trash flew around the parking lot. The street lamps all appeared to have been shot out. Teenagers and old men hung out in front of the few open stores. The liquor store on the other end of the strip seemed to have the most loiterers. The place gave Rainey the creeps, and she was armed. She had a newfound respect for any woman who would venture down here at night, alone. Katie Wilson must be a saint, risking her life in a place like this to help other people learn to read. Rainey made another note; this one to ask that JW make sure Katie carried mace with her at all times, especially when she came to the Literacy Center.

There were a few more addresses on her list. Mostly where Katie shopped for groceries, the doctors' offices they went to, the malls and stores she liked to visit, and JW's office in Raleigh. She checked the time on the car dashboard and decided she would visit some of them tomorrow while Mrs. Wilson led her minions in their pursuit of knowledge. Right now, she thought she should head back to the school and get a parking place before the parents descended on the area, blocking every outlet.

She arrived at the school just before the onslaught of over protective, frenzied, yuppie moms. Rainey watched as children poured out of every exit in her view. They were all dressed in the school uniform of white polo or short-sleeved, button-up shirts and blue or khaki shorts and skirts. She watched them scamper across the grass until a blond teacher caught her eye. It was Mrs. Wilson waving goodbye and granting last minute hugs to students. Rainey was not sure what grade she taught, but judging by the variety of the students' ages, Mrs. Wilson was beloved by all.

Katie Wilson looked as fresh as she would have when the morning bell rang. She was much more striking in person than the photographs Rainey had seen. Katie's light ash-blonde hair glistened with sun-bleached highlights of almost white. She was tanned, but not unnaturally so. She wore a simple cotton dress that was patterned after the bib overalls train engineers used to wear, gathered at the waist, with a white tank top underneath.

Rainey was sure the designer had Katie in mind when it was created. It hung on her body in just the right way, accenting her long, thinly muscular arms and legs. It was a conservative dress, but on Katie, the simple seemed to match her natural beauty, making conservative sexy in a way Rainey had never thought of.

Rainey watched as Katie reentered the school and then called Ernie at the office. A package containing the original notes and pictures had been delivered from JW's office. Rainey asked Ernie to scan the contents and email it to her, and then to lock the package in the office safe. After hanging up with Ernie, giving her time to scan the documents, Rainey used the opportunity to check the horizon for anything unusual. Nothing and no one stood out. After enough time had passed, she checked her email and read the notes from the stalker.

The notes appeared to have all been typed on regular computer paper, just a single line across the middle of the page. Someone had hand-written dates in the top right corner of each note. The notes began in late January, arriving once a month after that. The language was not outwardly threatening, just creepy, at first glance. The January note simply said, "Do you realize how lucky you are?" A note like this would have probably been dismissed and thrown away had it not accompanied a picture of Katie lying in a hospital bed. JW had mentioned an accident and losing a child. Obviously, the person who took the picture was in the room with her. If JW was not behind the camera, Rainey could see why this correspondence drew his attention.

The note dated February twenty-second asked, "Do you believe in fate?" The picture with this one was of Katie inside the Literacy Center, leaning over a young Hispanic boy, pointing at something on the page of the book in front of him. This time Rainey could tell the picture was taken through the front window of the Center at night, because the dust on the storefront glass distorted the image slightly. The picture in March showed Katie in what Rainey surmised must be the backyard of her home, judging by the familiar shrubs in the background. The attending note asked another question, "Should one laugh in the face of

30

providence?" This guy was warming up to something, but Rainey was not sure where he was going with the questioning.

The note from April was more alarming, because it indicated possible thoughts of action. The single line read, "Is a second chance worth taking?" This time, the picture was of Katie standing outside of her car with two bags of groceries perched precariously in one arm, while she fumbled with her keyless remote. The frustrated expression on Katie's face made Rainey laugh. She quickly looked at the next month's picture, which captured Katie alone on an isolated beach, her pants rolled up, carrying her tennis shoes in one hand and a bucket in the other. She appeared to be looking for shells, as the ocean wind whipped her light blue jacket out like a cape behind her. The note with this picture wanted to know, "Is it not a matter of fate rather than choice?"

Rainey was beginning to see a pattern in the wording of the notes. All of the questions contained similar words, such as luck, chance, destiny, or fate. The stalker believed something must be done. It was out of his control. Fate bound him, but to do what? The latest note was dated just two weeks ago, June twenty-fifth, which happened to be Rainey's birthday. The picture was unsettling in itself. Rainey must have overlooked it when she went through the envelope earlier. The angle of view suggested the person holding the camera was very close to a sleeping Katie, who was lying on a lounge chair, wearing a black one-piece bathing suit. An open book lay across her chest, her eyes covered by large dark sunglasses. She looked so vulnerable and absolutely stunning as she lay there, not suspecting that evil was so nearby.

Then Rainey read the last note. "Is it now the time when destiny is ours to hold?" A cold shiver crept up her spine. It was a primitive warning sign Rainey had grown to trust. This guy was probably going to make his move soon. JW was right to be concerned. The stalker might only be getting his nerve up to bring Katie flowers, or innocently introduce himself as an admirer, and simply disappear back into the woodwork. All this talk about fate and destiny indicated he felt he had been given a quest. Rainey knew he could not stop himself. He was driven to

31

complete the task. His psychosis would prevent him from veering off course. It was pushing him toward his goal, building pressure like a steam engine and soon it would blow.

Movement in the school parking lot broke her attention away from the computer screen. A woman opened the rear of her van, loading a heavy milk crate full of what looked like papers, the poor woman would probably have to grade tonight. As she shut the van's rear door, she turned to wave at someone coming out of the school. It was Katie, with a large purse hanging from her right shoulder and a canvas bag dangling from the other hand, also stuffed with papers. Mrs. Wilson appeared to have a long night ahead of her as well. Rainey cranked her car and prepared to trail Katie, moving slowly out of her observation spot toward the main road. Katie climbed into her car and was on the move in seconds. Rainey pulled out two cars behind her and the stalking of the stalker began.

CHAPTER FOUR

Rainey made mental notes of the vehicles around her as she followed the blue sedan through the late afternoon traffic. From the route Katie was taking, Rainey assumed that she was going home. Katie wound her way toward Franklin Street, through the throngs of students going to and from the university campus, which was located practically in the Wilson's backyard. There was always the possibility that one of those students was predisposed to stalking behavior, had seen Katie around her house, and formed an obsession. Rainey would need to check the taller buildings, on this side of campus, to see if Katie's house was viewable with a telephoto lens. The canopy of old growth trees made that unlikely, but the utility companies cut back growth at certain times of the year, opening holes where none had been before.

She was glancing up at the trees when her personal cellphone rang. She pressed the hands free button on the rearview mirror and answered, "Rainey Bell."

"Rainey?" It was Ernie. She always asked, as if it might not really be Rainey on the other end.

"Yes, Ernie, what's up?"

"How's it going?"

"Fine. I'm following Mrs. Wilson home right now," Rainey said, while stopping to allow a car to back out of a driveway in front of her. Since she knew where Katie was going, she decided to blend back into the traffic, to avoid being noticed. There were plenty of black Chargers on the road, but if one followed Katie everywhere, she would probably notice.

"That's why I called you. Mr. Wilson would like your private cellphone number. I told him I could patch him through, but he wanted to call direct," Ernie said, adding, "He's a little paranoid, don't you think?"

"Ernie, he's a politician. They're all paranoid," Rainey said, laughing into the phone.

"Well, can he have your number?" Ernie asked.

Rainey kept her personal cellphone number a secret from all but her most trusted associates. Her business card listed the office number and no address. She did not have a landline in the cottage. Ernie set the business line to ring through to Rainey's second cell, a business phone, when she left in the evenings. The business line had a permanent trap and trace put in place by the FBI, just in case the man who tried to kill her decided to call. Rainey wanted to be able to answer her private phone knowing it would not be him on the end of the line.

Rainey took other precautionary measures against that freak ever getting to her again. Besides the alarm systems and the fact that she was always armed, Rainey had installed GPS locaters in her cellphones that Ernie could track on the office computer. Her car was Lojacked. Someone always knew her location. If Rainey could help it, she would never again feel the absolute aloneness of knowing that no one knew where she was. Rainey really wanted an implantable GPS for humans and would be the first to buy one, if the technology reached the consumer outside of the military. Of course, the technology existed. It was just too expensive for the average person.

All the property she owned, including her car, was in the business name, William Bell Enterprises. All her credit cards and bank accounts ran through the business. Her Social Security number was listed under Caroline Marie Herndon, and only a handful of people knew her by that name, since she had not used it in thirty years. She moved to Charlottesville, Virginia when she was eighteen and had not lived in the Chapel Hill area, until moving back last July. She gave Quantico as a forwarding address when she left Virginia. Rainey rarely saw anyone she knew from the old days, since she mostly chased criminals, and did not travel in the golf club circuit anymore.

If this guy wanted to find her, he would. She was not naïve enough to think he was finished. Rainey only hoped he was caught doing something else, and was locked up or, better yet, dead. After her attack, he simply stopped killing or moved far away. The Bureau kept a watch out for crimes matching his particular proclivities, but so far, the man who almost took her life had gone to ground.

"Yes, go ahead and give him the number," Rainey said, although she felt uncomfortable doing it. "Make sure he understands he isn't to give that number to anyone else."

"Oh, I think he understands how private it is. I argued with him for fifteen minutes before I called you, but I'll explain it again, in plain language even a politician could understand," Ernie said sternly, gearing up for her next round with JW.

"Well, go easy on him. Don't use big words," Rainey said, teasing the older woman.

"Do you think he'll understand if I tell him Mackie will hunt him down, if that number gets out?"

Rainey appreciated Ernie's mother bear protectiveness. She smiled as she said, "Yeah, I think he'll get that. Thanks. I'll talk to you later."

"Okay, bye," Ernie said, just before the phone clicked off.

Rainey touched the hands free button, terminating the call, and watched as Katie's car turned into her driveway and disappeared around the house. At this time of day, there was a lot of foot traffic in the area. Frat houses, sorority houses, and rental properties popular with the university crowd were interspersed among the residences, making for a steady flow of people in and out of the neighborhood, until well into the evening. Rainey parked the car on the next street, deciding this would be a good time to explore on foot. No one would notice a woman with a camera taking pictures of the houses. It was a common occurrence on these picturesque streets.

The July heat had not released its grasp on the day. Even at five o'clock, it was eighty-eight degrees, but the weather on her laptop said it felt like ninety-four. The sweltering air hit her in the face, as if she opened a broiler instead of the car door. Deciding the jacket was just too hot, Rainey took it off and removed the shoulder holster. She took the Glock out of its holster and placed it in the side pocket of her camera bag. Her camera bag looked like a backpack, which would also allow her to blend in with the college crowd. The pad full of notes and a water bottle from the cooler went into the big zippered pocket. She put her personal cellphone back on her hip and dropped the business cell into the front of the bag. Finally ready, she stepped out on the brick walkway, and began her canvas of the block where JW and Katie Wilson lived, just as her phone rang.

"Rainey Bell," she answered.

"Did you get the package?" JW sounded breathless.

"Yes, and I have looked at the notes. I don't see anything really threatening in them, but I do believe he is ramping up to something," Rainey said into the phone, as she continued up the street.

"Yeah, that's kind of what I thought, too," JW said, breathing heavily through his words.

"Are you running a marathon?" Rainey asked, as the heavy breathing continued in her ear.

"No, I'm on the treadmill in my office. I have to exercise when I can," he gulped. "I'm on the last uphill section. Sorry about the heavy breathing, but I can't put you on speaker phone."

"I understand," Rainey replied. "I'm walking around your block. Katie just got home a few minutes ago."

JW stopped breathing so hard in her ear. He must be off the treadmill, she thought. She stopped and sat on the low rock wall that ran through the neighborhood. She put the backpack down beside her, removing the water bottle and taking a drink.

"Did you see anything today that worried you?" JW wanted to know.

"Nothing out of the ordinary. I do have a few questions," Rainey said, reaching for the pad in the backpack, where she had scribbled some notes earlier. "Do you have time to talk?"

"Sure. What do you need to know?" JW answered.

"I noticed your backyard is surrounded by those tall boxwoods. It's a great place for a perp to hide and take pictures. I was wondering, do you have an outside dog?" Rainey asked, and then crossed the question off the page.

"No, we don't. We're both so busy we opted for fish. They don't really mind our being gone from home," JW said.

"Well, if you're going to leave the boxwoods, and I'm sure the historic district organization would frown on their removal, you might consider getting a big dog, one with a loud bark," she said. Then she laughed a little, adding, "A black Lab makes a great family pet, and looks good on a political advertisement."

JW laughed, too. He said, "I'll take that into consideration."

"Okay, next," Rainey said, looking down the page. "Where is Katie's classroom located in the school?"

"She teaches first grade. Her room is on the front of the school. It's the first one on your left, when you go in."

Rainey made notes before asking, "So, her classroom windows face the parking lot, by the road, right?"

"Yes, that's correct," he answered.

"Okay. Does Katie carry mace or some kind of pepper spray?"

Rainey looked up, watching the cars and people, even as she was talking on the phone. It was her training. Be observant. Notice every detail. Remain in a state of constant vigilance. These things had been pounded into her at Quantico. The one time she forgot her training, she paid dearly.

"No, she's afraid one of the kids at school might get into it," JW answered.

"Well, I went to the Literacy Center and I'm recommending that she put some on her key chain and know how to use it. It's worth the risk, I think," Rainey said, trying not to scare him, but make the point anyway. "I can tell you what to buy, if you like."

"No, that's not necessary. I'll buy it and put it on her key chain myself," JW said, sounding forceful. "She'll just have to listen to me."

Rainey liked the image of big old JW being protective of his wife. He should be. Katie Wilson was stunning and charming. Rainey could tell that even from a distance. She guessed there was more than one man with his eye on Mrs. Wilson.

"Well, that's it so far." Rainey sighed. "I'll be around the house all night and follow her to work in the morning. I think she's safe at the school, so I'll pick her up again when she leaves work tomorrow afternoon."

"That sounds like a plan." He sounded relieved.

Rainey continued, "You have my private number. I don't usually give it out." She hesitated, and then blurted out, "You can give this number to Katie, in case she needs me in a hurry."

JW took a deep breath before saying, "I don't know Rainey. I thought we decided she shouldn't know about you."

"Just tell her I'm a friend she can call in an emergency. I can be there before the police. She doesn't have to know the particulars," Rainey assured him.

"So, she should call you instead of 911?" He sounded confused.

"No, she should put 911 on speed dial, if she hasn't already. I'm the backup, just in case," Rainey said, although she was thinking, "If she has a chance to call." She kept the thought to herself. Then she had another idea. "I'd like to give you a GPS chip to slip in her phone. I'll have her location at all times. If she gets in trouble, at least we'll know exactly where she is."

"That sounds like a good idea. I've always wanted to do that, just to be able to keep up with her." JW seemed a little too eager to track his wife.

Rainey quickly added, "The chip comes out when this is over."

"Yeah, I guess that would make me a stalker too, huh," he said, sheepishly.

Rainey was ready to move on with her surveillance, so she ended the call. "I guess that's it for now. Email me if you think of anything else. I'm online in the car."

"Okay, let me know if you find anything." He paused for a second, as if he wanted to say something important, but only added, "Be safe out there," before hanging up.

Rainey spent the next hour taking pictures of the vehicles parked in the area, careful to get tag numbers. She appeared to be snapping shots of the flowers blooming in the manicured lawns. With the powerful zoom lens on the digital camera, she was able to capture details from a great distance and then review them on the larger screen on her laptop. She always marveled at the things she missed at first glance, even though she took the picture.

Around six o'clock she headed back toward the car. Her stomach growled, as the smells of supper cooking in the South wafted through the trees. She stopped in front of JW's house and took a picture of the front lawn. She then took pictures going three hundred and sixty degrees from that vantage point. Rainey had just dropped the camera from her eye when she heard a voice behind her.

"May I ask what you are taking pictures of?"

It was not a demand, but a gentle inquiry, complete with Southern lilt. Rainey was shocked that she had been unaware of the woman, who somehow appeared on the other side of the wrought iron gate. It was Katie and she was glowing in the evening sun. Not only was Rainey surprised by her presence, she was taken aback by the sheer attractiveness of this woman. Katie had changed her clothes and was now wearing old gray shorts, rolled up at the waist, and a Tar Heel tank top. She must have been pulling weeds, because she was wearing gardening gloves and carrying a small spade. She had a little dirt on one cheek, which only made her more attractive.

Rainey smiled and put the camera away, before she answered, "It's such a wonderful street, and I love your wild flowers."

"Why, thank you," Katie said, extending her hand in greeting. "My name is Katie Wilson."

"I'm Caroline," Rainey replied, shaking her hand. "Caroline Lee."

Rainey lied, because she could not say her real name. It was too unusual, too easy to remember. Katie was not supposed to know Rainey was there. She removed her sunglasses from the top of her head, where she put them while she took pictures, and placed them over her eyes. She had to get out of there fast.

"It was nice to meet you, Katie," Rainey said, moving off.

"You too," Katie said. "Hope you got some nice shots."

Rainey looked back over her shoulder at the smiling Katie. "Thanks," was all she could manage to say.

Rainey berated herself all the way back to the car. How could she have been so stupid? She was shaken by the fact she did not hear Katie approach, and then she stammered like a nervous schoolgirl when Katie spoke to her. That was such an odd reaction, because Rainey was always in control in situations like that. She told herself it was because she let Katie get so close to finding out who she was and what she was doing. JW would not have been pleased. Rainey decided not to tell him about her little slip up.

Once in the car, she started it up and let the air conditioning blow on her face. She drank the rest of the water from her backpack, while collecting her thoughts. She drove around the block, finding a shady spot with a frontal view of the house. The tinted windows on the car made it nearly impossible for Rainey to be observed inside. At night, if she kept the laptop shut, she was all but invisible. She left the air running while she hooked the camera up to the laptop and downloaded the pictures. Usually the heat did not bother her so much, but she had to remember she was sweating out quite a lot of alcohol as well. It crossed her mind that she should stop drinking, but only for a second.

From Rainey's vantage point, she could see Katie occasionally, when she would stand, spade in hand, and then disappear again behind the Crepe Myrtles and Hydrangea bushes, in search of more weeds to pull. Rainey ate another sandwich and the watermelon from the container, while she watched the blond woman work in her garden. Rainey realized she had been staring at Katie for quite some time, when an alert tone sounded on her laptop. The woman was mesmerizing. Rainey was star struck and she had to shake it off. She could see right away, how someone could become obsessed with watching Katie Wilson.

The alert was for email, from Mackie. Everything was going fine on his end and he was just checking in with her. Rainey wrote back, telling him about her day and her plans to watch the Wilson house for the evening. She gave him the address, so he could stop by later if he wanted, but she knew he would be too busy picking up skippers tonight. Just after the first of the month was always a good time to hunt for a bail jumper. Momma would have the kitchen table full of food for her little baby criminal and maybe a little cash left over from her monthly check. Oh yeah, crooks love their mommas. She closed the email with, "I better let you go. It's almost suppertime in the hood." She knew he would read it right away, because his Escalade was tricked out with a built in laptop, and he was probably doing the same thing she was, sitting and watching.

It was true that they could instant message, text, or talk to each other on the phone, but none of those methods were as secure as the encrypted network she set up for their business. Her degree in Computer Forensics came in handy more than once in Rainey's line of work. She used it to secure her insulated life from outside intruders, to erase her existence. It allowed her to live apart from the world, venturing out only at the times and places of her choosing.

Rainey had chosen to be on this street, alone, at the coming of darkness. She removed the Glock from the camera bag and re-holstered it, sliding the leather straps back over her shoulders. She took the Taser out of the console, checked the charge again, and placed it on the passenger seat beside her. The message on the laptop screen said the pictures from the camera had been downloaded, so she removed the adaptor, and placed the camera back in the bag.

She took a small USB, night vision webcam out of the camera bag and hooked it up to the laptop. Snapping the camera into the holder already on the dashboard, Rainey opened a window on the

41

laptop screen and focused the camera on the scene in front of her. She pulled a second USB cable out of its hiding place next to the center consol. When she plugged it in, another window was called up, displaying the image from an identical webcam, permanently mounted in the rear window. It peered through a small square, cut out of the tint on the window, and had a wide-angle lens so Rainey's back was always covered.

Rainey settled into the seat and began reviewing the pictures she took earlier. She reached for the thermos of coffee and prepared for a long night of vigilance.

CHAPTER FIVE

The final rays of the sun slipped below the tree line and only then did the heat begin to relinquish its grip on the day. Katie Wilson had retreated into the house when JW's car pulled in the driveway. Rainey, knowing JW was in the house, took the opportunity to drive around the neighborhood with the webcams sending the images to the laptop. She would do this drive once an hour, throughout the night, recording each trip. Later she would compare the videos, looking for vehicles and people moving in the night.

Twice she had to drive over to Franklin Street to locate a restroom and get more coffee, but for the most part, Rainey remained in front of the Wilson house, watching. She sat in silence, windows rolled down just enough to catch the breeze and so she could listen to the sounds of the neighborhood. As the hours grew later, the streets around her quieted. Chapel Hill was a college town, so it never completely went to sleep, but the pace slowed and parts of the town, not occupied by bars or athletic venues, took on a hushed, studious mood. It was summer, which meant the student population had taken a significant dip. Rainey thought she could almost believe she was in a quaint little southern village, if she did not know the mighty Tar Heel basketball team resided right next door. People either loved them or hated them, but even non-basketball fans knew what that tar heeled foot represented.

You could not live in North Carolina and not know something about basketball. With Carolina, Duke, Wake Forest, and North Carolina State all within its boundaries, this state worshipped basketball, like they did football out in Oklahoma. Ask anybody where Michael Jordan played college ball. Rainey laughed at the old joke, "Who is the only person who could stop Michael Jordan from scoring?—Dean Smith." Dean Smith, the coach, the legend, and the man who built the Dean Dome. Rainey was a closet Tar Heel fan, but refused to attend the University under her mother's nose.

Rainey heard two girls approaching. She watched as they laughed and talked, passed right in front of her, and never once looked around, not aware of her presence. She wanted to get out of the car and scare them. She wanted to shake them both, telling them how stupid it was to walk out here, in the wee hours of the morning, without once checking to see who else might be there. She wanted to rip off her shirt and show them what happens when you do not pay attention. Instead, she peered into the darkness at who might be watching them, the silent guardian of this tiny block.

Rainey checked the cameras, stopped the recording, saved it to a file, and started another recording. This way she could review the earlier recordings while she waited in the car. She opened the file she just saved. Using the fast forward key, she scanned the video for any vehicles that drove by more frequently than others. She looked at the foot traffic for anyone repeatedly passing the Wilson house. From her position, the camera had a clear view of the front door and boxwood hedge on the right side of the property line. Even with the night vision, the tall shrubs cast dark shadows the camera could not penetrate. If this was her house, Rainey thought, those bushes would be down. It would not be pretty, but it would be so much safer.

Rainey fast-forwarded through five hours of video, stopping the playback to listen and look around every few minutes. By the time she finished, it was deep into the night. Rainey raised her eyes from the laptop and listened. The distant traffic sounds punctuated the summer insect cantata going on all around her.

She heard nothing unusual. Still, the hair began to prickle on her arms and down her neck. She did a quick three hundred and sixty degree check of her surroundings. She looked at the feeds from the webcams, nothing moving.

Rainey fought off the thoughts that it was her own paranoia again. Something was not right. She could feel it and she had learned to respect that primal instinct. She peered into the shadows cast by the boxwoods. There. Something was moving. She blinked her eyes and sat up, so her face was closer to the windshield. Her left hand automatically checked that the Glock was there and ready in its holster. Again, she saw the low crawling shadow creeping down the hedge. He was coming closer.

Rainey's left hand went to the door handle. She had disabled the interior light so the car would not glow when she opened the door. Her right hand took the keys out of the ignition and slowly dropped them into her front pocket. Gradually she opened the door and stood up. All the while, her eyes never left the shadow. She did not shut the door, but stepped around it, steadily moving toward her target. She removed the Glock from the holster and held it down at her side. If she went directly at him, she would have to cross under a streetlight.

Rainey decided to come up behind the moving mass. She walked down the street a few paces and then turned, crossing over to the Wilson's neighbor's yard, avoiding the direct light from the streetlamp. While she accomplished this, her eyes lost contact with the shadow. She crept closer to where she had last seen him. He was not there. Rainey looked down the boxwoods. The darkness swallowed her, as she inched her way down the shrub line. She told herself to take deep, slow breaths, but her breathing quickened with every step. She felt her scalp crawling and the chill bumps forming on her arms. She could almost smell him.

Rainey crouched down, listening. The only sound she heard was her own heart beating in her ears. She had to calm down. She took several deep breaths and listened again. She heard a faint sound, back by the street. There were footsteps coming closer, running down the brick sidewalk. He had not seen her. He was coming right at her. Her breathing quickened again as she moved, now using the shadows, inching closer to the sidewalk. She crouched again and waited for the right moment. When she could hear his heavy breathing, just steps from her hiding place, she sprang up, stepping onto the walkway in front of her prey.

"Jesus, God! You scared the shit out of me."

It was JW, dressed in sweats with the hood pulled up over his head. He was sweating profusely, as he grabbed his knees and tried to catch his breath.

"What the hell are you doing out here in the middle of the night?" Rainey snapped, the adrenaline coursing through her body, causing her hand to shake a little, as she re-holstered her pistol.

"I couldn't sleep," he said, followed by more heavy breathing. "I went for a run." He finally stood up, wiping the sweat from his brow with his sleeve. "Why did you jump out of the bushes like that? You could have killed me."

"I wouldn't have shot you," Rainey said, defensively.

"No, but I could have had a heart attack," JW shot back.

The adrenaline rush was subsiding. She tried to sound calmer. "I saw something moving by the hedge. I was checking it out and then you came running down the street. I thought you were him."

JW looked around. "Did you see a man?"

Rainey shook her head. "No, more of a shadow. I didn't get close enough to see clearly."

JW had finally gathered himself. "Rainey, you can't be jumping out of bushes brandishing a weapon. Suppose it had been a neighbor or some kid out for a run?"

"I didn't aim it at you," Rainey said, thinking no way was she going to be out here unarmed.

"Well, I'll give you that, but I don't want to draw attention to this thing, you know," JW said. "Can you try to be more subtle?"

Rainey laughed. "I'll just bring the Taser next time."

JW started backing away. "Just try not to kill anybody," he said, smiling. Then he waved and ran back to his house.

Rainey walked back to the car and got in. She was still on edge. She knew something or somebody had been out there. She stopped the video recording from the dash camera and rewound to the moment she left the car. She watched herself cross in front of the car and walk down the street. She stared at the dark place, where she had seen the movement earlier. Rainey's heart almost stopped when she saw the dark figure of a man rise up, watching her walk across the street, before running down the hedge line and out of view.

She stopped the video and rewound it to the spot where the darkness rose and took the shape of a man. He was dressed exactly as JW had been, in sweats and a hoodie. It was a good disguise for a stalker. If the police stopped him, he was just a guy out for a run. Again and again, Rainey watched the man watch her and then vanish. He had been so close and now she knew he had seen her. He knew someone was watching Katie. Maybe it would scare him off. Rainey did not think so. It was the way he watched her, coming after him, that let her know he liked the game.

For the remainder of the night and into the morning, Rainey was alert and focused. Even though she knew the guy probably would not come back that night, the way he had watched her kept her vigilant. At seven fifteen, Katie Wilson left her home and headed back to work. She drove east on Franklin and then turned onto Estes drive, stopping for gas and coffee, and then straight to school. No one followed Katie, as far as Rainey could tell. Once Mrs. Wilson was safely inside her classroom, surrounded by her eager minions, Rainey headed home for some much needed rest.

She drove under the cottage, just as Ernie was pulling into her parking place. It was Ernie's, because she painted a sign that made it so and nailed it to the building, right in front of her spot. Ernie waved to Rainey, who was crossing the lawn to the office, then unlocked the door and went in. Rainey watched her through the windows, flipping over the open/closed sign, and then going to her desk. She set down her purse and went straight for the coffee maker. Such a creature of habit, Rainey thought.

She walked into the office, headed straight for the couch, and flopped down on it with a loud sigh. "Damn, I'm tired."

Ernie looked up from her coffee making. "You should go get some sleep."

"I will." Rainey brushed the suggestion off. "Hey, is there any more watermelon?"

"I think so. Let me look," Ernie said, finishing the coffee and heading to the back room.

Rainey laid her head back and closed her eyes. She listened to Ernie's heels clicking on the concrete as she walked around in back. She opened her eyes again when the clicking grew louder, as Ernie reentered the room. She was carrying a bowl piled high with cubes of watermelon.

"Will this do you?" Ernie said with a smile, handing the bowl and a fork to Rainey.

Ernie sat down on the couch beside Rainey. She did not say anything. She just looked Rainey up and down and shook her head. Rainey ate the watermelon, careful to keep her mouth full, because she really did not want to talk to Ernie right now. Rainey did not want to tell her how she had discovered the man in the bushes and how he had watched her. She did not want Ernie to worry any more than she already did.

Ernie bore her silence as long as she could, then stood, and walked back to the coffee pot. While she made a cup of coffee, she spoke quietly to Rainey, not looking at her.

"Rainey, you need some real rest and a few good meals in you. I am not nagging. I am truly worried about you –"

The bowl in Rainey's hand grew heavy. The words Ernie was saying became a distant murmur. She leaned her head back and closed her eyes. Her ears were ringing from too much caffeine. She chewed the mouthful of watermelon slowly, letting the cool juice bathe the inside of her mouth, before swallowing. She tried to lift her head, but gave up easily and relaxed into the couch, the bowl perched precariously on one leg.

In the last moment, before she slipped off to sleep, she felt Ernie's gentle hands taking the bowl away. Her eyelids fluttered and she briefly glimpsed Ernie standing over her with a worried smile on her face. Rainey could fight it no longer, dreamland awaited.

CHAPTER SIX

Rainey's eyes blinked open. A searing pain was telling her to wake up and move her neck. She slowly brought her head up from the back of the couch and then rolled it from side to side, trying to relax her neck muscles. The office was quiet. She did not see Ernie and looked out front to see that her car was still there. Rainey thought she must have been really out of it, because Mackie's Escalade was in the parking lot. She could not believe she had slept through him coming in. They must be outside, because she didn't hear them inside.

Rainey stood and stretched out the kinks from sleeping sitting up on the old couch. She looked down at the coffee table and saw a yellow sticky note with a message from Ernie.

"Rainey, call this number," was all it said, and listed a number Rainey did not recognize.

Rainey used the business line to call the number, not wanting her private number on any callback list. She dialed and waited for the phone to ring on the other end. Her attention was drawn to her closed office door, which was never closed unless she had a client in there. A ring from inside her office followed the ringing in the receiver next to her ear. As soon as the second ring came through the phone in her hand, another ring echoed from behind the closed door.

Rainey slowly set the receiver down on the desk, letting it continue to ring. She reached for her Glock, but the holster was empty. She must have taken it out in the car. She had been distracted and tired on the way home. She looked out the window toward the Charger parked under the cottage. The rings continued behind the door. Maybe they were just trying to surprise her. They both should know better than that, she thought.

Very carefully, Rainey approached her office door. She listened, but only the ringing could be heard from the other side. She touched the doorknob softly, trying to avoid the click from the latch. The latch clicked anyway, forcing her to enter the room quickly, before whoever was in there could react.

The scream left her throat before she was fully able to take in exactly what she was seeing. There on her desk was the ringing phone and above it was the mutilated body of Ernie, strung up from the ceiling. The gaping Y-incision spilled the contents of Ernie's body on her desk, still dripping blood on the ringing phone.

She heard him behind her before she had time to act. He grabbed her and shook her, all the while yelling her name over and over. Her arms and legs refused to move. She screamed in terror at the familiar black mask, inches from her face. She screamed until she had no breath left. She closed her eyes and waited for the pain to begin.

"Rainey!" she heard him shout her name. "Rainey!" Her name was being shouted again, but this time the voice was recognizable.

Another voice, a female, yelled, "Caroline Marie Herndon, wake up this instant!"

Rainey's eyes flew open. Mackie's face was inches from her own. He was shaking her and calling her name. Ernie's face glowed red behind him. Her voice finally broke Rainey out of the nightmare.

"That is not my name," Rainey said, groggily.

"Well, the other name wasn't working," Ernie said, visibly upset.

Mackie's big paw brushed the hair from her face. "You were screaming, baby girl. I had to shake you."

Rainey looked back and forth between the two worried faces. "I'm sorry," was all she could say.

Mackie stopped pawing at her and asked, "Are you okay, now?"

"Yeah, yeah, I'm okay. Just give me a minute," Rainey said.

He knew better than to ask what she was dreaming about. She would not have told him, if he did. She certainly would never tell Ernie what she saw. She excused herself to the restroom, feeling both sets of concerned eyes follow her all the way out of sight.

When Rainey closed the bathroom door, she fell back against it. Running her fingers through her hair, she tried to erase the images she just saw from her mind. It was only a dream, but her reaction had been real. She was horrified. Terrified that, if and when the time came, when that monster reappeared, she wouldn't be ready. She knew that was what drove her dreams. The thought that he would find her, stepping out to grab her when she least expected it, to finish what he started.

Rainey bent over the sink, splashing cold water on her face. She toweled off, and then reached in the medicine cabinet where she kept a spare toothbrush. She brushed her teeth and hair, pulled the chestnut waves back into a tidy ponytail, and took a good look in the mirror. Better now, she thought. She took out her cellphone and checked the time. It was after one in the afternoon. At least she slept some, before the nightmare came crashing through her unconscious mind.

Her stomach growled as she exited the bathroom. She was hungry and knew mentioning that fact to Ernie would set her off on a mission to whip up something good to eat. This would also keep Ernie too busy to ask questions. She rubbed her belly as she stepped back into the main office, performing for Mackie and Ernie.

Rainey said, in her best Southern redneck drawl, "Y'all got any food around here?"

Ernie went right into motion, hustling in and out of the back room with a huge salad bowl, plates, and napkins.

"I knew you'd be hungry when you woke up, so I called Mackie and asked him to go by the farm and bring us some fresh vegetables and eggs off my back porch," she said. "I just finished making this chef salad in the back room. Do you want to eat in your office?"

"No," Rainey said, too loudly. She saw their reaction and, in a much calmer voice, added, "No, I'd rather eat out here, if it's all the same to you."

Ernie filled the counter behind her desk with fresh fruit along with the salad and a loaf of fresh bread she made the night before. Rainey thought it was smart of her father to leave the full size kitchen intact when he bought the building. New appliances had gone in over the years, because in truth her dad spent more time in the office than in the cottage. She realized that she had done the same since moving in last July.

The three of them sat balancing plates on their laps, while Rainey told them how she thought that JW's wife might be in real danger. She glossed over the story of the stranger in the shadows, and how she almost shot JW, making it sound much less exciting than it was. They got out the notes and pictures the stalker sent, laying them out on the coffee table. Rainey munched on the salad, listening to Mackie and Ernie banter back and forth about the meaning of the notes.

Mackie reached out to pick up one of the notes. "These have been dusted for prints?" he asked.

Rainey nodded and then swallowed a mouthful of salad. When she could speak again, she said, "Yes, the only prints found on the notes were JW's."

Mackie held the paper up in the sunlight. He checked the paper front and back.

"Looks like regular printer paper to me," Ernie said, squinting over her reading glasses. "I don't see a watermark, do you?"

Mackie answered her, "No, nothing identifiable on this sheet. Are they all printed on the same paper?"

They spent some time examining each note, looking for any distinctive marks on the paper. They concluded, after much passing of paper, that there was none. They also agreed that it looked like the same printer had produced each note. There was a characteristic shadow of smudge after each period. If they could find a suspect, they might be able to match the notes to a printer to which he had access.

"Lord, JW went and got him a fine looking woman," Mackie said.

He had just picked up one of the five by seven photographs from the table. When Rainey saw that he was looking at the picture of Katie in her bathing suit, she unconsciously nodded in agreement. Then, feeling odd about the way Ernie was looking at her, she felt the need to qualify.

"That one gives me the creeps. It looks like he was standing right over her," Rainey said.

Ernie leaned in to get a better look. "How could a stranger get that close?"

"If she was my woman, I wouldn't let a man get within a mile of her, much less close enough to touch," Mackie said matter-of-factly.

Rainey answered Ernie, "I'm beginning to think it may not be a stranger. He knows too much about where she goes and what she does. And you're right, I don't think a stranger could have been close enough to take that picture."

Mackie thumbed through the other shots, "Did you ask JW where the bathing suit picture was taken? Maybe he can tell you who else was there."

"I didn't see it when I first went through the envelope and I forgot to ask him about it when I talked to him," Rainey answered.

She could not believe she had not thought to ask JW about the bathing suit picture. What else had she overlooked? The memories and dreams of her attack were interfering with her thought processes. Her inability to concentrate was why she left the bureau. The image of Ernie filleted over her desk flashed into her mind. She closed her eyes and pinched the space between her brows.

"Are you all right, honey?" Ernie asked.

Rainey covered with, "Yeah, just a headache."

"Can I get you anything for it?" Ernie asked, at the same time beginning to clean up the lunch dishes.

"No, I need to go to the house and take a shower. That will probably take care of it," Rainey responded.

Rainey opened her eyes and stood up. She walked over to the counter and put her empty plate and fork down. She finished off her bottle of water, leaving the bottle in the recycle bin so Ernie would not gripe.

"I'll be at the house for the next thirty minutes at least, and then I need to get back to the teacher," she said, heading for the front door.

Mackie unfolded his considerable frame. "Let me walk you over," he said.

Once they were out of Ernie's earshot, Rainey told Mackie the truth about her encounter with the stalker last night. He agreed that JW's wife was definitely in danger.

"If this guy is that bold, he won't stop until he has made face to face contact with her," he grumbled out in his deep bass voice.

"Yep, he will not be deviated from his plan," Rainey said. "These guys can't stop themselves, they have to be stopped."

Mackie added, before she left him at the bottom of the cottage steps, "I don't care what JW said, you keep that Glock on you all the time."

Rainey laughed. "You didn't think I would go anywhere without it, did you?"

A laugh rumbled out of his barrel chest, then he said, "Rainey, call me before you get out of the car next time, okay?"

"Sure Mackie, I'll call you next time," Rainey said, smiling down at the big man from her front deck.

Mackie backed away, smiling up at her. "You'd better, because I'd hate like hell for your father to come back from the grave and haunt my ass, if I let anything happen to you."

"Don't worry. He's too busy making my grandmother's afterlife a living hell to worry about us. He's probably messed with Constance a few times, too," Rainey said, laughing at the image of her mother screaming through the mansion.

Mackie waved goodbye, shouting, "No doubt about that. Call me when you get parked tonight."

She waved goodbye, then picked up Freddie, who had come out to greet her and was purring, rubbing against her legs.

"I sure hope you didn't leave me any presents in there, I don't think I can take any more surprises today," Rainey said, hugging the big cat to her chest.

She looked around the property from her tree top vantage point. From here, she could see out onto the lake and far down the approaching road. The property was truly out-of-the-way. She could not see another soul. It was the perfect place for her to heal. Now if she could just get on with it. Just as she turned to unlock the door, Freddie sprang from her arms.

Freddie was the kind of cat that did what he wanted when he wanted, and only then. Evidently, he did not want to go in the house. Rainey found him one day hanging out behind the office. He could have only been six weeks old, at the most. A cast away someone had dumped out nearby. He was solid black with wild hair shooting in all directions. He had a tail, but it was so twisted and curled, it looked like a nub. His tail never grew out, and the nub was currently flicking back and forth, while he stood on the railing of the deck. His fur had flattened out into a sleek black coat and he grew so large, he looked like a miniature panther, with a nub tail, of course. His wide gold eyes were staring across the parking lot, his chest rumbling in a low growl. Rainey believed Freddie thought he was a panther, or at least a dog.

"Whatever it is, leave it outside," Rainey said, running her hand along his back.

Freddie jumped down and hurried down the steps, beginning the long slow stalk toward his prey as soon as his feet hit the ground. Rainey scanned the edge of the woods holding his focus. She could not see what he was after, but she hoped he would not catch it. His prizes for her tended to be messy. Rainey looked back down at him and smiled, turning toward the door, happily anticipating a much-needed, long soak in a hot tub.

CHAPTER SEVEN

Contrary to popular belief, substantiated by the entertainment industry, profiling could not somehow magically identify the offender the police were looking for. The process simply indicated the kind of person most likely to have committed a crime with the unique characteristics involved in the case. The Bureau stopped using the terms "psychological profile" or "criminal personality profile" long ago. The analysis of the type of criminal who would have committed a specific crime was a vital tool to law enforcement, but a small part of the services offered by Rainey's old unit.

The Behavioral Analysis Unit or BAU, a component of the National Center for the Analysis of Violent Crime, was located at Quantico, Virginia. The BAU assisted local law enforcement agencies all over the country, providing criminal investigative analysis, by reviewing the cases using methods developed from years of studying criminal behavior. Through this research, a process in which to study crimes developed. The criminal act itself was evaluated, along with a comprehensive look at the specifics of the crime scene. Complete background information on the victim was analyzed and the police reports were scoured for information. The Medical Examiners report was evaluated as well. The information was then hashed out and a profile with that particular criminal offender's characteristics was developed. The BAU was not finished with the process until suggestions were made to the investigators as to how to proceed in the subsequent search for the offender. It was akin to making a medical diagnosis and including a treatment plan. Rainey's current treatment plan for Katie's stalker was to go back through the evidence, while she kept her vigil over JW's wife.

Rainey arrived at Katie's school before the parents again, and watched as Mrs. Wilson led her little troops out of the school. When she dismissed them, some of them tore away to waiting parents, but most hung around to get a hug from their teacher. Katie smiled at the children and gave them each a special moment of her time. Katie Wilson appeared to love her job.

Katie did not go home after school. Instead, she drove to a bookstore on Chapel Hill Boulevard. Rainey could not follow her in, because she had been seen yesterday. She was still kicking herself for that one. Katie appeared in a window in the café section, sipping coffee, and eating a bowl of soup. She read a book while she ate, once pausing the spoon just inches from her partially opened mouth, as what she read captivated her attention. When she finished eating, Katie left the bookstore and drove to the strip mall near North Miami Street, in one of the most crime-prone areas in the city of Durham.

Rainey found a parking place where she could watch Katie through the storefront window. She used her digital camera to take periodic shots of the cars and people who came and went. While she waited, Rainey brought up the file on the laptop containing copies of the notes and pictures. Her training told her the wording in the notes was a key factor in figuring out who this guy was. The perpetrator spoke of fate and destiny, in some form or another, in each note. He believed the fantasy he conceived was a predetermined future. The powers that be had put Katie Wilson here at this time and this place, just for him. In his twisted mind, he must fulfill whatever the fates have destined for him.

Rainey scribbled her thoughts on a legal pad, checking every few minutes to see that Katie was still hard at work molding minds. She noticed the grammar and style in the notes indicated the author was educated, probably at least some college education. The note from June, "Is it now the time when destiny is ours to hold?" sounded like a quote Rainey had heard before. She typed it into Google and the results came up Paul Martin.

She wondered aloud, "Who the hell is Paul Martin?"

The name went into the search engine, resulting in two likely candidates for the quote. It was either a hockey player or the former Prime Minister of Canada. Rainey decided it was probably the politician. She noted no contractions in any of the messages and the order of the words suggested formality in the writing, an affect probably. If the guy was not educated, he wanted people to think he was.

The sky was overcast, with storms moving up from the south. The cloud cover lowered the temperature into the low seventies and a steady breeze was keeping the humidity at bay. Rainey had her windows down half way and could hear the winos and young bloods talking loudly and laughing, down at the other end of the strip mall. She kept an eye on them and noticed on several occasions that they were watching her as well.

"They probably think I'm a cop," she said to herself, knowing the black Charger was a favorite with law enforcement.

Rainey turned back to the legal pad. She began formulating a list of characteristics of the unknown suspect in this particular crime. In addition to at least some college education, he was following Katie at all hours of the day, as evidenced by the pictures. He must have a job that allowed him to be unaccountable for large blocks of time. Katie had to be in her mid thirties. Since most victims are near the same age of their assailants and due to the kind of language in the notes, Rainey guessed him to be thirty-five to forty-five years old. He could be a bit younger, maybe even mid-twenties, but her instincts were leaning to older. She had learned to trust those instincts after nine years of profiling.

Rainey had seen him, she was sure, so she knew him to be athletically built, about six-foot-two or three, maybe two hundred and twenty-five pounds. She had not seen his face, but assumed he was probably average or better than average looking. He was able to move around Katie without being noticed, so he could blend in. Not only could he blend in, Rainey believed Katie and

JW probably knew him. No stranger could have been that close to Katie, unless she was at a public pool and Rainey highly doubted that, but she would check.

Again, she looked back at the notes. JW said that the notes were sent to him at his office. Were the notes directed at JW or Katie? If they were meant for Katie, why were they sent to JW? Was the stalker asking if JW believed in fate? Why would he target JW with the notes when his obsession was with Katie? Maybe part of his fantasy was to antagonize the male in a relationship with his victim. Maybe Katie was just the pawn in his game, his real obsession being with JW.

Having done all she could with the notes, she turned her focus to the pictures. There did not appear to be anything else to learn from the photos. She looked at them so many times, she was sure she had absorbed all she could. She was drawn repeatedly to the picture of Katie in the black bathing suit. Something stirred in her; something she recognized as sexual attraction, but told herself it could not be that. Rainey was not, and never had been, a lesbian. Sure, she had the normal adolescent crushes and had no problem finding other women attractive, but Rainey loved men.

She loved the way a freshly showered man smelled and how his cologne blended with his natural scent. She had a healthy appreciation for the athletic build of baseball players, big guys with lean muscles. Rainey liked the way it felt to lie in a man's arms, to have him pull her tight in close to him, his warm hairy legs wrapped in hers. In addition, the sexual aspect of the woman on woman relationship had never been anything with which Rainey considered experimenting. She was a behavioral scientist and deemed the female fantasies she had from time to time normal and nothing to be concerned about. Rainey enjoyed having sex with men, bottom line.

So why was she becoming so enamored with Katie Wilson? Rainey had only spoken with her for ten seconds. She looked up just in time to see Katie jumping up and down, clapping her hands at some accomplishment made by her student. Her smile animated her whole face, her expression of joy so genuine. Who could resist a face like that? Rainey realized she was grinning back through the windshield. Katie's smile was infectious.

Maybe Rainey just needed a friend her age. One like Katie, to make her laugh and forget all the horrible things she had seen. Katie seemed to represent all that was good and wholesome in the world. That must be what attracted Rainey, she thought. Here was someone so beautiful and unsoiled by the ugliness of life. Katie could still smile the smile of childlike wonder, something Rainey had not been able to do since her first days with the FBI.

Rainey looked at the bathing suit picture again, this time thinking that it was the way Katie slept so peacefully unaware of the danger, which attracted her. The last time Rainey slept like that was when she was still with Bobby. He was a cop in Alexandria, Virginia, and a wonderful guy who loved her. She felt safe with him, there in the darkness of their little one bedroom apartment, but ultimately the relationship could not compete with her job. He called last month to say he was getting married. She dated some, since they broke up four years ago, but nothing serious, and after the attack, the last thing Rainey wanted in her bed right now was a man.

Headlights flashed across the windshield of her car, drawing Rainey's thoughts from the picture on her laptop screen. She watched as the sleek black luxury sedan rolled slowly toward her. It looked just like the car JW drove. The crowd in front of the liquor store shouted at the driver, who kept coming closer to where Rainey watched with heightened interest. The car's windows were tinted and rolled up tightly. The night sky, now in approaching darkness, was made darker by the impending storm. Glare from the naked fluorescent lights along the storefronts splashed over the windshield of the oncoming car, making it impossible to see the driver.

Rainey's nerves prickled. She sat up taller and set the legal pad down in the seat next to her. The Glock was securely in its holster, fully loaded and one in the chamber, but she felt for it anyway. The approaching vehicle made a wide sweeping turn in front of her and then pulled to a stop next to her, the driver's side windows of both cars facing one another. Rainey peered through

61

the tinted glass as the window of the other car came down slowly. She recognized his perfectly combed hair before the window was down halfway.

"Damn it, JW! What the hell are you doing here?" Rainey said, through clinched teeth, not wanting to be overheard.

"I had to talk to you," he replied.

"You do have a phone, don't you?"

Rainey did not want Katie to see them out here talking. She glanced toward the Center and saw Katie with her back turned, talking to a tall woman.

JW stuck his hand out the window, offering her a small manila envelope. "Here, look at this. It was in the mail at the house. I found it when I got home, just now."

Rainey did not want to touch the envelope, in case of prints, but she had no choice. A man in a black expensive car, handing a package to someone in a black Charger with tinted windows, could look suspicious in this part of town. Rainey did not need any more attention than JW already stirred up with his arrival. She quickly took the envelope from his outstretched hand.

"You know you could have waited to give this to me, until I was parked outside your house tonight," Rainey said, before she looked in the envelope.

JW replied flatly, "I didn't think it could wait."

Rainey looked at JW, confused by his tone. "Why, what does it say?"

"Look for yourself," he said. The look he gave her made Rainey uncomfortable.

She used a pencil to extract the note from the envelope. A picture fell out of the folded paper onto her lap. There was an audible gasp when she saw the image. Somehow, the stalker had snapped a picture at the exact moment she shook Katie's hand, yesterday. There was Katie smiling, hand extended, with the little smudge on her cheek, and Rainey grinning broadly back at her. Rainey picked up the picture from her lap by the edges. She looked back at JW.

"I thought you didn't know my wife," he said.

Rainey felt like she had been caught smoking in the bathroom, at school. She defended herself weakly, "I didn't—I mean, I don't—I just met—I mean—she surprised me yesterday. I made up a story about taking pictures of the flowers. I even gave her a fake name."

"So, I'm not being set up or anything," he asked in all sincerity.

"No, why would you ask such a thing?"

JW sat up taller in his seat, glaring at her. "Why didn't you tell me Katie saw you?"

"Because I was stupid and let her sneak up on me like that," Rainey said, honestly. "Don't be so paranoid."

Rainey saw him visibly relax, his entire demeanor changing back to the charming southern gentleman. She was glad. She did not like the way his questioning had made her feel.

"I'm a politician, Rainey. We're all paranoid. That doesn't mean someone isn't out to get me."

Rainey smiled reassuringly at him. "Trust me. I'm on your side." She looked down at the paper draped over the pencil. "So, what does the note say?"

"I don't remember. The picture freaked me out so much, I just took off to find you."

Rainey took the legal pad from the other seat and laid the note out on it. She unfolded it with the pencil.

On one single line, across the center of the page, was the question she read aloud, "Why do you tempt fate?"

She heard JW ask, "What do you think he means?"

Rainey thought for a moment, before she answered, "I think Katie isn't the only one with a stalker. The only way he could view me as a threat is if he knows who I am and what I do, and to know that, he had to have followed you to my office."

JW perked up. "Do you really think so?"

Rainey looked at the picture again. "Why else would he send this picture, one with me in it? Katie was in the yard long enough for him to take a picture of her alone."

"And you never saw him?" JW asked.

Rainey sounded dejected, "No, I never saw him," then she brightened, "but I haven't finished looking at the pictures I took yesterday."

JW sat silently. Rainey saw him glance in his rearview mirror. She imagined he was trying to decide if his wife was really safe with Rainey watching over her. She tried to imagine how conflicted he must feel, weighing his wife's safety against his political career. The average person would see nothing threatening about going to the police, but after living near Washington, Rainey understood how the most innocent circumstances could be twisted against a young politician. JW probably had a few skeletons he would rather leave buried.

Finally, he turned back to her. "Okay then, I should probably leave before Katie sees me."

Rainey felt sorry for him. He did not look as if he believed what he was doing was the right thing, but he had to. She tried to comfort him.

"Go home, get some rest," she said, and then added, "I'll be right outside all night."

Instantly, he put back on his charming veneer. "At least, that is a comfort. Be safe, Rainey."

Rainey watched JW roll away, passing the jeering crowd, on his way out of the parking lot. She hoped he would be able to get some rest. She certainly did not want a replay of last night. Had he not said he was running because he could not sleep? JW had a lot going on, with his law practice and his duties as a State Representative, not to mention someone was stalking him and his wife. Rainey wanted to end that worry for him.

She looked down at the picture of Katie shaking her hand. They looked like two old friends greeting each other. She put the picture in the visor above her head, taking one last look at it, before flipping the visor up and out of the way. That is when she noticed the lights were off in the back of the Center, and people were filing out the front door. Katie was among one of the last to exit.

Two of the young-bloods, from in front of the liquor store, were making their way toward the people leaving the Center.

Rainey watched as the two teenagers, hats on sideways and pants sagging down, exposing at least a foot of boxer shorts, moved closer to where Katie was parked. She came to full attention when one of the youths said something to Katie, who by now was almost alone, most of the others having found their cars. Rainey relaxed when Katie waved and went toward the teenagers. She hugged each of them and talked with them for a few minutes, before it started to rain, forcing Katie to run to her car and the teenagers to seek shelter. Katie started the Lexus sedan and drove out of the parking lot, Rainey's Charger not far behind.

Rainey followed Katie from a distance, as she drove toward her home, all the while thinking what an amazing person JW's wife seemed to be. She looked forward to the day she really had the chance to get to know Katie Wilson. She hoped it would be very soon.

CHAPTER EIGHT

It was nine o'clock by the time Rainey parked the car outside the Wilson home. The hard rain had subsided to a soft drizzle. Rainey had a different vantage point tonight, but she could still see the right side of the house and hedges. She did not have a good view of the front lawn or the driveway side of the yard, but both areas had outdoor lighting that would probably prevent anyone from trying to enter there unnoticed. She settled in, got the webcams rolling and called Mackie.

"Mackie," he growled into the phone.

"Hey there, hope your evening is going well," Rainey said, cheerfully.

"It'd go a whole hell of a lot better, if I could get this asshole to come out of this damn house."

Rainey laughed. "And which asshole would that be?"

"I got Charlie 'Butterbean' Beasley laid up in his girlfriend's house," he grumbled, "but the little fucker's been in there for four hours and I know he's got to come up for air sometime."

"Maybe he's sleeping over," Rainey suggested.

"Nope. She's got a husband and I know he gets off work in an hour, so Butterbean better get done with his business."

"Well, stick around," Rainey said, "You might see some action, if he waits too long."

Mackie's chuckle rumbled through the receiver. "I hope the husband comes home and shoots his fat ass. I'm tired of tracking him down every time he skips. How's it going over there?"

"Got another note today," she paused before adding, "with a picture of me shaking hands with Katie."

Mackie remained surprisingly calm, for the moment, and then asked, "What did the note say?"

"Why do you tempt fate?" Rainey answered.

Mackie was quiet. She could hear him breathing. Rainey knew he was thinking it through before making a decision. Mackie liked to mull things over. She had learned to be patient.

Finally, he broke his silence. "Look, after I get old Charlie locked up, which should be any minute now, I'm going to come over there so we can talk. You up for company?"

Rainey was glad he suggested it. She did not want to ask him to come and sit with her, but she really wanted to go over the case with him, get his feel for this guy. Mackie could have been a criminal analyst with no problem. He had a keen knack for knowing how their twisted minds operated.

"I'm parked on the south side of the block. Park on the other side and walk up," Rainey told him.

"Okay, I gotta go now. It looks like Butterbean's finished gettin' his groove on. He's coming out the door now. See you soon."

After her talk with Mackie, Rainey pulled up the pictures she took yesterday. She clicked through the files until she found the three hundred and sixty degree shots in front of the Wilson home. This was when the stalker had taken her picture, so there was a good chance she got a shot of him or his vehicle. She flipped the visor down and looked at the picture again. From the angle of the shot, the person who took it had to have been standing somewhere across the street, near where Rainey was currently parked.

She looked out the window at the row of hedges that nearly came to the edge of the sidewalk. The guy could have been lurking on the other side and she would never have seen him. Damn these people and their old boxwoods. Rainey found the picture of the area where she suspected the stalker had been standing. She looked carefully at the hedge, zooming in on a dark spot behind the thinning leaves. There, just off the sidewalk and hidden by foliage, the shape of someone blocked the sunlight coming through the hedge. The stalker had been right there, watching, listening to them.

She checked the images before and after she met Katie, but there was no way to tell if any of the people belonged with the shadow behind the hedge. She paid very close attention to the males who fit the description that she developed while waiting at the Center. She made notes on her legal pad and labeled a folder on the laptop screen, "possible suspects," dragging the pictures into it. He had been there and she missed him. She probably walked right past the guy. She would show the pictures to JW. Maybe he would recognize someone.

"Damn it! I forgot to ask about the bathing suit picture," Rainey said, slapping her fist down on the legal pad resting on her knee.

Rainey checked the time. It was now after ten and most of the lights were off in the Wilson home. She would have to ask JW where the photo was taken tomorrow. She hoped he was resting comfortably in bed, holding his beautiful wife. They did make a handsome couple. JW had George Clooney good looks that seemed to age so favorably. Katie was stunning all by herself. Rainey was sure they turned every head in the room, when JW walked in with Katie draped on his arm, his dark good looks complementing her fair-haired beauty.

She glanced at the picture on the visor, and was catapulted away from her imagery of Katie and JW making their grand entrance.

"Start with the victim you idiot," she said aloud. All those years of training and she had not yet utilized a major tool of the investigator. Faced with a seemingly motiveless crime, law enforcement took a hard look at the victim. Sometimes the victim's particulars could tell all that was needed to establish the type of person who would commit a crime against this individual victim. She needed to ask herself who the victims were and what attracted the stalker to them? Rainey was sure both JW and Katie were being stalked, but it was not clear who the real target was. She had to look closely at both Wilsons and the nature of their relationship.

JW turned out better than Rainey imagined he would. He was a wild child, rebellious, always taking risks. He and Rainey were never romantically involved or even best friends. They were part of a neighborhood group that watched each other's backs. She was along on many of his misadventures from the time they were in elementary school until high school graduation. None of their misdeeds were serious, more mischievousness than malice was involved, but JW found himself in serious trouble in high school.

Both Rainey and JW were highly skilled jocks. He played football, basketball, and baseball, while she played volleyball, basketball, and fast pitch softball. Of course, they both played golf, having grown up in the clubhouse during the summers. JW's hopes for a career in baseball were crushed when he broke his leg in two places, during a snow skiing accident, in January of their senior year. Later that spring, the "misunderstanding" happened.

Because of his legacy status, his father, and his father before him having been members, JW attended fraternity parties long before he was ever a college student. After a hard weekend of drinking with his future frat brothers, JW did not come back to school for several days. Rumors swirled around his involvement in a rape. Rainey had not believed JW would rape anyone. Why would he? He had girls falling all over him since grade school. Usually, all he had to do was ask.

The details of the event began to emerge, as the days went by, with no word from JW. Someone fitting JW's description had allegedly beaten and raped a college freshman. In fact, everyone was pretty sure it was JW. When Rainey finally saw him days later, she confronted him with what she had heard. That is when he explained it had all been just a "misunderstanding."

"I was drunk," he had said. "She kept coming on to me and insisted that we go upstairs and make out. We had sex and then she said she was going to tell everyone I raped her."

JW was so calm when he said it that Rainey had found it hard not to believe him.

He continued, "The docs had me on steroids for my leg. I've had trouble lately with my temper and I got really angry at this chick. I knew she was just after money. I guess I just lost it and hit her. I didn't beat her up, like everyone is saying."

Rainey had been shocked. She knew JW had a temper, but he had always been such a gentleman around her. She believed, in her heart, it was a one-time thing. Anyway, the whole mess just went away. Money talks and it can also shut people up. Soon everyone found something else to gossip about and the incident turned into a forgotten "misunderstanding." Rainey had not thought about it in years. She was sure it was something JW wished he could erase from everyone's memory.

When Rainey left for Virginia, she and JW lost touch. She kept up with him through her mother, during the infrequent times she talked to her each year, mostly around holidays and birthdays. She knew about him becoming a partner in his father's law firm and his political career. She had even been invited to his wedding, but work prevented her from attending. That was pretty much what she knew about JW, except what she read in the newspapers about his politics.

Rainey Googled JW and when the results came up, three images appeared at the top of the page. One was the standard Representative shot, sitting in front of a blue backdrop, flanked by the national and state flags with the North Carolina State seal in the background. The next shot showed the handsome politician cutting a ribbon on some property. The last image was of JW and Katie together. Rainey clicked on the image. A page came up showing JW in a tuxedo with his exquisite bride by his side. She wore a simple black evening gown and pearls, but there was nothing simple about the way Katie Wilson looked. Rainey had been right. They were stunning.

The hyperlinked caption under the picture read, "Representative JW Wilson and wife, Katherine Meyers Wilson (shown here at a Republican fund raiser last year) involved in auto crash. Wife in critical condition. Details on page 2."

Rainey clicked the link for more details. An article came up on the screen, dated January fourth. A picture of a crumpled sedan, the passenger side embedded in a tree accompanied the text. Rainey read the article. It explained how JW and Katie had been coming home from a fundraiser, when a teenager on a bike had come out of nowhere, crossing directly into the car's path. A popular off-road bike trail was located nearby. In an attempt to miss the biker, JW crashed into a tree. Katie, who was sleeping in the passenger seat, was ejected from the car when, unexplainably, the door had flown open and her seatbelt had come undone. JW survived with minor injuries from the airbags, but Katie had not fared so well. Along with the bruises and lacerations, she suffered from internal bleeding. She was six months pregnant and subsequently lost the baby. She remained hospitalized in stable, but critical condition. The teenager was not found and there were no witnesses. JW referred to this accident in Rainey's office.

Rainey looked at the picture in the visor again. Wow, she thought, you would never know Katie had gone through such an ordeal, just six months ago. Rainey could understand feelings of loss and the pain of recovery. Katie bore no outward signs of trauma, at least none that Rainey had seen, even in the bathing suit picture. Looking again at the crumpled car, Rainey thought it was a miracle that anyone survived. It was hard to say, but Katie may have been lucky her seatbelt failed and she was thrown away from the car.

Rainey looked away from the picture, because it made her feel queasy thinking of the anguish the Wilsons had gone through, especially Katie. It was obvious, from watching her interact with her students, that Katie loved children. How cruel it must have been, to lose a baby JW said they had wanted so much. She looked out through rain-streaked windows, at the traffic slowly passing. The glistening, wet roads were black as night. The drizzle kept the foot traffic to a bare minimum. Still Rainey took a hard look at everyone who even came close to matching the stalker's physical description.

The rest of the results on the search page were mostly about JW's politics. He was a rising young star in the Republican Party, a family values candidate, who did not mind giving people a hand up, but he was staunchly against what he called "Obama's handouts." A short biography on his State webpage contained no new information for Rainey. She switched her focus to Katie.

She typed in the name from the newspaper article, Katherine Meyers Wilson, and hit search. The same pictures from JW's search popped up on the page. There was a link to her elementary school, a link to an article about the Literacy Center and one concerning the accident. All the other links were redundant or were related to JW. The elementary school link turned out to be a bust, just a picture, so she tried the Literacy Center article. This article contained some personal details about Katie. It turned out that Katie was the former Katherine Anne Meyers, a granddaughter of one of Durham's tobacco mogul families. She had earned both Bachelor and Masters degrees in Early Childhood Education. The focus of the article was on the opening of the Center and the fundraising efforts of Mrs. Wilson and her husband. Katie had been instrumental in opening that one and two other Literacy Centers, in the Triangle area.

Rainey now had enough information to start a victim's analysis, which she would discuss later with Mackie. Ernie had packed another cooler, but Rainey wanted something hot, and she had to go to the bathroom. She decided to leave her post, slide over to the Franklin Street, for a hot sandwich and coffee. She would also use the time to cruise the neighborhood a few times, just to take a look. She hoped she would get back before Mackie came looking for her. She thought about calling him, but changed her mind. Rainey did not want Mackie to think she was worried about being alone, after last night. She would not be gone that long, and he would know she was probably just doing surveillance around the area.

Her cell rang on her way back to the car, after stopping at the closest fast food restaurant. She checked the caller I.D. and seeing Mackie's name flashing in the window of the phone, she opened it.

"Hey Mackie, I'm on my way back from a potty break. Can I get you something?" She said this while trying to open the car door and balance the coffee, without dropping the hamburger.

"No, I just stopped for coffee. Finished locking Mr. Beasley up about ten minutes ago," Mackie answered. "Wanted to let you know I'm on my way."

"What took you so long? I thought you had an eye on him two hours ago," Rainey asked.

Mackie laughed. "That damn fool tried to run on me. We had to stop by the twenty-four hour clinic before we went to the jail."

"You didn't run over another one with your truck, did you?" Rainey teased Mackie.

"No, this time I let Junior tackle him," Mackie said, followed by a loud chest rumbling laugh.

Junior was Mackie's twenty-two year old nephew. He was as tall as Mackie and built like the defensive end Mackie had been, back in the day, and Junior was bad fast. He worked for his uncle, because he just would not buckle down on the books in high school and missed his chance to play college ball. Mackie rescued him from the streets when he was nineteen and he had been working his way back to football ever since. Junior was not the college type, so he was training for the arena football league tryouts, next January.

"He sure does come in handy, doesn't he," Rainey said, laughing along with Mackie.

"Yes, that he does," Mackie, said through more rumbles of amusement. "See you in a few."

"Great, I'll be back in my parking place in five minutes. I've got lots to talk over with you," she said, finally getting situated in the car. "See ya'."

Mackie arrived before Rainey. She passed his parked Escalade. The rain had stopped and the streets were beginning to dry. When she turned the corner, she saw the giant man standing in the street, where she had recently been staked out. In his hand, he was carefully holding, by one corner, what appeared to be a manila envelope. It looked like the one JW handed her earlier.

73

Mackie turned when he saw Rainey's car coming. He stepped back up on the sidewalk, so she could pull in and park.

Rainey popped the lock on the passenger door and the tall man twined his broad body down into the seat. Good thing Rainey kept the seat pushed back as far as it would go. He shut the door and held out the envelope.

"I found this in the street. Look who it is addressed to." His tone was ominous.

Rainey looked at the envelope. She tried to be careful of leaving her prints or smudging possible prints from the suspect. It was unsealed and appeared to have one sheet of folded printer paper inside. She turned it over. On the front, where the address would be, there was only one word typed out in capital block letters, CAROLINE. Rainey's heart began to pick up the pace. She carefully removed the piece of paper from inside the envelope. She expected to see a picture fall out, but none did. The plain white sheet of paper appeared to be blank.

Rainey checked the inside of the envelope again. There was nothing left inside. Mackie peered over her shoulder at the blank sheet of paper.

"That's it, just a blank sheet of paper?" Mackie commented.

Rainey took the flashlight from its holder on her waist. She clicked it on and examined the paper closely. She had not seen it at first, but there, in the center of the page, was a single letter, Y.

Rainey froze. She stared at the letter in disbelief. Then, as a reflex, her eyes darted around her in every direction. Mackie saw her reaction and immediately placed his hand on his hip, where his own Glock rested in its holster.

"What is it?" he asked, his eyes darting from the paper to his surroundings.

Rainey looked back down at the paper then turned to Mackie. In words that revealed her deepest fears, she simply said, "He found me."

CHAPTER NINE

A little over a year ago, a detective contacted Rainey's unit. He was working cases that involved the rape and murder of three women near the Capital, in downtown Raleigh. Due to the nature of the killings, the detective was positive he had a serial murderer on his hands.

The unusual signature of the killer had linked the murders. The murdered women were high priced escorts, beautiful women who kept company with the rich and powerful men of the Capital city. Each of the bodies was found in Lake Johnston, wrapped in contractor trash bags closed with duct tape. The most striking element of the murders was what assured the detective that the same suspect had committed all of the killings. The women had Y-incisions, like the medical examiner used during autopsies, their chests and abdomens sliced open.

Three more escorts had been reported missing during the same time as the other murders. The detective was sure the bodies of these women would soon surface at the lake. He contacted the BAU through the local field office, in hopes that they would assist his department in searching for this killer. Rainey and her colleagues were dispatched to help analyze the crimes and develop an investigative plan to catch the murderer that the press had now dubbed, "The Y-Man Killer."

The BAU members evaluated the victims, examined the dumpsites, the initial crime reports, and closely analyzed the

Medical Examiner's report, which included viewing the bodies. The information was compiled and analyzed. Their conclusions helped direct the course of action taken by the investigators. What they found reiterated that the Triangle had a very sick boy on their hands.

The victims were high-class call girls, the kind of date a rich, lonely man could buy in any upscale restaurant or hotel bar. Although the women were all beautiful and Caucasian, they were different physical types, one blond and petite, and the other two tall and brunette. After talking with friends and associates of the victims, the investigators learned each of the women worked solo and usually took their dates to expensive, nearby hotel rooms. The victims were last seen in different locations. One disappeared from The Men's Club in Chapel Hill, one from the Homestead Spa in Cary, and the third was last seen at an upscale steakhouse in Raleigh. No one remembered seeing the victims leave with anyone. The location of the killings was still a mystery.

The autopsy reports revealed the cause of death as manual strangulation. The bruising on the victims' necks showed large hands had squeezed the life out of them. The victims' stomach contents suggested each had last eaten strawberries, chocolate, and champagne. This indicated the women had gone willingly with the assailant and shared an identical last meal, shortly before their deaths.

At some point, a stun gun was used, leaving burn marks on the victims' necks. There were no signs of defensive wounds or skin beneath the nails, indications that the women were rendered unconscious. Toxicology reports stated the women were drugged with a sedative given by intramuscular injection and commonly used by dental surgeons, before the practice of oral sedatives took its place. These drugs could also be found in a hospital or veterinarian office. The dosage indicated he used just enough to render the victims unconscious while he gained complete control over them and then re-dosed them later. There were ligature marks on the wrists and ankles where the victims were tied and marks in and around the mouth, indicating a gag had been used.

The women were beaten, the pre-mortem bruising suggesting the killer used his fists in a fit of rage. The killer probably strangled his victims during the initial rape, but indications were the murderer had sex with the corpses shortly after death. There was no semen recovered from the bodies. Perhaps he used a condom or was unable to complete the sex act, for whatever reason. A few dark head-hairs were found, but contained no viable DNA. The Y-incisions were sliced into the victims' skin postmortem. The depth of the incisions ended just below the skin, leaving the organs undamaged, the skin pulled back, as if the killer were peeking inside. It was the killer's signature.

A timeline developed when the approximate time of death had been determined. One of the victims had been killed the previous November, followed by one in December and then another January. The three missing escorts disappeared in consecutive months starting in February and ending in April. It was assumed the missing women would soon be found to be victims four, five, and six. It was May and everyone was waiting to hear of the next missing woman or floating body.

The summation; they were dealing with a sexual murderer, an organized killer who planned and orchestrated his crimes. The man they were looking for was probably of average to above average intelligence, a white male, and in his mid-twenties to late thirties. He was probably the first born or only son of an ambivalent mother and would have had a poor relationship with his father. He would have a poor quality of attachment with other family members as well. The discipline he received as a child would have been inconsistent and he was probably abused physically or sexually during his childhood and or adolescence.

The suspect would most likely be above average in looks, over six-feet-tall, and well built. He would be socially competent, able to move among people without suspicion. The organized killer would usually be involved in a relationship and live with that person. This suspect would be from the upper class and have disposable money. He would have a car in good condition and have a skilled job. The killer would also need a place to take his victims in order to ensure privacy, while he committed his crimes.

The investigators were told to talk to and give a physical description of the killer to the local escorts and call girls. Female officers were placed undercover in high-end restaurants and hotel bars. Since all the bodies found so far had been dumped in Lake Johnston, more than likely tossed off the Advent Ferry Road Bridge that dissected the lake, stakeouts were scheduled in hopes of catching him drop off his next victim. Every single person involved was positive there would be a next victim.

It was at this time, on May tenth, that Rainey's father was killed in a drive by shooting, while apprehending a gang banger who had skipped out on his twenty-five thousand dollar bail. Billy Bell stepped in front of Junior when he saw light flash off the gun barrel from the open window of the low-rider crawling by. Junior was not hit, but Billy Bell took a bullet straight in the heart and died instantly. Rainey had just eaten breakfast with him the day before. They were both happy she was working so close to home and spent as much time together as possible.

Rainey took two weeks off after her father's funeral and then returned to the task force working the Y-Man murders. The fact that she was just a little over twenty miles from the bait shop office made taking care of her father's estate business easier, but it did not ease the devastation she felt at the loss of the most important person in her life. Her mother's side of the family was merely a supplier of genetic material, as far as Rainey was concerned. She hated everything they stood for, most of all their pretentiousness. Billy Bell had not only been her father, he was Rainey's best friend. It was the first time she felt truly alone in her whole life. In hindsight, she was too emotionally disconnected to have returned to the field so soon, but she had asked to stay near home to close out her father's business.

On the twenty-eighth of May, Rainey was sitting in a black SUV observing the Advent Ferry Bridge's north entrance. The co-occupant of the vehicle was her fellow agent and longtime friend, Danny McNally. They joined the BAU at about the same time and had a brother-sister relationship that meant they loved each other, but sometimes they fought. They were parked near the boathouse since midnight and it was now almost four in the morning. Danny had obviously eaten something awful, because his stomach rolled incessantly. Rainey was one of the boys most of the time and suffered through their bathroom humor, but she drew the line at sharing farts. It particularly made her angry when they farted and did not warn anyone.

"Fuck you, Danny," Rainey said, "You could at least warn somebody."

Rainey exited the vehicle, slammed the door behind her, and walked past the boathouse, out on the footbridge that crossed the lake and paralleled the bridge. She was angry at the world these days. She stared at the moonlight sparkling across the hundred and fifty acre lake. Evergreen forest surrounded it, complete with miles of greenway trails. Lake Johnston was beautiful that evening, but Rainey did not see it. Her mind was racing with unfulfilled revenge. Mackie and his posse tracked down the gunman, four days after he killed her father, only to discover he was a fourteen-year-old boy earning his way into a gang. He did not even know at whom he was shooting. Rainey's revenge had no outlet, so it smoldered under her skin.

Rainey knew she had over reacted with Danny. His behavior was atrocious, but did not warrant her stomping off like that. She wondered if she should take some more time off to get her head straight. She could not concentrate or focus on the job, as she should, and she snapped at people, which was totally out of character for her. She couldn't remember the last time she had a good night's sleep. She stayed on the footbridge contemplating her situation for the next twenty minutes.

Rainey decided to head back to the vehicle, thinking she probably had been gone long enough for the air to clear. Maybe they should leave and find Danny a bathroom. She was just coming to the edge of the boathouse, still hidden from the view of the parking lot, when she heard something that made her stop. That was the last conscious thought she had until she awoke sometime later, in the killer's lair.

Rainey knew she had been drugged. Her arms and legs were too heavy to move and her eyes could not focus on the room around her. She could tell she was in a bedroom. She could tell that she had been raped. She felt the mattress through the plastic under her naked body. Her wrists and ankles were tied to the bedposts, leaving her splayed out and completely vulnerable. A cotton cloth was tied in a knot and stuffed in her mouth, the ends tied behind her head. She could hear music playing in the other room, but the Doppler effect from the drugs made it impossible to make out what the song was.

She felt the burning ache on the side of her neck where she must have been hit with a stun gun. A shadow moved just out of her view. She could feel his presence, just inches from her. Her heart pounded in her ears, her breathing rapid and shallow. She tried to scream, but only primal, muffled, guttural sounds left her throat, blocked by the gag in her mouth.

"Oh goody, you're awake. We can play now," a voice said, over her right ear.

It was a man's voice, but it sounded like an imitation of a small boy. The man moved into view. He was tall and muscular, completely naked, except for the black leather, sadist mask he wore over his head and face, latex gloves on his hands, and a condom on his erect penis. He carried a scalpel in his hand as he climbed on the bed and straddled her. He placed the scalpel on the bed, by her head. She was tied so tightly she could not move at all. Rainey was completely defenseless and about to die. No one knew where she was. She was alone with a psycho killer with no hope of rescue. Rainey's only thought was she hoped he killed her fast.

The childlike voice squealed out in joy, "I'm so happy you were able to come over and play today."

Then the torture began. He started with her nipples, squeezing and twisting them, pulling on them until Rainey thought he would tear them away.

"I love boobies," he sang, over and over, to the made up tune of a child.

He slid down her body and examined her vagina like a boy examines a bug. He poked and prodded, pulling her labial lips, stretching the skin to its breaking point. He jabbed his fingers into her, ripping her skin. Rainey screamed in agony under the gag, but he paid no attention to her muffled protestations.

He cheerfully sang out, in his childlike singsong, "Don't make too much noise. Mommy will catch us playing doctor and she won't like it."

Rainey pulled on the restraints, fighting for her life. She thrashed from side to side, bucking her attacker off balance, while he tried again to straddle her.

His singsong stopped and he whined like a child, "I don't like it when you move."

The first fist slammed into the side of her face, snapping her head to one side. A wave of nausea accompanied the searing pain. It was not until the second fist crashed into her temple that she lost consciousness. She awoke to her eyes almost swollen shut, her mouth full of blood, and the man raping her. He had beaten her unmercifully and continued her torture while she was unconscious. When he realized she was awake, he stopped. He lay down on top of her, his face close to hers. She saw tears in his eyes when he looked at her. Suddenly he sat up, his knees on either side of her hips.

His voice trembled, as he said in his little boy cadence, "I'm sorry, but it only works when you play dead."

Rainey saw him pick up the scalpel from the bed. She knew what was about to happen and she steeled herself against the pain. The cold metal cut into her skin above her right breast. Wait, wasn't he supposed to kill her first, strangle her? She bit down hard on the cotton in her mouth and growled with pain, as he continued to slice down to just above her belly button. This was all wrong. He wasn't cutting her deep enough to expose her like the others. He was off his script. He plunged the scalpel in again above her left breast, sending a new wave of pain through her body. She arched her back against his weight on top of her. She tried to buck him off, but he drew the second slice to meet the first, joining them into his signature Y.

Rainey thought she would pass out from the pain. She prayed that she would. Just when she thought she could take no more, he stopped. He jumped up from the bed and ran out of the room. A few seconds later, she heard a door shut somewhere off in the other part of the living space. Rainey fought to stay conscious, but lost the fight as the edges of the room turned to blackness and slowly closed around her.

She woke to Danny's voice screaming her name, "RAINEY!" His fingers were on her neck, checking for a pulse.

She opened her swollen eyes a crack to see his face, desperate for some response from her. The room grew louder with other voices barking out orders.

Danny saw her eyes open. He yelled, "She's alive, get those paramedics in here."

He removed the gag from Rainey's mouth, very careful not to cause her more pain. Through her badly cut and swollen lips she whispered, "Thank you."

Danny stood up and let the paramedics get to her. He pulled out a knife and cut the restraints from her arms and legs. She could see that he was crying.

"We're going to get him, Rainey. He couldn't have gotten far, we'll get him," was the last thing she heard someone say, before she was out again.

The next day in her hospital room, Danny explained that he had needed a restroom badly and was unable to wait for her to come back, after she stormed off. He came back and checked that she was still on the footbridge. A few minutes later, he saw a town car pull away from the boathouse, and made a note of the license plate, as it left the parking lot. When Rainey had not come back, he went looking for her. When he discovered her badge and gun, lying behind the boathouse, he had called for help.

From the license plate number Danny wrote down, they were able to track the car to a Chinese corporation that turned out to be a dummy company. Luckily, they had eventually found an address for a house that the corporation also owned, off Advent Ferry Road and near Lake Johnston. They arrived only moments after the would-be killer escaped. Danny blamed an inadvertent siren from a local law enforcement vehicle for warning the suspect of their pending arrival, giving him just enough time to disappear out the back door and into the woods. He must have had a car waiting somewhere nearby. Danny didn't realize the siren saved Rainey's life, but she knew how close she was to dying.

There were no fingerprints. The guy must have worn gloves the entire time he was in the house. They did find plenty of hair samples, again dark, but the techs thought there was no viable DNA. The previous victims' driver's licenses were taped to the bathroom mirror, including those of the three missing women. There were newspaper articles about the Y-Man taped on a wall in the living room. The suspect was in the wind.

They were still no closer to knowing his identity, over a year later, as Rainey sat in the Charger staring at the single "Y" on the otherwise blank page.

CHAPTER TEN

At first, Rainey did not know what to do. Her instincts said start the car and get the hell out of there. All the anxiety and fear of the past year crashed into her bones so hard, she felt weak, unable to move. She could feel her body start to tremble and tried desperately to gain control. That one single letter, on the paper she held in her hands, represented every frightening image that terrorized Rainey for months, only this image threatened to push her over the edge. She wanted to run and hide, never coming out again. Nevertheless, he would find her, she was sure of that. For that one reason, she fought the primal urge for flight and, at that moment, Rainey Blue Bell decided to fight.

She was up and out of the car before Mackie realized what was happening. She un-holstered the Glock and crossed the thirty yards to JW's front door, in a matter of seconds. Mackie unhinged himself from the front seat of the Charger, and sprinted after her.

"Damn it Rainey, stop! What are you doing?" he yelled between gasps for air.

Rainey banged on the Wilson's door like cops do, loudly and persistently.

"JW, it's Rainey. Open the door, it's urgent," she shouted at the glass windows in the top of the door.

Mackie arrived, breathless and repeated his question, "What are you doing?"

"I'm letting these people know there's a maniac out here somewhere and then I'm calling the BAU," Rainey said, gaining steam, "and then I'm going to kill that motherfucker."

Rainey banged on the door again, more forcefully.

"Calm down, Rainey. You're going to scare these poor folks to death and wake up half the neighborhood."

Rainey turned on Mackie, her face hot with rage, her voice booming. "They should be scared!"

The door to the Wilson residence flew open. JW stood on the other side of the opening, eyes wide, and a panicked look on his face. Behind him, Katie appeared pulling on a silk housecoat over her matching pajamas.

"Jesus, Rainey, what the fuck?" JW said, moving aside as Rainey and Mackie pushed their way into the foyer.

JW shut the door behind them. Rainey came face to face with Katie Wilson for the second time in her life. She saw a flash of recognition in Katie's eyes.

"I thought your name was Caroline," Katie paused, looking down at Rainey's hand, "and why do you have a gun?" She glanced at her husband. "JW, what's going on?"

JW ushered everyone into the den, where it was obvious he had fallen asleep on the couch watching TV. He crossed to the coffee table, retrieving the remote, and clicked off the television. Katie turned on the end-table light and went to stand by her husband. Her mouth hung open as she took in Rainey and the giant Mackie, armed and out of breath.

JW was the first to speak. "Okay Rainey, what in the hell has happened?"

"Why do you keep calling her Rainey?" Katie said. "Who is she?"

"I'm sorry to have frightened you, ma'am," Rainey answered, going immediately into Bureau mode. "I'm afraid I wasn't honest with you yesterday. My name is Rainey Bell. I'm an old friend of your husband and a Special... former Special Agent with the FBI. Your husband hired me to protect you. This is my partner, Mackie."

Mackie interrupted, "I'm sorry, but Mr. Wilson, I need you to show me all of your outside windows and doors." JW hesitated, then Mackie added, "Now, Mr. Wilson."

Katie slumped down on the couch, her fear more apparent, as the color drained from her face. Rainey checked the locks on the windows in the den. She peered through the curtains into the backyard, seeing only the shadows cast by the tall boxwoods surrounding them. He could be out there and she would never see him. Rainey turned back to the couch, holstered her pistol, and sat down facing Katie, who was squeezing herself into the corner of the couch, her knees pulled tight up to her chest.

"I'm sorry we had to formally meet under these circumstances," Rainey said, in a quieter, calmer tone.

Katie reached out and clasped Rainey's hand. A tear rolled down her cheek as she pleaded, "Please, tell me what's happening."

Katie's fear was so real and her plea so genuine, Rainey made her mind up instantly that she would defend this woman with her life, if it came to that. Something in Katie triggered a protective instinct Rainey had never felt before. She wanted to hold her and tell her everything would be okay, to shield her from what came next. For Rainey knew, she would have to tell Katie about the maniac, the one who almost killed her, the same man who had been stalking Katie for months. Sweet innocent Katie was about to be introduced to the ugliness of the world. Rainey wished she could spare her that.

It helped Rainey focus, having someone else to worry about. She had been watching Katie to help out JW, but now she wanted to help Katie. For the moment, Rainey's fears came second, as she tried to think of the right thing to say.

"Katie, please know that I am here to keep you safe. I will do everything in my power to make sure nothing happens to you," Rainey said, patting the frightened woman's hand. "I'll explain everything when JW and Mackie come back."

Katie said nothing and only nodded. Rainey saw a box of tissue on the coffee table. She lifted it to Katie, who took several sheets. She let go of Rainey's hand, dabbing the tears from her eyes and cheeks. Rainey took the opportunity to send a text message from her phone. She stood, walked across the room, finding Danny's name in her contacts list and sent a two-word text, "HE'S BACK."

Rainey hung up the phone and slipped it back into its holder on her waist. She saw her reflection in the big hall mirror, and realized what she must look like to Katie. She was dressed in her black tactical pants, black tee shirt, and shoulder holster with the big black pistol at her side. Katie must have thought the SWAT team was invading her house when they pushed through the door. Now, Katie looked anxious enough to spring up on the ceiling at the least little noise.

The ponytail was making Rainey's head hurt. She removed the hair band and ran her fingers through her hair. She made a show of calming down, as if the danger had passed. Her chestnut waves fell down around her shoulders. She took a deep breath and sat down, sighing loudly, as she relaxed back into the couch.

Katie put her feet back down on the floor and adjusted her gown. She too took a big breath and let it out slowly. Sometimes when people were in a crisis, they would mimic behavior instinctively, because they were so overloaded they could not think for themselves. Rainey had used the technique before. She was glad to see Katie responding.

Katie looked at Rainey. "You have lovely hair."

It was odd what people thought about in situations of emotional pain and uncertainty.

Rainey smiled at Katie. "Thank you," she said, and then added, "So do you."

They heard Mackie's rumbling bass before the two men reappeared. Rainey stood up when they entered the room. Mackie moved over and stood in front of the windows, where he periodically checked the backyard.

"Now, Rainey will you tell me what's going on?" JW asked.

"Sit down JW," Rainey indicated the recliner near where he was standing.

JW sat down. Rainey resumed her seat on the edge of the couch cushion. Katie leaned forward, placing her elbows on her knees. All eyes looked eagerly at Rainey for answers. She thought again about how Katie was going to react to the news. She tried to be as calm as possible, while she told the Wilsons what real danger they were in.

"Katie, JW has had me following you for the last two days. He wanted me to catch the guy who has been sending the pictures of you and the notes."

Katie looked stunned. She quickly said, "What pictures? What notes?"

Rainey was as stunned as Katie was. She did not know what to say. She looked at JW for answers.

"Katie, I didn't tell you, because I didn't want you to worry. You were trying to heal from the accident and the baby. I didn't know how much more you could take," JW explained.

"That's why you wanted me to have a bodyguard, not because of your Senate campaign. If I had known about this, I wouldn't have thought it was so silly," Katie shot at him.

"I'm sorry. I did what I thought was best," JW answered a little more sternly than Rainey had expected.

Katie's retort was just as snappy. "That's what you always do, isn't it?"

The happy couple was not so happy inside the beautiful home. It was hard not to notice the animosity between the two. Rainey imagined it was not the first time Mr. Wilson slept on the couch. She needed to get them to focus.

"Look, you two can discuss JW's decision not to tell you another time. Right now I need you to concentrate on what I am saying," Rainey said. When she had their attention, she continued, "Tonight we uncovered information that leads me to believe the person stalking you is a serial killer the FBI has been looking for, for more than a year."

JW sat up. "What serial killer?"

Rainey went on, "You may remember the women who were murdered and found floating in Lake Johnston, in the spring of last year."

"The Y-Man Killer," Katie said, her eyes widening again. "He almost killed that FBI agent and then disappeared."

"Yes," Rainey answered, "that's him."

"I heard a rumor that FBI agent was you. Is it true?" JW asked.

"Yes, I'm afraid that is true," Rainey paused, "and now he has seen me and knows that I am watching Katie. He left a note on the street for me, sometime in the last half hour."

"He was here, outside of the house, tonight?" Katie said, obviously mortified.

"I've contacted the Behavioral Analysis Unit working on the case. We should hear back from them very soon as to what action they recommend we take," Rainey explained. "Till then, I suggest we all make ourselves comfortable."

"Make ourselves comfortable!" Katie stood up, excited. "Why haven't you called the police? Why aren't we surrounded by cops? What about the neighbors? Shouldn't somebody warn them?"

JW stood up, trying to grab Katie by the shoulders. "Calm down, Katie. We don't want to attract that kind of attention."

Katie flashed with anger. "Don't you dare patronize me." She backed away from him. "I think that's exactly the kind of attention this situation calls for."

Rainey tried to refocus the two, before the disagreement escalated. "Katie, I'm afraid that JW is right in this particular scenario. If you'll both sit back down, I will try to explain what will probably happen next."

Rainey took a quick look at Mackie. She looked at Katie's angry, terrified expression. She thought about it for a second, and then turned back to Mackie.

"Wake up Junior and the boys," she directed him. "Put them around the block in groups of two, always together." She repeated, "Always together, remind them. Make sure they dress to blend in with the college crowd. They should call, if they see anything suspicious. Nobody goes after this guy alone. Oh, and ask Junior to move my car around to the driveway and park it out back. I left the keys in it."

"What are you smiling at?" Katie was speaking to JW

Rainey turned around to see that JW was actually smiling, an odd response under the current circumstances. He must have seen the questioning expression on Rainey's face.

He shrugged his shoulders. "I was just thinking I picked the right person for the job." He turned to his wife. "I think she has everything under control and I think we should respect her expertise, in this matter."

"Don't be condescending, I'm not one of your tort juries," Katie snapped.

"I don't know what you're so angry about. I was trying to protect you," JW shouted back, the old temper just under the surface.

Katie screamed back through tears, "You were trying to protect your goddamned career, JW, at least be honest about that."

Katie stormed out of the room and down the hall. Rainey heard footsteps pounding up an unseen staircase. JW watched his wife leave and then looked at Rainey. He made a move to go after Katie, but Rainey raised her hand and waved that idea off. Rainey dropped her eyes to the floor, thinking how best to diffuse the situation. Mackie had been watching intently the whole time.

He finally spoke up, "Mr. Wilson, I could sure use your help setting my boys up."

JW pushed the dark bangs out of his eyes. He nodded, saying, "Sure, sure..." as he followed Mackie back out into the foyer.

"Call Ernie," Rainey said to Mackie. "Tell her not to go to the office alone. I will contact her later."

Rainey headed off in the direction Katie had disappeared. She found the stairs, just off the kitchen and followed them to the second floor. She looked in several rooms before finding a locked door at the end of the hall. She knocked softly.

"Katie, it's Rainey. May I come in?"

She heard Katie's bare feet coming toward the door, the hardwood squeaking with her steps. The lock snapped back and the door handle slowly turned. Katie opened the door and immediately turned her back to Rainey, walking across the room to sit in an armchair near the window. Her face remained turned away, as Rainey entered the room and closed the door behind her.

"Lock it, please," Katie said, sniffling. She reached for the tissue box, on the table, as Rainey turned back and set the latch.

Rainey came over and leaned against the window casing, facing Katie. Katie's tears embarrassed her and she waved Rainey away.

Rainey reached down and brushed some stray hairs from Katie's brow. She wasn't sure why she did that, she wasn't normally so familiar with other women, but it just felt like the thing to do. Rainey spoke softly, "Go ahead and get it out. It is an honest response to stress. You'll feel better, if you just go with it."

Through her tears, Katie said, "I'm sorry that you had to see that outburst. I'm not usually so out of control."

"This is an extreme circumstance, you're allowed at least one outburst." Rainey tried to lighten the mood.

Katie was suddenly seized with the giggles. She began to laugh and cry at the same time.

Rainey continued, "Good, laughter through tears, another excellent way to relieve stress."

This caused Katie to double over. Rainey smiled down at Katie, watching as the giggles subsided and Katie began to take deep breaths, trying to regain her composure. After a few minutes, Katie sat up straight, smiled up at Rainey, and excused herself to the restroom. She came back, after having splashed some water on her face and running a brush through her hair. Her eyes were lined in red from the crying, and her cheeks were a bit splotchy, but other than that, she looked like she had her act together.

She smiled at Rainey. "Thanks, I needed that." She sat back down in the chair.

"Anytime." Rainey smiled back.

"So former Special Agent Bell, what happens next?"

"May I?"

Rainey reached for the chair under the desk near the window. Katie nodded in agreement. Rainey moved the chair close to

Katie and sat down. Katie leaned in to listen. She was calm now and focused. Rainey wanted to ease Katie's mind somewhat, but not downplay the seriousness of the circumstances the two women found themselves in together.

"I think we are done with our stalker for the evening. My experience with this guy is he does not want to be caught. He knows I will probably contact the BAU and has gone to ground to watch and plan his next move."

Katie calmly asked, "So, you think we are safe for the moment?"

"He will want to catch either of us when we least expect it. He will assume the cavalry is coming, so yes, he is gone for the time being," Rainey reassured her.

Katie thought for a second. Then she asked, "So you think you are a target too, because of what happened?"

"He left the note for me," Rainey said. "He wants me to know it's him. He wants me scared, that's part of his sick game."

Katie creased her brow and looked into Rainey's eyes. She seemed curious and empathetic at the same time, asking in a quiet voice, "Are you scared?"

Rainey hesitated to answer, and then she responded softly, "Yes, I'm scared. I'd be lying, if I said I wasn't. However, fear can keep me focused. That's what I'm counting on."

Katie smiled. "I'm counting on you."

Rainey met Katie's smile with her own. "Your safety is my number one priority."

Katie reached over taking Rainey's hand in hers. "We'll do this together, okay?"

The cell ringing on Rainey's hip suddenly ended the moment they shared. She looked at the caller I.D. and saw Danny's name flashing in the window.

She stood up and walked toward the door, saying, "I need to take this. It's my contact at the BAU."

Katie nodded that she understood. Rainey unlatched the door and went into the hallway, closing the door behind her. She did not want Katie to overhear this conversation.

She flipped open the phone, talking into the receiver, "Damn, it took you long enough."

"What do you mean, he's back?" Danny sounded out of breath.

"Where are you?" Rainey asked him.

"I'm running up the stairs, because the fucking elevator in this old ass building is not working at the present time. What do you mean he's back? Are you talking about our guy?"

Rainey felt the fear surface at the back of her throat. When she tried to speak, her voice came out dry and harsh. "Yes," she crackled out, and then cleared her throat. "Yes, it's our guy and he knows where I am."

The man who nearly killed Rainey had become "our" guy, because Danny blamed himself for the attack. Rainey never blamed him. She knew it was her fault. She was tracking a serial killer in his territory, and allowed herself to be distracted. Danny still felt guilty. He sat beside her bed for weeks, refusing to leave even when she went home to her apartment in Bethel, Virginia. When she left the Bureau last July, he was grief stricken that he had caused it all. He made her swear to call if she ever needed anything. Rainey needed something from Danny right now. She needed him to rain down FBI agents from the skies all over "our" guy, before he succeeded in killing her this time.

"We're on the way. Send me all the particulars. I'll go over it with everyone on the way down," Danny said, still running from the sounds of things.

"Thanks Danny," she said, feeling the emotions well up in her throat.

Her eyes began to burn and water. She told herself it was just the stress release, from hearing his voice.

"Hang on Rainey, I'm coming," she heard him say, before she flipped the phone shut and fell against the wall.

Rainey buried her head against her arms and sobbed. She had not cried in almost a year. The built up tension released from her chest, in breathtaking retches. She did not hear the door open, but did not fight the hands that gently lead her back into the bedroom. The door shut and latched behind her. She was tenderly led to the bed, where Rainey buried her face in the pillows and cried until she had no more to give. A cold washcloth was applied to her neck. A soft hand stroked her back until she rolled over. She opened her eyes, as Katie softly brushed the tear-dampened hair from her face. Katie smiled at Rainey.

"I'm glad you got that over with," Katie said, "I've heard it will make you feel better."

CHAPTER ELEVEN

Rainey gradually pulled herself together, while Katie excused herself to take a shower, leaving the bathroom door open a bit, should Rainey need anything. She lay back on the down pillows Katie had carefully fluffed for her, feeling stupid for breaking down and yet, lighter from the release. Rainey should have broken down more often, but she could not let the tears begin, for fear they would never stop. She lost the most important person in her life and shortly after, lost all of her dignity. The rapist degraded her into a piece of meat for his perverted pleasure. He left her scarred both inside and out, to be constantly reminded of him and what he had done to her body and soul. Rainey had been made what she feared most, a powerless victim.

She sat up and threw her legs over the side of the bed. Her shoes were on the floor. She did not remember taking them off. She slipped the shoes on and walked over to the window. The sun was just starting to lighten the sky, turning the blackness to a deep rich purple. Though the clouds had cleared, only the brightest stars could penetrate through the haze created by the city lights. Even out by her house, the lights of the Triangle area shrouded the tiniest stars from view.

She looked at her surroundings. The scene analyst in her began to take mental notes. This was a woman's room. There were no outward signs of a man's presence. Colorful, freshly cut flowers sprung out of various sized vases, on every flat surface.

There were no pictures of JW anywhere. The only pictures Rainey saw were of the smiling faces of children tucked into the dresser mirror. It appeared one person had been sleeping under the covers. Magazines and books were stacked on the floor, on the unoccupied side of the bed. JW had not slept in this room in a very long time. She heard the water in the shower shut off.

Katie's voice came from the bathroom, "You doing all right out there?"

Rainey walked nearer to the door. "Yes, but I really need to use the restroom."

"Oh my gosh, you poor thing. Come on in."

Rainey pushed the door open slowly, saw the toilet, and made a beeline for it. For some reason, when her eyes saw the toilet, her bladder decided need had now become desperation. She rushed to get her pants down and barely made it in time. When she looked up, she saw Katie's reflection in the mirror. She was toweling off behind the opened shower door and glanced up, just in time to see Rainey looking at her. Rainey felt the rush of embarrassment flush her face, as she quickly looked away.

"Don't be embarrassed. You're not the first to take a peek," Katie said, from behind the door.

Rainey was mortified. "But I'm not..." she stammered, before Katie cut her off.

"I'm not either, so I guess it really doesn't matter then, does it?"

Katie came out of the shower with the towel wrapped around her and pranced like a sorority girl into her bedroom, where Rainey could hear her opening and closing drawers. Rainey sat on the toilet, in shock. She *had* been looking. Rainey had seen that Katie was naked and looked anyway, not diverting her eyes until she was caught. It was an entirely new reaction to a female nude body, since Rainey had been in and out of women's locker rooms her entire life. She had never responded with any sexual curiosity to a woman, but she was sure that was exactly what had just happened. What she did not need right now was for her mind and body to start exploring a new sexuality, especially without her full attention. She had quite a lot on her plate as it was.

"Are you ever coming out of there?" Katie inquired.

Rainey finished on the toilet and flushed it, before answering, "Yes, I just need a moment to splash some water on my face."

"Take your time, I just want to brush my teeth," Katie chimed.

Rainey washed her face with cold water several times and toweled off. She looked in the mirror over the sink. Her hair was now a wild tangled mess. She ran her fingers through it and stuck it back in a ponytail. She rinsed her mouth out, splashed cold water on her face again, and dried off.

"That's as good as it gets," she said to her reflection in the mirror.

Her tear reddened eyes stared back. She dropped her gaze and left the bathroom. Katie had slipped into a pair of gray sweats and a pink tee shirt with a "Girls Kick Butt" logo across the chest. Her hair was still wet and pulled back with a clip, pinned to the back of her head. Even dressed this casually she was beautiful. She was on the phone.

"Who are you calling?" Rainey asked, concerned she may alert the wrong person to their predicament.

She held up a finger, signaling Rainey to wait while she punched numbers into the phone with the other thumb. Katie put the receiver back to her ear again, listening. She punched several more numbers and then put the receiver down.

"I had to call for a substitute. It's an automated service, so I didn't have to make any excuses."

"Good," Rainey said, "the less people that know what we know, the better."

Katie brushed her teeth and then opened the bedroom door for them, asking Rainey, "What did your contact at the BAU say?"

Rainey smiled again for the first time since she broke down. "He said the cavalry is coming."

Katie surprised Rainey by hugging her. She whispered against Rainey's chest, "God bless John Wayne."

Then, just as quickly as she hugged her, Katie released her and went down the stairs. Rainey followed, still tingling where Katie's body had been against hers. This could not be happening, not with a serial killer on the loose, not to mention this was JW's wife. She needed to put some distance between herself and Katie for a few moments, clear her head. While Katie went into the kitchen to make coffee, Rainey went to the den to find Mackie and JW sitting quietly.

JW stood up. He looked at Rainey, brows raised in a question.

"Yes, she's okay. She's making coffee. She should be back in here soon," Rainey answered his silent inquiry. "I don't know what's going on between you two, but you have to find a way to form one front against this guy. Don't give him the satisfaction of driving you any further apart."

"Maybe I should go try to smooth things over," JW said, moving toward the kitchen.

Rainey stopped him, by saying, "Don't piss her off. I need her focused on her safety, not on killing you."

JW smiled a half smirk, before he continued toward the kitchen, calling back, "Yeah, now wouldn't that make headlines."

Mackie waited until he was sure JW was gone, before he said, "That is one weird duck."

Rainey sat down on the couch beside him. She patted his enormous thigh. A silent sign, letting Mackie know she was glad he was there. She looked in the direction JW had taken.

"I remember JW as a little irreverent. It was how he dealt with stress."

Mackie shook his head. "No, it's more than that. His responses are all wrong."

Rainey leaned in conspiratorially, before she whispered, "Look, from what I can tell, these two haven't slept together in a long time. They lost an unborn child just six months ago in an accident that nearly killed Katie."

Mackie tried to whisper, but was not exactly successful, "I think I remember reading something about that."

Rainey signaled for him to keep his voice down, even though she knew he could not.

She continued, "He's worried about being the strong male for Katie and an upcoming Senate campaign he's worked for all of his adult life. There's no telling how much stress he's dealing with. He could be reacting oddly, because he is so used to keeping his emotions in check."

Rainey turned her head toward the kitchen. She thought she heard someone coming. She let Mackie know with a look and then changed the subject.

"I need my laptop. I have to email Danny."

Mackie caught on quickly and almost spoke too loudly, "So, you've talked to the BAU."

Rainey grinned at Mackie's attempt at nonchalance.

She kept going, "They're on the way. Danny wants me to send him the latest information I have. They should be up in the air by now."

"I brought in your laptop. Locked your car up, too. Got to thinking about how mad Ernie would be if it got stolen with the keys in it. It's around back." Mackie laughed and tossed her keys to her.

Rainey looked at the big man with surprise. He chuckled even louder.

"No, I didn't squeeze my fat ass into your ride. I made JW move it. Junior and the boys are already walking the block. Nothing moves without us knowing it." Mackie stood up. "I think I'll go check on things myself. Your laptop is in the kitchen, on the table."

"Mackie, don't go into the shadows alone," Rainey said quickly.

"Now Rainey, do you seriously think some punk ass white boy is going to jump a three hundred pound black man in the dark?"

"I think you forgot a few pounds there," Rainey said, teasing him.

"Go on, wiseass. See if you can keep them two from each other's throats. I'll let you know when Danny gets here." Mackie opened the front door. "Make him turn the alarm back on, after I leave," he said and shut the door behind him.

Rainey smelled the bacon cooking, as soon as she started for the back of the house. She entered the wide open-spaced kitchen through the door, where she had last seen Katie. It was completely furnished in stainless steel appliances and marble counter tops. A large center island offered refrigerated space underneath and a small wet sink on top. Katie was standing on the other side of the island surrounded by multiple pots, pans, and bowls of all sizes. She was working feverously on chopping something that was blocked from Rainey's view by a large bowl. She looked up when she heard Rainey come in. Her cheeks were once again damp with tears.

"What happened?" Rainey questioned her. "Where's JW?"

Katie looked surprised, rubbing her chin with the back of her hand. "Nothing happened. He went to take a shower."

Rainey took a step closer. "Then why are you crying?"

Katie looked down at the surface in front of her. Rainey took another step. She was now able to see the large mound of onion on the chopping board. Katie laughed at her and Rainey joined in. Rainey asked Katie to arm the alarm. Katie went to a pad by the French doors that led to the blue slate patio. Rainey could see the Charger parked under the covered carport.

"I thought I would make some breakfast and judging by the size of Mackie, if his boys are anything like him, we're going to need a lot of omelets," Katie was saying, returning to her chopping.

Rainey put her hands on the edge of the counter opposite Katie. She said, "You don't have to do this. We can fend for ourselves. Just coffee would be fine."

"Nonsense, I love to cook and I am glad to have someone here to eat it."

"It smells delicious. Can I help?"

"Just my luck, a volunteer after I finished the onions," Katie teased. "I need to send someone to the grocery store, but I don't guess that's going to be you."

"No, but one of the boys can go for you." Rainey saw her laptop on the kitchen table. She retrieved it, saying, "I'll just sit over here on this stool." She sat at a counter that served as a breakfast bar. "Let me know if you need me."

Rainey opened her laptop and waited for it to wake. She watched Katie hustle from the refrigerator to the island and then over to the stove.

"Who taught you how to cook?" Rainey asked.

Katie kept moving while she talked. "I taught myself mainly, something to relieve stress and living with JW, I had lots of reasons to practice."

Rainey laughed. "Most people eat when they're stressed."

"Well, I like to feed them. I've been completely responsible for the significant total weight gain of my school's faculty, in the last six months."

"You don't look like you have any weight issues," Rainey commented. She enjoyed their banter back and forth.

Katie popped several small ceramic pie dishes out of the oven, while she talked. "I eat healthy and exercise. I don't eat half the stuff I cook. I just like to make it."

Rainey looked over at the pie dishes. "Are you making pies, too?"

"Well, I was going to make quiche, that's why I started the pie crusts, but then I decided on omelets. Now, I have these piecrusts, so I thought I would make some summer pies. You know the creamy ones, like lemon and key lime…"

Rainey threw her hands up. "Okay, okay Julia Child. I'll just let you cook and I'll sit over here and write my email."

The two women worked in silence, Rainey keenly aware of Katie's presence, and trying to ignore it. She needed to get this email to Danny, as soon as possible. She already let too much time elapse since their phone call. Once she focused on giving the BAU as many new facts as she could think of, her ability to concentrate returned. She told them all she knew about the stalker and how she had discovered it was the same man who attacked her. She attached copies of the notes and photos that had been sent to JW, except for the one he had given her last night. She had not had a chance to scan it in.

Katie brought over a cup of coffee and set a pitcher of cream beside the sugar bowl, already on the counter.

"What would you like in your omelet?"

101

Rainey knew she had to eat, but her stomach was tied in knots from the stress. "Can I just have a piece of toast? My stomach isn't ready for a meal, just yet."

"When did you eat last?" Katie asked, with her hands on her hips, questioning Rainey like an adult speaking to a wayward child.

"I had a hamburger around midnight," Rainey answered, sheepishly.

"Okay, I'll make you some toast, but you're getting some fruit, too. I don't want you crashing on me." Katie paused, and then added quietly, "I might need you."

Rainey felt an unfamiliar tightening in her chest. She looked Katie directly in the eyes. She said, "I promise, I will not let anything happen to you."

Katie leaned across the counter. She reached for Rainey's hand and surrounded it with both of hers. She looked deep into Rainey's eyes and said softly, "Promise me you won't let anything happen to you, either."

Rainey swallowed hard and felt her vocal chords tighten. She had never dealt with a woman who physically touched her so much. In a hushed whisper, she said, "I promise."

Katie held on to Rainey's hand. Rainey felt her head spinning again. She felt the heat from the flush of her face. Katie smiled, still holding Rainey's gaze with her own crystal blue eyes. Rainey thought to herself that those eyes could make her promise anything.

The sound of JW bounding down the stairs fractured their moment. Katie released Rainey's hand and turned back to her cooking. She did not acknowledge JW entering the kitchen.

"That smells delicious," he said, moving over to Rainey. "I'll take an omelet with everything," he called to Katie.

Katie did not react to his request. She kept her back turned and continued to cook, dropping slices of bread into the toaster. Rainey watched Katie as JW began speaking to her. Katie's body language had completely changed since he walked in. Whatever had happened to their marriage, Rainey could see Katie could not stand being in the same room with JW.

"Two of my favorite women in the same room before breakfast, life is good," JW said, sitting on the stool next to Rainey.

JW was in his good ol' boy persona, the backslapping politician, "just glad to be here folks" guy that everyone loved so much. Rainey had witnessed JW slip in and out of characters as long as she had known him. When they got in trouble, he could "ah, shucks" them out of it, most of the time. She remembered the smooth talker, the one the girls melted for, the tough guy protecting his turf, and so many more. He was a marvel. He should have been an actor. Maybe that was what Mackie picked up on, JW's ability to hide, from the people around him, the reality of his situation. Two of his favorite women, as he put it, were in mortal danger and he was smiling, as if it was just another morning.

"Why are you dressed like that?" Rainey was referring to the designer shirt and tie he was wearing.

"I have to go into the office for a few hours. I have some things I have to deal with this morning."

Rainey looked at him in disbelief. "You can't do that. The BAU guys will be here soon, and they are going to want to talk to you. Not to mention there is a maniac out there who might be trying to kill you."

"You say it's this Y-Man character. He doesn't kill men, so I should be okay, don't you think?" JW asked her, and then took a sip from the coffee cup Katie set down for Rainey earlier.

"He didn't stalk his previous victims, either," Rainey countered. "He's changed his method of operating. We don't know what he's planning."

JW sounded like a lawyer giving a summation to the jury. "Well, this guy is a sexually motivated serial murderer. He has already killed six women that you know about. They don't usually change their victim choice. I don't think I really have any reason to worry."

His thought process floored Rainey. He had completely ignored the most important thing. She could not stop herself from sounding disturbed by his disregard for the reality of the

103

situation. Katie slid a plate of toast and fruit in front of Rainey, and put a fresh cup of coffee down for her.

"What about your wife?"

"I know you won't let anything happen to her. The house is surrounded and the FBI will be arriving soon. I'll have to explain this to my father, and tell him I'll be away from the office a few days."

Katie interjected, "And he has to figure out how he can spin this to the media in his favor."

JW smiled at Katie. "Now there's a thought."

"Oh, for God's sake, just let him go," Katie snapped.

Katie turned away disgusted. Rainey had to think. She could not let herself get drawn into the tension between the two people she was trying to protect.

"Okay, but you can't go alone. Take Mackie with you," Rainey finally said.

"Are you kidding me? He'd scare the daylights out of everybody," JW said.

"That's the point," Rainey said.

"I'd rather him be here to protect Katie, she's the one in danger, and you for that matter. Shouldn't he be here watching your back?"

"I think my back is pretty well covered, and as you say the FBI will be here soon," Rainey said.

JW had lost the argument and he could see no way around it. He finally conceded, after Rainey watched his brain trying to figure a way out of her proposition.

"Okay, I'll take Mackie."

Rainey pulled out her cellphone. "I'll call him and get him in here. Then we can go over a plan for this morning. I want to know where you are at all times. We make a plan and you don't deviate from it, got it?"

"Why don't you put one of those chips in my phone, like you were talking about for Katie?"

Katie arrived with JW's omelet. "What chip?" she asked.

"She has a chip for your phone, so she can track your movement," JW said, just before taking in a mouthful of egg, dripping with cheese.

"You didn't put a tracker on me, did you?" Katie asked.

"No, I didn't. I didn't get the chance," Rainey said.

"Well, don't give him any device to track me. I don't want him spying on my every move," Katie said, emphatically,

"Why? Do have you have something to hide?" JW said, still chewing.

"I don't want you to know which divorce lawyer I'm going to contact, when this little campaign is finally over," Katie quipped, going back to her pans on the stove.

JW swallowed. His mood darkened. His voice was much less congenial when he said, "Katie, that's a private matter. I would appreciate it if you would leave it that way."

Katie turned quickly and charged at him. "Don't you get it? There isn't going to be any more privacy. These people are going to come in here and tear our lives apart. They'll question everything. There won't be any skeletons left in the closet."

JW glowered at Katie. He gripped the fork in his hand tightly, frozen between the plate and his mouth. Suddenly, there was a loud banging on the front door. Everyone jumped. Rainey could hear Mackie's voice, on the other side of the door, calling her name. She realized at that moment that she was still holding her opened phone in her hand. She had dialed Mackie's number, but when the fighting escalated between Katie and JW, she had forgotten to say anything. He must have thought something was wrong. She jumped up quickly.

"JW, disarm the alarm. I'll get the door," she said, sprinting toward the front of the house.

She threw open the door to find Mackie, breathless, and scared.

"I'm so sorry," she offered.

"Goddamnit, Rainey. I thought he was in the house," he shouted at her.

"I'm sorry. Those two started going at it again, and I got distracted," Rainey explained.

Pushing passed her, Mackie said, "That distraction is going to get you killed."

Rainey did not argue. There was no point. He was right. The Wilsons were a huge distraction, especially Katie. Rainey needed to distance herself from the two of them. She was too close and being drawn steadily deeper into their dysfunctional personal drama.

She tried to smooth things over. She used the one thing she thought would brighten Mackie's mood. "Katie has food for you, in the kitchen."

She followed the big man, as they made their way back to the back of the house. Katie was at the stove again, silently cooking. JW had finished eating and was standing by the French doors, drinking coffee. The tension hung in the air like dense fog. Katie turned, as they came in.

"Hello, Mackie. What would you like in your omelet?"

"Anything you can throw in it will work for me," Mackie said, a big smile on his face.

"Just sit down at the table and I'll bring you some coffee," Katie said, going to work on the omelet.

"I'll get the coffee," Rainey said, retrieving her cup from earlier and grabbing one for Mackie from the cup-tree on the counter.

Rainey poured the coffee, taking it to the table, where Mackie was standing behind a chair. He was looking down at the spindly legs of the colonial reproduction and, Rainey assumed, trying to gauge if the chair would hold his massive frame.

"Go ahead, I don't think it's an antique," Rainey teased.

"Just for that, you're paying for it, if it breaks," he said.

The wooden chair creaked, as he lowered himself onto the seat. JW joined them and they discussed the plan for Mackie to go with him to his office for a few hours. Mackie raised his brow, questioning Rainey with his eyes, but remained silent on the subject of how odd it was that JW was leaving the house. He listened intently as JW outlined his morning and agreed to ride along. Katie came to the table with Mackie's plate, piled high with a glistening fluffy omelet, cheese oozing from the ends. She also brought Rainey's untouched plate from before, raising one eyebrow at Rainey, which said, "Eat your food."

Rainey did as she was told, eating everything on her plate. The room grew silent, except for the appreciative moans from Mackie, after every bite. Katie smiled and patted his huge shoulder.

"Send the rest of the boys in, before you leave. I'm sure they are hungry by now," Katie said.

Mackie nodded, but did not stop eating. When his fork finally clanked onto his empty plate, he thanked Katie and complimented her ability to fluff the eggs just right. It was high praise from a food aficionado such as Mackie. He and JW left together and then the boys trailed in, two at a time, to be fed and fussed over by Katie. Rainey stayed busy, checking doors and window locks a second and third time. She got a feel for the layout of the house, admiring the antiques and decorative choices Katie had made. It was a showcase of good taste, done well enough for a display in a design magazine.

The third story was merely an attic storage space. An artificial Christmas tree stood at one end surrounded by boxes of ornaments and decorations. Several boxes, labeled baby things, were stacked inside a crib at the other end. A teddy bear slept in a stroller nearby. Rainey's heart broke for the woman, who had packed her dreams away in those boxes, with hopes of needing them again. Rainey never wanted children, never had the time really, but she could certainly understand the pain of loss.

In the basement, she found the washing machine and dryer, a treadmill, weights, and not much else. A wooden door with paned windows was the only exit to outside. She checked the bolt was securely in place and went back upstairs. She found Katie alone, loading the dishwasher. She saw a list on the counter with a stack of twenty-dollar bills.

"What's this?" Rainey asked, pointing at the paper and money.

"One of the boys volunteered to do some shopping for me. They were all so nice. I hope JW is paying you enough to take care of them, too."

107

"Oh, yeah," Rainey answered, "He's paying enough."

"There isn't enough money to pay you for what you are doing. Thank you again for all of this," Katie said.

Rainey refilled her coffee, turning back to Katie. "We're in this together. I want this guy caught so we can all go on with our lives."

"Amen to that, sister," Katie said, wrapping her arms around Rainey, pulling her in for an embrace.

Katie was a hugger. Rainey was not used to a woman other than Ernie hugging her. Rainey's heart thumped against her chest. She returned the hug and was met by a tighter squeeze. They both jumped when they heard the French doors open. They released each other and turned to see Junior poking his head in the door.

"Rainey, the FBI is here."

"Thanks, Junior," she said, and then looked at Katie. "Well, the cavalry has arrived."

CHAPTER TWELVE

The suspect had made one mistake, as far as Rainey could tell. He attacked an FBI Agent, making this a federal case. The BAU did not have to be invited to participate. Their jurisdiction superseded that of local police departments. The killer brought the full force of federal law enforcement and all the tools at their disposal down on his head. Three big black SUVs pulled into the driveway and a small army of agents descended on the house, coming to avenge one of their own.

"Let the games begin," Rainey whispered under her breath.

She opened the French doors, stepping out on the patio. She waved at Danny when he exited the first vehicle. Danny McNally looked just like his Irish name made him sound. He was tall and broad, with red wavy hair and freckles to match. His childlike face and cherub cheeks made him appear younger than his forty-two years. He looked out of place in the blue suit he was wearing. He preferred jeans and tennis shoes, although he could be persuaded to wear a tie and jacket with them. The suit had come with a promotion. He was now a Supervisory Special Agent and he was heading the team on this investigation. Danny saw Rainey and walked quickly to her.

"You look great Rainey," he said, squeezing her into a bear hug. "It's good to see you. I wish I were here under different circumstances."

"Me too, Danny, me too," Rainey said.

"I put a call in to that detective we worked with last year. He's going to liaison for us with all the local jurisdictions," Danny said, looking back over his shoulder. "Do you think we could work here until they clear a space for us downtown?"

Katie, who had been standing in the doorway answered, before Rainey had a chance, "Yes, of course. Make yourselves at home. There is coffee in the kitchen and I can make you something to eat."

"Special Agent Danny McNally, this is Katie Wilson," Rainey introduced them.

"It's a pleasure to meet you, Mrs. Wilson," Danny said, shaking Katie's outstretched hand.

"Please, call me Katie," she said. "Come on in, you can put your things on the kitchen table."

Katie turned, going back through the open doorway. She had charmed him, and like the pied piper led Danny and his fellow mice streaming into the house behind her. Rainey smiled, watching Katie through the panes of glass in the doors as she flitted here and there, making room for laptops and pouring coffee. Rainey shook hands with the other agents. She knew most of them, but had only worked personally with James the tech guru and Roger the strong and quiet one standing guard behind the last SUV. They waved and smiled at each other, and then Rainey followed the last agent in and closed the door behind her.

The agents went about setting up, while Katie bustled about making muffins in the kitchen. Danny called Rainey to the side. He wanted to talk somewhere more private, so Rainey took him to the living room, at the front of the house. They sat down in matching wingback chairs, across from each other.

Danny spoke first, "Where is Mr. Wilson, may I ask?"

"He went to his office. Mackie is with him." Rainey replied.

"When will he be back?" Danny asked.

"He said he only needed a few hours. I can call Mackie and see how much longer they'll be."

"That's okay. We can interview him when he gets back." Danny looked around the room. "These people are loaded," he said, followed by a whistle. He looked at Rainey for a second, then added, "How are you, Rainey?"

"I'm all right, considering," Rainey said.

"Are you sleeping? What about the dreams?" He knew her too well.

"They have been better since I moved down here," she lied.

Danny slept near her for two months, after the attack. He slept on the floor of her hospital room, until a nurse saw him and brought a cot. He slept on her couch when she went home to her apartment. He was the calming voice she awoke to, when the terror filled her dreams. He was always there, holding her, soothing her until she could regain control.

"Don't lie to me, Rainey. You are an important witness in this investigation. I need to know where your head is," Danny said, locking her eyes with his.

Rainey sat back against the Laura Ashley, pink and blue, floral patterned cushion, "A witness? I hadn't thought of myself in those terms."

Danny leaned in closer to her. "You are a vital witness. You are the only one of his victims to have survived."

"Wow, witness and victim," Rainey said.

Danny cleared his throat. "I know it's hard for you to think of yourself as a victim, but you know as well as I do that you are the most important piece of evidence we have on this guy."

Rainey responded sharply, "I am fully aware of that, Danny. I know where this is going. You can't shut me out of the investigation. I'm not in the Bureau anymore."

"Technically, you are on medical leave and besides, you know you can't be objective," Danny countered.

Rainey stood up and paced the room. She knew he was right, but she wanted to be out there hunting this guy like a cop, not a tool for the cops to use. Danny could not make her follow orders. She would just quit the Bureau completely. She had to believe in Danny, though. Rainey had worked side by side with him for seven years. She knew he was a sharp investigator and he had good instincts. Rainey had to relinquish control and follow his lead. It really was the best thing to do. She stopped pacing and leaned on the back of the armchair she recently vacated.

"I'll do what you need me to, Danny. I trust you."

"That's all I want, Rainey, is for you to trust me. We'll get this guy."

"Okay, how can I help?" Rainey asked. She sat back down.

"One of the other agents is going to take your statement. She'll want to go over your stalker investigation with you in detail. I'll need the note you received last night, from JW, and the one addressed to you." Danny said, and pulled a pad from his pocket. He thumbed through a few pages, before he found what he was looking for. "You said the originals are in a safe, in your office."

Rainey answered, "Yes, I can get them for you, but they've already been run for prints. Only JW's prints showed up."

"I'd still like to have a look at them. We'll send someone with you to get them later." Danny looked at the pad again, asking, "Do you think he targeted your friend's wife to get to you?"

"No," Rainey answered quickly, because she had thought about that already. "I think it was just a fluke. If he knew enough about me to know JW and I were friends, then he didn't have to involve them, did he? He could have come straight for me and I wouldn't have seen it coming."

"Maybe he did it to draw you out of your comfort zone. He wants to play the game."

Rainey thought about that. "His MO has changed. He was stalking Katie. Why? It just makes more sense that I showed up in his radar by accident."

"Okay, I thought it was worth asking." Danny went on, "Anyway, I'm going to need you to give the video of the guy you saw the other night to James. Maybe he can enhance it."

"Sure, anything else?" Rainey stood up.

Danny rose from his seat and moved in close to her. "You never answered my question, how are you?"

"Tired, angry, frustrated and yes, scared," Rainey answered him.

"And the dreams?" Danny persisted.

"They did go away soon after I moved, but I started having them again around my birthday."

"Maybe you've experienced something recently, something you are unaware of, that triggered the return," Danny suggested.

"It's possible, I guess," Rainey said, thinking of the prospect that she may have subconsciously picked up on something she had seen or heard.

"Okay, then, after the agent has talked to you, we'll see about getting those notes and pictures from your office," Danny said, putting an arm around her shoulder.

Rainey leaned into him and put an arm around his waist. They stood there for a moment then went back to the kitchen. Some of the agents were eating fruit and nibbling on toast while they went over investigative reports. Rainey recognized the names on the folders, the killer's victims. She saw her own name and felt her stomach turn over. In that folder were the details of what she had endured the night she was attacked. Pictures of her brutalized body were clipped to the inside. She had not seen the pictures. She was not even aware they had been taken, but she knew they were there. There were always pictures of the victim.

Katie was leaning on the kitchen island, pen in hand, writing on a pad that said, "Teach from the Heart," across the top.

Rainey moved over to the island and leaned down on her elbows next to Katie.

"Making another list I see," Rainey said.

"I need more supplies, even with the ones Junior brought in a little while ago," Katie said, tapping her head with the end of the pen.

"You really don't have to feed everybody."

Katie turned her face to Rainey. "It keeps me busy. I couldn't just sit around. I'd rather not have the time to think about a crazed man out there hunting us."

They were inches apart. Katie's eyes were even more dazzling up close. The starburst patterned colors of her irises ranged from a deep midnight blue to sky blue, with golden highlights.

113

"Rainey, I asked if you have any requests." Katie was looking at Rainey, who was lost in the other woman's eyes. She had not heard Katie speaking to her.

"No, I'm fine, but thanks for asking," Rainey managed to say, though she was beginning to panic.

What was happening to her? Rainey was developing a major crush on this woman. Not now, she thought, not while I need to be focused on keeping us both safe. Rainey knew what falling for someone felt like. She did it with Bobby and a few others along the way, but never with a woman, unless she counted the schoolgirl crushes she had experienced, but they never felt like this. She felt an electrical charge between them, a physical heat that kept rising. Rainey had to get away, but she wanted to stay right here beside Katie. She was so conflicted it must have shown on her face.

"What's wrong?" Katie asked.

Rainey stood up. "Nothing's wrong. I was just thinking."

"It must have been something important. You looked so worried," Katie said, studying Rainey's face.

Rainey thought quickly. "Danny called me a victim. I have a hard time thinking that way."

"It must be hard, going from the hunter to the hunted," Katie said. Her look of empathy was genuine.

"Yes, it is. I'm not looking forward to going over it all again," Rainey said, moving away from Katie.

Katie remained focused on Rainey, forgetting her list. "I'm a good listener, if you need to talk, not about what happened, just if you need a shoulder to lean on."

Rainey smiled. "I appreciate that."

Katie went back to her list and Rainey wandered over to the agents at the table. A tall, athletically built, cocoa-skinned woman with close-cropped hair asked if she could take Rainey's statement now. Rainey remembered her name was Paula, but she only knew her in passing. She was a new member of the BAU and Rainey had not had time to get to know her before she left. Rainey showed Paula to the living room where they talked for an hour. Rainey went over every detail she could remember about the stalker investigation. Paula did not ask any questions about her attack, to Rainey's relief.

She went out to the Charger and retrieved the notes, passing them off to an agent wearing latex gloves. She gave her laptop to James so he could copy the video file and the pictures she took while on the stakeout. Rainey asked if there was anything else she could do for them, and they said no.

Rainey decided to call Ernie and give her the details of what was happening. She told her to stay home and keep the doors locked. Rainey was not sure how far this lunatic would go to terrorize her. She did not want to think about Ernie being in danger, but she told her to load her gun anyway. Ernie, though petite and very feminine could shoot the eyes out of a gnat. Rainey's father had a gun for the office, because their clientele were, after all, criminals. Ernie insisted he teach her how to use it. She was a crack shot from the beginning, having grown up on a farm surrounded by guns. She was very capable and willing to use one.

"Now, don't you go trying to be a hero. Let those other agents do their jobs," Ernie scolded.

"I won't do anything crazy, I promise," Rainey said. "You be careful, too."

"Don't worry about me. My boys will take care of me and I will shoot the little bastard, if he tries to come in my house. I guarantee you that."

Rainey believed her. Not only would Ernie shoot someone, that person would have to get past her four sons, who were all over six feet tall and loved their momma. She thought about Freddie.

"Could you get the boys to take you to the cottage to feed Freddie for me? I might be gone for a couple of days. You don't have to go today. I'm going to get the notes and pictures out of the safe and I'll feed him."

"He can feed himself from all the stuff he drags up, but I'll go out there anyway," Ernie said.

Rainey laughed. "He doesn't eat them, they're gifts."

"Gifts, my behind," Ernie said. "That cat's a killer, no question about it. I think he's part bobcat."

"I've thought that myself, from time to time," Rainey said. "You take care now and I'll see you, as soon as this is over."

"Rainey, you know I love you, don't you?" Ernie said softly.

"I love you too, Ernie. I'll be careful," Rainey said, almost tearing up. "I gotta go," she added, so she would not have to say anything else.

"Be safe, honey. See you soon," Ernie said, and then hung up.

Rainey found Danny chatting with Katie, in the den. He had just finished interrogating her, but she really had little to offer in the way of successfully identifying her stalker. She had been completely unaware of his existence until last night. They were talking about her teaching career when Rainey came in. Katie was going on about how she loved her job and the challenge of molding young minds. Rainey listened as the animated Katie told amusing stories about the mess six-year-olds could get into. Most involved scissors and glue.

When Katie finished, Rainey said, "Danny, do you think I can go home now, take a shower, and grab some clothes? I would really love to brush my teeth. I can grab the stuff out of the safe while I'm there."

Katie brightened. "Do you think I can come along, so we can go to the grocery store?"

Rainey and Danny responded simultaneously, "No."

"Please? I don't think he's going to try anything in the store," Katie argued.

Danny thought, and then said, "Okay, we have to go meet Detective Griffin. He's got a room set up at the police department. We're moving most of the agents down there."

Rainey asked, "How many are you leaving here, with us?"

"I'm assigning Roger and three others to watch you. Their only job is to keep you covered at all times."

Rainey looked at Katie. "Roger is a good agent. He'll keep us safe."

Danny continued, "I think four agents ought to be able to take a lady shopping, if she needs to."

Danny had fallen under Katie's spell. Against his better judgment, he was doing what would make her happy. Rainey probably would have given in, too. They loaded up, Katie and Rainey in the Charger, and the four agents trailing in an SUV. It took twenty minutes to get to the cottage. Rainey listened as Katie talked about growing up just outside of Durham, with her parents and sisters, and where she had gone to high school. She never once mentioned JW. She questioned Rainey about her childhood and Rainey told her the story of discovering her real father at age ten. They arrived at the cottage just as Rainey was finishing up the story.

"That must have been a real shock at that age, well, at any age, for that matter," Katie commented.

Rainey parked the car under the cottage. "It all turned out for the best in the long run," she said.

They exited the car and walked down to the office, followed by four large men in suits.

Rainey went in the office to retrieve the file containing the notes and pictures. She handed it to Roger, who put it in the SUV when they went back to the cottage. Katie looked out at the view from Rainey's front deck.

"This is really nice and I love the cottage look. It reminds me of Nags Head," she said.

Rainey unlocked the door and disabled the alarm. She turned back to Katie. "It should. My father copied the plans from a place down there. He loved the beach."

"You must miss him terribly," Katie said.

Rainey answered, "Every day."

They entered the cottage, Roger first, then one other agent. They checked the place out and determined it was safe to enter. Roger stationed two agents on the back deck. He and the other agent would stay by the front door. Rainey and Katie went inside together. The memorabilia immediately enthralled Katie.

"This is some great stuff. Your father collected it all?"

Rainey called out from the kitchen, where she had gone to get them each a bottle of water, "Yes, it took him years. I think I'm

117

going to donate most of it to a museum, except for the things that actually belonged to him when he was in combat."

Rainey returned from the kitchen and excused herself to take a shower. She left Katie examining a helmet from World War II, complete with bullet hole and blood stained webbing. Rainey went into her bedroom, found her overnight bag, and put some things in it. She was used to packing a travel bag, not knowing when she would return. When she was in the Bureau actively, she had a "go" bag packed at all times. She picked out some jeans and a tee shirt to wear today. No need to be uncomfortable, she thought.

Rainey checked on Katie, before she went to the shower. Katie was lost in the hundreds of artifacts strewn around the cottage's large main room. She told Rainey to take her time and went back to her sightseeing. Rainey shut the door on the bathroom, and then shed the clothes she felt she had on for days. She put them on only yesterday afternoon, so it had not been as long as that. The hot shower helped release the tension in her neck, as the water pounded down on her. She rolled her neck and moaned when it popped, relaxing her muscles. She was really tight.

She took the time to think about her feelings for Katie. This was all so new and exciting, yet inappropriate, considering three major factors. First and second, Katie said she was not gay and neither was Rainey. Third and lastly, she was JW's wife. Although unhappy, Katie was still married to JW. Maybe, when this was all over, Rainey would examine her unexplored attraction to women, but now was not a good time. Besides, she did not think it was all women, just Katie that pushed her previously unknown buttons. She wished she had someone to talk to about it, but there was no one she was willing to trust with this. She was on her own.

After the shower, she stepped out of the tub and began to dry off. Rainey heard something hit the door, then the latch opened, and the door swung open slowly. Freddie came around the door and began rubbing on her recently dried legs. He purred loudly as he twined himself between her ankles. The bathroom door handle was the type you pulled down to open. Freddie had learned the trick of opening it, at an early age.

"Hey there, little man," she said, bending to rub her hand along his sleek back.

Rainey stood up and was horrified to see Katie standing outside the bathroom door. Rainey was completely naked in front of someone for the first time since the attack. She pulled the towel up to cover her chest. It was too late. Katie had seen the scar. Rainey could see it in her expression. Rainey stood frozen on the bathroom floor mat, unable to speak. Katie did not turn away in revulsion, as Rainey thought she would. Instead, she walked into the bathroom and right up to Rainey. Rainey still did not move, only clutched the towel closer to her breast.

A single tear flowed down Katie's cheek as she looked into Rainey's stricken face. She pulled the towel from Rainey's hands and examined the scar with her eyes. Rainey remained still and watched Katie's face, reflecting the sadness in her heart. When Katie reached out and touched the spot where the top of the Y came together, Rainey flinched and drew in a quick breath. The sensation was electrifying. Katie's finger and eyes followed the scar down its path to her navel. When she looked back at Rainey, her cheeks were wet with tears. Then she did something so much more unexpected. She leaned over and kissed the scar between Rainey's breasts.

Rainey had a hard time fighting the impulse to run. She was then seized with the urge to grab Katie and kiss her, to hold her against her naked body. No other thought could penetrate the want she felt. The sensation overpowered her mortification at showing the scar.

Katie raised her head again. She whispered, "I'm so sorry this happened to you."

Rainey could not speak. She remained silent, while Katie handed her back the towel and left the bathroom without another word.

Rainey was in a daze. Freddie continued his figure eights around her legs, while Rainey just stood there, staring at her reflection in the mirror. What just happened? It was all just too much to take in. Her brain had finally overloaded and left her dumbfounded. She replayed the moment over in her mind. Rainey felt the thrill again, as Katie's lips touched her skin. The scar seemed to be burning where she had gently kissed it. It was not her imagination, it really happened. Now Rainey just needed to figure out what to do next. Get dressed, was what she came up with.

She finished drying off and then dressed, going through each task automatically, her mind lost in Katie's kiss. She brushed her hair and teeth, leaving her hair down to dry. She took the hairbrush and toothbrush back to the bedroom, and threw them into the overnight bag. She checked herself, in the dresser mirror, and decided against the tee shirt she was wearing. She found a French-blue, cap-sleeve, button-up and put it on. The white tee shirt she always wore, to cover her scar, stuck out at the neck. She took the blouse off, removed the tee shirt and dug around in a drawer until she found a lace trimmed, cotton and spandex camisole she used to wear. It was a complimentary blue, so when she put the blouse back on, they matched perfectly. Rainey had not taken this long to dress in years, but she had the desire to look nice, which was a new feeling since the attack. She stopped caring what she looked like until just a few minutes ago.

When she emerged from the rear of the cottage with her bag, she found Katie sitting on the couch. Katie was staring into space. She seemed as freaked out as Rainey was by the whole encounter. Rainey decided the best course of action was to pretend it did not happen.

Katie heard Rainey behind her and stood up quickly. She turned to Rainey, saying, "I'm sorry if I made you uncomfortable. I don't know what came over me."

Rainey was glad someone else was feeling confused, but only said, "It's okay, really. Forget about it."

Rainey was not about to forget about it, any time soon. From the look on her face, Rainey did not think Katie would forget it either. Rainey excused herself to feed and water Freddie, who had begun to whine and cry, prancing around her feet. She went to the kitchen and filled his bowls. She rubbed his head a few minutes while he ate. Rainey explained that Ernie would be coming by and that she might be gone for a few days. She did not know if he understood, but just in case, she told him anyway. She collected her bag and they left the cottage in silence, both women lost in their own thoughts.

Katie gave directions to the grocery store where she liked to shop, and they drove in almost total silence. There was some light banter about different kinds of lettuce and their nutritional value, but neither woman was as comfortable as before. They drew lots of attention entering the store, with the four black suits hot on their trail. Katie asked for help and, of course, the guys said yes. Soon two men were pushing carts, following Katie through the aisles while she filled them. Rainey tagged along, lost in her own thoughts. Roger fell in step with her.

"How you been, Rainey?" he asked in his soft baritone.

She smiled up at him. "Pretty good until recently."

"We're not leaving until we catch him," Roger reassured her.

Katie came up to them. "Do you think I should get chocolate milk, too?"

Roger shrugged, leaving Rainey to answer, "Sure, I guess." Rainey looked at the two nearly full carts. "I do think you should leave some food on the shelves for other people."

Katie laughed for the first time since the bathroom incident and the two women finally relaxed. Roger went to check out the front of the store. The veil between them lifted, Katie and Rainey finished the shopping together, laughing and joking as if they had not a care in the world. The agents put the groceries in the back of the SUV and they headed home. The pleasant mood continued until they turned onto Katie's block.

Rainey heard Katie sigh loudly. She glanced at Katie and saw that she was staring out the window. Katie began to talk without looking at Rainey.

"Maybe it's the stress, maybe it's the situation we find ourselves in together, but I feel like I've known you my whole life. I'm not sure what's going on here, but I don't want to lose you as a friend, now that I've found you."

Rainey's breath caught in her throat. She pulled into the driveway and parked the car. She turned to Katie and waited for her to turn around.

When she did not, Rainey said, "Katie, turn around."

Katie slowly turned her head and finally made eye contact with Rainey.

Rainey took a deep breath and said exactly what was on her mind, "I'm not sure what's happening either, but I am sure of one thing. I'm not going anywhere."

Katie reached out and squeezed Rainey's hand. Rainey tightened her hand around Katie's, nothing else needing to be said.

CHAPTER THIRTEEN

When Rainey, file in hand, and Katie entered through the French doors with their entourage, a frantic JW met them.

"I was worried about you. Are you all right?" he said.

Katie looked around her at the four large men, all holding grocery bags. "Why wouldn't I be?"

Katie walked away from him and into the kitchen, instructing the men on where to set their bags. Rainey was left with JW.

He turned to her, flushed with excitement. "I got another note and a picture of you sitting in the parking lot, at the Literacy Center."

Rainey met his excitement. "Where is it?"

"Danny has it, in the other room." JW said, leading the way.

Danny was standing with Mackie and another young agent in the den. All the others, except for the four men loading bags of groceries into the kitchen, had moved their operation to the police station. Danny was looking at a piece of computer paper in latex-gloved hands. He looked somber when he met Rainey's eyes.

"What does it say?" Rainey asked.

He turned so she could see the writing on the paper. She grew closer and the words came into focus.

"Can you keep fate from its path, once it has been set in motion?"

A million thoughts crowded Rainey's brain. Whose fate, Katie's, JW's, her own? What game was this guy playing?

"How did you receive this?" Rainey asked JW.

"It was under the door of my office when I got there."

Rainey questioned Mackie with her eyes. It was a natural response of an investigator to question every possible witness. She did not doubt JW. It was just so unbelievable how freely this suspect moved around, unnoticed.

"I was right behind him when he picked it up from the floor. I didn't let him touch the note. We waited until we got in touch with Danny," Mackie said.

"How long have you had this? You've been gone for hours," Rainey asked.

JW answered her, "I had to go to my Raleigh office first. I remembered leaving a brief on my desk, after we left this morning. We didn't find the note until just a little while ago. We brought it straight here, as soon as I did some quick paperwork."

Rainey's anger and frustration needed an outlet. It found one in JW. Her anger flashed and she raised her voice. "I told you not to deviate from the plan. How can I protect you, if you won't listen to me?" She turned to Mackie next. "How could you let him do that? Why didn't you call me?"

Mackie looked ashamed. He lowered his eyes, when he said, "My cellphone battery died. The charger is in my truck. We were in JW's car."

Rainey realized Danny was looking at her. He was studying her reaction and the look on his face said he thought Rainey might be losing it. She had to calm down. She took several deep breaths, before she spoke again.

"I'm sorry, you didn't deserve that," she said, trying to appear much calmer than she really was.

Danny put the note in a plastic evidence bag and handed it to the other agent. He picked up a picture from the table. He turned it so Rainey could see. It was taken during daylight, but the overcast sky gave the atmosphere in the picture an ominous appearance. The suspect printed it in black and white, creating a kind of Hitchcock feel to the image. The picture showed Rainey's car in the foreground, the tinted windows shielding Rainey from view. The storefront of the Literacy Center appeared in the background. Rainey knew that was Katie's blurred image behind the glass, only because she remembered her standing there, just like that.

Danny asked her, "Do you remember about what time this picture could have been taken?"

"It could have been any time after five and before sunset yesterday. He had to have some kind of long-range lens, because I know I would have seen him. He must have been in one of the tall buildings on the next block to shoot from this angle."

Danny was listening intently to her. He added to her thought process, "This guy has to be loaded. Lenses like that don't come cheap. We know he set up a phony bank account in China and paid cash for a house and a car."

Rainey kept going. "The way this guy moves around unnoticed, I'd bet you he knows JW. He has to run in that social structure. The real money in this town sticks together. It's a tight circle."

Danny turned to JW. "I'd like to speak to you in private, get a statement from you, if that's all right?"

JW responded, "Sure, whatever you need to catch this guy. I'm tired of him terrorizing my family—and Rainey, of course."

Danny picked up another evidence bag, placing the picture inside. He handed it off and picked up a yellow legal pad from the table.

"Your living room will do fine," Danny said, and indicated for JW to lead the way.

Rainey was still holding the file she retrieved from the safe. She turned to the other agent. "I guess I should give these to you. It's the original of the other notes and pictures. I'm sorry. I don't remember your name."

"It's Eric ma'am. I'm just an intern. I was only with the BAU a month before you went on leave."

The intern went to do something with the evidence. Mackie went outside. Rainey suspected he was going to his truck to charge his phone. Suddenly Rainey felt very old and tired. She sat down on the couch and closed her eyes. Her head fell back against the cushion. She must have fallen asleep, because she awoke to Danny gently shaking her shoulder and saying her name softly.

"I hated to wake you. You've been out for two hours," he said.

Rainey rubbed her eyes. They were burning and scratchy from lack of rest. She blinked several times, before she was able to focus and her head cleared of the fog of sleep. She had not had a nightmare, but the sleep left her feeling heavy and drugged.

"What time is it?" she said, groggily.

Danny checked his watch. "It's almost four. I need to talk to you and the Wilsons."

Rainey stood up on still sleepy legs. She wobbled a bit before she caught her balance. She followed Danny to the kitchen, where JW and Katie sat at the kitchen table. Two guys in suits stood by the French doors. Rainey found a chair and plopped down on it. She rubbed her eyes again, making them worse. She needed eye drops in the worst way.

She asked the room, "Does anybody have any eye drops?"

Katie stood up. "There's some in the downstairs bathroom. I'll get it."

Katie hurried out of the room. JW was focused on what he was writing on a legal pad. Danny brought Rainey a cup of coffee. Rainey took a sip. He had added cream and sugar, just as she liked it. Working stakeouts together so many times, he had learned how she liked her coffee, and could probably order a deli sandwich for her, with just the right toppings. Katie returned with the eye drops. Rainey put the drops in and felt the fire burning under her lids. She waited a minute and then added more drops. This time the burning was not as bad and she actually started feeling some relief.

Danny waited until Rainey was ready, before he started, "I've been over the recent evidence, and I believe the suspect is escalating. He's gone from sending notes once a month to three in two days. His actions are more daring. He is devolving and his behavior will become more unpredictable."

JW, who had stopped writing, asked, "What does this guy want?"

"He's playing a game and he wants to win. His goal is to terrorize you, until he catches his quarry alone," Danny said, and then continued, "We're not sure, at this point, if it is one of you, or all of you he is after. We need more time to evaluate the notes. A forensic linguist is looking at them now. We'll know more when the report comes back."

He took a second to let that sink in, and then went on, "What I'm getting at is I don't think you're safe here. Even with four agents, there are so many ways to get in. We took the liberty of covering the basement door and windows, so that's more secure, but I still can't guarantee your safety. I think we should move all three of you to a safe house, at least until we get more analysis of the evidence we have. JW has given us a list of people fitting the general description of our suspect. We need time to check out each one of them. I would just feel better if this guy didn't know where you are right now. It could cause him to make a mistake."

Rainey challenged him. "Or it could send him over the edge. He could wind up killing more people, out of frustration. I'm the bait; use me. Let me draw him out. You can take Katie and JW, but I'm not going."

"Me, either," Katie said. "I'm staying with Rainey."

JW spoke next, "I can't go to a safe house. I have meetings with the budget committee, next week."

Danny knew there was no reason to argue. He could tell they were not going to take his advice. "Okay then, these agents will stay with you. Please keep the doors locked and the alarm on, after I leave. I'll be back in the morning."

Danny left through the French doors. Rainey followed him out to the patio. They stopped together by the wrought iron table set.

"I'm serious about being bait," Rainey said. "I know we can bring him out, if we show him an opportunity he can't resist."

"I'll think about it, Rainey," Danny replied. He sounded tired.

"I'll see you in the morning," Rainey said.

Danny started for the SUV and Rainey turned to go inside. Just as her hand turned the handle on the door, Danny's voice stopped her.

"Hey Rainey, sleep with your gun," he said.

Rainey smiled at him and replied, "Always."

Rainey entered the kitchen area. JW was not sitting at the table anymore. Katie was standing, in the open door of the refrigerator, lost in thought. Rainey watched her for a moment, until she became aware of an agent sitting at the end of the table. She moved to the kitchen island.

Rainey inquired, "Where's JW?"

Katie did not turn around, her voice flat as she said, "In his study, I suppose."

"Can't make up your mind?" Rainey said to Katie.

"I want to fix something that will last, so the guys can munch on it during the night. I think I'm going to make pizza. How does that sound?"

"I'm sure it will be fine. Can I help you?" Rainey asked.

Katie turned around with a big onion in her hand. "You get to chop this time."

They hurried around the kitchen, Rainey watching closely, as Katie talked her through the recipe for authentic brick-oven, Brooklyn-style pizza. Katie had purchased the dough crust already made, that was the hard part, she explained. She made it from scratch before and it took sixteen hours for the dough to rise. They used a pizza stone on the lowest rack in the oven, setting the temperature at five hundred and fifty degrees. Katie showed Rainey how to place thinly sliced pieces of Mozzarella cheese on the crusts and ground black pepper over it. Katie brushed Rainey's arm and the electricity shot to Rainey's heart. Next Katie sprinkled oregano on the crusts and had Rainey randomly arrange crushed tomatoes around on top. Katie drizzled extra virgin olive oil over all four pizzas, telling Rainey that was the key to the recipe.

Rainey enjoyed the time she spent cooking with Katie. They worked together very well, she thought. She was proud when the pizzas came out of the oven, bubbling with melted cheese, looking like a picture in Bon Appétit magazine. Rainey helped Katie set out the food, stacking plates and napkins at the end of the table. The agent, still in the room, ate a piece and gave it the thumbs up. Rainey and Katie each took pieces and sat on stools at the counter. Rainey thought the pizza was outstanding and ate another large slice.

The entire time they worked together Katie kept touching Rainey. She would brush up against her when they worked side by side, at the island. When they sat down to eat, Katie repeatedly touched Rainey's knee or thigh to make a point. Every time a part of Rainey came into contact with Katie, she felt a tingling sensation and streaks of electricity crashed through her body. Rainey looked at the agent stuffing pizza in his mouth, glad he was there watching their backs, because all Rainey was watching was Katie.

JW reappeared with the other agent in tow. "Mmm, that pizza looks great," he said, when he arrived at the table. He, and the agent with him, sat down to eat. The other agent, who just finished his third slice, made plates for the guys outside, thanked the women for cooking, and went to deliver the pizza. Katie and Rainey cleaned up the kitchen and then took glasses of sweet tea to the den and settled in on the couch.

Rainey's eyes began to get heavy again. She was spent emotionally and physically. She needed a long sleep to recoup her strength. The agent came back from delivery duty and joined them a few minutes later. JW went back to his study, accompanied by his shadow agent. There was small talk, but nothing interesting. They really could not talk with the agent in the room. The news channel they were watching started repeating stories, so Katie turned the channel to PBS and they watched a show on museums of music in New Orleans. Rainey did not really pay attention. Her head was spinning with thoughts of Katie, only Katie. She could think of nothing else. She finally asked if there was someplace she could lie down.

Katie stood up and crooked her finger at Rainey. "Come with me," she said, and it had the pied piper affect on Rainey.

Rainey grabbed her overnight bag from the car, and then followed Katie up the stairs to a bedroom across from the master suite. The ever-present agent followed too.

"Will this be all right?" Katie asked.

"This is great, thank you," Rainey replied. She looked at the agent and said, "I think I'll be okay up here. You can wait downstairs." She patted her gun, to remind him she was armed.

"I think I'll go to bed, too," Katie said. "Good night, Rainey. Sweet dreams."

"Goodnight, Katie," Rainey said and watched her walk away.

Katie went to the master bedroom and locked the door. Rainey heard the latch click over. The agent went downstairs. Rainey changed her clothes and crawled into bed, leaving the door open, so she could hear. She was lying there, thinking about Katie and the serial killer lurking around outside, but soon the heaviness of her eyelids forced them closed, and she drifted off to sleep.

Some time later, she felt someone's weight press down on the bed. She sprang up in a sitting position, reaching for the Glock she had placed on the bedside table.

"Don't shoot. It's just me," Katie said.

Rainey looked at Katie, blinking the sleep from her eyes. "It's not a good idea to walk up on me when I'm asleep," she said, still a little shaken.

"I'm sorry," Katie said, and then explained, "I couldn't sleep in there alone. I hope you don't mind if I share your bed."

Rainey let out a sigh, releasing her heart to resume a normal beat. "Yeah, sure. No problem," she said, still thinking she was dreaming.

Katie settled down into the covers and Rainey followed suit. They did not talk. They were both exhausted and soon sound asleep. Rainey woke up again later, sensing someone nearby. She looked out the open door into the hallway and saw JW standing there, watching them sleep. When he realized she was looking at him, he turned and went back down the stairs. She closed her eyes again and slept better than she had in months. She did not wake up until early morning. She had no dreams at all that she could remember. She rolled over and saw Katie sleeping beside her. She thought to herself, "Wouldn't it be wonderful to wake up to that face every day?" That was a dream Rainey was beginning to think she could live with, and it frightened her.

CHAPTER FOURTEEN

Rainey slipped quietly out of the bed. Katie was sleeping so soundly, Rainey did not want to wake her. She grabbed her bag and found the guest bathroom, where she showered and dressed for the day. Rainey had purchased some tank tops back in the spring, which did not show her scar. She was glad because she was running out of old tee shirts to cut up. She put on a blue tank, adding a simple white, short sleeve, cotton shirt over it. She left the over shirt unbuttoned and folded the sleeves up a little. She wore khaki shorts, tennis shoes and of course her shoulder holster. She was glad she wasn't still in the Bureau, forced to wear those dark blue and black suits, while strolling around the piedmont of North Carolina in the height of summer. She brushed her hair and put it up in a ponytail. She put everything back in her bag, surveyed the room, and deciding it was clean enough, Rainey walked out to start the day.

When she came back into the guest bedroom, Katie was gone. There was no trace that either of them had been in the immaculately made bed. She turned to look down the hall and saw that Katie's door was closed. The aroma of fresh brewed coffee filled her nostrils, winding its way up from the kitchen downstairs. Katie must have awakened shortly after Rainey left the bedroom. Rainey put her bag down and happily bounded down the stairs. She felt better than she had in months. Last night she slept nearly ten hours of the most peaceful rest imaginable.

No terrifying nightmares, no waking for unknown reasons only to stare at the ceiling, just the sleep of babes. It must have been because she felt safe with all the extra security in the house. It could not have been because Katie was sleeping by her side, could it?

Rainey did not care why she slept so well, only that she had. Now she was about to hang out with Katie for another day. She let the fact that a serial killer was after them take a backseat for a few minutes. She had a huge grin that she could not control on her face, as she turned the corner into the kitchen. The grin died on its own, when she saw JW, not Katie, standing by the coffee pot.

"Good morning, Rainey. You look as though you slept well."

"I did, thank you. I must have been exhausted," Rainey said.

She took the cup from JW's outstretched hand and poured herself some coffee. The cream and sugar bowls were there by the coffee maker. She added some of each, while she took in JW, who had moved to the breakfast counter. He was leaning on his elbows, reading the paper. JW was dressed more casually today, in a polo shirt and slacks, but he still looked like he walked out of a golf magazine advertisement. Rainey could smell his cologne and, although it was nice, had been applied a little heavily this morning. He was completely engrossed in the newspaper.

Rainey heard a noise behind her and turned to find Katie smiling at her. She too looked refreshed from yesterday's drama. Katie left her hair down, pulling only some of it back away from her face. She was wearing a simple, Carolina blue, cotton tee with little flowers sewn in the same color around the scooped neckline. She wore white tennis shorts, styled like the men wear, but fitting her perfectly. The bright white against her skin made her smooth, tanned legs glow. Once again, Rainey found herself spellbound.

Katie said, "Good morning. I hope I didn't keep you awake, I just couldn't fall asleep in that room by myself, for some reason."

"No, I hardly knew you were there. I slept like a log."

JW did not look up from his paper, but added, "Don't let it become a habit, Rainey."

132

Rainey looked at his back. "What?"

JW reached for his coffee cup, on the counter. He did not look at it, he just reached for the cup and found it robotically, while saying, "Don't let my wife make a habit out of sleeping with you—"

He paused just long enough for Rainey's heart to jump into her throat. She had a blurry memory of JW watching them sleep. What was he accusing her of?

JW finally let her off the hook, by adding, "– she snores."

Rainey was sure she felt the blood flowing back up to her brain, after having drained to her toes just seconds ago. She said, laughing to cover her nervousness, "I don't think I would have heard her, if she did. I was out of it."

JW still did not turn around, concentrating on the paper in front of him. He saluted her with his coffee cup and said, "I'm just saying—"

Katie poured a cup of coffee for herself. She turned to Rainey and said, "I snore terribly, but really, all you have to do is roll me over."

"Good luck with that," Rainey heard JW say, still engrossed in what he was reading.

Katie stuck her tongue out at his back, which made Rainey giggle. She covered her mouth, so JW would not hear her. One of the French doors opened and the two agents, who had been outside, came in to retrieve the other two, who were standing just off the kitchen. Rainey had not seen them when she first came in; they were standing just out of sight. Four fresh agents were here to relieve them and they were as big as, or bigger, than the first group. Rainey did not know any of the new men. They were probably locals. Rainey thanked Roger and the others, as they passed her leaving the kitchen.

By the time Rainey made it back to her coffee cup, Katie had begun cutting slices of cantaloupe and toasting bagels. Rainey heard Danny coming, before he entered the French doors. He was red-faced and angry, his Irish temper looking for a vent. He slapped his briefcase down on the table, his eyes searching for

Rainey. When he saw her, he marched up to her with a newspaper in his hands.

"Have you seen this yet?" He barked at her.

He opened the paper to the front page. "Y-Man Killer Returns," screamed across the headline, in bold black letters. JW finally looked away from his paper, to see what all the fuss was about. Rainey's jaw dropped. It had been only twenty-four hours and the media was all over the story. Danny paced the room, while Rainey scanned the article with Katie reading over her shoulder. When Rainey finished, she handed the paper to Katie, so she could continue reading and took Danny into the den.

Once they were alone, he started, "Who did this, Rainey?"

Rainey was confused. "What? Do you think I know something about this?"

Danny's anger had not subsided. It flashed throughout his next accusation. "Other than the UNSUB, there are only two people alive that know the details of what he said and did to you, and I am one of them. I sure as hell didn't contact the media, so that leaves you."

Rainey could not believe this was happening. "Are you serious? Do you think I told anyone what he did to me? What about you? Did you write it down and leave it lying around somewhere?"

"What are you talking about?" Danny said, topping her incredulous tone.

"I saw a folder on the table, clearly marked Rainey Bell, just lying out for anyone to see. How would you like your deepest secrets lying in a pile of folders, like just some old file, like those files don't represent real human beings, real feelings?"

Danny lowered his voice. "Rainey, that file never contained all the details you told me, never. I am the only one that has a file with that information and it is locked in my briefcase."

"If I didn't do it and you didn't do it, there is only one way some of those facts made the paper this morning," Rainey said, calming down, too.

Danny put his hand over his brow and let out a, "Shit!" followed by, "I hate this fucker."

"It's the only way," Rainey said and sat down on the couch, amazed at the audacity of this killer.

Danny plopped down beside her with a sigh. "We're already getting the writer, an editor, and a judge together for a first amendment pow-wow. We should have his source soon."

"It won't help us," Rainey said. "He's too smart to get caught that way."

"They all make mistakes," Danny replied. "That's how we catch them."

"We'll catch this one when we figure out what he's planning," Rainey said, beginning to think more like an analyst than a victim. It was the only way she was going to survive this. "He must be experiencing some significant stress right now. Something has brought him back to me after almost a year of apparent inactivity."

Danny got on board. "He is escalating at an accelerated pace. He's gone from one serial murder a month, to nothing—that we know of. Now he's turned to long term stalking, but his contact with his victim has multiplied since he recognized you."

Rainey wrinkled her brow, saying, "Why does he contact the media? He's never done that before."

"He wants credit for being the one who attacked you. He thinks he'll humiliate you by publishing some of the more gruesome details of what he did to you," Danny said to her, more as a fellow agent than a victim.

Rainey continued, "And he's trying to show that he's smarter than the FBI. After all, he nearly killed an agent and he got away. In fact, he is responsible for bringing the FBI back to his case. He had to know, when he identified himself to me, I would call you immediately."

Danny stood and began to pace the room. "So, you're convinced that it's just dumb luck that he stumbled across you. Why doesn't he just try to kill you? Why bring this heat down on himself again?"

Rainey sat up on the edge of the couch. "Because he needs to feel that rush again. When he saw me, he remembered how exhilarating it felt to capture an FBI agent. He can't get the thrill

135

from the hookers he killed that he got from taking on the most powerful federal law enforcement agency in the country, and winning."

Danny countered, "But he didn't win. He didn't kill you."

"No, but he got away," Rainey answered. "Imagine what he must have thought it would feel like to get a second chance to outsmart the FBI and accomplish his goal of killing me. It would be too much for him to resist."

"So, your conclusion is that he is now using the Wilsons as a ploy, and has switched his focus to you? You are the real target?" Danny wanted to confirm.

"Yes, and you need to take advantage of that knowledge. Let me go home, set up surveillance, he won't be able to resist. You know I'm right," Rainey argued.

"And what about the Wilsons, do you think they are out of danger?" Danny said.

Rainey had an answer. "Leave the four guys you have here now. Make sure that at least two of them go with Katie, everywhere, even to school. JW is too much of a threat for this guy. The UNSUB doesn't get off on playing doctor with men. I really think they would be safer, if I wasn't with them."

"Will you stay here one more evening, until I can get my guys set up in the woods around your place? We're going to want to video all the activity coming and going, even from the boat dock day and night. I need time to get the equipment here," Danny said, without any further argument.

He had to know Rainey was right. He knew it when he barged in here this morning. He needed to hear her say it. If the Wilsons were not targets, then they would just get in the way of catching this guy. They were the killer's distraction. If they were removed, he would have to come after Rainey directly. She did not mind spending another night with Katie, and Rainey would be glad to have Katie out of the crosshairs of this maniac when she finally went home. She wanted the UNSUB to stay as far away from Katie as possible. Rainey had to believe she was right. Katie was safer with the other agents, than being guarded by his real target.

Danny and Rainey talked a few minutes more about the set up at her place. She told him where the best angles and vantage points were. Danny asked for Mackie's number, so he could call him to help with the local traffic, maybe turn the boaters away for a day.

"We don't want to be seen," he said.

Rainey told him, "He can say it's rented to a private party. My dad used to do that sometimes." She wrote Mackie's number on a sticky note from a pad by the phone, handing it to Danny.

Danny tucked the note in his shirt pocket. "You know I didn't really think it was you," he said.

Rainey questioned him with her eyes.

He continued, "I never thought you were the one who contacted the media. I had to ask."

Rainey was sorry she said those things about him being the leak. She knew he must have some real pressure from up high to make sure it was not her.

"What? Do the guys at Quantico think I've cooked this whole thing up as an attempt to draw attention to myself?" Rainey asked.

"Yeah, something like that," Danny replied.

She was more sad than angry, when she said, "Those fucking assholes don't have a clue, do they?"

"Nope, not a one," Danny said, matter-of-factly.

The crash of glass breaking and raised voices sent Danny and Rainey running, guns drawn, to the kitchen. They met two of the new agents in the hall, giving the slow down hand sign, indicating that everything was okay.

Rainey heard Katie yell, "I know you did it, you sick bastard."

When Rainey made it into the kitchen, there was a cup in pieces and coffee flowing down the wall, near where JW had been standing. JW backed across the room and one of the agents was trying to prevent Katie from getting to him.

"Whoa, what's going on?" Rainey demanded.

"He did it, Rainey. He's the one," Katie said, making another attempt to get to her husband.

Rainey stepped in between the agent and Katie, who was doing a dance back and forth in front of JW.

"Katie, calm down. Talk to me," Rainey said. "Tell me what you think he's done."

JW answered for her, "Your girlfriend thinks I called the media. That I've tried to spin this thing somehow."

The word girlfriend stung a little. Because of the sexual attraction she was now feeling for Katie, a simple word she had used last week had taken on a whole new context. She tried briefly to determine which one he meant, but then quickly got back to the matter at hand.

"Katie, JW isn't the leak. He couldn't be. There is no way he could have known some of the things written in that story," Rainey said. "The Y-Man is the leak."

Katie looked puzzled. "Why would he do that? Why would he want everyone to know he's out there?"

"Because he gets off on the attention," Rainey answered.

"Aren't you going to apologize to me, now?" JW asked, and Rainey wished he had not.

Katie lashed at him, "Oh, shut up! You know you're glad he did it. You would have done it yourself, if he hadn't. Tell me you didn't count the number of times your name was mentioned."

JW threw his hands up, saying, "There's just no winning with you."

Katie was not finished. "That's right. It's about time you gave up, don't you think?"

Rainey wanted to separate these two and was so relieved when JW said he had an early tee time. JW took one of the new agents as a fourth, after giving him a polo shirt and assuring he would get him clubs and shoes at the pro shop. Danny reminded the agent to return the borrowed merchandise, before returning to the house. JW said he would just donate them to a charity auction, assuring Rainey they would end up in a Republican fundraising raffle. Whatever was going to happen to the clubs and shoes, she was so glad when JW finally left.

Danny followed shortly behind him, heading off to coordinate the move to Rainey's house. Katie excused herself, after telling everyone there were fruit slices and bagels for breakfast, then returned upstairs. Rainey cleaned up the mess from the shattered coffee cup. She told the agent not to bother, when he was about to follow her, as she started up the stairs. Rainey felt his services would be more useful downstairs, since there were no entrances on the second floor. He was young and did as he was told. Rainey went to Katie's door and knocked.

"It's Rainey, Katie. May I come in?"

Soft steps hurried toward the door and the latch threw. Rainey heard the soft steps move away from the door again. She slowly opened the door. Rainey latched the door behind her. She found Katie face down in her pillows.

"It's okay, he's gone," Rainey offered, as a way to help ease Katie's hurt.

"Oh, fuck him!" was the muffled sound out of the pillows.

"I've got to say, you two have a strange way of communicating," Rainey said.

Katie did not say anything.

Rainey tried again, "You know, I'll listen, if you need to get something off your chest."

Rainey was not expecting what came next. Katie sat up and turned to Rainey.

"I'm not crying because of JW. I'm crying for what that madman did to you, and then to tell everyone what he did in the paper. How could they print that?" Katie cried, as the tears fell and slid down her cheeks.

Rainey sat silently in shock. Somehow, she had transferred to Katie all the hurt and indignation she felt, when Rainey herself read the article. She did not know how or have time to react.

"How can you sit there, so calmly?" Katie ranted.

Finally, something Rainey knew the answer to. "I have to, Katie, if I want to survive."

Katie arms flew around Rainey and she cried into her shoulder. "I'm so sorry, so sorry."

Rainey put her arms around Katie and could not resist pulling her closer. For Rainey, the next few moments went by in slow motion. Rainey felt Katie push back against her arms, pulling away from her. She had done the wrong thing. Katie did not want her to hold her tightly. She did not do it consciously, it just happened. Now, what must Katie be thinking? Rainey let her arms fall down by Katie's sides.

Instead of running from the room in terror, Katie pulled back until her face was inches from Rainey's. She stared into Rainey's eyes, as if searching for something. Rainey held her gaze, seeking her own answers in the other woman's eyes. What was happening and why? Rainey had no answer to the questions Katie's expression asked, nor did she know the answers to her own. But then, all of Rainey's questions vanished from her thoughts. Katie placed her right hand behind Rainey's head and pulled her down softly to her waiting lips.

Rainey had never felt a sweeter kiss. She closed her eyes and felt herself kissing Katie back, in almost an out of body experience. The room began to swim around her and desire tightened in her chest. Her arms found Katie's body again and pulled her tightly to her. The breath caught in both of their chests, when what started so sweetly, quickly became a long deep kiss. Neither woman could control the soft sounds emanating from their throats, the sounds of want and need.

Katie slid the shoulder holster from Rainey's shoulders and began falling back onto the bed, pulling Rainey down on top of her. Rainey fell into Katie's arms and kissed a woman for the first time in her life. It did not feel funny or weird. It felt as natural as coming home, after a long journey. Katie's body felt warm underneath her. She felt Katie arch into her, causing a longing between her legs, something she thought she would never feel again. Rainey was alive from end to end with feelings and emotions she had not thought she would remember.

Katie began to move under her, sending shock waves through her body. Then a single thought flashed through her mind. Rainey stopped. She pulled away from Katie and stood up. She crossed to the window, peering outside.

Katie sat up in the bed. "Rainey?"

Rainey did not look away from the window. Instead, she stared out into the sunlit backyard and spoke softly, "Katie, I can't do this."

"Why? I thought it was what you—what we wanted," Katie said. She seemed confused by Rainey's reaction.

Rainey stared straight ahead, trying to get control back. Her eyes burned as she fought back tears.

"Rainey, turn around," Katie said, softly.

Katie got off the bed and walked to Rainey. Rainey slowly turned to her. Katie saw the tears welling in Rainey's eyes. She reached out to Rainey.

"Talk to me. I need to understand."

The dam broke and the tears flowed from Rainey's eyes, not in torrents, but in slow falling raindrops from her lower lids.

Rainey spoke softly, because if she tried to speak normally, she would lose more control, "He just keeps taking things from me," she paused, "and—and because of that, I can't let this happen between us."

"Why, what does he have to do with us?" Katie asked.

"I can't be distracted, it could wind up killing us both," Rainey answered her.

Katie was undeterred. "Don't let him do this to you."

"Katie, he's already done it. I can't put your life at risk. Don't you understand that?"

Katie put her hands on her hips and said, "How would I be in any more danger than I am already?"

Rainey had to tell her, "Danny and I think he's now switched targets, to me solely. I have to distance myself from you and JW, to keep you safe."

"What about you? Where are you going?" Katie looked frightened. Her hands slid from her hips and hung by her sides.

"I'm going back to the cottage."

"When?" Katie asked.

"Tomorrow afternoon."

"You're going to leave me alone? I thought we were in this together," Katie said, jabbing her hands back on her hips.

"Katie, I'm not leaving you alone. The agents will still be here with you. They're going to stay with you until this is over."

"Rainey Bell, you are not going out to that house alone," Katie was adamant.

"I won't be alone, either. I'll be protected," Rainey tried to explain.

"You are setting yourself up as bait." Katie was aghast and then incensed. "That is insane. Haven't you given enough to the investigation?"

Rainey felt herself flush with anger. It was not aimed at Katie, but at him. "I will give every last breath of my being to send this son of a bitch straight to hell, if that's what it takes."

"That's what I'm afraid of," Katie said.

The color from Katie's face drained. She took several shaky steps back and dropped into the armchair. The implications of what Rainey just said were written in Katie's expression. Rainey felt her chest tighten. She hurt Katie without meaning to, unable to see past her own rage the influence her actions had on the emotions of others. Rainey moved to Katie and knelt down on the floor in front of the chair. She looked into Katie's face and listened, as her mind raced with thoughts, so many, she couldn't stop one long enough to reflect on it.

Rainey did not think about what she said next, she just let the words stream from her mouth, in a steady calm voice. "Katie, I'm not going to risk my life unnecessarily. I truly believe that the best chance we have of ending this safely, for all of us, is to separate myself from you, to draw his focus and allow Danny and the other agents to catch him. I'm not going out alone to hunt him."

Katie started to speak, but Rainey raised her hand to stop her.

Rainey leaned in closer to Katie. She continued, "My mind is telling me that what is happening between the two of us is merely the product of two very wounded women, who find themselves in a life and death struggle. Our subconscious recognition in each other, of the depth of want and longing, is driving us together."

Once again, Katie started to speak, but this time quieted on her own. She listened intently to Rainey's soft voice.

"On the other hand, my heart is saying, fall, fall hard into her arms, and don't look back. Find out if it's just the circumstances we find ourselves in. It's so overwhelming and confusing, and wonderful..."

Katie interrupted, "I hear a 'but' coming."

Rainey nodded. "But, when I'm thinking about you, I lose focus. I can't be objective. I can't keep us safe, if I'm distracted by your very presence in the room."

Katie smiled at Rainey. "May I say something?"

Rainey nodded her head yes.

"Rainey, I have never done anything like what just happened, in my entire life. I am as confused as you are. I have no explanation for the attraction between us and I'll admit it has been a distraction, because I haven't been able to get you out of my mind."

"That's what I've been trying to tell you," Rainey said.

Katie had been thinking while Rainey was talking and had evidently formulated a debate in her mind. "What makes you think that separating us will keep you from thinking about me? What if you're more distracted worrying about where I am and who's watching me? I know that's what I'll be doing, worrying about you."

Rainey had not thought about that. She pondered for a moment and then added another element to her side of the argument. As it turned out, it was a very poor choice.

Rainey stood up and looked down at Katie. "That maybe true, but besides the inappropriateness of having a personal relationship with someone you are supposed to be guarding, there is the small matter of your being married to the man who hired me to protect you."

"He hired you to protect his career," Katie spat.

"He loves you, Katie. He was genuinely worried about you," Rainey argued.

Katie got up and stomped toward the bathroom door. Rainey followed her.

Katie said, over her shoulder, "Oh, please. Don't tell me you've fallen for his act, too?"

143

"I've known JW longer than you. I think I know when he's playing one of his characters," Rainey said, defensively.

Katie turned at the door to the bathroom, her expression fierce. "You have no idea who he really is." She slammed the bathroom door in Rainey's face.

Wow, Rainey thought. Katie had gone from zero to pissed in no time, when JW's name was mentioned. Whatever he had done, Katie was not about to forgive him. Rainey made the mistake of defending him, one she would not make again. She listened outside the door for a few minutes. No sounds other than Katie mumbling under her breath could be heard. Rainey decided Katie was not coming out, so she went to the armchair and sat down heavily. The range of emotions she had experienced since coming into this room was exhausting.

Rainey had felt the soaring thrill of Katie in her arms, only to crash against the thought of Katie losing her life to a sadistic killer, because Rainey was not paying attention. How could she make Katie understand the responsibility she felt for having left him free to wander amongst them, the guilt that loomed over her for being distracted the first time she had a chance to catch him? It was more powerful than the physical and emotional damage he had done to her.

No matter how Katie felt, Rainey also felt guilty about what she was doing with JW's wife. Having an affair with a married man or woman was just not something with which Rainey felt comfortable. Rainey was not a cheater. She did not like people who were. The thought that Katie might be just using her to get back at JW crossed her mind. It loomed there and then took on a life of its own. Before long Rainey had convinced herself to get up and leave, untangle her life from this dysfunctional chaos.

Katie remained behind the closed bathroom door. Rainey went to the bed, retrieving her Glock and over shirt, which she put on quickly and let herself quietly out of the room. She crossed the hall to the guest room, where she grabbed her overnight bag and took it with her down the stairs. She located her laptop and charger in the den, and then called Mackie from her cell.

He answered quickly, "What'cha need?"
"Where are you?" she asked.
His bass voice growled out, "Down the block."
Rainey said, "We're going home."
"When?" rumbled through her receiver.
With no hesitation, Rainey said, "Now."

CHAPTER FIFTEEN

Rainey talked with the agents still at Katie's house. She explained that she was leaving and their only priority was the safety of Mrs. Wilson.

"If anything happens to her, I will personally see to it that you won't even be able to find a job as a security guard in an empty parking lot, got it?" she said to the wide-eyed agents.

Rainey left through the French doors. She slid into the Charger and was down the driveway and out on the street in seconds, with Mackie falling in tightly behind her in his Escalade. Rainey could see Junior in the passenger seat. Rainey glanced back at the house once more and saw Katie standing, unmoving, on the front landing, bookended by two agents. Rainey slowed down. She almost stopped. Her heart ached and tightened her chest. Rainey thought for a second she was making a mistake, but then she pushed her foot down on the accelerator and sped away.

Rainey called Danny from the car. His Irish temper exploded over the phone, one expletive after another. She could not explain to him why she had to leave the Wilson's house. She promised to keep Mackie and Junior with her and to stay inside the cottage with the alarm on no matter what happened. Danny said he would send Roger and his team to her cottage, as soon as they had some rest. He reluctantly calmed down and agreed it would be good to have her at the cottage, while the surveillance was being set up.

Rainey had a little surveillance equipment of her own, strategically placed around the office and her cottage. In the large, wood-paneled main room of the cottage, her father had built a bookcase along the wall separating the living area from Rainey's room. The shelves housed some of his memorabilia and books. There was a space in the middle for the old television Rainey had replaced with a new flat screen. From her remote, she could pull up eight day and night-vision camera images at the click of a button. Those images were of the front and back decks with views of the exterior doors of Rainey's cottage, two wide-angle views of the yard around the cottage, both outer doors of the office, the docks, and the area under the cottage. She could call them up individually or stack them across the screen. The cameras were equipped with motion detectors and alerted her with a message on the TV screen, if she was watching some other program. The Bureau guys would probably tie in to her feed from the cameras and add a few more.

A special weapons and tactics team would be put in place around the cottage. If anything moved, those guys would be on it before it ever knew what hit it. This dead-end road was the perfect place to lay a trap. Danny would release a statement saying Rainey had refused FBI protection. Rainey would comment, through a protected source, on how she did not want anything to do with the agency that allowed her to be attacked in the first place. Danny would add that the Bureau's main concern was the safety of the future senator and his wife.

The illusion would be that law enforcement believed the Wilsons were the Y-Man's real targets and former Special Agent Bell had simply stumbled upon him. The Bureau's stance was that this type of offender would not knowingly go after an FBI agent, former or not. The first attack on Rainey had merely been a crime of impulse. They believed emphatically that the Y-Man would not make another attempt on Rainey's life. The snare laid, all they had to do was wait.

Rainey arrived at the cottage, went in, and turned the TV on. She clicked a few buttons and the eight images from the cameras spread across the screen. Mackie followed her in and made

147

himself at home in the big Lazy Boy her father had bought, just for Mackie. He special ordered it extra large and presented it to the big man one Christmas. Mackie moved it into the cottage, because the two men spent so much time there together. They used up hours talking and watching old John Wayne movies. They never watched Vietnam War movies, because they did not have to. They witnessed it up close and personal.

A routine patrol had become a nightmare ambush in seconds. Deep in the jungle, away from any hope of reinforcements, the patrol stumbled across a series of tunnels in the hills above them. Pinned down, they fought through the night, together. In the morning, they discovered they were the only two left alive of an eighteen-man patrol. Mackie had been wounded several times and Billy could not walk, having had shrapnel rip through his flesh, splintering bones in both his legs. They patched each other up, as best they could. Only a few of the enemy had remained behind to finish them off. Mackie carried Billy Bell on his back for two miles through the jungle, all the while, Billy shooting at the Viet Cong trailing them to the evacuation zone. After that, the two men were inseparable, recovering in the hospital and the next year going back in the dark jungle together.

Mackie now watched over Rainey for the man he had loved so much. Their friendship had been deep and unwavering. He took the responsibility for Rainey's safety seriously, the weight of it showing on his face. Junior sat on the front deck drinking the sweet tea Rainey fixed for him. She was inspired by her thoughts of Katie to cook steaks, the only thing she knew how to do well. Rainey asked Junior to go to the office and retrieve the fresh vegetables from the back room refrigerator. She would make a salad and grill some squash for her protectors, the activity keeping her from thinking so much about Katie.

Katie had been right. Her absence distracted Rainey. She replayed that first sweet kiss over in her mind, each time experiencing a tightening, hollow feeling in her chest. Mackie remained in his seat diligently monitoring the video feeds. Junior returned from the office with a paper bag full of fresh vegetables from Ernie's garden. He refilled his tea and resumed his post on the porch. Rainey cut up the squash and made salads. When it was time to cook the steaks, Mackie would not allow her to go out on the back deck, where her gas grill was located. Instead, he insisted grilling was man's work and took the plate containing the steaks and squash from her hand.

When he left out the back door, Rainey was alone for the first time in days. She had become accustomed to a solitary life. She usually enjoyed the peace and quiet, but not today. Freddie came in from his morning wanderings for his midday nap. He was happy to see her home and rubbed against her legs incessantly, until she had to pick him up and love on him a little. She fed him, refreshed his water, and after a snack, he went to his favorite spot in the front window for a snooze.

The quiet began to close around her and the thoughts in her head became so much louder. Left alone, with nothing more to do after setting the table, she wandered into her bedroom and sat down on the bed. She looked in the mirror at her reflection for a long time. She left Katie with no goodbye, no explanation. What could Katie be thinking? Now that Rainey was gone, Katie might have time to reflect on what happened between them earlier. Maybe she would decide she really was not attracted to Rainey. That Rainey had been right, it was the circumstance they found themselves in that caused this to happen.

A horrible thought crossed Rainey's mind. What if she never saw Katie again? What if that had been their one moment? What if she had just lost something she had not known she wanted so badly, until this morning? The ache she started to feel overwhelmed her. She needed to do something, get her mind thinking about something else. Rainey had to come to terms with her feelings for Katie or they were going to get her killed. Finally, she told herself, the best way to handle this situation, whatever the future held for them, was one step at a time. First, she had to get rid of a major obstacle between them, concentrate on catching the Y-Man.

"Here kitty, kitty," Rainey whispered, to the unknown killer.

She changed into sweats and a tee shirt and returned to the kitchen as Mackie was coming in the back door. They called

Junior in to eat, with Mackie insisting on sitting in his chair in the main room, so he could keep an eye on the monitors. Rainey set up a TV tray for him, and he happily munched away while Junior and Rainey sat in the kitchen. After eating, Rainey filled the dishwasher with the dinner dishes and cleaned up.

Roger and his team arrived shortly after, deploying around the residence, relieving Junior of his post on the deck. Rainey and Junior spent the afternoon cleaning all the guns in the house. Her father had a M1 carbine, two shotguns, a thirty-aught-six, a 357 Smith and Wesson revolver, and a Ruger forty-five. Billy Bell was a true believer in the second amendment. Rainey retrieved her other two pistols and shotgun from the Charger, under the watchful eye of an agent. They cleaned them and added them to the other weapons strategically placed around the house. There was enough firepower in the little cottage to take on a small army.

Danny called during the gun cleaning fest. "Rainey, we got the source from the newspaper guy. You were right. It leads nowhere. He used a disposable phone."

"When did he call?" Rainey asked.

"The same night you called me. The paper guy was going to contact us, after the story went public. That was generous of them," he added, sarcastically.

"The media is so helpful, don't you think?" Rainey said, joining him in his disgust. "So, let's use them. Did you plant the story?"

"Yep," Danny said, "They lapped it up. They now have the inside scoop on your disdain for the FBI and our concentrating the investigation on the Wilsons. You are merely a distraction, and we are glad to be getting you out of our way."

"Do you think he'll go for it?" Rainey asked.

"I think so. Once we pull all visible support it will work," Danny said.

"How are you making sure he knows I'm here, alone?"

"We alerted the media that we were removing our support as of three tomorrow afternoon. That will give tactical time to set up. There should be helicopters watching us leave you on your own. We'll make a big show of it. It'll play on every newscast in the area," Danny said, proud of his plan.

"Do you think I should do an interview? Tell them I don't think he'll come after me?" Rainey wanted to help more.

"I included that, in the anonymous statement, quoting you," Danny answered, delighted he had thought of it already.

"We should have Junior drive Mackie's Escalade away too, but I want Mackie to stay with me. You couldn't make him leave anyway," Rainey said.

"Okay, are you locked down out there?" Danny asked.

"Oh, yeah," Rainey said, checking the slide action on the shotgun she was holding, while balancing the phone on her shoulder, "locked and loaded."

"Be safe," he said and hung up.

About six o'clock that evening, a large black SUV pulled down the driveway and parked. Everyone was alert, because there had been no call to say someone was coming. Men's voices were raised outside. Rainey went to the front window to see what all the fuss was about. She was shocked to see Katie leading two agents, with boxes of what appeared to be food, toward the cottage steps. Roger and one of the younger agents were in a heated argument.

The agent was saying, "We didn't have a choice, sir. We had to bring her or she would have come on her own."

Katie paid no attention to them. She marched up the stairs, unconcerned about the commotion she was causing. Rainey disabled the alarm and unlocked the door. Katie walked through the door, passing Rainey and went straight to the kitchen. With her hands on her hips, she ordered the agents around and in no time organized a spaghetti dinner buffet. She did not speak to Rainey, just fed the troops, and ignored Roger's protestations. It appeared that Katie spent the time they were apart cooking. Rainey filled her plate and ate with the rest of them, silently watching the blond woman filling plates with second helpings. Mackie was as appreciative as he had been of the omelet. With every mouthful, he praised Katie's sauce and salad dressing.

Rainey made eye contact with Katie only a couple of times. They held each other's gaze for a moment, and then looked away. Rainey had no idea what to expect next. Katie had not just come there to bring food, even though her excuse was that she knew Rainey would not have enough at the cottage and wanted to make sure the agents were fed well. When the food was consumed and the dishes cleared away, the agents left for their posts outside. Mackie resumed his vigil at the camera monitors, leaving Katie and Rainey alone in the kitchen.

Katie finally spoke directly to Rainey, "Is there somewhere we could talk privately?"

The master bedroom was the most secluded place in the house, so Rainey led Katie into the room and shut the door. When they were alone, they stood and stared at each other until Rainey broke the silence.

"This sort of defeats the purpose of my leaving you at your house."

Katie snorted. "A little rudely, I might add."

Rainey was quick to retort, "You slammed a door in my face."

"I came here to explain that," Katie said.

"You couldn't have called?" Rainey asked.

Katie looked down at the floor. "What I need to tell you can't be said on the phone."

"Okay, let's have a seat," Rainey said, motioning to the dressing chair in the corner for Katie, and taking a seat on the trunk at the foot of the bed.

Katie sat down, looking around the room, obviously trying to find the right words. Rainey waited patiently. In a moment, Katie began, "I don't remember the accident or much of what happened just before it. I must have fallen asleep. At that time in the pregnancy, I was so tired. I had been on my feet all night. Really, the last thing I remember was JW handing me a bottle of water when we got in the car."

She looked around the room again. Rainey knew not to say anything. Katie was opening wounds she must have tried to close for the last six months.

Katie swallowed hard. "I woke up in the hospital. I was told right away, I lost the baby boy that I had carried for six months. I was in so much pain. They kept me doped up for days. When I finally came home, I couldn't sleep, so they gave me more drugs."

She was approaching a difficult part of her story, even though Rainey could not think of anything worse than the loss of a child. Katie swallowed hard before she continued.

"JW begged forgiveness for the accident, which I didn't have the strength to blame him for. He tried to make me comfortable. He dutifully gave me pills around the clock and was by my side always. I didn't notice him. I couldn't feel anything. The doctors prescribed more drugs. I was dead inside."

Rainey's heart broke for Katie. She knew that feeling all too well. She had experienced it after the attack, a deadening numbness enveloping her being. It was her mind's way of not letting her feel the depth of her pain.

"I stayed drugged for weeks. It wasn't for the physical pain, which had passed. I just couldn't function. I barely moved. I had to be helped to wash, to eat, simply to get out of the bed. I really don't remember much from that time. Then one night –" she paused, "one night, I woke up with JW on top of me."

Rainey held her breath. She did not want that image in her mind. She concentrated on shutting it out.

Katie continued with much difficulty, the tears flowing steadily now. "I was under heavy sedation and barely remember it. I couldn't move my arms and legs. I was unconscious as far as he knew and he was raping me."

"Oh my God, Katie, I'm so sorry," Rainey softly said, her own eyes beginning to well up.

Katie went on, "I blacked out. I woke up the next day and began to remember. From that moment on, I refused to take any medication. When I was strong enough, I told him I knew what he had done. He said he thought if I got pregnant that I would be happy again. I told him he was disgusting. I despise him and I've told him so, and I will never trust him again."

153

Katie let that sink in, and started to pull herself together. She said, after a moment, "Our marriage is finished. I agreed to stay until this proposed Senate campaign is over, but now I'm leaving as soon as I can get a divorce lawyer and file the papers. I am done with JW Wilson. I told him that this afternoon, before I left."

That was a lot of information for Rainey to process at one time. She was horrified at JW's behavior. Rainey assumed the accident and the loss of a child caused the distance between them, a common occurrence in couples when that happened. The reality of Katie's situation was worse. Rainey would never look at JW the same way again. Katie had every right to hate him. It took a lot of courage for Katie to tell her about this. Rainey wanted to hold her and tell her everything would be all right one day. She was frozen there on that trunk with Katie sitting across from her. Rainey knew nothing she could say would erase the pain Katie was feeling. Only time could do that.

Rainey stood up and crossed the room to Katie. She stopped in front of the chair and Katie stood up. Rainey wrapped her arms around Katie and held her close. Katie fell into her arms and laid her head on Rainey's shoulder. They stood there in the embrace, Rainey just holding Katie as long as she needed to be held. No words were needed. They understood each other completely.

Rainey waited for Katie to release their embrace, before she let her go. Katie took a step back and looked up at Rainey.

"I needed you to understand why I reacted the way I did and to apologize for it," she said.

Rainey brushed a stray hair from Katie's brow, saying, "No apology necessary."

Katie put her arms back around Rainey's waist. She said, "Now, about the other elephant in the room."

Rainey smiled down at her. "One thing at a time, okay? I can't focus on you and keep a killer at bay. Katie, you're not safe here."

"My god, there's an arsenal in this cottage. I think I'm pretty safe here." Katie laughed when she said it.

"For today, yes, but tomorrow they all go away." Rainey could not let anyone know what was happening with the tactical team, not even Katie. "You're going to hear some things on the news attributed to Danny and me. All I can say is don't believe everything you hear."

Katie's jaw dropped. "They're going to leave you alone as bait. What kind of fucked up plan is that?"

"I can't talk about it, but I'm fine with the plan and I'm sure we'll catch him. Then we can go on with our lives," Rainey said.

Katie was about to protest, but Rainey silenced her by kissing her deeply. She surfaced for air and said, "Katie, if I'm what you want, you have me. Just let me finish this."

Katie searched Rainey's eyes. Rainey tried to let her know that she had regained control. She was a highly skilled Special Agent and she was prepared to do what it took to end this. Rainey would not be caught off guard, not this time. She had a goal and was focused on it. Kill this fucker and put it to rest, all of it.

Rainey did not speak the words. She just squeezed Katie a little tighter and whispered, "I'll be all right, I promise."

Katie took her hands from Rainey's waist and put them gently on Rainey's cheeks, her eyes still searching back and forth between Rainey's. Her mind apparently made up, she pulled Rainey's mouth to hers and kissed her as passionately as Rainey had ever been kissed. It left Rainey weak-kneed and breathless. It had the same consequence for Katie. They let go of each other and caught their breaths.

Katie smiled up at Rainey. A grin began to form and then took over Rainey's face. Katie got the giggles, which caused Rainey to erupt, too.

When Katie could finally speak, she said, "If what comes next feels anything like that last kiss, I can't wait to find out what it is."

You could cut the sexual tension between them with a knife. They had to get out of that room, before God knows what would happen. Rainey suggested they go back to the main room and sit with Mackie for a while. They watched some submarine movie with a B actor playing the part of Steven Segal. Katie and Rainey sat together on the couch, while the videos from outside flipped by in succession on the picture in picture screen. It was a constant reminder of why they were really there.

They sat on opposite ends of the couch with their legs side by side on the cushions. Katie got a chill and Rainey pulled the blanket from the back of the couch, draping it across their legs and torsos. Katie took the opportunity to tease Rainey incessantly, rubbing her legs against Rainey's, under the covers. The sensation was electrifying when Katie slipped her foot inside the stretched out elastic around the bottom of the legs of Rainey's sweats, running her toes along Rainey's calf. She stopped moving and left it there, burning a hole in Rainey's leg.

Rainey could not tell what was happening in the movie. She was so tense with sexual desire she could barely breathe. The two-hour movie ended, after an eternity to Rainey. Roger knocked on the door and Rainey got up to let him in. It was ten o'clock and time for a shift change. The agents following Katie wanted to know if she was ready to go back home.

Rainey spoke for her, a little too quickly and with tension in her voice, but Roger did not seem to notice. "No, she's staying here tonight and going home in the morning."

Katie winked at Rainey. Rainey hoped no one noticed. She was not ready to let the world know that they were—well, whatever they were, she was not sure.

Rainey and Roger made decisions about where everyone would be for the evening. Two agents would stay in the main room to monitor the videos, while the others patrolled the area outside. They would switch off from time to time, so Rainey gave Roger the code for the alarm. She could change it later, when this was over. With that taken care of, she did not have to get up and let them in and out during the evening. Rainey had no intentions of coming out of the bedroom once she and Katie were locked away inside. She did not know exactly what was going to happen next, but Katie had her so wound up, Rainey knew she would not be able to control herself once they were alone.

Rainey sent Mackie to bed in the Master bedroom, and Junior joined him in there on a pallet Katie helped make for him on the

156

floor. The agents were all settled in the main room and Katie made sure they would spread the word about the leftovers in the refrigerator. Rainey put out paper plates and plastic utensils and pulled a trashcan out close to the table, where Katie set up the cut vegetables and dip she brought from home. Rainey knew what pigs agents could be and wanted the trashcan clearly visible.

When everyone was in their places, Rainey and Katie went into Rainey's room and locked the door. They flew at each other, Katie more aggressive and hungrier than before. They kissed all the way across the room, Katie leading Rainey backwards, until she pushed Rainey down on the bed. Rainey sat with her feet on the floor and buried her face in Katie's chest, as Katie stepped between Rainey's legs. Katie removed the ever-present shoulder holster and laid it down on the table next to the bed.

Katie pulled Rainey's head up to look into her eyes. She whispered, in a sultry voice, dripping with desire, "Something that feels this right can't be wrong." She bent her head and kissed Rainey softly again.

Then Katie did something Rainey was going to remember for the rest of her life. She slipped out of Rainey's arms and stepped back a few feet. Rainey was not sure what was happening, and then Katie slowly pulled the Carolina blue tank top she was wearing over her head, and tossed it away. There was a thin, faint scar about six inches long running down Katie's stomach. It must have been from the car accident. Rainey barely noticed it, because of the blue lace bra Katie was wearing. Ladies' lingerie had never sent shivers down Rainey's spine like this particular little lace number was doing. Katie then unbuttoned her pants, sliding the zipper down ever so slowly. Then shaking the shorts from her hips, she let them fall to the floor, revealing a matching pair of blue lace panties. Katie was so beautiful it took Rainey's breath. Rainey stopped breathing completely when Katie stepped back between her legs, and placing her hands on Rainey's shoulders, pushed her down onto the bed.

Katie straddled Rainey and crawled up her body. Rainey pulled the smaller woman down on top of her, arching her back, pushing into Katie with unfettered desire. She wanted this woman so badly, she felt she was going to orgasm from just the feel of Katie's soft skin on hers. Then it all came to a screeching halt when Katie tried to lift Rainey's shirt. Rainey stiffened and grabbed at the bottom of the tee shirt, holding it down against her abdomen.

Katie stopped and looked deeply into Rainey's eyes. "It's okay," she whispered. "You are beautiful and I want to feel your body against mine."

Katie gently placed a hand over the one Rainey was tightly gripping the tee shirt with. Slowly Rainey relinquished her hold on the shirt and allowed Katie to pull it over her head. Katie bent and began kissing Rainey's scar, following it down to just above her belly button and back up to her chest. The sensation of Katie's soft lips against her skin was almost more than Rainey could handle. She began to tremble uncontrollably as she lay back against the mattress. When Katie's mouth closed around her nipple, Rainey moaned and arched off the bed.

That was it. Rainey stood up, with the smaller Katie still in her arms. She threw back the covers and laid Katie down on the cool sheets. Rainey took off her sweat pants and climbed in beside Katie, pulling the covers up over them. As soon as Rainey was lying down, she reached for Katie and pulled her back on top of her. She fumbled with the bra snap, having never undone one from this angle, and finally released Katie's perfect breasts and pink nipples, hardened with excitement.

Katie was light as a feather to Rainey. She pulled Katie's body up higher so she could take one of Katie's nipples into her mouth. Katie arched her head back and smashed her breast against Rainey's mouth, beginning to grind her hips into Rainey, in a steady rhythm. Rainey spread her legs and Katie slid between them. Rainey pushed back against Katie's hips, growing with desire with every rock of the rhythm they created together. They kissed again so hungrily, each woman was moaning with pent up passion.

Katie then pulled herself up and straddled Rainey on all fours, never letting her lips leave Rainey's. She took one of Rainey's hands and shoved it into the front of her panties. The hair between Katie's legs was soft and fine, and wet. Katie began to grind against Rainey's hand, her breath coming shorter and faster against Rainey's lips. Rainey parted Katie's hot labial lips and moaned loudly when she felt the wetness on her fingers. She instinctively knew what to do. Katie stopped kissing her and buried her face in Rainey's hair, on the pillow. She rocked back and forth against Rainey's fingers until she came in a crashing orgasm and fell on top of Rainey, jerking with each wave of pleasure.

Rainey felt like she had climaxed with Katie and when Katie's hand slipped between Rainey's legs, it didn't take long for Rainey to reach a mind blowing orgasm, holding onto Katie so tightly, with each wave of spasm Katie moaned with her. They lay there spent, each breathing fast, trying to get a deep breath. Rainey held Katie there on top of her, Katie's face buried in her neck. They lay like that until their breathing slowed.

Rainey, finally able to talk, simply said, "Wow."

Katie said, with a wicked grin on her face, "I hope they didn't hear us."

"Maybe not that time," Rainey said.

Katie teased her, "Oh, you think there will be a next time?"

Rainey rolled Katie over onto her back and looked down at the beautiful blonde in her arms. She smiled a devilish grin and said, "Oh, I know there will be a next time."

They spent the night alternately talking, making love, and falling asleep, only to wake up and make love again until they were too exhausted to open their eyes. During those few hours, there was no Y-Man, nor FBI agents in their world, only the two of them cocooned together. Rainey fell asleep with Katie in her arms and slept like an angel for the rest of the night and into the morning. No terror invaded her sleep; only visions of making love to Katie entered her dreams, carrying her peacefully through the night.

CHAPTER SIXTEEN

Rainey awoke to Katie kissing her face softly. She opened her eyelids to see Katie's big blue eyes sparkling in front of her. She was gorgeous. It was the way Rainey wanted to wake up for the rest of her life. In just a few short days, Rainey had done what had been unimaginable to her. She never thought this would happen to her again, because after the attack, she could not or would not let anyone beyond the walls she built around her heart. Rainey was falling in love.

She smiled up at Katie, who was leaning on one elbow, inches from Rainey's face. Katie smiled back. They lay there looking into each other's eyes, both answering the other silently. Yes, this had been the right thing to do.

Suddenly an expression of sadness crossed Katie's face. She whispered, "I don't want to lose you, now that I've found you."

Rainey pulled her tightly to her. "You couldn't lose me now, if you tried. I'd stalk you," Rainey said, trying to lighten Katie's fears.

Katie asked, "When are they leaving you?"

"Three o'clock this afternoon. There will be media. You need to be gone by then. You don't want to be on the news," Rainey answered.

"I don't want to leave you, but I understand you need to be alert and focused." Katie smiled, sliding her hand between Rainey's legs.

Rainey moaned with pleasure and they made love, this time slowly, exploring each other's bodies with hands and mouths. Rainey investigated every inch of Katie's body and then brought Katie to a shuttering climax. Rainey thought that sex would be something she would have to work up to, but desire took over and it felt as natural as anything she had ever done in bed before. Rainey got as much enjoyment out of pleasuring Katie as Katie did.

They finally had to stop fooling around and get up, though neither one of them wanted to let the outside world into their secluded bubble. They showered together, which took longer because they could not keep their hands off each other. Rainey turned Katie around in the shower, pushing Katie's chest against the glass stall. She reached around, running her hand up Katie's thigh until Katie spread her legs and pushed back against Rainey, her hands braced against the glass. Rainey moved against her, both coming together even though Katie was not touching Rainey with her hands. Just the grinding action of her hips against Rainey's was enough to send Rainey into waves of ecstasy.

They finally got out of the shower and dressed. Rainey gave Katie a tee shirt and some gray cotton gym shorts, both of which were much too large for the smaller woman, but Katie pulled it off. She rolled the pants up at the waist and tied the tee shirt up, looking as sexy as ever to Rainey. Rainey put on her standard black BDUs and black tee shirt and slid the holster with the Glock over her shoulders. She was ready for battle. They kissed passionately one more time, at the door, neither wanting to let go of the other.

Katie finally said, "Please be careful, and when this is all over I want you to come for me, do you understand?"

Rainey smiled down at her sweetly. "There is nothing in the world that will stop me from coming for you and my only priority will be to make you happy for the rest of my life."

Katie looked deeply into Rainey's eyes. She hesitated a bit before saying, "I feel like I've been waiting for you all my life, like we've known each other before. I have fallen so hard for you, so fast, it's indescribable. As unbelievable as it sounds, at this moment, if you asked me to spend the rest of my life with you, I would say yes. I think you are my missing piece, Rainey."

Rainey's heart sent waves of electricity through her body. She loved this woman and before she could stop herself, she said, "Katie, I fell in love with you the first time I laid eyes on you, but I didn't recognize what the churning in my gut meant every time I saw you. Now, I know what falling in love was supposed to feel like, all along. Does that sound crazy to you?"

Katie did not hesitate this time; she answered, "I love you, too. Please be safe. Don't be a hero. Come back to me."

They kissed sweetly, one more time, then unlocked the door and went out to face the unknown together.

They fixed pancakes and sausages for breakfast, which the agents gobbled up in no time. Rainey was glad that Ernie's husband had killed some hogs and given her the mound of homemade sausage she had stored in the deep freeze, in the laundry room. Her dad had kept the freezer full of deer meat, from his and Mackie's hunting trips. Rainey did not eat deer meat and had cleared the freezer for the half a hog she bought from Ernie's farm. She gave the deer meat to a church, to give to the poor. No need to let it go to waste.

After cleaning up from breakfast, the whole time flirting conspiratorially, they snuck back into the bedroom for a passionate goodbye. Katie had to leave soon and it was breaking her heart and Rainey's. Rainey tried not to be too emotional, but when she saw the tears on Katie's cheeks and felt her sobbing softly against her chest, Rainey's tears began to fall down her face, landing in Katie's hair. Rainey did not wipe them away. She just held Katie until her sobbing subsided.

Katie raised her head from Rainey's chest. She said in a hushed whisper, "I'm so scared to leave you, but I know I have to."

"Very soon, you won't have to be scared anymore. You have to trust me," Rainey said.

"Okay," was all Katie could manage to say.

They went to the bathroom and splashed cold water on their faces, trying to erase the tearstains. One last kiss at the door and then Katie was gone. Rainey watched the SUV, with Katie in it, until it disappeared from sight. She stood there, staring out the window for a long time after Katie left. Mackie's voice jolted her out of her thoughts.

"She's something, isn't she?" he said, with a knowing grin.

He knew her too well to try to hide her true feelings and she was not afraid of disapproval from him. He loved her too much to be judgmental.

Rainey answered him with a matching grin, "You have no idea."

Danny arrived shortly after, with the tactical team. The team commander talked with Rainey about the layout of the land and the best places to set up. The team placed their equipment on the kitchen table and began laying a virtual net over Rainey's property. Mackie took the old wooden, roadblock sawhorses from the back of the office, setting up a command post of his own across the road where the pavement disappeared under a canopy of trees. He parked his Escalade behind the barricade and waited. No one would get by Mackie and Junior until Danny wanted them to.

It took all morning to set up the surveillance equipment. By noon, when they stopped to eat the barbeque take-out provided by one of the agents, all the cameras were in place. The snipers' nests were located and prepared. Rainey warned all the agents to take lots of water and bug spray with them. If they did not, the mosquitoes and deer flies would eat them alive, if the humidity and heat did not get them first. It was approaching the longest day of the year, when the sun was at its closest to this part of the earth. The Carolina sun would shine brightly for nearly fifteen hours today.

All of the local television and other major media outlets were leaked the story that something big would be happening out at Rainey's place of business. It was two o'clock when Mackie moved his barricades and the way was clear for the hordes of reporters sure to show up any minute. The first TV truck pulled up at two fifteen. Soon there were media people of all kinds, being held back on the road by several large men in black suits, and at least three helicopters flying over Rainey's house.

Other agents made a big show of packing up electronic equipment and moving it to the SUVs parked in the driveway. Rainey stood on the front deck with Danny, having an animated argument for the benefit of the press. By three o'clock, all the visible agents piled into the SUVs and made a very fast, public exit from Rainey's property. Junior followed in Mackie's Escalade and the illusion had been cast. The media got tired of waiting for Rainey to come out and talk to them, so they left, thinking Rainey Bell was now alone, in an isolated cottage, out in the woods. The media people had no way of knowing that the tactical team was in place and Rainey was anything but alone.

So much activity had taken place since Katie left, Rainey did not have the time to let thoughts of her invade her focus, but now that the activity had come to an end, Rainey could think of nothing else. She went into her bedroom, just to be alone for a few minutes with her thoughts. Her face flushed hot when images of Katie flashed in her mind. Katie on top of her, her eyes locked on Rainey's, smoldering with desire. Rainey had never known that sex could feel like that.

Rainey had not really thought about sex much since the attack. In fact, the thought of it made her sick. Rainey had been around enough victims to know that was a natural response to being raped and as time went by, she would eventually get back to a healthy sex life. Rainey was in no hurry, until she met Katie. Craving Katie the way she did, Rainey never once thought of the rape while in bed with her. Though the attack was still vivid in her mind, the pain was a little more palatable today.

Rainey's phone began to ring on her hip. She answered it immediately without looking at the caller ID. Rainey was pleasantly surprised, when she recognized the voice on the other end.

"Rainey, it's Katie. Is everything okay out there?"

Rainey burst into a smile. "Yeah, we're okay. Nothing happening, probably won't till after dark."

"What do you mean, we?" Katie was confused. "I saw you on the four o'clock news. I saw all those agents leave, even Mackie left."

"Do you really think Mackie would leave me?" Rainey said to ease Katie's mind. "He's right out there, in his chair, watching the video feeds."

Rainey wanted to tell her the truth. There was no way this guy could get to her. Armed SWAT guys surrounded her and the virtual net would see the killer long before he got within two hundred yards of her. Rainey couldn't tell Katie the truth. She could not take the risk that somehow this guy would find out that a trap had been laid for him. No one knew what was going on, except Danny and the few agents that had been at the cottage. Even the local police had been fed the same story as the media.

"I'm so worried about you. I have been cooking all day. There are pies on every surface in the kitchen," Katie said.

Rainey laughed, which unsettled Katie even more.

"I'm serious Rainey, I don't know if I can take this."

"Hang in there," Rainey said. "It will all be over soon."

"Promise me you'll be safe," Katie demanded.

"Katie, as long as I don't leave here, I promise you I am as safe as I could possibly be."

Rainey was not lying. She could not be any safer, as long as she stayed home. The only way she would be in danger is if he lured her away somehow, but even then, she would never go alone.

"Okay, I'll just keep telling myself that." Katie sighed.

Rainey wanted to change the subject. "How are things at your house?"

"Oh, fine. When the agents left your house, they descended on mine. So, I've had people to feed. I haven't seen JW. I assume he's in his study brooding," Katie said.

"So, you are completely covered by agents. That's good." Rainey ignored the JW comment.

"I've been trying to figure out what to say to a room full of first graders tomorrow, when I walk in followed by two big guys in suits," Katie said.

Rainey panicked. "You're not going to school, are you?"

"I have to, Rainey. We have a program for the parents tomorrow night. I can't abandon my babies."

"No way are you going into a public place tomorrow night," Rainey said, growing more desperate.

"Rainey, you don't understand. I have to go. There isn't anything that could stop me."

"Even if I asked you not to?" Rainey said.

"I asked you not to hang yourself out like a piece of meat to slaughter. Okay, that was not a good illustration, but you have made yourself bait," Katie argued.

"Touché," Rainey answered, because she had become the lure.

Katie went on, "And besides, I have these goons that follow me everywhere. I'll be fine."

Rainey became dead serious. "You listen to me. Do not go to the bathroom, the copy room, anywhere without them. Do you understand?"

Rainey was frightening Katie. She could hear it in her voice, when Katie answered quietly, "Okay, okay, I understand."

"I'm sorry, Katie," Rainey said. "I didn't mean to scare you. I'm worried, that's all."

"I know the feeling," Katie quipped.

Rainey did not want to waste the time they had discussing how scared they both were.

"I miss you, Katie."

"I know that feeling, as well," Katie said, more softly this time.

They sat quietly listening to each other breathe for a moment.

Katie broke the silence. "I pray this will all be over soon."

"Amen to that," Rainey said.

Rainey talked with Katie for the better part of an hour. They spent the time learning things about each other, what they liked and did not like, books they read, it was all new and exciting to Rainey. They laughed at each other's stories and pretended nothing else in the world existed, but the two of them. Rainey was sorry to have it end, but Mackie was knocking on her bedroom door.

"Katie, I have to go. I'll call you in the morning, okay?"

"Can't I call you later?" Katie asked.

"I need to stay focused," Rainey said, laughing, "and I cannot do that, if I'm talking to you."

"I guess you're right," Katie conceded. "Be safe, I love you," she said.

"Me too," Rainey said and they hung up.

A truck had pulled down to the boat ramp, while Rainey was on the phone. Mackie did not recognize it and wanted to go down and check it out. A debate ensued as to whether Mackie should give away his presence or remain in the house. Finally it was decided that Rainey would walk out on the deck, look at the truck long enough to make the driver nervous, and if that did not make him leave, then Mackie would go down there. It worked like a charm. The two teenagers immediately backed up and drove away, as soon as they saw Rainey. Evidently, the girl and boy were looking for some privacy.

After that, there was no activity until dark. Then a few vehicles pulled down to the landing and were met by a set of powerful floodlights Rainey's father had installed with motion detectors. He did it to help the fisherman at night, he said, but Rainey knew he did it to discourage teenagers from making it a hangout. When the lights would come on, the cars would leave like roaches fleeing back beneath a kitchen cabinet.

Every time she saw car lights, Rainey's heart sped up. The adrenaline pumped through her veins as she gripped the Glock in her hand. Then the car would leave and she would have to breathe deeply to calm herself down. Mackie was the same way, up and down from his recliner, looking out the windows. He occasionally checked the windows and doors all over the entire house, and then returned to the recliner to watch the video feeds. The agents in the kitchen kept up a steady banter with the ones outside of Rainey's house, talking into their earpieces, as the night grew deeper.

Rainey's skin began to crawl about three in the morning. The hair on the back of her neck stood up when Freddie began to growl from his perch in the window. Rainey peered through the darkness, trying to see what he saw.

"You guys see anything in the woods out front?" she called to the kitchen.

Rainey waited for the reply, listening as the agents questioned the men outside in the woods. "Nothing on the monitors, nothing but our guys on night vision or heat signature. There is a small animal, possibly a raccoon near the road, but that's it," the agent in the kitchen responded.

"Okay, thanks," she said and rubbed Freddie's back. "It's just a raccoon, remember what happened last time," Rainey said to the cat, who was still growling at something out the window.

The first and last time Freddie tangled with a raccoon Rainey ended up at the vet getting him shots and stitches. From then on, he would growl when he thought one was around, but Rainey could not force him outside to see. He met his match and was giving the raccoon population a wide birth.

Freddie remained on high alert. He stood in the window staring, as if he were watching someone move about. Rainey figured he saw one of the agents and finally relaxed back onto the couch. She started thumbing through a stack of Our State magazines, the state magazine of North Carolina. A former teacher gave her a subscription, before Rainey left for Virginia. The teacher said she always wanted Rainey to stay in touch with her roots. When the subscription ended, she liked it so much that her father gave her a subscription every year in her Christmas stocking. She took over buying it this past year, because it really was a slice of home.

She paged through the June issue, reading the article about Highway Twelve, the Beach Road that wound its way through the outer banks islands of the state. She took the state trivia quizzes in several preceding issues, even though she had done them before. It was usually the first page she turned to each month. She was always surprised at what she did not know about a state she thought she knew so well. She knew the eastern part of the state, but the mountain area was a bit of a mystery to her.

Rainey tried to read other articles, but could not concentrate so she got up to pace from room to room, checking and rechecking the slides and ammo of weapons around the house. There were only a few lights on, as if she had gone to bed, so walking amongst the memorabilia was tricky. She was looking at the bookcase, trying to find something to read, when she saw the small dagger tucked behind a helmet. She picked it up and looked at it. It did not have a fancy blade or ornate handle. A plain knife, with dirty, grayed, cotton fabric wrapped around the base, was unusual among all the other collectables. She always meant to ask her father about it, after she found it on the shelf one day, but she never did. Therefore, she did the next best thing and asked Mackie.

"Your father never told you about that dagger?" his big voice rumbled.

"I never asked him," Rainey said, still standing by the bookcase.

"Well, see, we were in these fox holes, March 30, 1972, in Quang Tri province, where we were helping the South Vietnamese Army fortify the area around Hue, before we pulled out. Most of the US ground forces were gone by then, except a few of the units like ours, special guys, you know." Mackie winked, because Green Berets and other Special Forces did a lot of things no one in the media knew about.

He continued, "There hadn't been any action in days, so we were hanging out, eating, listening to music, shit like that. Generally, no one was paying attention. It was after three in the morning. Your dad was standing down in the last hole, sort of by himself. He was looking for a place to get some sleep. He chose that hole, because it was away from all the noise we were making. Out of the blue, this gook jumps into the hole with your father and tried to stab him with that very knife. Right then all hell broke loose with regular NVA everywhere and mortars raining down on us. The North Vietnamese Army had launched a large-scale assault across the DMZ."

169

"Dad always said they were sneaky little bastards," Rainey added.

"Your dad didn't have time to grab his gun. He popped that pajama-wearing piece of shit right in the face with his fist, took his knife, and slit his throat. Billy jumped out of that hole and did a John Wayne, right through the middle of those little fuckers. He killed, I don't know how many with it, before he picked up a M1 and started mowing them down. He kept the rest of us from getting killed, until we could get back in our holes and return fire. We were air lifted out later. Billy kept that knife the rest of the time we were in country. It was his talisman, because he should have been shot to pieces running through those guys and he came out without a scratch."

"That's amazing," Rainey said, looking down at the knife. She could see now that the dark stains on the fabric were blood, not dirt.

"Your dad was a crazy fucker," Mackie said, laughing

"He was always so calm and caring. I can't picture him doing that," Rainey said.

Mackie sat back in the recliner. He said, "It was a different world over there." He grew silent and looked out the window.

Rainey knew that look. Her father got it, too, sometimes. He would become real quiet and stare into space. She wondered what they saw, in the images flashing through their heads and yet, at the same time, she probably really did not want to know all they had seen. Rainey had experienced enough human depravity right here in the United States. She could imagine what they had observed, without knowing the details.

Rainey returned the dagger to the shelf. She went back to pacing and looking out windows until the sun began to rise. A shift change took place at dawn, so they could get in and out without drawing any attention. Once the fresh team was in place, Rainey went to her bedroom and closed the door. She was exhausted from little sleep and the activity the night before. Rainey crawled into bed in her clothes. She thought about calling Katie, decided it was too early, and then changed her mind. She dialed Katie's cell, so she would not accidently get JW. Katie answered before the first ring was completed.

"Rainey?"

"Yes, I hope I didn't wake you," Rainey said.

"No, I've been up since before dawn, waiting for you to call," Katie said, sounding relieved.

"Well, everything's okay. No sign of him, yet."

Katie asked, "What do you do now?"

"I get some sleep," Rainey said. "Somebody kept me up all Saturday night and I'm exhausted."

"Somebody, huh?" Katie teased.

"Yeah, this good looking blonde stopped by and took me for a spin," Rainey played along.

"Was it worth it?" Katie continued.

Rainey answered with enthusiasm, "Oh yeah, most definitely."

"Do you think she'll be back?" Katie asked.

Rainey smiled to herself, the thought of Katie in her arms, giving her a thrill. She said, "I hope so, real soon."

Katie kept going, "Sounds like you like her."

"Yes, I do, actually. She's very nice and really hot," Rainey said.

Katie giggled and then said, "I bet she thinks you're hot, too."

"Really?" Rainey asked.

"Oh, I think she thinks you are extremely sexy," Katie said, giggling some more. "Your work outs are paying off. Your ab muscles alone are worth every sit up, if you know what I mean."

Rainey laughed. The flirting was fun and making her hornier than she already was. She had been since Katie left. She tried not to think about it, but her body kept reminding her. It craved Katie as much as Rainey did. She almost wished they had waited until the manhunt was over, because now that she knew what she was missing, she wanted it more. It was out of character for Rainey to express what she was truly feeling, but she seemed to have no barriers with Katie, no walls to keep her emotions in check.

"I want you," Rainey heard her own voice saying. It came out in a sultry whisper unfamiliar to Rainey's ears.

Katie chimed in, "Oh honey, tell me about it."

They laughed again. Katie told Rainey that she had contacted her two older sisters—both lived on the west coast—explaining what was happening at home with the stalking, because in this day and age electronic media made it a very small world. Katie also called her mother and father, who were on an extended holiday in the Mediterranean. Rainey did not have anybody to call. The people she really cared about already knew.

"Honey," Katie said, after a few more minutes of chatting, "I would love to stay here and talk to you all morning, but I have to get dressed for school."

Rainey grew serious. "You remember what I said. You don't go anywhere alone."

Katie teased her. "Yes ma'am, Special Agent Bell."

Rainey was slightly amused, but said, "I'm serious. Promise me."

Katie stopped teasing and answered firmly, "I promise."

"Katie, please be careful and call me after school, before the program," Rainey paused, and then added, "I love you."

"I love you, too. Get some rest. Sweet dreams," Katie said, before hanging up.

Rainey knew her dreams would be sweet, because her mind was completely inundated with thoughts of Katie. She closed her eyes and was gone within minutes, dreaming of Katie in her arms.

CHAPTER SEVENTEEN

Rainey awoke at four o'clock that afternoon to the phone ringing on the table by the bed. She was still fully clothed, having only kicked off her black Nikes before she lay down. She was still lying in the exact same spot. She had surfaced a couple of times from the land of nod, only to have the exhaustion pull her back down into her dreams, where Katie baked pies, wearing only an apron and a little French maid's hat. In the dream, Rainey sat on a stool watching her, as Katie explained her every move, like Julia Child on a cooking show.

She reached for the phone groggily and hoarsely said, "Hello."

"Hey," Katie said, cheerfully, "Are you still asleep?"

Rainey looked at the clock. She had slept nine hours. Rainey considered five hours a good night's sleep. This had been a marathon nap. She was hungry and had to pee. Rainey sat up on the edge of the bed, wiping the sleep from her eyes, and was reminded immediately of her need for a bathroom.

Rainey managed to say, "Hang on, I have to go to the bathroom," almost forgetting she could take the cellphone with her. She made it just in time, holding the phone to her ear with her shoulder. After a yawn she asked, "How was your day?"

Katie was excited, as she said proudly, "I have the smartest and most talented first grade class in the school. We are going to shine tonight."

Rainey yawned again. "Sorry about the yawning, nothing personal. I'm glad to hear your class is doing so well."

Rainey sat on the toilet, even after she had finished, quietly talking to Katie. She was still groggy as she listened to Katie relaying stories of her "babies" and the program they practiced for today. Katie was pleased with how well they had all done. Even their mistakes were cute and fixable. Katie obviously adored her job and her students. As she talked about her kids, Rainey could hear the love in Katie's voice.

Rainey's head began to clear, so she stood up and walked to the sink. She looked at her nappy hair and sleepy eyes. She had slept like the dead, one of those heavy sleeps from which it is hard to emerge. Katie prattled on about costumes and forgotten lines, while a thought crept into Rainey's head. Was Katie ready to give up her career to be with Rainey? This was the Bible belt, even if Chapel Hill was much more liberal than the rest of the state.

When Katie gave her a chance, Rainey said, "You obviously love teaching. Have you thought about what consequences our relationship might have on your career?"

"Rainey, there are gay men and women, at least one, on every hallway at my school. They're good teachers and wonderful people. As long as I don't walk around with a sign saying I'm a lesbian and bring you to show and tell, I think I'm okay."

Rainey was hit with a question. "Does sleeping with just one woman make you a lesbian?"

Katie answered with a scholarly tone, "I believe it is the quantity of sex, not the number of women you sleep with that makes you a lesbian."

"Do you think we qualify?" Rainey asked, playfully.

Katie continued, in her laboratory voice, "I think you should have a few more goes at it, collect more data, before I make that qualification."

"I'll take your recommendation seriously and I hope very soon," Rainey said.

"Oh God, I know. Isn't it driving you crazy? I guess not, you've been passed out, but I've had to walk around all day with my crotch on fire," Katie said.

Rainey laughed loudly at Katie's predicament. Katie had a tendency to ask a question and then answer it herself. It was cute the way she talked fast, her accent dripping with just enough Southern sugar to keep the listener mesmerized, or at least it had that result for Rainy. Her own body started reminding her again that it wanted Katie in the worst way.

The dichotomy of Rainey's position was bewildering. Here she was experiencing falling in love with the woman of her dreams, at least the ones she had lately, and on the other hand, using herself as bait for a serial killer. Rainey was sure that she would just split into two people, at some point, if this situation did not work itself out quickly.

They talked for a few more minutes. Rainey made sure Katie was following the rules about being alone. Katie promised to call after the program and then she was gone. Rainey showered and changed into fresh BDUs and a tee shirt. This one said FBI on the back in bright yellow letters. With the shoulder holster in place, she opened the door on another evening of surveillance.

Mackie was up making breakfast, the day having been turned upside down for them. The tactical team took care of themselves, but did not turn down the offer of a hot biscuit. Rainey ate the eggs and bacon ravenously. She jellied two biscuits and gobbled them as well. She drank two glasses of orange juice and a bottle of water. She could not seem to get enough to quench her dehydration. Coffee came next, creamy and sweet, just as she liked it.

It had been a beautiful day in the Triangle, the agents reported to Rainey. An older lady identifying herself as Ernestine Womble, and her two sons, had come by earlier. She left when the agents told her that Rainey and Mackie were asleep. She left some fresh vegetables and the agents put them in the refrigerator. Rainey had forgotten to call Ernie and was pleased to find out Mackie had, but she still needed to let her know she was all right.

Ernie worried about Rainey, as if she was her own child. She came to stay with Rainey in Virginia, that first week home from the hospital. Mackie wanted to stay, but Rainey did not want another man around; she already had Danny sleeping on her couch. She needed a mother and her own was the last person she wanted in her cramped apartment. She wished for a "mom" and Ernie came to her rescue. Rainey had always treasured her relationship with Ernie, but after that, Rainey cherished her even more.

She went out on the front deck, just to get some air. There were too many people in the cottage, which was locked up tight, no movement in and out for hours, and all those people breathing the same air. The air conditioning helped, but only so much air moved about, and the smell of men penetrated every molecule of oxygen, in Rainey's opinion. She had to get out of there and the deck was her only source of freedom.

Rainey dialed Ernie's number. She picked up on the second ring. "So you finally remembered my number?" Ernie said sarcastically.

"I'm sorry, Ernie. It's been a circus. Mackie told me he talked to you," Rainey offered in apology. It did not work.

"Yes, at least he had the courtesy to call," Ernie shot back.

Rainey tried again. "I'll make it up to you. We'll do a spa day, just me and you."

Ernie started coming around. She loved spa days. "Okay, but you have to report once a day, preferably before you go to sleep in the morning, so people don't think you're dead and drive all the way over there, thinking they're going to find God knows what."

Rainey's tone was repentant. "I really am sorry, Ernie, and I promise to call every day, at least once."

Ernie finally let it drop and they went on to other things. Rainey thanked her for the vegetables and asked if Ernie could pick up a few things at the store, and then bring them by tomorrow. She had not been shopping lately, and needed most of the staples and something to go with the vegetables Ernie supplied. She had to feed Mackie and that took some doing, not to mention all the other hungry men wandering around. Rainey knew what it was like on stakeouts. Everybody ate from boredom. Thank goodness, she had a deep freeze. Ernie was happy to do it. It made her feel involved in the investigation.

"All right, I'll come by about this time tomorrow," Ernie said. "I'll bring you some watermelons, too. Henry's best ones just got ripe."

"Thank you, Ernie. I love you. Be careful," Rainey said.

"I'll cut his pecker off if he comes near me," Ernie said, in one of the rare moments when she said anything remotely off color.

"I'll bet you would," Rainey said, laughing.

Rainey hung up with Ernie and told Mackie about the watermelons she was bringing. Henry Womble grew fantastic melons. They were so sweet, Rainey could eat half of one all by herself, and these were big watermelons. Henry called them African watermelons. He said he got the seeds off a man in Wilson County, and that is what he had called them. They were gigantic round watermelons, dark and light green stripes encircling the rind, and were legendary in these parts. Mackie was as excited as Rainey. It was good that they had something fun to anticipate, surrounded by the FBI's tactical team and a maniac out there somewhere, with Rainey his only obsession.

At six o'clock, her cellphone rang. It was Katie again.

"I only have a second, but I just wanted to call to tell you I was thinking of you," she said.

"I was thinking of you, too," Rainey said, stepping out on the deck for some privacy.

"I'm almost at the school, so I don't have much time," Katie said, quickly.

"Where are the agents, the ones watching you?' Rainey asked, concerned.

"They're right behind JW."

"Where is JW?"

Katie's tone reflected how she felt about the following statement. "JW is tagging along behind me, in his car. He decided it was too good a chance to slap backs and shake hands to miss."

Rainey saw the politician character, JW, in her mind and knew he could not resist showing up at a public place. Free votes had to be collected where they could be found. The high level of income that the majority of the students' parents enjoyed was probably a major enticement, as well. There could be donations out there for the picking. Katie was not happy about it, that was for sure.

Katie's voice broke Rainey's train of thought. "I just wanted to ask if I could call again at eight-thirty? That's not too late, is it? I think that's still early enough that you could afford to focus on me for a few minutes."

"Yes, that would be nice. I'd love to focus on you for a few minutes," Rainey said, smiling inside and out.

"Okay, I have to go now. Talk to you soon," Katie said, and then she was gone.

She did not say, "I love you," Rainey thought and then dismissed it as something typical of a teenage reaction to a supposed slight. Rainey was turning into a little girl, tender to the touch, overwhelmed with the mere thought of Katie. This was a heavy-duty crush. Rainey knew why it was called a crush, because it crushed your brain and made you stupid.

Rainey convinced Mackie to go down and get some files out of the office, so she would have something to do. When he got back, Rainey began the same routine as last night, watching the sun go down and then alternately reading, eating, or anxiously pacing the floor from room to room. Mackie did some phone tracking of skips, and was able to convince two of the ones he located to come in voluntarily. Mackie sweet talked a girlfriend into giving up the whereabouts of her worthless banger boyfriend and sent Junior to pick him up with the boys. Rainey anticipated Katie's call at eight thirty. It was all she had to look forward to, while waiting for the maniac to make his move.

Rainey expected him to come soon. Today or tomorrow, he could not wait much longer. The bizarre flight of fancy he was living would not allow him to ignore this chance of fate, Rainey stumbling across him and him her, outside of Katie's house. He had to have Rainey to relive the thrill of out-smarting the FBI. He would be getting sicker with his psychosis; it would be in control of him by now, constantly driving him, nagging him, pushing him toward his goal, the capture and murder of one Rainey Blue Bell. He considered her death critical to completion of his sexual fantasies. He was a need-based killer. He would not stop, until he was caught or dead. Rainey still held out hope for the latter.

Eight thirty came and went with no phone call. The anticipation was beginning to turn to anxiety as the minutes clicked by. Rainey paced her bedroom floor, until her cell rang. It was only eight forty-five, just fifteen minutes late, but it felt like hours to Rainey. She yanked the phone open and shoved it to her ear.

"I was getting worried," she said into the handset.

A familiar voice, but not the one she was expecting, came from the other end of the connection.

Danny said, "Were you expecting a call?"

"As a matter of fact, I was," Rainey said, wanting him off the phone, so Katie could call. She forgot all about call waiting. Her failing reasoning was a symptom of her crush.

Danny hesitated, and then said, "I'm afraid I have some bad news."

"What, is DC pulling the plug on the operation, too much money being spent?"

"Katie Wilson is missing," Danny said, but the words did not sink in for Rainey.

"What did you say?" she asked

"Katie Wilson went missing from backstage an hour ago. I just now had a chance to call you. I've been dealing with her shithole, 'I am somebody' husband, and a bunch of locals trying to get the area locked down. I wanted to call and let you know. I guess we were wrong."

Rainey only heard the first sentence and then her knees buckled to the floor. All she could hear was the roar of her blood rushing to her heart. She froze in place, unable to move, to think, to react.

"Rainey—Rainey—Did you hear what I said?" Danny was talking in her ear. "Rainey! Answer me!"

She found her voice, only it was weak and shattered, "We have to—we have to find her."

Danny spoke rapidly, "You stay put, Rainey. That's why I called, so you wouldn't hear it from one of the guys at your house and run out to look for her. We have it covered. We'll find her. He did not get out of this neighborhood, no way. We locked it down seconds after she vanished. Hang on a sec."

He pulled the phone away from his head to speak to someone else. Then he was back with her, talking fast again. "Hey look, I gotta go deal with Mr. Wilson. It seems he's going out on his own to search for his wife. Probably get shot. Serve him right. He's a real piece of work. Stay put, Rainey. I'll call you when I know something."

He hung up. Rainey continued holding the phone to her ear. She did not move for a while, she could not. All the blood had rushed to her heart and stayed there, not letting her brain or limbs share. When the feeling started coming back in her arms and legs, she dropped the phone on the floor. Her arms hung limp by her sides, as she tried to stand up. Then a wail started in her gut and fought its way out of her throat. A guttural, primal sound of grief crawled from her body. It was so distressing that Mackie burst through the door, seconds later.

Mackie rushed to her side and lifted her from the floor, as if she were a feather. He placed her on the end of the bed and made her put her head between her legs. He brought a cold, wet rag from the bathroom and held it on her head. She was racked with silent sobs and rocked back and forth on the bed. He waited a few minutes for her breathing to become more regular.

He did not speak until he was sure she could understand him. "Rainey, the guys out there told me what happened to Katie. You have to get it together. Don't let it take you down."

Rainey could hear him now. His voice rumbled through her brain. She took the cloth from his hand and began wiping her face. The worm had turned and the rage began to boil from the depth of her being. Mackie must have seen the tension building in her muscles.

"Rainey, we're not going to do anything stupid, because if you go, I'm going and I ain't letting you go off half-cocked."

Rainey did not answer. She had her breakdown and cry and it was over, for now. All she could think about was finding Katie. Rainey stood up and went to the closet. She found the extra holster that attached to the shoulder harness she wore. She added it and the Beretta, from the car, to the harness. She checked that her flashlight worked and added extra batteries to a side pocket on her pants. She grabbed the ballistics vest she kept in the closet. She took down the dark blue windbreaker from the coat rack on her bedroom door, where it had been hanging untouched for a year. Emblazoned on the back, in large, block, yellow print, were the letters FBI. Rainey put on the vest, tightened the Velcro straps, adjusted her holster harness over it, and then slid the thin blue jacket on, feeling its coolness brush against her arms. She found her other nine-millimeter in the bedside table and dropped it into the waistband at the back of her pants.

Mackie watched, silently, the guardian at the door. Rainey was aware of his presence, but said nothing. She knew she could not leave here without him. He would not let her. Rainey went to the dresser, stopping to pick up her cellphone from the floor, and retrieved her old FBI cap, from where it hung over the mirror. She pulled her ponytail through the hole in the back, sliding the cap on her head.

Rainey looked at her reflection in the dresser mirror. Her eyes shown back at her, full of hatred and rage, and yes, guilt. She saw it there for an instant, but had to shut it out. Rainey could not let the guilt she felt consume her. She had left Katie alone, so sure that Katie was not his real target. Rainey let the rage focus her on the one thing she had to do, the only thing she could do, find Katie.

Special Agent Rainey Bell turned to the big man, waiting by the door. "Let's go."

Mackie stepped in front of her. He said, "Has it crossed your mind that he could be luring you out, where he can get to you?"

Rainey picked up the shotgun, leaning against the wall by the door. She looked up at Mackie, her jaw set and focused. "I hope so."

CHAPTER EIGHTEEN

The agents in the outer rooms of the cottage were involved in a blur of activity. All movement ceased when Rainey and Mackie stepped out of her bedroom. All eyes were on Rainey, as she made her way toward the front door, Mackie right on her heels. No one tried to stop her. She was armed and being followed by a former NFL defensive end. Nobody wanted to tell her she could not go. They would all be doing the same thing, in the same situation, even if they didn't know the whole story. What the agents in the cottage did not know was that Rainey was not going after the killer, because of what he had done to her, not entirely. Rainey had to find Katie, before he had the chance to do more to her than he probably already had.

Rainey had to think like a trained analyst now, not emotionally attached to the facts she had at hand. Separating her fears and anxiety over what the sadist was doing to Katie, she tried to think like him. Where would he go? He would need isolation to do what he did. He would have found a house where the neighbors were not too close or friendly. It would have a garage he could pull into or a hidden entrance, so no one could see the occupant of the house coming and going. He had stalked and kidnapped Katie in Chapel Hill. Rainey guessed it became too hot for the psycho in Raleigh, after the attack on her last year. He was probably living in Chapel Hill now. His torture chamber would be located nearby. He would have to visit it, prepare for his victims, and revel in his memories. The Y-Man may have continued killing all along, learning from his mistakes and concealing the bodies from discovery. The only thing she could not wrap her mind around was why he deviated from his usual behavior. Why had he begun to stalk Katie?

Rainey could not answer that question. She only knew she was leaving the cottage to find the house, where the kidnapper had taken Katie. Her mind raced through the neighborhoods and cul-de-sacs of Chapel Hill. Finding his lair was all Rainey could let herself think about. There was so much new building since she had lived here, the old wooded areas were now speckled with houses. She needed her laptop and picked it up from the coffee table, as she went by. If Rainey looked at Google Earth images of the town, she had a better chance of finding a secluded area, with widely spaced houses, near Katie's school. If Danny was right, and the kidnapper had not escaped the area, the piece of shit had to be nearby, holed up in a residence.

Just as Rainey's hand hit the handle of the front door, after shutting off the alarm, one of the agents said, "Who are we supposed to watch, if you're not here?"

"I think your services would best be used searching for this fucker, but that's just me. You should ask your supervisor."

The agent who asked the question immediately pulled out his cellphone and frantically punched in a number. Rainey did not wait to find out what the supervisor said. She and Mackie went out the door, leaving the confused agents to work it out on their own. When she reached the car, she heard footsteps and turned to see two agents running down the stairs. The agent who had been making the phone call stood at the top of the stairs, with the phone pressed to his ear. A big black SUV was coming down the road, from where an agent had been stationed out of sight. The guy with the phone yelled, "Stay with her!" at the agents, now standing in the yard waiting for a ride.

Rainey said, under her breath, "Good luck."

She and Mackie climbed into her car. Rainey put the shotgun on the floor of the back seat and positioned the laptop in its holder. She fired up the engine on the Charger, just as the other agents were climbing into the black SUV. They had no chance to catch her. The Charger had already started down the driveway, before the big SUV turned around. She left rubber on the road, where the driveway met the pavement, kicking up a cloud of smoke that trailed off behind her. The Charger vanished from sight, slipping into the shadows where the trees closed in over the road.

Rainey floored the car down US Highway 64 to the junction with Highway 15, called Chapel Hill Road by the locals. Mackie got on the phone with a buddy in the highway patrol. By the time she turned onto Chapel Hill Road, Rainey had an escort cruiser speeding in front of her, lights flashing, leading the way. She headed the Charger north, counting off the time in her mind that the bastard had already been holding Katie.

Rainey knew the guy probably stunned and drugged her. At least Katie would not remember the first part of her captivity, Rainey thought. The Y-Man liked to take his time, which was helpful to the investigators searching for Katie, but the more time that ticked by brought Katie closer and closer to death.

Rainey's cell rang. She knew it had to be Danny, before she even answered it.

"Goddamnit, Rainey. I told you to say put," he shouted at her when she answered.

Rainey hit the button on the rear view mirror and hung up on him. He could shout at her to her face when she got there, but she was coming. Rainey was coming too fast to listen to Danny barking at her through the radio speakers.

She told Mackie to fire up her laptop and pull up the satellite image of the neighborhoods around Katie's school. While he did that, Rainey drove the car right on the cruisers tail, weaving through the early evening traffic. Darkness was enveloping the sky completely, as they flew by the downtown area of Chapel Hill, and out to the last place Katie Wilson had been seen alive.

Rainey's cellphone rang again and she almost did not answer it, but she had to, in case it was important. Maybe Danny had calmed down. She hit the button again on the rearview mirror and answered, "Don't yell at me, Danny."

185

The faked little boy voice that spoke next sent chills down her spine. Every hair on her body stood up and the color drained from her face. She looked quickly at the mirror, as if she could see him in it. What she saw was her own white pasty face and frightened eyes staring back at her.

"Hi Rainey, do you want to come out and play?" the excited little boy voice said.

Mackie's head snapped up from the laptop. He looked at Rainey, his eyes wide with the recognition of who the voice belonged to. He could tell from Rainey's reaction.

Rainey thought quickly. She needed to play his game. She said, "Yes, I want to play." Then pressing him, she asked, "Is Katie there with you? Can she play with us?"

"Yep, she's here... but she's asleep now," the eerie voice answered.

Rainey's breath caught in her throat and then she asked, softly, "Can you wake her up?"

She heard him moving around. She listened to him trying to wake Katie, like a kid waking an older sibling, because mom is on the phone. "Hey, wake up! Wake up, Katie. Rainey wants to talk to you."

Then Rainey heard the sound for which she was praying. After a few moans of protest, Katie's heavily sedated voice, barely audible, whispered, "Rainey... help... me."

Rainey's heart leapt against the wall of her chest. She had to stay calm and though she wanted to scream it, Rainey said softly, "I'm coming Katie, hold on, I'm coming."

"She's gone back to sleep," the voice said, in singsong.

"What's wrong with her?" Rainey asked.

"I played with her and now she's tired." Rainey could almost see his preschool shrug when he answered.

Rainey needed to focus him on her, not Katie. She had to keep him talking. "You know my name, but I don't know yours. I have to know your name so we can play together," she said.

"It's—Johnny," he spit out reluctantly.

"Good, now I know what to call you, Johnny. So Johnny, how do we play the game?" Rainey asked. She repeated his name to pull him in closer to their conversation and distract him from Katie.

"First, we have to have some rules to play the game." He said, like a six-year-old organizing a group of kids in the backyard. "Rainey, you have to come by yourself. If one other person tries to play our game, then Katie loses, and you know what that means." He added quickly, "That big guy is with you, I know it. You have to drop him off, before you get here. He scares me."

"I have an idea, Johnny," Rainey said, in the tone that adults use with small children. "Why don't you let Katie go home and you and I can really play alone together, just like before?"

He thought for a moment, then said, "Okay, I'll let her go when you get here, if she can walk, she's kind of tired." He paused to let that sink in. "Yeah, I'll let her go," he was bargaining, "but you have to leave your guns in the car. I'm not allowed to play with guns."

Mackie was motionless, wide eyed, staring at her, while she talked to the maniac on the other end. His first move was to grab his cellphone, which he flipped open in his hand. He started to punch a number, but Rainey stopped him, by silently placing her hand over his.

Rainey answered the boy inside the man, "That's a deal, Johnny, no guns, but you have to let Katie go, or I won't play. You have to promise." She had to talk only to the boy, not remind the childlike creature on the other end that he was insane. He probably knew it, when he was not living a fantasy, but right now the child was in control.

"Okay, I promise," he said, a little whiny. As always with children, some codifications had to be added. The boy said, "You have to pull over and let the big man out, so I can hear him leave."

"Do you want me to do that right now, Johnny?" Rainey eyes darted around her. They were on a busy highway.

The child became insistent. "Do it now, Rainey, or Katie can't go home."

"Okay, I'm pulling the car over, Johnny." Rainey did as she was told and slowed the car, pulling off onto the emergency lane. The highway patrolman stopped about three hundred yards further down the road.

Mackie was shaking his head no. He was not about to let her go off alone, especially since he did not know where she was going. Rainey looked at him, mouthing the words, "Get out."

Johnny was impatient. "I didn't hear the door open."

Mackie opened the door, but did not move. Rainey begged him with her eyes to get out. She was even more insistent when Johnny said, "I can still see you."

Rainey looked around her, eyes flashing on every vehicle.

"No, silly," Johnny said, "I can see the inside of your car."

Mackie and Rainey both checked every surface of the car. They found the small camera above the windshield, cloaked by the black cloth interior, almost invisible. It was wireless, sending a signal to the killer. He had to be close, in a car driving by, or parked on an overpass, or in a house nearby, and she had driven into his range. He knew she had to come this way to get to the school. Rainey knew the specs on the best wireless cameras on the market. She knew that meant the man calling himself little Johnny was within at least two thousand feet of her location. She could not tell Mackie that Johnny could see her hands and face probably, but someone would know. Someone would know where to look for them.

Johnny's voice took on a more sinister tone. "Tell him to get out, or we don't play the game, and I go back to playing with Katie and you will never see her again."

"Get out, Mackie," Rainey said.

He stared at her helplessly and slowly got out of the car. Mackie gave her one last look, pleading with her not to go alone, before he closed the door.

"He's out," she said to the voice in the speakers.

"Now, drive ahead and turn east on Cleveland Road."

Rainey did as she was told. She passed the highway patrolman backing down the highway to pick up Mackie, who was waving his arms in her rear view mirror. What a sight it must have been to people driving by, seeing the huge black man with a pistol showing at his waist, flagging down a highway patrolman. The 911 calls were probably hammering the switchboard.

Rainey turned right onto Cleveland Road at the next junction in the highway.

"Now turn left onto Hampton Road and follow it around to the farmhouse at the end of the road. Stop in the big turn and throw the guns you're wearing out the window. I'll be watching," the boy instructed, his voice having taken on a more sadistic tone. He now had Rainey alone and the game had begun.

She was right. He was close. She hoped Mackie and Danny would figure that out. Still there were hundreds of houses south and west of where she turned onto Hampton Road. There appeared to be no development in the wooded area to the right of her and the highway was on her left. She followed the paved road to where it turned into a gravel path and made a sweeping wide turn back to the south. How would they find this one isolated old farmhouse? Maybe Mackie would remember her saying to look for isolated places around Katie's school on the satellite image.

Rainey was trembling with adrenaline when she took off the shoulder holster and dropped it out the window. It landed in the middle of the road, the guns clattering against the pavement. She hoped someone would see it, someone who was looking for her. The camera could not see the Sig Sauer pistol in the waistband of her pants. Little Johnny did not know it was there. Rainey slid the jacket back over her shoulders to keep it that way.

"Goodie, we can play now," Johnny, said.

Rainey needed to take control away from him. She said, "Bring Katie out of the house, so she can take my car home."

"Rainey, I don't think she should drive. She doesn't look like she feels good."

Rainey lost the control game. She raised her voice. "What did you do to her?"

He laughed, enjoying himself. "I gave her a shot. Maybe I gave her too much."

189

"Bring her outside, Johnny. She can sleep in the car," Rainey said. She needed to get Katie away from this guy. "Don't you want to play with just me?"

"You know, I changed my mind. I want to play with both of you. It will be twice as much fun," he responded, happily.

Rainey was at a disadvantage. He had Katie and he knew Rainey would come for her, no matter what. She could see the farmhouse now. It was a two story, dimly lit old home, the roof of the porch sagging with the weight of its years. It needed painting. Many years after it was built, someone had added a three sided, aluminum carport on one side, sheltering an exterior door, Rainey suspected. She slowed the Charger down, rolling to a stop a hundred yards from the driveway.

Rainey could hang up now, call Danny, and be surrounded by law enforcement in minutes. From the rolled down window, she could hear distant sirens. They were looking for them. They were coming. Rainey could wait here for backup. That would be the smart thing. The maniac in the house must have sensed her thoughts.

His voice rang out in the singsong pattern, "If you hang up now, I'll give Katie another shot, and she will go to sleep forever."

He must have heard the sirens too. Rainey was running out of time. Rainey had no choice. She took her foot off the brake and rolled slowly forward.

"Okay Johnny, here comes Rainey."

CHAPTER NINETEEN

Rainey's every nerve was on high alert. She slowly rolled the Charger into the driveway. She parked right at the end, near the gravel road, blocking the exit of the old Jeep she saw parked under the carport. He could still drive through the thin carport walls, but at least he wasn't coming back out the driveway. A single bare light bulb lit a door leading into the house, near the jeep. Rainey opened the car door slowly. She took the phone from the clip on her hip and flipped it open. She now had control of the call on her cell. Just before she stepped out of the car, she ripped the small camera from above the mirror and threw it as far as she could from the car.

Sirens blared in the neighborhood nearby. Rainey watched the house for any signs of life. She listened to his breathing growing faster in her ear. He was moving around again, probably watching her through the stained, faded sheers, in the windows.

"Come in the front door, it's unlocked," the excited little boy said.

Rainey eyed the side door again. She would rather go that way, less open yard to cross. A yellow bug light cast an amber glow across the lawn, lighting the front door. Rainey would be out in the open, with no back up. He could just shoot her, but she knew he would not do that. This killer liked his victims up close and personal. No, he was waiting somewhere in there, holding Katie hostage. She took a few steps toward the front door.

Through the heavy trees, on the south side of the house, she could see the faint flashes of blue and red lights. A helicopter was closing in on her position, but from the sound it was making, it was still a few miles away. If Rainey could just get to Katie, before he killed either of them, they might survive.

"Rainey, I have to hang up now so we can play the game, but you know what I thought would be fun?" he paused, and then added with a giggle, "If we played hide and go seek, in the dark."

The lawn and house were plunged into darkness. There were no streetlights to cast a glow on the yard and the moon was in its darkest phase, not visible at all. It was pitch-black and Rainey was alone about to take on the psycho that nearly killed her. The connection ended with childish, sadistic laughter, ringing in her ear. Rainey flipped the phone shut and put it back on her hip mechanically. She crouched down instinctively and slowly removed the pistol from her waistband, bringing it around, aiming it in front of her.

Rainey tried to control the trembling and her breathing. She crossed the few remaining feet to the steps and shielded herself, her back against the side of the house, near the front door. Her flashlight was on her waist, so she pulled it out and clicked it on. Rainey tried the door handle behind the old screen door. It turned easily. She let go of the handle and the door slowly opened itself, creaking in a low slow whine all the way.

Rainey yanked the screen door open and rushed in, jerking the light to every corner of the front room. There was nothing there but an old ripped up couch against one wall. Across the room from her, an open doorway led to the rest of the house. The trembling in her hands was growing worse. Rainey once told a fellow agent that Jodie Foster's hands shook too much, when she was tracking the killer in the dark basement scene, in "Silence of the Lambs." Rainey would have to change her mind about that, because her own hands shook uncontrollably and her breathing was shallow and fast.

Rainey had been in on the capture of some very sick and dangerous criminals, always remaining calm and in control throughout. However, this time it was different, she was not the only one hunting. In this dark house, Rainey was prey too, and she knew what lurked in the shadows. She checked the floor in front of her and saw dusty footprints leading to the hallway. She followed them to the central part of the house. Rainey stepped into a passageway dominated by a staircase leading to the second floor. Partially opened doors, which led to the rest of the rooms on the first floor, were evenly spaced around her. There were so many places Katie could be and so many traps that could be waiting to be sprung. There were footprints in the dust, going in and out of each doorway. Rainey would have to check them all. She listened to the house for a moment, trying to pick up any sound other than her own beating heart.

Rainey's attention was snapped to the top of the stairs when she heard music begin playing on the second floor. It was a familiar tune somehow and then it came to her. It was the same music she vaguely remembered hearing, when he captured her the first time. Only she could never place the tune, because of the drugs he gave her. Now she could hear it clearly. It was an old children's song. A needle was scratching out an old warped recording of, "Hush a Bye Baby." The playback speed fluctuated, giving the music a psychedelic trippy sound, because the only person who could appreciate it would have to be on acid or a stark raving lunatic. Guess who was upstairs?

Rainey moved quickly, shining the flashlight on every door she passed, pulling them closed, one by one. She did not want anything coming out of one of those rooms behind her without making some noise. Rainey reached the bottom of the stairs, pressing her back along the wall. The flashlight jerked everywhere, as she tried to make out anything, anything at all. The house had been shut up and empty for a while; she could smell it in the stale, hot air and see it in the dust clouding into her beam of light. Rainey wiped away the sweat, now pouring from her forehead into her eyes, with the back of the hand holding the flashlight. Her light flashed widely about and then returned to the top of the stairs.

Rainey peered into the darkness surrounding the beam of light. She took the first step slowly, near the side, close to the wall, hopeful of preventing any sound from the old wooden stair. She made the first step with success, but the second step complained loudly, screeching under her weight. Rainey stopped to listen again. She checked the doors on the first floor once more, before proceeding to the third step. The music was loud and unsettling, a favorite FBI technique for disturbing hostage takers. The record played through and then, after a short pause, it started all over again. Rainey could hear the needle dropping on the record with a loud pop, then more scratches, followed by the children singing their warped lullaby.

Rainey took the next three steps quickly, stopped to listen again, and thought she heard movement above her and to the left. She could not see yet where it was coming from. She had seven more steps to go to reach the landing at the top of the stairs. Her blood was pumping through her body at an enormous rate. Rainey gripped the gun with both hands, still holding the flashlight, trying to reduce the uncontrollable shaking. She held them both out in front of her, as she made the next five steps rapidly. Her light searched above and below her, still no sign of movement.

Rainey stayed frozen two steps from the top, sensing he was very close to her. She heard a door creak open and then shut again. It was muffled, as if it had come from behind one of the closed doors on her left. The music was coming from a small Bose CD player, placed at the far end of the hall behind her. From where she was standing, she could see that it was a simple floor plan. Four rooms, with doors set one in front of her on the right, and one behind her around the stair banister, also on the right wall, both unopened. The other two doors, located on her left, were closed, as well. One of those two rooms on the left contained Katie and the killer she was hunting. Rainey was pretty sure it was the far one, when she heard the loud sound of something wooden hitting the floor hard.

Rainey took the last two stairs in one leap and was in front of the suspicious door in three steps. She quickly pressed her back against the wall that stood between the two doors. As she was about to test the door handle, she heard a loud thud from downstairs. She ran to the railing, in time to see a shadow flash past the stairs and toward the carport side of the house. She fired her weapon twice, but could not get a good angle on him. She knew it was Johnny. It was too big to be Katie.

Rainey tore around the banister and was on the first stair down, when she heard the only thing that could have stopped her from chasing after the man who had raped her and scarred her for life.

"Rainey!" Katie screamed hoarsely, but weakly over the music. Her voice came from inside the room where Rainey heard the wood hit the floor. Rainey forgot all about the man downstairs. She rounded the banister again and crashed through the door hiding Katie.

The beam of Rainey's flashlight hit the bottom corner of the bed first, and then traced upward to find the ropes binding Katie's right foot and then traveled up her naked body to her face. Rainey forgot all the rules about checking the corners and closets in the room. She rushed to Katie. The light searched Katie's body for wounds or injuries. Katie was on her back, tied just as Rainey had been. Her face was red and swollen, already bruising from the beating she had taken, but there was no Y cut into her skin.

Katie was semi conscious, in and out while Rainey frantically cut the ropes from her limbs. In the moments when she was more aware of Rainey's presence, Katie whispered, repeating, "You came for me—you came for me."

"I'm here, Katie. Hold on baby, I'm getting you out of here," Rainey whispered to the softly sobbing woman lying in front of her.

Rainey finished cutting Katie free. She flashed the light around the room, looking for something to cover Katie. There were no sheets on the plastic covered, oddly stained mattress Katie was lying on, so Rainey took her jacket off and wrapped Katie in it. She put the flashlight in her mouth and lifted Katie into her arms, while still holding the pistol in her hand. The smaller woman draped her arms around Rainey's shoulders and buried her head into her neck and wept. Rainey was taking Katie out of this house, and she would blow a hole the size of Texas in anyone who tried to stop her. Rainey had almost taken the first step out of the room, when she heard a vehicle start outside.

It must have been the old jeep parked under the carport. The vehicle came to life and roared away from the house. Katie lay limp in her arms, as Rainey approached the head of the stairs. She peered over the banister and saw nothing. She did not expect to. For some reason Johnny had given up the game and was escaping from the house, as she made her way down the stairs, carrying Katie. The sound of a helicopter circling overhead grew louder. Rainey now heard sirens approaching and saw the emergency lights flashing on the thin worn curtains covering the old glass panes downstairs. The noises from outside could have scared off Johnny, or he may have seen the police coming through the upstairs windows.

Rainey was still aiming the flashlight with her mouth in every direction, steadily heading for the open front door. She reached the portal, kicked open the screen door and sprinted across the yard to her car, holding Katie tightly as she ran. The fuchsia-pink strobe lights, pulsing through the red flashing light bar of a trooper's car split the dark like lightning in the sky, as it pulled in behind Rainey's Charger. The helicopter overhead trained its powerful light on the two women, blinding Rainey, as she tried to open the door of her car.

A young trooper burst from his vehicle, shotgun in hand. "Where is he?" he shouted over the noise from the helicopter.

The trooper was so excited, Rainey was glad she had the FBI hat on, or he might have shot her. She looked at him and yelled, "Help me open this fucking door!"

The trooper immediately ran to her side and opened the passenger door. Rainey shouted again, "Lift the seat; I need to put her in the back."

He hesitated, questioning Rainey again, "Where's the suspect?"

"He's gone," Rainey screamed at him, "Now, help me or get the fuck out of the way."

The trooper did as he was told and then stood guard outside the car, while Rainey laid Katie down, covering her with the thin jacket as best she could. Vehicles from at least three law enforcement agencies were screeching to a halt in the road, in front of the house. Officers and agents were running and shouting in every direction.

Katie was cold and shivering, going into shock. Rainey kissed her on the forehead, whispering, "You're safe now, Katie. The cavalry's here."

Rainey tried to stand up, but Katie reached for her, saying, "Don't leave me."

"I have to get you warm, I need to start the car, turn on the heater," Rainey said, in the most soothing calm voice she could muster. As the light from the helicopter continued to glare through the car windows, Rainey could now clearly see the bruising on Katie's face and the thin, crooked lines of blood trickling from her swollen lips.

Katie lost consciousness again, which sent Rainey running around the car to the driver's side, after closing the passenger door. The trooper watched her and then went back to guarding the car from the invisible offender. Rainey threw open the door, dove into the seat and started the car. She turned on the heat and revved the engine, trying to warm the car up quickly. Even on this warm night, Katie's body temperature was plummeting. After popping the trunk, Rainey got out and closed the door behind her. She found an old blanket she kept for cold nights on stakeouts and dropped her ballistics vest in the trunk. Rainey re-entered the car, closing the two of them inside. She lifted Katie, so she could sit in the back seat and hold her. She wrapped Katie in the blanket, hoping her added body heat would help warm the shivering woman in her arms.

Rainey whispered, "I love you, Katie," repeating it in Katie's ear, while she watched the men and women in matching FBI jackets descend on the house. An SUV took off across the grass fast, following the tracks left by the jeep. It disappeared down a muddy path that led back into the woods. The light from the helicopter led the SUV, as it tracked the jeep. The agents poured into the house. Rainey could see the beams of dozens of flashlights reflected through the windows.

No one seemed to realize Rainey and Katie were in the car. When she saw the paramedics approaching, she tapped on the window. The trooper, still on guard duty, opened the door and looked inside.

"Get the paramedics, she needs help, now!" Rainey shouted above the sirens and helicopter blades.

Two paramedics removed Katie from the car and placed her on a gurney. One of them covered her with a white sheet and took vital signs and hooked up monitors to Katie's chest, while the other started a saline drip, put an oxygen mask over Katie's mouth and nose and pulsox meter on her index finger. Then they began searching Katie for other injuries. Katie could only respond to their questions part of the time, mostly mumbling the answers, slipping in and out from under the influence of drugs.

Rainey told the paramedic, "If he's still using the same drugs, he shot her up with a mixture of pentobarbital, an opioid, and an anticholinergic." Rainey knew this from reading her own medical reports. She also knew something else. She leaned into the paramedic's ear, whispering, "She's most likely been raped, too."

Rainey had a good idea of what had gone on in that house, before she arrived. It would take Katie a long time to recover from this. Rainey's only hope was that he had given Katie more drugs than he had given her, so Katie wouldn't remember any of what happened to her. The doctors told Rainey in the hospital, if he had given her just a little more of the mixture of drugs, she would not have remembered anything about her own attack. Rainey remembered thinking she wished he had given her more. She wished it for Katie now, but she also hoped he did not give her too much.

Now, covered from her neck to her toes in the white sheet, with wires running to monitors everywhere, Katie came out from under sedation for a moment. She opened her eyes long enough to see Rainey and recognize her, through swollen slits left from fists smashing into her face. Her beautiful face was a mass of swollen lumps and abrasions. She slowly moved an unsteady hand out from under the sheet, reaching for Rainey.

Rainey took her hand and squeezed it tight. Katie pulled weakly on Rainey, until Rainey bent down, placing her ear near Katie's mouth. Katie's breathing was shallow and weak, under the oxygen mask. It was hard for her to speak, her voice thin, slurring the words, "Stay—with—me."

"I won't leave you, I promise," Rainey said, and kissed the top of Katie's head. Katie passed out again. She turned to the paramedic. "What's wrong with her? She's having trouble breathing."

"It's a side effect of the Pentobarbital, too much can cause respiratory depression. Her blood pressure is low. I've given her Narcon to counteract the narcotics. It will help, but we need to get her to the hospital now."

Rainey said, "I'm going with her."

The paramedic started to say something, but did not get the chance.

"I'm going with her," Rainey said again, this time more firmly, with an edge in her tone.

There was no further argument. Katie was not going anywhere without Rainey. When the paramedics were ready for transport to Memorial Hospital, Rainey let go of Katie's hand just long enough to reach back inside the Charger, retrieving the pistol she dropped behind the passenger seat earlier. She grabbed her FBI credentials, in case she needed a way into Katie's treatment room, and her car keys. She took the pistol and placed it in her waistband, checked to make sure she had an extra clip, and then locked the car. She handed the keys to the trooper still guarding the car, even though no one was in it now. They would need to process the car for any evidence that could have fallen off Katie or Rainey.

There was still a killer running loose out there and she was not going anywhere unarmed. The only reason she did not bring the shotgun was because she probably would not get into the hospital with it. She found her jacket being stuffed into an evidence-bag, and borrowed one from another agent. She slid it on to conceal the weapon poking out of her pants. Rainey took

Katie's hand back in hers and walked with the gurney toward the back of the waiting ambulance.

Rainey had not had time to cry, but the let down from the adrenaline spike she had just experienced was making it hard to fight back the tears. She was relieved to have Katie alive, but the wretchedness of what she had been through enveloped Rainey, sending waves of throbbing pain across her chest.

Rainey heard Danny calling her name. He was running after them, shouting for her to stop. She did not care and kept walking. He could take her statement later. Rainey was taking Katie to the hospital. Katie was her only priority. The FBI could go fuck itself for all she cared. Katie was safe with her now, and Rainey would remain by her side, forever watching over her, giving her time to heal. If she had ever doubted it, she knew now that Katie was the love of her life and the only thing that would ever matter to her, for the rest of Rainey's days.

CHAPTER TWENTY

Rainey had no trouble following Katie into the treatment room. When she told the nurses the attacker was still at large, they were more than happy to have someone with FBI emblazoned on a hat and jacket there to guard them. Katie was whisked into a trauma room and quickly surrounded by doctors and nurses, buzzing about her body like bees in a hive. The pace in the room was almost hectic. Rainey stood back, out of the way, as the doctor, who seemed to be in charge, called out orders that people around him quickly followed. A pretty dark-skinned nurse with closely cropped hair, and about Rainey's age, must have realized what the agonized expression on Rainey's face meant. This was not just an agent guarding a victim.

She touched Rainey's arm gently and said, "She's going to be okay. She's turned the corner already. Her vitals are getting better."

Rainey could stop fretting over whether Katie was going to die of an overdose or shock and start thinking about Katie's recovery. The constant activity slowed down and the doctor declared Katie stable and ready to be moved to the Intensive Care Unit, but first they had to do the sexual assault examination. Rainey stepped out of the trauma room while that was being done. Rainey knew how humiliating the process was, and she did not want to see it happening to Katie. She waited outside until the procedure was over and then went back inside.

Katie's body was worn out from fighting the drugs and the insane man who held her captive. She would rest comfortably in the trauma room until the bed in ICU was ready. The doctor, who had been barking orders, came back in, checked Katie's vitals again, and then talked to Rainey. He told her once Katie was moved upstairs, she would be monitored through the night and probably two to four days after, depending on her progression. They wanted her to rest and give her body the time it needed to expel the drugs. In the morning, a plastic surgeon would look at her face, but the doctor told Rainey that the x-rays showed no broken bones, as far as he could see. Only the cartilage in her nose had been displaced, and he had already popped it back in place. He thought that once the swelling went down, there would likely be no permanent disfiguration.

After the doctor left the room, a lone nurse, the one who had spoken to Rainey earlier, stayed behind, watching Katie's vital signs, hovering over the bed. Rainey did not pay any attention to the nurse's presence. She sat by Katie's bed, talking softly to her, even though she was asleep now. Rainey told Katie about how, when she was released from the hospital, Rainey was taking her home with her to the cottage. She promised never to leave Katie alone until this maniac was caught, and even then, she might never want to let Katie out of her sight. Tears rolled down Rainey's cheeks, as she tenderly stroked Katie's hair and told her how she had fallen so very deeply in love with her.

She was shocked when Katie did not open her eyes, but said in a quiet whisper, "I love you, too."

The nurse looked over at Rainey, from across the bed. She winked and said, "See, I told you she was going to be all right." She smiled and tucked the covers around Katie, once again. "You need to let her rest now. Go get a soda or something. You look as though you could fall out yourself." The nurse saw Rainey's expression of protest and said quickly, "I promise I'll come and get you if she wakes up, but I really think she's going to sleep for awhile."

Rainey reluctantly walked out into the hallway, just as Mackie showed up at the hospital. He had been at the farmhouse scene, but could not get to Rainey, because the cops would not let him through. He did not get across the barricade until Danny saw him and let him pass. Mackie saw Rainey get in the ambulance with Katie and after talking with Danny, came to check on them. Rainey collapsed on a chair outside the trauma room, suddenly drained of all her energy. Mackie remained standing next to her, while they talked.

"Is Katie going to be okay?" Mackie asked.

"The doctor seems to think so, physically anyway."

Mackie hesitated and then asked Rainey anyway, "Did he cut her?"

Rainey had relief in her voice when she answered him. "No, I think he ran out of time."

"Good thing," the big man rumbled. "Are you okay?"

"Yeah, I'm fine. By the way, how did they find me so fast? There were hundreds of houses out there," Rainey asked.

Mackie smiled a wide-open grin. "Ernie," was all he said.

Rainey was befuddled. "How could Ernie have known where I was?"

Mackie beamed with pride at what Ernie had done, on her own, without being asked. "She loaded that tracking system software, from the office, on her home computer. She's been watching our every move for days. When she saw us take off, flying down the highway, she knew something had happened."

Rainey smiled at Mackie and let him continue his story.

"So, when she saw the two phones separate, she knew that wasn't good and then you stopped out in the woods, from what she could tell. Ernie called me right away, but couldn't get me, because I was talking to Danny and some other people."

Mackie did not have call waiting, because he considered it rude, and hung up on anyone who tried to put him on hold to catch another call. "When she finally got through, she was hopping mad and worried sick, but she had a GPS signal from you and told us almost exactly where to find you."

"God I love that woman," Rainey said. "Remind me to buy her a year's worth of spa treatments when this is over."

Mackie was enjoying telling the story, only because nobody was dead, and that was a happy ending to Mackie. He knew Katie was scarred, at least emotionally, but they were both alive. That deserved an Amen and Hallelujah, as far as Mackie was concerned.

He continued, "We had a little trouble at first, because the coordinates are only good to within one hundred meters of the phone. We made the mistake of looking in the neighborhood, south of the trees from where you really were. Nobody saw the house on any of the maps. No one noticed the gravel side road until we pulled up a satellite image of the area, and then a trooper found your shoulder holster. Nice play, by the way."

"Thank you. I was trying to leave a large bread crumb for you to find."

Mackie had a sudden thought that brought his mood from happy to angry in a flash. "I can't believe you went in that house alone."

Rainey was sure she had done the right thing, and she told him so. "I didn't have much of a choice, now did I?"

Mackie grumbled, "I still can't believe it," but conceded.

They remained quiet for a moment. Rainey stood up and walked to the window in the trauma room door, so she could look at Katie. She did not turn around when she asked, "Did they find him?"

There was a pause, followed by a deep bass, "No."

The nurse was still hovering and watching Katie, while Rainey was out of the room. She turned back to face Mackie, satisfied that Katie was in good hands.

"Tell me," she said.

"He must have seen us coming. He dropped down an old emergency trap door, in the closet upstairs, landing in a room below you."

Rainey added, "That must have been the loud noise I heard, him slamming the trap door open."

"From what I gathered, the asshole took off down a path in the woods. They found his jeep parked in the community center parking lot on the other side of that patch of woods, to the north.

He must have had another car waiting there, because he vanished."

"Goddamnit!" Rainey said, loud enough to draw attention from the people down the hall. She said it a second time under her breath and stared down at the floor. What could they do now? The suspect was in the wind, and the last time this happened, he did not surface for over a year. Rainey could not face another year of looking over her shoulder. This had to end soon.

At that moment, a loud argument erupted at the nurses' station. It was JW demanding to see his wife immediately. He spotted Rainey and charged down the hall toward her. He was enraged and she was his target. Mackie stepped in front of him before he could reach Rainey. Still, he reached around Mackie, pointing a finger directly at Rainey.

"This is your fault," JW shouted. "I should have known better than to hire an ex-FBI agent who was stupid enough to get caught by a serial killer. Now look what you've done!"

Rainey backed away from JW, while Mackie restrained him. She did not know what to say. She knew nothing she could say would ease the rage JW was feeling. His fury had to have an outlet and Rainey had become his choice. Yet, his words rang true and hurt Rainey terribly, because she felt the guilt already. Never mind the guy was stalking Katie before Rainey ever got involved. It was because of her presence that the stalking had escalated into attempted murder, and Katie had become the bait to lure Rainey.

"Get her the hell away from my wife," JW was shouting at Mackie.

Mackie could not and would not be bullied by JW. He said, "I think that's up to Katie and she wants Rainey here."

How was Mackie so sure he was right? Rainey had not said anything to him about promising Katie she would stay with her. The big, rough man had a tender heart and he evidently saw how much Katie meant to Rainey and vice versa. He understood what was going on between them, without being told, and he was protecting Rainey, knowing it would kill her to have to leave Katie alone.

"Get her the hell out of here, or I will sue this goddamn hospital into the stone ages. You won't have a bed pan to piss in when I'm through," JW shouted at the Emergency room staff in the halls.

The nurse came out of Katie's room. She looked JW up and down and sized him up right there, a privileged pretty boy with anger issues. She started by saying, "Mr. Wilson, calm down. You are disturbing my patient. She needs to rest."

JW turned his attention to her. "Is she awake? Can I see her?"

"No, you may not. She just now told me, and I quote, 'Don't let that asshole in here.' According to the HIPAA privacy act, I must respect my patient's wishes and ask you to leave."

By that time, two very large security guards, almost as big as Mackie, but leaner, appeared behind JW. The future senator was livid. He took one more shot at Rainey. "You'll pay for this, Rainey Bell. I swear you will. This isn't over."

The hospital cops asked JW to leave and he complied, though not happy about it.

The nurse turned to Rainey and patted her on the arm. She whispered conspiratorially, "Katie woke up and said, 'Asshole,' when she heard his voice. With all that raging he was doing, I put two and two together and knew exactly what she meant. That white boy has some problems and that child in there doesn't want him around."

"Well you hit that one on the head," Rainey said. "They're getting a divorce."

The nurse whispered, so only Rainey could hear, "It's a good thing, girl. Bad as you got it for that woman in there, she's going to need that divorce real soon." She laughed and added, "Y'all ought to just go on out to Reno and get that done, get the hell away from that man."

Rainey smiled at the nurse. "We might just have to do that. Thanks for the advice."

The nurse laughed again. "The advice is free, but that divorce is gonna cost you."

Rainey half smiled. "I'll bet it does."

CHAPTER TWENTY-ONE

Almost an hour after JW left the hospital, Katie was moved up to the ICU. Rainey followed the rolling bed into the elevator, while Mackie walked to the waiting room located on the second floor of the Pavilion. Mackie hated elevators. Rainey was sure it had to do with his size and the amount of weight he calculated in his brain, every time he saw people getting on the elevator. He just could not take the risk, he once told Rainey. So, he walked to the waiting room, where someone would come and get him if Rainey needed him. She told him to go home and get some sleep, but she knew he was not leaving. Mackie would be passed out in the waiting room, but he would still be at the hospital if she needed him.

Before they left the emergency room, Katie was lucid enough to tell the nurses that Rainey could have access to her medical information. All Katie did was nod her head in agreement, as the nurse explained it to her. She managed to get out, "Rainey, stay with me," when she understood they were trying to make that possible, because Rainey was not family, and Katie had to say it was okay. That was enough for the nurse who told off JW, and had witnessed the two women's affection for each other. Confidentiality was waived for Rainey and she was then informed of the medical decisions being made concerning Katie's recovery.

Rainey hugged the nurse who had been so helpful, thanking her for all she had done for them, before she stepped on the elevator. A few minutes later, she was introducing herself to a new nursing staff, explaining that she was Katie's bodyguard, as well as her best friend. Rainey did not know if Katie was ready to let the cat out of the bag, so she kept their true relationship from the nurses. There was a recliner by Katie's bed, so Rainey plopped down and watched the new batch of nurses hover over Katie.

Rainey was told that Katie was now going to be assigned to a Critical Care Physician named Dr. Henry P. Marsden, III. He specialized in trauma and care of critically ill patients. Dr. Marsden came in about five minutes later. He introduced himself to Rainey, who in turn explained who she was and why she was there, almost. Dr. Marsden told Rainey that Katie was still not all the way out of trouble. The combination of the amount and the kinds of drugs Katie had been given were slowing the effectiveness of the Narcon, the chemical used to counteract the barbiturates and opium based drugs. Katie had been given all the Narcon she could have, for her body weight, at this time. The lunatic in the farmhouse had given Katie nearly seventeen parts per million, an amount that could have been lethal, not to mention the other two narcotics. Katie was very lucky.

Dr. Marsden explained that Katie was being given Sodium Bicarbonate intravenously, two bags, wide open. This fluid therapy would help her body get rid of the drugs through elimination from the bladder. In other words, Rainey thought, it would make Katie pee like a racehorse. The medical staff had inserted a catheter during Katie's stay in the trauma room. The doctor told Rainey that the more she filled up the bag hanging under her bed, the better Katie would feel. They were monitoring Katie's breathing, in case it became necessary to hook her to a ventilator to assist her lungs, since the drugs the assailant gave her depressed the respiratory and central nervous systems. So far, she was doing okay with just the oxygen mask.

Dr. Marsden was a little older than Rainey, but not by much, she guessed. He was about five foot three inches tall and wore red canvas, Converse tennis shoes. He looked like Peter Pan in his green scrubs. He was cute, funny, and serious about his job. Dr. Marsden put Rainey at ease immediately. The staff respected him and his bedside manner was charming. He checked Katie's x-rays and looked at the swelling on her face. He agreed Katie would heal nicely. She may have a few small scars, but they would fade with time. Luckily, when the bastard had hammered Katie with his fist, he had not split her skin open too badly. The deeper cuts had been closed with butterfly bandages or medical glue in the Emergency Room. Dr. Marsden told her that they had done an excellent job downstairs and he thought Katie would be happy with the final results. The plastic surgeon would still look at her in the morning.

Dr. Marsden said, "We're going to take care of her physical injuries first. Then we will address the emotional trauma of the kidnapping and rape. That may be harder to deal with, and will be a much longer and slower process. We need to make sure she is physically well enough for the coming emotional challenges." He smiled at Rainey, reassuring her. "We'll take good care of her."

Dr. Marsden skipped off to another patient. Now, only one nurse remained. She told Rainey her name was Janet and if Rainey had any questions at all, she could ask her. Janet was there to help and she was enthusiastic about it. Rainey was glad when Janet left her and Katie alone for a few minutes. Katie slept the whole time, but Rainey was glad to hear just Katie's breathing, between the beeps on the monitors. Rainey held Katie's hand and read the News and Observer someone had left on the tray table.

All of the feeds from Katie's monitors sent signals to a bank of monitors at the nurses' station; still, every few minutes, Janet came in to check on them personally. She began to grow on Rainey; the tender way she handled Katie and the Coke and cup of ice she brought Rainey did not hurt. Janet must have been able to tell that Rainey needed sustenance. The next time she came into the room, she brought a cup of fruit and some crackers, silently setting them on the tray table, a cue to Rainey that she needed to eat. Rainey followed nurse's orders and ate the fruit.

She started feeling better right away. She had not noticed how much energy the stress had taken from her.

Rainey read the Monday morning paper, finding a Y-man article just under the fold on the front page. He had been knocked from the major headline by an article about misconduct in the state police. Still, there he was on the front page. The article basically rehashed everything from the weekend editions. Rainey could only imagine what the headlines would look like tomorrow morning. FBI loses killer for the second time, former agent involved.

Janet came in to tell Rainey someone was waiting outside to talk to her. It was Danny. Rainey hesitated to leave. She did not want Katie to wake up and not find her there.

Janet, sensing Rainey's reservations, said, "You go ahead. I'll stay with her until you come back, okay?"

Rainey thanked Janet and went to talk with Danny in the hall outside of Katie's room. Danny was standing there looking worried and stressed. He was running the fingers of one hand through his thick red hair, the other hand resting on his hip. His back was to Rainey, and she could see from his posture that the pressure of being the lead agent on this case was bending him at the waist. Rainey knew from experience that Danny carried his stress in his lower back. He was probably in excruciating pain from the tension in his muscles.

"Danny," Rainey said, to get his attention.

He turned to her and forced a weak smile. "Are you okay? How is Katie?"

"I'm fine. Katie has another twenty four hours before she's out of the woods, but she's stable."

"Rainey, I think we got a break this time," Danny said. "Katie's sexual assault kit came back positive for sperm, and if she wasn't having sex with her husband, then it has to be our guy."

Rainey answered quickly, "She wasn't. I understand she hasn't had sex with JW in months."

"Okay then, now, we need a suspect." He looked at Rainey's jacket and hat. He smiled and said, "That hat looks good on you."

"It opens doors," Rainey said.

"How about we reinstate you for the time being, clear up any gray lines, in case we need you in the investigation officially?"

Rainey thought about it. If she had to use her gun, there would be less paperwork. She said, "Okay, temporarily though. I'm not back. Do you understand that?"

Danny asked her every time he called when she was coming back on active duty. He really wanted her back. Rainey figured it would ease his guilt if she resumed her normal life, but her normal life had become Mackie and Ernie, and she did not think she wanted to go back to the Bureau, not now especially.

Danny nodded, "Yeah, you're on active duty, temporarily. I'll make the call."

Danny took out a pad and pen. This was an investigation, Rainey reminded herself. He was about to question her in his official capacity. It felt violating to Rainey, one of the reasons she did not think she could go back on active duty and do the job. She would feel the violation every time she had to question a victim or a grieving family member. Rainey did not want to answer Danny's questions, but she knew he had to do it.

He began, "Mackie gave me all the information up until you left him on the side of the road. Can you go over what happened after that?"

Rainey gave Danny what he wanted. Every detail of what had happened was clear and sharp in Rainey's mind. The only detail she did not have was what Johnny looked like. She had only seen him for a brief second, and that was when she caught him in the shadows, just out of the beam of her flashlight. He told her his name, but she knew nothing that could help them identify this man, nothing.

Danny wrote it all down. "The jeep was stolen, so it was a dead end," he said. "We're tracing the ownership of the property. It's been abandoned for years."

Rainey offered, "He wasn't set up there, like the other house. I think it was a place of opportunity, but he was familiar enough with the property to feel safe there, and he did know about the trap door."

"He doesn't do things without a reason. There has to be a reason he picked that place. He was familiar enough with it to have the escape route planned," Danny said.

Rainey had an idea. "Talk to the local cops. It had the feel of a hangout. Maybe they have caught some teenagers out there. It might be worth looking in to."

Danny wrote on his pad and then looked back at Rainey. "We are tracing the Bose CD player. That's a pretty high-end item. It should lead somewhere, if it doesn't come up stolen. I sent the CD to the lab boys. See what they can make of it."

"Fingerprints?" Rainey asked.

"No, nothing yet. There are tons of prints in the house, but we're pretty sure he wore gloves. There were only the owner's prints on the jeep. It was stolen a week ago from campus."

"I left my car unlocked, on the street outside the Wilson's, Friday night. That must have been when he put the camera in my car," Rainey said. "He knew I would have to come by the farmhouse, if I was headed to Katie's school. He kidnapped her to get to me. He didn't count on Ernie knowing how to find me so fast."

"It doesn't make sense, Rainey," Danny said. "He knew we were all over you. How did he know you would try to find Katie?"

"I guess he thought I would have a strong sense of guilt, leaving her alone like I did," Rainey answered. There was no way this guy knew about Rainey and Katie's real relationship. The only person Rainey thought knew was Mackie, and he would not say anything.

Danny went on, "Then the other thing that bothers me is he knew he wouldn't have that long before we came looking. He had to know Mackie saw where you turned off of the highway. That limited the places we had to look. He would not have had the time to live out his fantasy with you."

"The amount of drugs he gave Katie was intended to kill her. She was a means to an end. He probably planned to use the opportunity of having me alone, to capture me, and take me in the jeep to another location, his real lair."

Danny agreed. "That would make more sense, but he's getting sloppy. He left DNA. He almost got caught."

Rainey added, honestly, "He almost got dead."

Danny had all he could get from Rainey. He peeked into Katie's open door. He turned back to Rainey. "Let me know when she wakes up."

Rainey said, "I don't think she's going to remember much, but I'll call you."

"I'm putting two agents outside the ICU doors. I guess you aren't leaving her side, am I right?" Danny asked.

"No, I am staying with her until she leaves the hospital. She will be going to my cottage when she is discharged."

Danny cocked his head and raised his eyebrows in a question.

Rainey answered his silent inquiry, "JW is blaming me for Katie's attack. He's on the warpath, because Katie refuses to see him. Katie and JW are getting a divorce and she wants nothing to do with him. He's at her house, so she's coming with me."

Danny accepted her explanation, but Rainey could tell he did not think she was telling him the whole story. Luckily, Danny's phone rang, so he could not ask her any more about it. Rainey listened as Danny took the call. He became increasingly excited as he listened to the voice on the other end.

"I'm on my way," he said, and hung up the call.

Rainey asked him, as soon as he hung up, "What's happening?"

"We were able to trace the owner of the property through the caretaker. The owner's name matched a name on the list JW gave us of his social circle," Danny said, and then continued, "It's a lead, so I'm going over to his home address now to meet with the team. We're going to question him at his house first, before we bring him in. It could be a coincidence."

Rainey smiled. "You don't believe in coincidence. What's his name?"

Danny looked at the pad where he had written notes while on the phone. "His name is John P. Taylor."

Rainey recognized the name. She had gone to school with him. He was a year younger and hung out occasionally with

Rainey's crowd. "I know him," she said, "or rather I knew him, in high school."

"There's the connection," Danny said, more excited, now.

Rainey thought back to the last time she had seen John Taylor. It was at the graduation party JW's parents had thrown for them. Rainey had danced with John, she remembered.

"He's the right height and build, or he was the last time I saw him," Rainey told Danny.

Danny was ready to leave. "Look, I'll call you if I find out anything."

"I can't have my phone on, in Katie's room. Call the ICU nurses' station, they will come get me," Rainey said.

"Okay, I'll get the number. Stay here. I'll let you know what's happening, I promise," Danny said.

Rainey answered quickly and she meant it this time, "I'm not leaving Katie's side until you catch this guy. I'll be right here."

CHAPTER TWENTY-TWO

Katie slept peacefully for several more hours before she awoke. Her body had been flushing the drugs from her system at a steady rate, filling the bag beneath her bed. She was still very groggy, but aware of her surroundings, for the moment anyway. Katie looked at Rainey, who was standing leaning on the rail of Katie's bed, still holding one of Katie's hands.

"What happened?" Katie said, in a weak voice, through the plastic mask and swollen lips.

Rainey's eyes were filling with tears, she was so happy to see Katie responsive. Rainey had to tell Katie what happened. She would probably have to tell her several times before she would remember asking. It was a side effect of the drugs that almost killed her.

Rainey said, "Katie, you are in the hospital, in the ICU. You were kidnapped and given an almost lethal injection of sedatives. The doctors are running fluids through your body to flush them out. You're going to be okay, Katie."

Janet interrupted, "Katie, my name is Janet. I'm your nurse. Are you in pain?"

Katie lifted the hand Rainey was not holding to her face, indicating she felt pain there. She whispered, "My head hurts."

Janet nodded. "Okay, I'll go get the doctor and we'll do something about that right away, sugar."

Katie's tears were beginning to leak from her eyes, down the sides of her face. Rainey took some tissue from the bedside table and wiped the tears gently. Katie squeezed Rainey's hand, letting her know with her eyes that she was glad she was there.

"You're going to be okay, Katie," Rainey repeated. "I'm not ever letting you out of my sight again, I promise."

Katie was getting groggier. She closed her eyes for a second then opened them again.

"Catch him?" Katie asked, in a whisper.

Rainey hated to tell her the truth, but she did, her expression of sorrow written all over her face, because she knew what Katie would feel, having been told the same thing by Danny after her attack.

She answered Katie, "No, he got away."

Katie closed her eyes and turned her face away, her hand tightening around Rainey's fingers, as she processed the information. Rainey was patient, returning the squeeze, and waiting.

Katie opened her eyes and turned back to Rainey. "I don't remember," she said, and the tears came harder. She took a deep breath and quietly she asked, "Raped?"

Rainey squeezed Katie's hand and answered, "Yes."

Katie cried harder now. Rainey comforted her, wiping her tears, repeating, "It's okay, Katie, it's okay."

Katie only stopped sobbing when Dr. Marsden came in and introduced himself to her. He was concerned about her emotional state, but happy to see her progressing so quickly. He checked her vitals and looked into Katie's eyes with a light.

Dr. Marsden said, "Katie, you've experienced a tremendous trauma to your body and your mind. I am working on repairing your body so you can deal with the rest. The best thing for you right now is to sleep and let your body heal."

Katie took a deep breath and nodded that she understood.

He patted Katie's hand, saying, "You are doing very well, Katie. You should be out from under the influence of the drugs within twenty-four hours. I will give you something for the swelling and it should help with the pain."

"Thank you," Katie said, weakly.

Janet, who had come in with Dr. Marsden, stepped back out to the doorway with him. While they discussed the treatment plan, Rainey tucked the covers around Katie.

"Are you cold, baby?" Rainey asked.

Katie nodded yes, so Rainey pulled the folded blanket, at Katie's feet, up to her neck, tucking it in over the others. As Rainey worked around the bed, Katie followed her with her eyes. Rainey kissed Katie on her forehead, the only place not swollen badly. Katie reached for Rainey's hand again and held it tight.

"Rainey, stay with me," Katie said, as if Rainey had not told her repeatedly that she would.

Rainey looked deeply into Katie's blood shot eyes, and said, "Katie, I'm not leaving you, ever. Do you understand what I'm saying? I'm staying right here, I promise."

Katie's eyes blinked a couple of times. She was fighting to stay awake.

Rainey smoothed Katie's hair, saying, "Go to sleep. I'll be here when you wake up." Just before Katie slipped back under the heavy veil of slumber, Rainey said, "I love you, Katie."

Rainey let go of Katie's hand and put it gently under the covers. She turned to go back to the other side of the bed, where the recliner sat. That is when she realized Janet had been standing there. She did not know for how long. It was clear from the expression on her face that she had been there long enough. She smiled at Rainey as she walked back to the chair. Janet crossed the room to one of the tubes in Katie's arm and inserted a syringe, slowly adding medication to Katie's IV.

Janet looked over at Rainey and said, "I know you're worried sick. I would be, too, if someone I loved was lying here, but I promise you Dr. Marsden knows what he's doing. She's going to be fine."

Rainey was shocked at Janet's remark about Rainey loving Katie, but was so appreciative that Janet understood. It felt better somehow that Janet grasped their real relationship.

Rainey said, "Thank you."

Janet looked at Rainey, cocking her head, and then she said, "You are the FBI agent from that article in the paper Saturday, aren't you?"

Rainey simply nodded yes.

"This has to be extra hard on you, knowing what she's been through," Janet said, sympathetically.

"Yes, it is," Rainey answered plainly.

Janet looked at Rainey hard for a minute and then made up her mind to take care of Rainey, too. She said, "You have to remember to take care of yourself. She's going to need you strong. Let me order you a tray from the cafeteria. It's really good food. It's chicken breast and roast tonight. Which will it be?"

Rainey could tell from Janet's expression that she was not taking no for an answer. Rainey said, "Roast will be fine, thank you."

"Okay," Janet said, finishing with the syringe and dropping it into the biohazard red box on the wall. "Roast and potatoes, coming up."

She left Rainey alone with Katie and the beeping monitors. Katie was sleeping soundly again. Rainey sat there watching Katie breathe until Janet returned. When Janet came back with Rainey's tray, she ate hungrily, not having realized she missed dinner. She thanked Janet profusely for the food. Once they were alone again, Rainey drifted off to sleep in the recliner.

Rainey slept lightly, opening her eyes each time Janet came in the room. Janet brought Rainey a pillow and a blanket, still looking after both her patients. Rainey opened her eyes several times to check that Katie was still sleeping and then faded back to sleep. The stress and excitement had taken its toll. Janet was right. Rainey needed the rest, so she could be there for Katie when she needed her.

Three hours later, Janet woke Rainey to tell her there was a call for her at the nurses' station. Again, she promised to stay with Katie while Rainey was out of the room. Rainey rubbed her face to wake up and went out to take the call.

"This is Rainey Bell," she said into the receiver.

"Special Agent Rainey Bell to be exact," Danny said, sounding happy on the other end.

"You know something, don't you?" Rainey asked, getting excited.

"It turns out our John P. Taylor is a veterinarian, giving him access to the drugs used on you and Katie. His wife is out of town, and it seems she goes out of town once a month on business, stays a week in New York, some design business she's into," Danny said.

Rainey's heart picked up the pace. "Have you talked to the wife?"

"Yes, she gave us the dates she has been out of town for the last three years. All of the murders and attacks have happened when she's been in New York," he said, more excited now.

Rainey joined his excitement. "How about the rest of the profile?"

Danny checked off his list. "He's wealthy. His parents left him tons of money. He's good-looking, dark hair, married, he knows both you and Katie, and to top it off, they moved to Chapel Hill from Raleigh, right after your attack last year. He lives just a few blocks from the Wilsons."

"What about the farmhouse? What's his connection?"

Danny was checking his notes, she could tell. After a moment, he said, "Belonged to the family for years. He inherited it and a trust takes care of it. Says he hasn't been out there since he and some buddies used it as a party pad when he was in high school. He used to play in the house as a child, when an aunt lived there. He was aware of the trap door. Said his aunt put it in because she was scared she'd get trapped upstairs in a fire."

"Does he have an alibi for the time of the attack?"

Danny almost giggled. "Nope, he was alone from four thirty in the afternoon until we knocked on his door. Said he was working in the yard at home and then he watched TV all evening."

Rainey could not believe it. "Is it him, Danny?"

"I think it is, Rainey. I want to see how he reacts to you, but I think it's him. We are taking him to the station now."

"I can't leave Katie," Rainey said, immediately.

"I'll bring him to you if I have to. Right now, we're going to get his DNA and have it hand delivered to the lab in Quantico in a couple of hours. I've asked for a push on the results, should take less than seventy-two hours. I'm going to let Johnny cool his heals in lockup until his lawyer comes to get him. Then I'm going to blanket his ass with surveillance, talk to his friends and neighbors, and basically make the son of a bitch as uncomfortable as possible."

"That sounds like the best plan at this point," Rainey said, lost in her own thoughts.

"It's him, Rainey. It's got to be," Danny said, again.

"Okay, call me when something breaks," Rainey said. She needed to hang up. She felt sick.

Danny sounded concerned. "You okay, Rainey?"

"I have to go now," she said, and hung up. She ran into Katie's room, went into the bathroom, and threw up. Rainey did not know why she was throwing up, she just was. It felt like all the ugliness she had seen in her life was leaving her soul. Janet came in and turned on the water in the sink. She pulled Rainey's hat off and helped her to the sink. Janet wet a washcloth and handed it to Rainey. She patted Rainey on the back until Rainey had regained control.

"Thank you," Rainey finally managed to say.

"You go sit down in the recliner and I'm going to get you some Sprite," Janet said.

Rainey made her way to recliner. Her legs were weak and she felt like shit. Rainey marveled at her body's reaction to what Danny said. They might have the guy in custody right now. This could all be over soon. It was the day she had prayed for, and yet, she was sick from the thought of coming face to face with the man responsible for so much pain, not only for her, but also for his other victims. Rainey began to cry softly, not sobbing, just releasing the pent up emotions from the last three days, the highs and lows of it all.

Janet returned with the Sprite and a small cup containing a pill. She did not comment on Rainey's tears, she simply said,

"Here, this will help settle your stomach, it's just an over the counter antacid."

Rainey took both items from Janet, took the pill, and chased it with some Sprite. "Thank you, Janet, for everything."

"I'm going to turn the lights down, so you two can get some rest. I'll be right outside if you need me." Janet walked to the doorway. She turned the lights down and looked back at Rainey, paused and said, "That must have been one hell of a phone call."

CHAPTER TWENTY-THREE

Rainey slept until daybreak. When she awoke, Katie was awake and looking at her. The bruising had taken on darker shades of black and blue. The swelling had not increased, but had not receded much either. Katie's eyes peered out from the bruising, focused on Rainey. Rainey sat up.

"Hey," she said softly.

"I was watching you sleep," Katie said, better able to form the words now.

"I'm sorry. I wanted to be awake for you," Rainey said. She stood up and moved closer to Katie's side.

"Tell me what happened," Katie asked again.

Rainey knew the drugs had erased their previous conversation. She took Katie's hand and repeated what she told her previously. She left out the rape, but Rainey could tell from Katie's reaction that she already knew that it had happened. This time Katie did not cry, she steeled herself and said nothing for a few minutes, just absorbed the information.

Rainey waited for Katie to settle down and then asked, "Do you know John Taylor?"

Katie was confused. "Yes."

Rainey needed information. "Katie, do you remember anything?"

Katie's eyes started to puddle, now. "I only remember getting ready for the program. I was arguing with JW backstage, that's it."

"Do you remember seeing John Taylor at the school?" Rainey persisted.

"No. Why are you asking me about John?" Katie asked with more confusion in her eyes.

"He's being questioned about the murders and your kidnapping," Rainey said. "I just need to know if you've seen him around at all."

"Not John, he's so nice," Katie said.

"How well do you know him?" Rainey asked.

"He was in our wedding, we've known John and Ann for years, JW has known him even longer," Katie was growing agitated, the realization that she had been intimate friends with a man who may be a killer hitting her hard.

"Don't get upset, Katie. We're not positive it's him. We have to wait for DNA to be sure."

"How long will that take?" Katie was anxious.

"Seventy-two hours, at least," Rainey answered.

Janet came in the door, just then, saying, "What are you two up to? Her heartbeat is really rapid. Whatever it is, you need to stop."

Rainey smiled at Janet's attempt to lighten the mood in the room. "We're just talking, Janet. Katie, do you remember Janet? She's your nurse."

Katie said, "Hello."

Janet smiled at Katie. "You look a little more with us now."

Katie said, "Yes, I think so."

Janet checked the monitors again. "Whatever you were talking about, let's just leave that alone for now. I don't want Dr. Marsden coming in here finding you all excited. He will be coming in to check on you in a few minutes. Then we'll hand you off to the day shift."

"Will the next nurse be as nice as you?" Rainey asked, smiling at Janet.

"Aren't you sweet," Janet said. "Oh, you'll love Margie, everybody does."

Margie was just like Ernie, direct, but loving at the same time. After Dr. Marsden saw Katie and pronounced her progress very good, better than he had expected, he introduced them to Dr. Lawrence, who was on call today. Dr. Lawrence was young, blond, and handsome, with an easygoing air. He and Rainey hit it off right away and Katie seemed to like him, too. Margie was adamant Rainey take a break from the room, while she bathed Katie and cleaned her wounds. Rainey left reluctantly, at Katie's insistence. Margie made her promise not to come back for an hour. Rainey kissed Katie's forehead and told her she loved her before leaving.

Katie said, "I think you're kind of cute, in that ball cap." She tried to smile and it hurt her.

Rainey smiled down at her. "Oh yeah, I think you're going to be just fine."

Before leaving the ICU, Rainey spoke with the two agents outside of the doors. They were two of the guys that had been with Danny at JW's house. She told them she would be gone for an hour, and to be alert. Even though they thought they knew who the suspect was, Rainey was cautious. Something gnawed at her. How could he have been so stupid, to use his own property? This guy had been very careful to hide his identity. Why change that now? In his devolving, he may have just made a mistake. That was usually how criminals got caught, she told herself. Still, she would not be positive it was him until they showed her the DNA results, then she would relax.

She found Mackie, just as she had predicted, passed out in a chair in the corner of the waiting room. He was by himself, because he was snoring so loudly. To the relief of the other occupants of the room, Rainey woke him and they went to the cafeteria for some breakfast. They talked on the way. Danny had called Mackie and told him what was going on. It was a favor Danny thought he owed the big man. When they got in line at the buffet, they both piled their plates high with eggs, bacon, and grits and sat down by one of the big windows.

They ate for a few minutes before Mackie said, "So, Katie never suspected John Taylor?"

Rainey swallowed. "No, she was shocked that it could be him."

"What about you, what do you think?" Mackie asked.

"I couldn't identify him. What memories I do have are blurry," Rainey said.

"No Rainey, what do you think? Is it the right guy?"

"He fits the profile, he had the opportunity and the means, but you can't convict him on that alone. We have to wait for DNA, before I'll be sure," Rainey said.

"Okay, we wait," Mackie, said, taking another bite of eggs.

Rainey ate some more, relieved that her stomach could take it, after last night. After a few bites she said, "Have you talked to Ernie?"

"Yeah, she's up to speed," Mackie said.

"I need to call her and thank her for helping last night. She really saved the day," Rainey said.

Mackie laughed. "Oh, she knows. She reminded me several times when I spoke to her."

Rainey smiled at Mackie, happy to see him relax a little. "I hope you thanked her sufficiently."

"I told her you promised her a year's worth of spa treatments, and she's ready to collect," Mackie said.

Rainey noticed the headlines on the newspaper a man at the next table held. It read, "Senator's Wife Kidnapped." Under that in smaller letters it said, "FBI agent risks life to rescue her." Rainey got up and found the newspapers stacked by the cashier. She bought two and returned to the table, handing one to Mackie.

Rainey read the first article with its incorrect facts and suppositions. First, she was not an FBI agent then, and she did not rush Katie to the hospital in the back of her car. She did not "possibly" wound the guy. She missed. The article was accompanied by the same picture Rainey had seen when she Googled JW, Katie and JW arm and arm looking like the perfect couple. JW was quoted as saying, "The former FBI agent that you are referring to is the reason Katie was kidnapped in the first place. Rainey Bell brought that maniac into our lives."

There was a smaller article about a local veterinarian being questioned, but no name was released. Rainey threw the paper down in disgust, glad she did not have the business phone with her. The mailbox was probably full of messages from media wanting interviews. That was not going to happen. Rainey never talked to the press after her own brush with the killer. She certainly was not talking to them now.

Rainey grabbed the paper in front of Mackie, pulling it down so she could see his face. "Don't tell anybody where I am except Ernie. Tell her, if the media contacts her, my comment is, no comment."

"Where are you going?" Mackie asked, as Rainey stood up from the table.

"I don't want to run into one of those media shits right now," Rainey said. "Hey, you should go home. Get out of here for a while. I have two guys upstairs watching my back." Rainey saw that Mackie was reluctant to leave her alone. "I could use some fresh clothes and my laptop. I also need some help finding out what happened to my shoulder holster and where my car ended up, too."

Once given a mission, Mackie was glad to leave the hospital. Rainey knew he wanted her to make him go. He would not do it on his own. Mackie knew the alarm code at the cottage, so he would have no trouble getting her things. She told him a new code to program in, after he was inside. Rainey did not like the idea of too many people knowing her code. She changed it frequently anyway, just to be sure. Rainey left the cafeteria, taking the elevator up to ICU. As soon as she stepped off the elevator, a microphone was thrust into her face and a bright light blinded her.

"Are you or are you not an agent with the FBI?" A pretty blonde, with too white teeth asked her. She was quite persistent. "Are you the agent who was attacked last year, are you Rainey Bell?" Rainey ducked her head and passed the reporter only to

227

run into JW, who was again furious, maybe even more so. JW was coming unwound.

He shouted at Rainey, "I demand to see my wife."

Against her better judgment she responded, "She doesn't want to see you." Rainey could feel the heat from the big white light of the camera on her back. She could see the reflection of it bouncing off the glass doors to the ICU.

JW was not taking that as an answer. "How do you know? She was drugged. Why can't I see her?"

Rainey flashed with anger. She stepped in close to JW, so no one else could hear what she had to say. "Because she told me why she hates you and if you don't want all these other people knowing your little secret, you will back off now."

JW's face lost all its color. For a moment, he was stunned and then he slowly stepped aside, letting Rainey pass. She heard the reporter ask him what she had said, and he replied, "No comment."

Rainey smiled and kept walking. Katie was ready to see her when she got back. She had eaten a little, coaxed by Margie, and was sitting up a little higher in the bed. Margie inquired if Rainey had eaten breakfast. Rainey assured her she had. Margie told her to feel free to use the shower in the bathroom and she could get her a toothbrush, if she needed one.

"My friend is bringing me some things from home, thank you," Rainey said.

Margie told Rainey the plastic surgeon had been by and declared Katie's nose set perfectly and the small cuts were not going to be permanent. Besides, he could get rid of scars, if any remained, with a couple of simple procedures. He left instructions for home care and wanted to see Katie in his office in a week.

Margie began leaving, saying as she went, "She's just had some pain medication, so she should drop off to sleep. I'm right out here, if you need anything. Katie, you get some rest now."

Rainey smiled at Katie. "You look a little more bright eyed."

"A sponge bath will do that to you," Katie said, through cracked lips. It appeared Margie had put some salve on the cracks, but it still looked extremely painful.

"How are you feeling?" Rainey asked her.

"Not too bad right now, the meds are kicking in," Katie said, her eyes rolling a little. She was fighting to stay awake.

"Don't fight it," Rainey said, "Go to sleep, we can talk when you wake up."

Katie's eyes shut involuntarily. "Will you talk to me until I fall asleep?"

"Sure, what do you want me to talk about?" Rainey said, leaning over the railing, stroking Katie's hair.

"Tell me how you're going to take me to Nags Head, fishing," Katie whispered. She was already fading out.

Rainey began, "When I take you out of here, you are going with me to my cottage. When you are well enough, I'm taking you to Nags Head. We'll get a cottage on the beach. I'll hold you while we swing in a hammock, watching the sun set, listening to the waves…"

Katie's breathing became steadily slower until she was fast asleep. Rainey sat down with the images of holding Katie in a hammock, in her mind. She sat in the recliner and daydreamed. For the first time, in a long time, Rainey had something to look forward to. A life with Katie was definitely what she had planned. It crossed her mind that she should ask Katie, but she knew in the looks Katie gave her, that she too, had fallen madly in love. Now, all they had to do was get through this healing process, something they could help each other with, because Rainey had never healed, not by a long shot, but she thought she might be able to with Katie.

The image of her attacker flashed in her mind, interrupting her sweet dreams. She saw him there in an instant of clarity she had not experienced since the attack. The physicians, who took care of her in a room not far from this one, told her she may get some memories back, but it would take time. For one brief second, she saw him kneeling over her, his eyes close to hers. Then she remembered a scent, something familiar, but she could

229

not place it. She had smelled it in the room where she found Katie last night, too. In the image, all she could see of him was the leather mask, his distorted mouth and nose, and his eyes. They were blue, she suddenly remembered, but his lashes were dark, like the rest of the hair she could see on his body. Dark hair, blue eyes, and maybe some kind of cologne, she had to tell Danny.

Rainey did not want to go to the nurses' station to use the phone. The reporter was probably still there and would see her through the glass. She checked the bathroom and sure enough, there was a phone by the toilet. Rainey left the door to the bathroom cracked open, so she could hear if Katie called out to her. She dialed Danny's number, surprised that she still remembered it after years of just punching a contact button on her phone. He answered on the third ring, still talking to someone else.

"McNally," he finally said into the phone.

"Danny, it's Rainey. I've remembered something, it could be important."

Danny was interested. "What is it?"

"The dark hairs found at my scene match in appearance the ones found tonight, right?" Rainey asked.

"Yes, they did, but we already knew that," Danny said.

"But I just now remembered seeing the hairs on his chest. They were black, not too thick. His eyelashes were black as well and his eyes were blue."

"You're sure about the eyes, they were blue?" Danny asked.

Rainey answered him emphatically, "Yes, I'm positive. What color are Taylor's eyes?"

"Blue, they're blue, Rainey. I'm going to send a picture to you, do you have a computer?"

"No, not here," Rainey said, "but Mackie is trying to locate my car and the laptop is in it. He's supposed to bring it to me, when he finds it."

Danny talked fast, "I can help Mackie with finding the car. I'll call him. In the meantime, I'll shoot you an email with

Taylor's picture. I know you didn't see much, but maybe it will ring a bell for you."

Rainey needed to know, "Do you still have him?"

"It's amazing. He hasn't asked for a lawyer and keeps saying he will do anything to help find the man who did this awful thing to his friend's wife. He's either the nicest guy I've ever met or he's getting off on the attention, throwing himself into the investigation," Danny said.

Rainey was starting to believe Taylor could be the guy. She said, "They almost always try to be involved in the investigation. Can he account for all the drugs in his practice?"

"That's interesting, too. He filed a complaint with the County Sheriff's office, way back before the bodies started floating up in Lake Johnston. Taylor said a large shipment of medications went missing. He said he had just signed for them, which the shipping company manifest backed up. He set the box down by the front desk, when a lady came in with a dog that had been hit by a car. When he came back, he said the package was no longer on the floor, where he left it. The staff didn't see anybody come in, they were all too busy helping with the dog."

"Convenient," Rainey commented.

"To top it off, he claimed JW could verify his story, because he had helped the woman bring the dog into the office and stayed until after the police had come and gone."

"Interesting, how he tied himself to JW as a witness, instead of his victim," Rainey said. "Speaking of JW, have you talked to him?"

Danny snorted. "If you mean, have I listened to him rant and rave, yes, I've spoken with Mr. Wilson several times. I haven't received many answers from him about Taylor, because he's so focused on crucifying you. He's got a hard on for you, Rainey. Watch your back."

Rainey laughed. "I saw him just a little while ago. I don't think he'll be calling me out anytime soon. I simply reminded him I knew where too many of his skeletons were buried."

"That's the Rainey I know and love. Tell the son of bitch to stick it," Danny said.

Rainey smiled to herself and then asked, "Is that the official Bureau position?"

Danny was feeling a little cocky himself. "As far as I'm concerned JW Wilson is a non-factor in this investigation. I can get as much information out of Katie about their relationship with Taylor and the rest I can find out from other sources. I'd just as soon not have to talk to the man again, I might punch him."

Rainey giggled. "I might shoot him in the ass, if he keeps bothering Katie."

Danny became serious. "Don't do that, Rainey."

Rainey laughed harder and then covered her mouth, afraid she might wake Katie. When she finally could, she said, "I was just kidding, Danny. Relax."

"I have to go in now and take another crack at Mr. Taylor. I'll let you know if anything breaks," he said, in a hurry to hang up.

Rainey said, "Okay, shoot me the picture and tell Mackie where my car is before you go in. Oh, and take the picture with his shirt off, it will help."

"Okay, Rainey, sit tight. It's almost over." Danny hung up.

Rainey returned to her post in the recliner. She watched Katie breathe and waited as the clock ticked away the morning. Margie brought coffee and offered her fresh scrubs until her clothes arrived. Rainey must have looked like hell. It was the second time Margie suggested a shower. Margie promised to stay in the room in case Katie woke up, and Rainey finally caved, took the scrubs, and went into the bathroom to shower. Margie even brought a hairbrush, toothbrush, and toothpaste, all in a sealed plastic sanitary bag.

Rainey closed and locked the bathroom door. She took the pistol from her pants and laid it on the back of the toilet. When Rainey finally looked in the mirror, she saw that her face was the only thing clean on her body. She had washed it last night after she got sick. Her tee shirt was stained with dirt and dark spots that must have been Katie's blood. Her pants were covered in thick dust, from the farmhouse. Rainey saw blood on her neck where Katie had rested her head, when Rainey carried her out of the farmhouse. Margie was correct. Rainey needed a shower.

The hot water beating on her back felt incredibly good. She stayed longer than she intended to. After washing her hair and body, she leaned on the shower wall, allowing the hot water to release the tension in her tight neck muscles. The fresh scrubs felt comfortable and clean, unlike the dirty clothes she placed in the plastic bag marked "Personal Belongings," she found on the back of the bathroom door. She put the pistol on top of her clothes and snapped the bag shut. Rainey brushed her teeth and hair and left her hair down for a while. Tying it back was beginning to give her a headache. She put the tie back around her wrist and exited the bathroom.

Margie smiled at her. "You look like you feel better."

"Yes, I do," Rainey said, going over to put the bag by the recliner. "Thank you for suggesting the shower. I really needed one. I hadn't noticed how dirty I was. No wonder people were staring at me in the cafeteria."

"You were focused on Katie," Margie said.

Rainey looked at the sleeping Katie. "I guess I was."

What Margie said next surprised Rainey. She looked at Katie and back at Rainey and said, "My granddaughter is gay. I can only hope she finds a love like the one you two have for each other. You were all Katie talked about this morning when we were alone."

Rainey did not know what to say. She had not thought about being a lesbian role model. Rainey could not tell Margie she had known Katie less than a week. She at last said, "Katie is a special person. I do hope your granddaughter finds someone like her."

Margie smiled at Rainey, saying, "I wouldn't mind if she found someone like you, a woman who carries a gun. I'd feel like she was safer and you're a special kind of person yourself, and pretty, I might add."

"Thank you, Margie. That is nice of you to say," Rainey said, feeling her cheeks blush.

"Well, I'll leave you two alone now. I'll bring you fresh coffee, the next time I come in. There's water and ice in the pitcher there, if you get thirsty. If you need anything, just push the call button."

Again, Rainey was alone with Katie. She sat in the recliner and turned the on TV. She watched the news channel, with the volume turned off. Rainey was not surprised to see her name go by on the news ticker at the bottom of the screen. They even showed an old FBI photo, from a very early field office assignment, years ago. She was much younger then and smiling. Then the image of her grim face appeared, pushing by the reporter and being accosted by JW.

Rainey was glad the volume was off, so she did not have to listen to the two analysts discussing her case. Pictures of Katie from the school web page, and a few of her in public settings with JW, faded in and out on the screen. Then JW's official State Representative photo zoomed in and stayed on the screen, while the analysts seemed to be discussing his political career.

Rainey turned the TV to an episode of The Andy Griffith show. She did not need volume. She knew them all by heart. Rainey thought to herself how nice it would be if they all lived in Mayberry, where the worst criminal was Otis, the drunk. Nevertheless, Rainey did not live in Mayberry, with the kind sheriff and goofy deputy. She looked at Katie's brutalized body and wished it so with all her heart.

CHAPTER TWENTY-FOUR

Mackie arrived two hours later with Rainey's clothes and laptop. The lab was finished with Rainey's car, so Junior drove it to the hospital. Mackie gave her the keys and told her where it was parked. He had updated Ernie, who was presently shopping for all the things Rainey would need when she brought Katie home from the hospital. She remembered taking care of Rainey and knew what it would take for Katie's recovery. Ernie had the code and was going over to change the sheets and clean up the cottage. She needed to do something and that was all she could really do at the time.

"Ernie said your mother called," Mackie told Rainey, while they stood outside Katie's door.

"What did Ernie tell her?"

Mackie laughed. "No comment."

Rainey laughed, too, drawing looks from the nurses in the hallway. They quieted down, well, as much as possible for Mackie, whose bass voice seemed to rumble down the hall.

"Thank you for doing all this," Rainey said.

"I was glad to get out of here. I stopped by the house to check in with Thelma," he said.

Thelma was Mackie's wife, a long-suffering woman, who was used to Mackie vanishing for days, and let him do it with no argument from her. Thelma knew she could not tie Mackie down.

Their marriage was a happy one, for the most part, and they had recently celebrated their thirty-fifth anniversary.

"How is Thelma?" Rainey asked, being polite. She was not expecting the long story that came next.

Mackie answered, "She's overloaded with tomatoes from the garden right now. They are everywhere in the house. I went to take a shower and had to take the tomatoes out of the tub first. I'm serious; there are hundreds of tomatoes in that house. She's canning as fast as she can, but she can't keep up. She sent a bag with me to leave at the cottage. She said to tell you her prayer group has you and Katie on their list."

A nurse passing them in the hall said, "Bring some tomatoes up here, we'll help her get rid of them." She laughed and walked away.

"Thank Thelma for me," Rainey said, "the next time you talk to her."

Mackie said, "I will," then asked, "Have you heard anything from Danny?"

"He sent me an email with Taylor's picture attached. I need to look at it," Rainey answered.

"Well, I'll let you get to it," Mackie said, preparing to leave. "I'll be in the waiting room, if you need me."

Rainey told him good-bye and took her things into Katie's room. Katie was still sleeping, so Rainey went into the bathroom, taking her belongings bag with her. She took the pistol out of the bag and redressed, this time in the jeans and two tee shirts Mackie had brought her. He knew about the undershirt she always wore to hide the scar. She tucked the pistol back in her pants and covered it with the FBI jacket she retrieved from the bag. She was not totally ready to believe that Danny had the killer with him. He could be turned loose any minute, if he asked for a lawyer. Rainey was taking no chances. She put her hair up and went back out to the recliner.

Rainey used the Wi-Fi signal from the hospital to access her email, and found the one from Danny. She clicked on the attachment and the picture of a dark haired, blue-eyed man appeared on her screen. He was handsome and had a dazed look in his eyes. Rainey zoomed in on his face and tried to imagine it covered in leather. She stared into his eyes. It could be him, but she was not sure. She looked at his body hair, trying to recognize a pattern of growth, anything that might spark a memory. Rainey simply had not seen enough of her attacker's face to make a positive identification. It was a dead end.

"What are you looking at?" Katie was talking to her.

Rainey set the laptop aside, closing the lid so Katie could not see the picture of Taylor.

"Hey there, you had a long nap," Rainey said, standing up and going to the side of the bed. "How do you feel?"

Katie touched her face. "I think the pain meds are wearing off."

"I'll call the nurse," Rainey said, reaching for the call button.

"Wait," Katie said, stopping her. "What day is it?"

Rainey let go of the call button. "It's Tuesday afternoon."

"Did someone call my school and tell them I wouldn't be there?" Katie asked.

"I think they knew, Katie. You were taken from the school Monday night," Rainey reminded her.

Katie thought for a second, trying to remember. "I forgot about that. Why can't I remember?"

Katie was growing agitated again. Rainey said to her calmly, "Katie, the drugs you were given can cause amnesia for the time just before, during, and after you have been injected. Don't try to remember. It will come to you slowly or not at all. Pray for not at all, you don't want to remember what happened to you, take it from one who knows."

Katie responded, "It's so frustrating."

Rainey tried again to make her understand. "Katie, please concentrate on getting well. You need to not waste your energy trying to remember something that will probably always be a black hole for you."

Katie looked at Rainey. "Is that what happened to you? You don't remember."

Rainey saw that Katie was trying to come to grips with the fact that she may never remember the man who attacked her.

237

Rainey spoke softly, "I don't remember very much at all and I was given a lot lower dosage than you received. I've come to terms with not remembering, because the parts I do remember are bad enough. I don't want you to remember. Do you understand that I'm trying to help you?"

Katie accepted what Rainey was saying finally. "I understand. You're trying to protect me."

Rainey squeezed Katie's hand and said, "I don't want you to hurt anymore than you already are. I want you to get well and come live with me for the rest of my life."

Katie smiled, letting the memory issues go for the moment. "Why Rainey Bell, are you asking me to marry you?"

Rainey laughed at herself. "I know it's crazy, we haven't known each other very long, but I can't think about a day without you in it. I've completely lost my mind over you, so yes, if you'll have me, I'll spend every moment making you happy. We'll eventually forget about all this, and I would like to live happily ever after with you."

Katie teased Rainey. "Well, that's a lot to process and I probably shouldn't make life changing decisions, in the condition I'm in."

Rainey was not deterred. "I'll wait. I'll wait as long as it takes. You've stolen my heart."

"Do you think you could steal my clothes from the house, so I don't have to see JW ever again, except when we go to court to end this sham marriage?" Katie asked.

Rainey smiled widely, when she asked, "Does that mean you're saying yes to living with me?"

Katie switched subjects. "I think I remember him arguing with you in a hallway. I told a nurse to keep him away from me. Did I dream that?"

"No, actually you called him an asshole. The nurse kind of picked up on the fact that you didn't want him around," Rainey said, still wondering about Katie's answer to her question.

"Even out of my mind on drugs, I didn't want him near me, I remember that," Katie said.

"He won't be coming back. I sort of threatened him," Rainey said.

Katie looked alarmed. "You didn't threaten to kill him, did you? He'll have you locked up for threatening a public official."

Rainey was proud of her answer; she thought she had handled JW nicely. "No, I just told him he didn't want me digging up skeletons. He got the picture pretty quick."

Katie was relieved. Then she asked, "What about my family, has anybody talked to them?"

"I'm sorry Katie, I don't know the answer to that, but I'll find out. I'll call them myself, if you want me to."

"Yes, please. Tell them I'm all right and not to come. I really don't want my family hovering over me in that little cottage."

Rainey brightened. "Does that mean you are saying yes?"

Katie touched her face again. She said, "Yes, I want to live with you, now please call the nurse, my face is throbbing."

Rainey immediately pushed the red call button. Margie appeared almost magically at the door, syringe in hand.

"I bet it's time for another pain shot," she said, knowingly.

"Yes, please," Katie said in desperation. Her pain level had increased significantly, in the short period she had been awake.

Margie inserted the needle in the tube and Katie visibly relaxed as the drugs began to circulate through her blood stream.

When Margie was finished giving the shot, she threw away the syringe and turned, calling Rainey to her. She said, "I'm going to bring you some ice bags. I want you to hold them on her face for ten minutes. It's time to get that swelling down. We couldn't do it before, because a side effect of one of the drugs she was on is hypothermia. Her body temperature is stable now, so we can start the ice."

Rainey did as she was told, holding ice bags on the sides of Katie's face, while she drifted under the influence of the pain medication. After ten minutes, Rainey removed the bags.

Katie whispered, "Thank you," without opening her eyes.

Soon, Katie returned to a deep sleep. Rainey went back to her laptop and shot Danny an email explaining that she could not identify the man in the photo. She also wanted him to get her the contact information for Katie's sisters and parents. Rainey was not going to call JW for their phone numbers, and Danny had more resources than she did at the moment. Rainey had forgotten to ask Katie what their names were. She spent the next few hours alternately holding ice bags against Katie's bruises and trolling the Internet, reading everything she could find on Dr. John P. Taylor. Rainey also checked her email for a response from Danny.

Rainey received Katie's family contact information from Danny about five o'clock. She called the numbers from the bathroom and got voice mail on all of them. She left a brief message, giving them Katie's room number and an update on her condition. She told them to call back on that number to speak to Katie. Rainey hoped that was enough to keep them away from Chapel Hill. Katie had to understand Rainey could not stop them, if they wanted to come.

Katie reawakened shortly after the phone calls were made. She felt better this time and the swelling had gone down quite a bit. Katie felt like eating and was given some soft foods, so she would not have to chew. Moving her jaws hurt. Rainey ordered a chef salad from the cafeteria and ate with her. More pain meds were administered and the cycle began again, Katie sleeping, Rainey applying ice packs and searching the Internet. Night fell and Rainey finally went to sleep in the chair, waking when Janet, who was back on duty, came in and out, and when Dr. Marsden came by to check on Katie several times. He thought her progress was remarkable and that she may be able to go home Wednesday afternoon. Rainey became very excited at the prospect of getting out of this hospital room.

The rest of the night, when they were alone, Rainey slept with her arm stuck through the railing, holding Katie's hand. For the first time in days, Rainey had sweet dreams.

CHAPTER TWENTY-FIVE

Rainey awoke again at sunrise, this time before Katie. She was standing over Katie's bed looking at the swelling that appeared to have mostly dissipated, in the night. Katie looked more like herself now, only with different shades of bruising on her beautiful face. Katie's eyes fluttered open. She stretched and smiled up at Rainey.

Rainey said, "Good morning."

"Good morning to you," Katie said, sounding much stronger.

"You sound like you're feeling better this morning."

"I do actually," Katie said, "and I think I could eat a horse."

That was good news to Rainey. The more food Katie could consume, the stronger she would feel. Maybe they would go home today. Rainey did not want to raise Katie's hopes, so she did not mention it.

"Your face looks better," Rainey said.

"I haven't looked in a mirror," Katie said. "I know I must look terrible."

Rainey smiled, again. "You look great, to me."

Margie walked in with Janet. Margie said, "Okay, Rainey, you'll have to leave for a few minutes. We're going to remove these IVs and the catheter and let you take Miss Katie here for a walk before breakfast. How does that sound?"

Katie answered for Rainey, "That sounds fantastic. I'm ready to get out of this bed."

Janet beamed. "Katie, you seem much more alert today. That's wonderful."

"No offense ladies, but I'm ready to go home," Katie answered.

Rainey laughed at Katie, who was so much more herself and entertaining the nurses, while they poked and prodded. Rainey stood outside the door, waiting. In just a few minutes, she heard Katie moan loudly. Rainey burst through the door, to find Janet and Margie changing the sheets. She turned toward the bathroom, to see Katie sitting on the toilet. That sound Rainey heard was the pure moan of ecstasy Katie let out, when she was finally able to urinate on her own. Rainey remembered well her own experience with the catheter and laughed aloud at Katie's contented expression.

Rainey took Katie for a couple of spins, up and down the ICU hallway. They went as far as they could go without the reporters, who were constantly coming and going, seeing them. Local news crews were filming the glass ICU doors for their evening broadcasts. Rainey held Katie's gown closed in the back, at Katie's insistence. Disconnected from the tubes, Katie's arms reanimated as she talked.

Katie waved her hands around, punctuating her plea. "Please, Rainey, you have to convince them to let me go home with you, today."

Rainey applauded Katie's enthusiasm, but she had no say in whether Katie would be released from the hospital. "I'm glad you're feeling better, but it really is up to Dr. Marsden."

"You have to back me up," Katie said, as if she were ramping up for a confrontation with a parent, "when I tell him, I want to go home and that you will take care of me. Deal?"

Rainey played the partner role well, she said, "Deal," with no hesitation. This made Katie too excited and she almost lost her footing. She had to grab Rainey's waist to maintain her balance.

Rainey, still holding the back of Katie's gown closed, said, "Whoa there, cowboy. Let's not get ahead of ourselves."

Katie lost some of the color in her face. She looked up at Rainey, saying, "I want to go lay down, now."

242

Rainey put her hand in the small of Katie's back and let Katie lean into her, the smaller woman wrapping her arm around Rainey's waist. The two women just rounded the corner leading to Katie's room, when Katie suddenly stiffened and froze in place.

A loud shriek of, "Katie!" followed.

The noise had emanated from a blond woman, who looked a lot like Katie, but not as well put together. She was about the same height and build as Katie, but heavier and older by at least ten years and she was heading straight for Katie. Another woman waited by the door. She was taller than Rainey and lean, with the body of a model and Katie's best features, blond hair, crystal blue eyes, and a dazzling smile. She was older than Katie, maybe five years at the most, in Rainey's estimate. This woman was a drop-dead knock out, and from her expression, she was completely embarrassed by the blonde heading for Katie, arms stretched out in an anticipatory hug.

Rainey heard Katie say, "Shit, it's my sisters. I thought you called them."

"I did," Rainey said defensively. "They could have already been on the way, caught the red-eye or something. JW could have called them."

The oldest sister was now close enough to see Katie's face clearly. She stopped charging at them and threw her hands up to her own face, sliding to a stop. She screeched out, "Oh my, sweet Jesus! Look what that monster did to that beautiful face." She turned back to the other sister and said, loudly enough to disturb everyone up and down the hall, "Helena, did you see what that monster did to our baby sister?"

"No Maria, I haven't yet, but I bet everybody in the hall is going to come out to see it, after your little announcement," Helena cracked.

To which Maria replied, "Oh, shut up!" and turned her attention back to Katie.

Her older sister's reaction to her face mortified Katie. She looked up at Rainey and asked, "Is it that bad?"

Rainey said, "She should have seen it yesterday," with all the seriousness she could muster.

Katie put her hands to her cheeks, saying, "Oh, my god."

Rainey started laughing. "No Katie, you are not scarred for life. You heard what the plastic surgeon said."

Katie appeared suddenly to remember the conversation with the plastic surgeon. "Oh yeah, that's right." Katie turned to the sister, still standing in front of them, frozen with a comical expression of horror on her face. "Stop being so dramatic, Maria. It will heal."

"I know that it will heal," Maria said, falling in step with them toward Katie's room, "but it just looks so horrible right now."

Katie, already tired of this sister, said, "I really don't care to know how I look, so thank you for your vivid imagery that will now haunt me in my dreams."

Rainey stifled a laugh. Katie and Maria took pot shots at each other all the way to the door. When they entered the room, Helena joined in, taking up for Katie. It sounded like laughing gulls fighting over a piece of food, about fifty of them, all three women talking at once, but no one was listening. Rainey stood clear of the main action, once she put Katie in her bed. She leaned against the doorframe, amused by the trio. Margie charged into the room. She looked at Rainey for an explanation. Rainey simply shrugged her shoulders and gave Margie one of those, "It's out of my hands," looks.

Margie stepped forward and in a commanding voice, said, "Ladies!"

The room fell silent. Katie, who was sitting in the middle of the bed, flanked by her sisters, was the first to speak.

"Margie, I would like for you to meet my sisters, Helena and Maria." She indicated each, when she said their names.

"It's a pleasure to meet you, but you must keep it down, this is an intensive care unit." Margie told Katie, "I'll be back with your breakfast," and left.

The next thing Rainey knew, the sisters were involved in a group hug. Rainey was glad she did not have a sister, at that moment. These three were involved in a very dysfunctional relationship, from what Rainey had witnessed so far. If this is how they handled one of them in trouble, growing up together must have been quite an experience.

Katie finally acknowledged Rainey's presence. "I want you to meet the woman who saved my life." She motioned for Rainey to come to her side. "Special Agent Rainey Bell, these are my sisters. I guess you figured that out." Katie's accent grew stronger as she went on, "This is Maria. She lives in Beverly Hills, with her millionaire husband, and she is my oldest sister." She added quickly, "By ten years."

Maria reacted immediately. "Thank you for broadcasting it."

Rainey grew up around Southern women like Maria. She might live on the West coast, but Maria had not forgotten from whence she came. She probably attended numerous charity events during the week and church on Sunday. These women were always impeccable in dress and manners. Yet, they did have a way of saying, "thank you," meaning, "fuck you" instead, and it was an acquired skill. Maria, Rainey thought, had achieved the mark.

Maria extended her hand to Rainey, saying, "It's so nice to meet you. Thank you so much for saving my baby sister."

Rainey shook Maria's hand and gave her a standard response from years of dealing with grateful families, "You are very welcome."

Katie was smiling at Rainey, seeming to realize how shy she really was, and how she had to fight it. Rainey had not always been that way. She was full of self-confidence until the attack and then she shut herself off from the world, for so long, Rainey was now enduring the difficult process of re-joining it. The mostly solitary life of a bail bondsman fit her better now, than that of the Special Agent she used to be.

Katie said, "And this gorgeous creature is the middle sister, Helena. She's a model and lives in LA."

Maria piped up, "Why don't you tell Rainey how old Helena is?"

Helena answered for Katie, "I'm forty-two. Rainey, it is a pleasure to meet you." She extended her hand for Rainey to take. Helena left the South in the dust and embraced her LA persona.

Only one thought crossed Rainey's mind, "I hope I look that good at forty-two," but she said, aloud, "The pleasure is mine."

Helena had a moment of recognition. "You are the one who left the message on my phone. Maria was coming anyway and I couldn't leave Katie defenseless against her, so I had to follow." She looked down at Katie. "I know you didn't want us here, but she could not be stopped."

Maria defended herself. "With Momma and Daddy in the Mediterranean, someone had to come take care of her. God knows JW wouldn't."

Helena snapped back, "He took care of her six months ago and she came out fine."

Rainey thought the sea gulls were about to erupt again, but Katie quieted them, when she said, "I'm divorcing JW."

Maria was thunderstruck. "What?"

Helena was much less dramatic, saying only, "Thank God." Rainey liked Helena right away.

Katie was in the hospital and under the influence of medications, so Rainey figured she was thinking, "What the hell. I can always claim the drugs made me say it, if it goes badly."

"That's not all of it," Katie said. "I'm moving in with Rainey."

"You're going to move in with a friend and let him have your house. Are you out of your mind?" Maria said, showing her true colors and totally missing the point of what Katie said.

Helena remained quiet, looking at Katie, trying to understand what she said. When Katie took Rainey's hand and returned her sister's gaze, the light came on for Helena.

"Congratulations! I'm so happy for you both, well, except for the fact someone kicked your ass," Helena said, bending to give her sister a kiss on the top of her head.

Maria was still trying to put the picture together in her mind. Rainey could visibly see Maria's mind trying to put the square peg in the round hole. It just was not working for her. Everyone

246

in the room turned to her. Maria was unable to make the puzzle go together.

Katie said, "Maria, I'm a lesbian."

Helena made Rainey laugh, saying, "Oh, thank god. I have a lesbian sister. That will be so hot in LA, you know with the whole Ellen movement."

Maria was not so supportive, asking, "When did this happen? You were just pregnant six months ago."

Katie gripped Rainey's hand tighter, but Helena saved her from having to say anything to Maria. Helena leaned across the bed and said, "You insensitive bitch."

Maria began to ring her hands. "I'm sorry. I'm just so confused."

Helena was breathing down Maria's neck. "What is so hard to understand? Katie has left that asshole JW and is now in love with a woman. Is that too unclear for you?"

"Katie, what will people think?" Maria asked.

"Oh, for fuck sake," Helena said, exasperated, "it's the twenty-first goddamned century."

"Maria, I don't care what people think. If I lose my job, my family, my friends, I will have gained one good thing in my life. One thing that I chose, one time that I threw caution to the wind, and lived my life the way I wanted to."

Helena was extremely funny and Rainey could not wait to get to know her, even though her Hollywood affect was a little too much. Helena started digging through her giant handbag, saying, "God, Katie, that was profound. I have to write that down. That would work so well in a screenplay."

Maria pressed on. "What about JW? You will ruin his career."

"Fuck JW!" Katie said, with venom enough for even Maria to understand.

"Okay, if that's what you think is best," Maria said, not convinced, but conceding.

Katie looked at them both. "Do not tell mom and dad. I will do it when they get back from their holiday."

Both sisters shook their heads back and forth, neither wanting to be the one to break that news to the parents.

"What can we do for you, while we're here?" Maria asked.

"If you really want to help, go by my house and pack some clothes for me. It will be at least two weeks before I go back to school. The bruising would scare my babies," Katie said.

Maria could not control her mouth. "I should say it would. Give them nightmares for weeks."

"You are just a fucking idiot, aren't you?" Helena asked Maria.

Once again, the squabble began and was silenced by Katie's voice. "Look, either help me or get back on the jet and go home. I can't deal with you two at each other's throats." Katie sat back on the bed.

Rainey decided it was time to intervene. "She's getting tired. She hasn't gained back all her strength yet."

Katie protested, "But I'm strong enough to go home, Rainey."

"Okay, honey, what do you need from the house?" Helena asked.

"I have nothing, so a little of everything, underwear, bras, socks and shoes, the basics, you know. Bring the toiletries from my bathroom and my makeup. I need pajamas, lying around stuff and some shorts and tanks. My luggage is in the walk-in closet."

Maria was a bringer of bad news. Rainey was beginning to understand it was just her nature. "What about JW? Won't he be angry?"

Katie paid no attention to Maria and spoke directly to Helena, who did not seem to care if JW was angry. "JW probably won't be there, so I'll give you the alarm code."

Rainey spoke up, "Just in case, I think you should take a police escort and one of my guys will come with you to carry things."

Maria looked more frightened than ever. She was not used to so much excitement and it was taking its toll. Margie came in with Katie's breakfast, which she ate, while relaying what details of the attack she wanted her sisters to know, leaving out some of the things she had been told happened to her.

Rainey went to the bathroom to use the phone. She called Mackie, arranging the sisters' escort to JW's house. He said he would take them over in the Escalade, and meet the police there. Mackie would arrange everything with the police, because he had such a long working relationship with the departments in the area.

Margie came in with pain pills and news that Katie may go home this evening when Dr. Marsden came for rounds. Katie drifted off to sleep, still talking to her sisters. Rainey took the sisters down to meet Mackie and couldn't wait for Katie to wake up so she could tell her about the look on Maria's face when she saw Mackie. Rainey wished so badly that she had taken a picture.

Katie's sisters were off on their mission and Rainey was glad to see them go. The air around her became more still. She grabbed a breakfast burrito and took it back upstairs, assuming her position in the recliner, once again the guardian of Katie's dreams.

CHAPTER TWENTY-SIX

Danny came in, just after Katie had awakened and eaten lunch. She was once again rejuvenated from her nap and wanted to hear everything Danny could tell her about the case.

Danny told them, "We had to release John Taylor. He finally asked for a lawyer, after his wife arrived from New York."

"Poor Ann, she must be so upset," Katie said.

"Pissed off is more like it. She nearly took my head off," Danny alleged.

Rainey was more interested in where the Veterinarian had gone. "What about Taylor? Are you covering him?"

With confidence, Danny said, "Like a blanket, he can't breathe without us knowing it."

"We might go home tonight, that's all. I don't want to be surprised by this guy in the middle of the night," Rainey said, warily.

Danny was adamant in his reply, "Trust me, Rainey. He will not get near you. I'll put a couple of agents out there with you, but this is our guy, I know it."

Katie was still mulling over John Taylor's arrest in her mind, she asked, "What kind of hard evidence do you have to link him to the murders?"

Danny's confidence waned a little. "Katie, this guy had the means and opportunity to commit every one of these killings and attacks. He fits the physical description. He fits the profile to a tee."

"But that's all you have, circumstantial evidence," Katie stated, like a lawyer. Rainey was reminded that Katie had been married to one. Katie probably helped him study for his law exams.

Danny wasn't out yet. He had one more play. "We have his DNA and when it comes back a positive match, he's getting the needle, no question."

Rainey was still on the fact that the guy was free. "Who's on Taylor's tail?"

Danny ran his fingers through his hair. "Don't worry Rainey. I got the best guys on this, Roger and Bobby. You remember Bobby, right? They aren't going to lose him."

"You got a tracker on his car?" Rainey was not listening to Danny tell her it was under control, she wanted details.

Danny was getting frustrated. "Yes, Rainey. If he moves, we will know it."

Katie piped in, "What about his wife's car?"

"Would you two relax? In twenty-four hours, we should get some preliminary reports back on the hair samples and DNA. Until then, we'll be watching you and Taylor."

Leave it to Katie to ask the question nobody seemed to want to hear. "What if it isn't him?"

"Then we keep looking. If it isn't Taylor, then it is one of his friends and yours. We will find the connection," Danny answered her, earnestly.

Danny thought he had his guy, but he was prepared to be wrong. Rainey hoped she and Katie would not pay the price for it, if he was.

Danny laughed to himself and then said, "You know what the kicker is? JW is representing Taylor."

Rainey reacted. "You have got to be kidding me."

Katie smiled and shook her head. "It's just the kind of thing he would do," she said. "He can make a name for himself and he'll have his face all over the media. It's perfect for him."

"He must not think Taylor is guilty. I can't see him taking on a losing cause," Rainey said.

Katie explained, "Right now, it's free publicity. He can always drop out of the case, if it sours for him."

Danny shook his head. "JW has some anger management issues, that's for sure."

Rainey told Danny that the agents outside the doors would go with them, if Katie did get discharged, and that he could switch them up later, if need be. Before he left, Danny assured them, once again, that they were safe. Rainey wished she felt as confident as Danny did.

Soon afterward, Maria and Helena reappeared with a pair of pajamas and slippers, from Katie's house. Mackie had the rest of Katie's things in his Escalade. There had been no confrontation with JW, only because he was not at home.

Maria started in right away. "Katie your house is a mess. There are dirty dishes and clothes everywhere."

"It's not my house anymore. Not my problem," Katie said, not bothered at all by JW's treatment of her former home.

Helena tried to put a positive spin on things. "Your yard is gorgeous, though."

"Thank you. It took a long time to get it that way."

Once again the voice of gloom and doom, Maria said, "Aren't you going to hate leaving it, after you worked so hard to make it nice?"

Maria's attitude did not deter Katie. "I can start over at Rainey's place. She has lots of property." She turned to Rainey. "May I plant a vegetable garden, too?"

"Whatever you want," Rainey answered her.

Katie cocked her head. "Do you have a boat?"

"Yes," Rainey said, wondering where this was going.

Katie ignored her sisters for a moment. "Can you pull me on water skis?"

"Yes," Rainey said, "I didn't know you skied."

"I love to water ski. I haven't been in forever," Katie said, excited at the prospect.

Maria, observing the conversation between Rainey and Katie, said, "Exactly how long have you known each other?"

Katie did not flinch. "About a week," she said, happily.

"Katherine Ann Meyers, have you lost your mind?" Maria turned to Rainey. "I'm sorry, Rainey. You seem like a nice person, but my sister is not a lesbian. If you seduced her while she was being chased by a serial killer, she might not have been thinking straight, no pun intended."

"Maria, you have the wrong impression." Katie was enjoying this. She continued, "Rainey wasn't a lesbian. I turned her into one. I seduced her."

Helena slapped Katie a high five, adding, "You go, little sis!"

Maria shook her head, in confusion. She said, "I just don't understand. How do you go from being not gay to gay, in a week?"

Rainey could not resist. She had to say it. "You sleep with a woman. Now, that I've done it, I'll never go back."

At that moment, Rainey learned a lesson about sisters. They can rag on each other all they want, but no one else gets to play.

Katie popped Rainey on the arm. "Be nice! Don't tease her. She's having a hard time with this."

Rainey rubbed her arm, saying, "Okay, okay. I'll be nice."

Katie's sisters visited for a few more hours. There were tears and hugs and promises to call and then they were gone. As Katie requested, they headed for the airport, boarded a jet, and flew back west.

Katie asked Margie if she could take a shower. After checking her steadiness on her feet, Margie agreed to the shower, but she still insisted on staying with Katie. Katie did not care who was in the bathroom with her, she wanted a shower and to shampoo her hair. Margie and Katie went into the bathroom together, so Rainey wandered out into the hall.

Sneaking a peek around the corner, Rainey saw that currently there were no reporters or cameras camped out by the glass entryway doors. Rainey spoke with the agents on duty, explained that they might be following her later, and made sure they were ready to take on the new assignment. In Rainey's mind, there was a big difference between guarding them inside a major metropolitan hospital and protecting them out at the cottage. These agents were not rookies and seemed to be very comfortable with the move. Rainey, reassured, went back to Katie's room.

Katie was freshly showered and back in the bed. She was dressed, in blue and white striped, men's style, pajamas and beaming, as best she could without splitting her healing lips. Her bed had been remade and she looked not to have a care in the world, just a plastic surgery patient on a weeklong stay to have a little work done.

"You look like that made you feel better," Rainey said.

Katie rolled her eyes. "You have no idea. There was so much blood in my hair, it turned the shampoo pink. I'm glad to have it off of me."

"Did you look in the mirror?" Rainey asked, remembering the first shower and the first look she had at her face and body, after the attack.

"Yes, and despite Maria's reaction, it really isn't much worse than the car accident and I recovered from that, so it's no big deal. Been there, done that."

Rainey laughed at her. "That's a healthy attitude to have."

"I'm thinking positive," Katie said. "I'm hoping to get out of here."

"That would be nice," Rainey agreed.

Dr. Marsden arrived minutes later. He came in early to see if Katie was ready to go home. He checked her, head to toe, and made her promise to take it easy, before signing the release papers. Katie was ecstatic and impatient, at the same time, because the discharge process took nearly an hour. Finally, after stopping at the pharmacy for Katie's medications, Rainey loaded Katie into the Charger, and the short motorcade pulled away from the hospital. Rainey and Katie led the way, followed by the FBI agents, with Mackie taking the rear.

Rainey had not realized how caged up she felt inside the hospital, until the Charger broke out of the main downtown area and moved into the countryside, for the fifteen minute ride out to her house. Even though it was hot outside, they rode with the windows rolled down for the fresh air and to get the chill of the hospital out of their bones.

When they arrived at the cottage, Rainey helped Katie up the stairs and into the cottage. Ernie had definitely been there. Rainey was not a messy housekeeper, but she had never seen the place so spotless. Ernie had cleaned and dusted every surface and piece of memorabilia in the entire cottage. The refrigerator and kitchen cabinets were stuffed with food. All the linens had been washed and the beds changed and remade. Ernie even left fresh cut flowers on the coffee table.

Katie had been in bed so long, she asked if she could just stay out on the couch for a little while. Rainey got out blankets and pillows, while Freddie twirled around her ankles. He was glad to see her, but when Rainey put the blankets on Katie, Freddie curled up with her on the couch, forgetting about missing Rainey. Rainey found picnic ham and potato salad already made in the refrigerator. She sliced some of Thelma's tomatoes and fed everyone, including the agents, rewarding them for helping carry all eight pieces of Katie's luggage up the stairs. Katie's sisters were not sure when Katie would get back into her house, so they went overboard on the packing.

Mackie took the agents on a tour of the area, since it was this duo's first trip out to the cottage. Rainey gave Katie a pain pill and left her happily on the couch, channel surfing. Rainey went to take a shower, in the big bathroom. While drying off in the master bedroom, she decided it was time to move into the larger room. With Katie living here now, there was no need for them to share the much smaller bedroom when the master suite was empty. It also had access to the deck, through patio doors, even though she added a massive hasp and padlocked them shut when she moved in. It was time to move on, Rainey told herself.

Rainey and Mackie moved her dad's old things out of the master bedroom. Rainey replaced the king mattress set, last year, anticipating moving in the room one day. Basically she traded the manly furniture for the more feminine and moved her clothes into the big walk-in closet. Once finished, it almost looked like a woman's room, but it could still use Katie's touch later, when she felt up to it. Rainey saw how well Katie decorated her own house and she was happy to let her redo this old cottage into a more livable space for two women. The thought of living with Katie was becoming a reality, much quicker than Rainey could have imagined.

Rainey left her dad's tall chest of drawers, using it for Katie's things. She hung up Katie's dress clothes in the closet and stored her luggage in the old bedroom. Rainey wanted Katie to feel comfortable and at home, especially since this was a step down from Katie's previous home. For the first time, Rainey thought about the empty lot next door to the cottage. Her father always said it was for when she was ready to build a house. Maybe she would build now, a real house with a porch and a swing. "Don't get ahead of yourself, Rainey, she's only been here a few hours."

In the meantime, Katie fell asleep, the remote still in her hand. The afternoon had been long and tiring for her and evidently Freddie, too. The two slept on the couch throughout the bedroom switch. Mackie went back outside, to spend the night in the Escalade, something he preferred to do, rather than stay cooped up in the cottage. The stay in the hospital had made Mackie feel caged, too. He was glad to have his freedom back and opted to keep the agents company outside, while the women were locked away behind an alarm, in the cottage.

Rainey handed out bug spray, a cooler with water and snacks, and locked the door. She called Danny to check on the location of Taylor, before she went to bed.

"Where are you?" she asked.

She could tell Danny was in a moving car, when he said, "I'm in a surveillance vehicle following our suspect to... we think... yes, to his lawyer's home."

Rainey heard the car stop and someone slide the transmission into park. "What's he doing?"

"It looks like he's going in for a consultation with JW," Danny said, sizing up the situation. Then he turned his attention to Rainey. "Everything all set out there?"

"Mackie and the other guys are down below, so I guess we're pretty safe up here. There are only two ways up and they have them both covered. You stay awake now. I'm going to sleep in a bed for the first time in days," Rainey said.

"Get a good night's sleep, Rainey. I'll call you in the morning,"

"Not too early," Rainey said, before hanging up.

Rainey woke Katie, so she could feed her again and give her a pain pill. Rainey had experienced pain pills on an empty stomach and would not do that to Katie. They shared a plate of ham, potato salad, and cubes of cold watermelon. The meal finished, Rainey gave Katie her pill and took her into the newly decorated master bedroom. Katie was delighted and hugged Rainey for all the hard work.

Rainey went around the cottage cutting off lights and getting ready for bed. She checked the locks on all the windows and doors one more time and double-checked that the alarm was set. When she came back into the bedroom, Katie was already in bed, but she wasn't lying down. Rainey looked at Katie's puzzled face.

"What is it, Katie?"

"Which side of the bed do you want?" Katie asked, as if it were a major decision.

Rainey thought for a second and then said, "It really doesn't matter to me, you pick."

Rainey could tell Katie had been thinking about this for a few minutes, when Katie said, "Well, I think, since you're the one with the gun, you should sleep on the side nearest the door."

"That's good thinking," Rainey said, turning her back to Katie, while she took off her tee shirt, near the dresser.

Rainey found a fresh white one and put it on, then took off her pants and socks. She was walking toward the hamper, when she noticed Katie wasn't talking anymore. Rainey stopped in mid-step, realizing Katie was watching her.

"What?" Rainey said, looking down to see if she had forgotten something.

Katie said, "Come here."

Rainey put the clothes in the hamper and walked to the side of the bed, where Katie now sat, dangling her feet over the side.

Katie put out her hands for Rainey to come closer. Rainey stepped up close to Katie, who spread her legs so Rainey could get as close as possible. Katie took the front of Rainey's tee shirt and pulled it up, exposing the scar. She leaned in and kissed it softly with her still cracked lips. She pulled the shirt back down and looked up at Rainey.

"Rainey, when you take your shirt off, you don't have to turn your back to me. That scar doesn't freak me out or bother me. I love you, all of you. You don't have to hide it from me."

Rainey hugged Katie to her and kissed her on the head. "Okay, I won't."

Rainey climbed into the right side of the bed and Katie lay down on the left. It worked from the first moment Katie spooned into Rainey's arms. Freddie joined them, curling up with Katie. Rainey fell asleep, with Katie's soft breathing and Freddie's purring the only sounds in the room. She said a silent prayer, before she dropped off.

"Watch over us, tonight, Dad. Watch over us, always."

CHAPTER TWENTY-SEVEN

Rainey was awakened at six o'clock in the morning by the ringing of her cellphone. She was now facing the door, with Katie behind her, snuggled up close. Rainey reached for the phone, trying not to wake Katie. She saw that it was Danny and flipped open the phone.

"I told you not to call too early," she said sleepily into the phone.

Her heart dropped at the first sound of his voice. "Rainey, he's in the wind."

Rainey bolted upright. "What do you mean, he's in the wind? I thought you were watching him."

Danny tried to explain. "He never left JW's house last night. Then the next thing we know, JW comes out this morning to tell us Taylor vanished."

"How is that possible, Danny?" Rainey said, looking at Katie, who was now wide-awake.

"JW said, when he went to bed, Taylor was on the couch passed out. When he woke up, Taylor was gone. We don't know how he got past us. We had four cars out here."

"Did JW not set the alarm?" Rainey asked.

"He said he forgot." Danny was upset. Rainey could hear it in his voice. She could tell Danny never wanted to make this call. "I interviewed JW and he said he thought Taylor got spooked. JW told Taylor he would get the needle, if he were convicted. JW doesn't believe Taylor did the crimes, but he thinks he was scared enough to flee the country. With his money, it would be easy."

Rainey asked, "Did you check his financials?"

Danny let out a sigh. "Yeah, he cashed a check for one hundred thousand dollars yesterday. He told his wife it was for JW's fees."

"And, I'm guessing, JW doesn't have it," Rainey said, letting out a sigh of her own.

"Bingo."

"Jesus, Danny," Rainey said, in exasperation. She could not look at Katie. She did not want to see the fear in her eyes, again.

"I know, Rainey, I'm sorry. We're checking all modes of transportation out of the area. We have a nationwide BOLO in the works. I'll find him, Rainey," Danny said, but his words, by now, were sounding hollow.

"Yeah, Danny, you find him," Rainey said, and hung up.

Rainey sat with her knees pulled up in front of her, her arms clasped around them. Katie rested a hand on Rainey's arm. Rainey turned to look into Katie's face. "Taylor's gone. He's in the wind."

"I gathered that from your conversation. What does it have to do with JW?" Katie asked.

"Taylor was at JW's last night. When JW got up this morning, Taylor was gone. He has one hundred thousand dollars cash on him and he has vanished," Rainey explained.

"Maybe he took the money and ran," Katie suggested.

"Let's hope so and that he never comes back," Rainey said, wishing against hope, that it was true.

Rainey got out of the bed and began to pace the room. Katie watched from her seat, on the bed, seeming to understand Rainey needed to vent.

"Goddamnit!—Fuck!—How can one fucking guy be so hard to watch? He got past eight agents, on foot. Once again, he's made fucking fools of all of us."

"I don't remember you being there. I could have sworn you were here with me all night."

"You know what I mean," Rainey responded.

260

"No, Rainey, I don't know what you mean," Katie said, arguing, "Who has he made a fucking fool out of? Certainly not me. He kidnapped me, he brutalized me, he raped me, but he did not make a fool out of me and, from where I sit, he didn't make a fool out of you either."

"No, of course I didn't mean you or me. It's just—I can't believe he got away, again. It's too fucked up for words," Rainey said, looking at Katie for an answer, because she did not have one of her own.

Katie got up from the bed and began making it. Rainey stopped agonizing long enough to say, "What are you doing?"

"I can't lie here with you freaking out," Katie said, pulling up the covers. "I'll go make some coffee so you can think straight."

Rainey pulled the covers away from Katie. "No, you're supposed to take it easy. Get back in bed. I'll make the coffee."

Katie yanked the covers back. "No, you get dressed and go work this mess out with Mackie. The sooner you do it, the sooner I can relax and vegetate on the couch."

Rainey saw there was no use arguing, once Katie decided it was going to go her way. Rainey acquiesced and got dressed. Katie had the coffee ready for Rainey, when she came out of the bedroom, once again in BDUs and black tee shirt. Rainey got on her cell and called Mackie to come upstairs. Katie sat down on the couch with her own coffee and flipped on the local morning news.

At six thirty, they broke with the news of the suspected Y-Man's escape from the clutches of the FBI. The news channel showed a picture of Dr. John Taylor, as the alleged killer, no more vague suggestive titles. Katie watched as images of her house flashed by on the screen and then a picture of the farmhouse, which was of more interest to her. It was stock footage from Monday night. Katie watched herself roll by on a stretcher, Rainey at her side, and then the screen image returned to the tanned face and white teeth of the reporter reading the story. Watching Katie watch herself felt surreal to Rainey.

Mackie tapped on the door. Rainey let him in. From the expression on his face, it was apparent he already knew what had happened. Rainey saw that new agents had arrived for a shift change, and figured they brought the bad news. Mackie said hello to Katie, then he and Rainey sat at the kitchen table to talk. They left Katie engrossed in The Today Show. Rainey poured Mackie a mug of coffee and sat down across from him. They sipped silently for a few minutes, both lost in thought.

Finally Mackie said, "I got you a new shoulder holster yesterday. They're keeping yours and your pistols as evidence. I did get your shotgun back. It's in the back of your car with the shoulder holster. You want me to bring them both in?"

"Yes," Rainey said, her tone defeated.

"Rainey, you can't get beat down. It won't help what's happening."

"I know, I just need a minute to finish my pity party and then I'll be okay," Rainey smiled and patted his big paw.

Mackie leaned in. "Don't let Katie see you feeling sorry for yourself." He motioned over his shoulder to Katie in the main room.

Rainey laughed. "Too late. She already has."

"What did she say?" Mackie wanted to know.

"She basically told me to get my ass dressed and deal with it, so here I sit with you, drinking coffee."

Mackie raised his head and laughed loudly. He said, "I like this girl."

Katie's voice came from the living room. "What's going on in there? I thought you were trying to figure out how to keep a madman from killing us all, not having a party."

Rainey shouted back, "It's not that kind of –" She stopped shouting, because Katie suddenly appeared, coffee mug in hand.

Katie raised her mug. "Refills anyone?"

Rainey stood up and took Katie's coffee mug, saying, "Please sit down. You are supposed to be resting."

"I was resting and now I need more coffee," Katie said, even though she sat as Rainey had asked her to.

Rainey poured everyone more coffee, while telling Katie, "If you don't behave, I'll take you back to the hospital."

Katie smiled at Rainey. "You wouldn't take me back. You like being out of there as much as I do."

"I'll have to take you back, if you collapse from exhaustion," Rainey countered.

Mackie started to laugh again. "You two sound like an old married couple, already."

Katie laughed as well. Rainey sat down, less amused. "I'm serious. She's supposed to be on bed rest."

Katie patted Rainey's hand. "Okay, I'll lie back down after breakfast. I'm starving." Katie started to get up and saw the look of disbelief Rainey was giving her. "Why don't you fix me something, while I sit right here and relax?"

Rainey smiled. She finally won a round. She asked, "Ham and eggs okay with everyone?"

Mackie and Katie agreed that ham and eggs would be great and Rainey began to cook. While she worked, the three talked about what to do, now.

Katie said, "I really don't see what's so different. We were going to have to stay in the house for a week, anyway, because as you say, I am supposed to be on bed rest."

"The difference is, we wouldn't be looking over our shoulders all the time, if we knew where he was," Rainey said, stirring the scrambled eggs. "Do you guys want cheese in the eggs?" she asked.

Mackie said, "Sounds good," and Katie agreed.

"We won't know for sure until the DNA comes back, if Taylor was the guy," Mackie said, adding, "Stay prepared until we know for sure, that way we're ready for anything. That was the plan originally, nothing's changed."

Katie said, "So stop being a grouch and let's just get through this."

"I am not being a grouch," Rainey shot back, though she was smiling, "I'm just a little pissed, that's all."

On cue, Rainey's cell rang on the table. Katie picked it up and said, "It's Danny."

Rainey turned back to the stove. "I don't want to talk to him right now; you talk to him, Mackie."

Mackie took the phone and went into the other room, where Rainey could still hear him rumbling, in his "quiet" voice. Rainey turned on the fan in the range hood, so she would not try to listen. She did not care what Danny had to say. Rainey had not blamed Danny for letting her get attacked or even not catching the killer, but she sure as hell could blame him for this latest debacle. She was fuming and the eggs were her only outlet.

Katie came up behind her, slipping her arms around Rainey's waist. Katie said, into Rainey's shoulder, "You know, those poor eggs never did anything to you."

Rainey placed a hand over Katie's hands, now clasped at her waist. She smiled, took a deep breath, and began to take it easier on the eggs and herself. If the truth were known, Rainey was really angry with herself for not killing the bastard at the farmhouse, when she had the chance. She was so emotionally involved with the victim that she let the killer go free. Rainey could have chased him, could have probably caught him, before he could get the jeep started, but she did not run after him. Instead, she went to Katie. Rainey came to terms with it, just that minute, because there is no way she would not do the same thing, if she had it to do all over again. She also knew, in that moment, she was never going back to the FBI.

Katie sat back down, because Rainey made her. Rainey put eggs and warmed up ham on three plates, adding bread from the toaster. She poured a glass of orange juice for everyone and refilled the coffee cups. When she sat down, Katie kissed her on the cheek.

"Thank you, sweetheart," Katie said, just as Mackie came back in.

Mackie sat down and told them what Danny had to say. "A man fitting John Taylor's description, using the name John Wilson, JW's driver's license and credit card, bought a ticket at five thirty this morning bound for Philadelphia. Also, a man fitting John Taylor's description and flying under the name John Tyler is on a flight to LA that left Philly, at seven a.m. The Philly Bureau office missed the flight by minutes. It's in the air, with no scheduled stops until it reaches LAX at twelve thirty our time.

The LA field office will board the plane, before it unloads and take Taylor into custody."

"Are they sure it was him?" Katie asked.

Mackie answered, "Well, we know that it wasn't JW at the airport here, and JW says his license and black American Express card are missing from his wallet."

Rainey said, "What about security video?"

"Guy wore a hat and sunglasses, most of the time. He had one carry-on, that's it, so he bought his ticket at the kiosk. Didn't have to speak to anybody," Mackie said, between bites of egg and ham, "And the same guy definitely got off the plane, in Philadelphia, but there were no clear pictures of him boarding the LAX flight. The gate crew was shown Taylor's picture and they say he is on board."

Rainey relaxed a bit. In a little more than four hours, they would know if John Taylor was in custody. All they could do was wait. Rainey made Katie take a pain pill and the anti-biotic she had to take twice a day. She fluffed the pillows on the couch and forced Katie to lie down at least, if she wouldn't go back to bed. Rainey washed the dishes and Mackie went back outside, with coffee for the new shift of agents, and sent Rainey's shoulder holster and shotgun back up with one of them.

Rainey introduced herself to the agent, whom she did not know, and thanked him for bringing her things to her. She shut the door, reactivating the alarm. She placed the shotgun in the corner behind the front door, and put the new shoulder holster on, trying to adjust the straps while wearing it. It was not working well.

Katie said, "Come here, let me help you."

Rainey sat on the edge of the couch and let Katie tighten and loosen straps until the holster felt right. She stood up, pulled the weapon from the back of her pants, and slid it into place.

"Now, there's the hot cop I fell for," Katie said.

Rainey said it aloud for the first time, "Not for much longer."

Katie was puzzled. "Not hot or not a cop?"

"Katie, I don't want to go back to the Bureau. My heart wouldn't be in it anymore."

"Are you sure? Maybe you shouldn't make that big of a decision right now," Katie reminded her.

Rainey laughed. "Not make a big decision? What in the world do you think sleeping with you was?"

Katie smiled and grabbed Rainey's ass. "That was not a decision, that was lust."

Rainey swallowed hard. "Take your hand off me woman," she said, laughing, "you are nowhere near well enough for that."

"Okay," Katie said, "under one condition, you don't quit the FBI because of me."

"It isn't what I want to do anymore, chase murderers and child molesters. I think I put in enough time doing that. I want to do what I do now. I set my own hours and make a hell of a lot more money," Rainey said.

"Whatever makes you happy is fine with me." Katie kissed Rainey's stomach before letting her go. "Oh, and by the way, don't worry about money. I have loads of that. I'm a trust fund baby." Katie smiled a wicked grin and returned to surfing the channels.

She left Rainey to ponder that information on her own and became involved watching an old Andy Hardy movie. Rainey did another final check of the doors and windows. She only quit pacing from room to room, when Katie whined enough to get her to sit down on the couch. Rainey sat with Katie's head in her lap, until the movie was over and Katie had dropped off to sleep.

Rainey slid Katie's head off of her lap and onto the pillow, barely waking her, before Katie fell right back to sleep. Rainey stood over Katie for a moment, watching her breathe. Katie really was extraordinary and Rainey felt blessed to have her in her life.

Rainey was bored. She went to the kitchen table and took apart the Sig Sauer. Rainey laid the pieces of the pistol on a towel and got out the gun cleaning kit. She had not cleaned the weapon since firing it Monday night. She busied herself with cleaning every nook and cranny of the weapon. About halfway through, she heard a car door slam.

Rainey heard a male voice outside, a familiar voice she did not expect to hear. It was JW. She went to the window to see him walking up to Mackie's Escalade window, holding four large Styrofoam cups with straws and lids. He appeared to be offering one to Mackie, who rolled down his window and accepted the cup. He disappeared from sight, under the cottage, where Rainey figured the agents were standing out of the sun, because she heard JW say, "Hello fellas, brought you some ice tea," rather loudly. After a moment, JW stepped back out and got in the passenger side of the Mackie's SUV. Rainey could tell they were talking, because one of Mackie's hands was gesturing, as it usually did, when Mackie was talking seriously. Rainey hoped Mackie was explaining to JW why he could not come into the cottage.

Rainey decided she should wake Katie and get her out of the main room. In case she had to talk to JW, she did not want Katie to listen to his ravings, as of late.

"Katie, honey, let me put you in the bed," Rainey said, shaking Katie's shoulder.

Katie barely opened her eyes, leaning on Rainey, as she walked to the bedroom. She climbed between the sheets and immediately returned to sleep. Rainey pulled the covers up around Katie and kissed her on the head, before leaving her in the bedroom. She went back out to see what had happened with JW.

She arrived back at the window, to find Freddie had come in. He was on his familiar perch, in the front window, growling. Rainey looked out to see JW, standing by Mackie's driver's side window again. All that Rainey could see of Mackie was his arm resting on the door, where the window rolled down. Rainey heard JW speaking, because he was using his loud politician, good ol' boy volume.

"Okay, Mackie, I won't be long, I promise," JW said. He now had his sleeves rolled up, with his jacket thrown over one arm, looking the part of a John Edwards "wanna be."

"Shit, Mackie's letting him come up here," Rainey said.

She went to the couch and gathered up the pillows and blankets Katie had been lying on and threw them into her old room. Rainey wasn't hiding the fact that Katie was there, she just did not want to rub JW's face in it. She was not sure what JW was planning, but she did not want to give him any excuse to lose his temper. Rainey was not afraid of JW. He was the least of her worries, at this moment, and she could always have the agents throw him out if he started getting out of control. Rainey would hate to have to shoot him.

CHAPTER TWENTY-EIGHT

Rainey heard the knock on the door and knew the time had come to face JW. She went to the door, peeked through the curtain, and saw him standing outside the door alone. The agents must have decided to let him come up by himself. He smiled and waved at her through the window in the door. Rainey deactivated the alarm and opened the door.

"Rainey, I am here to apologize to you for my recent behavior and to talk to Katie," JW said. He must have seen a look in Rainey's face that made him add, "I am not here to bother her. I want her to know I will not stand in the way of the divorce. She wants out of our marriage and I owe her that much."

Rainey thought he was just trying to cover his ass and keep Katie from going public with what she knew about him, but she did not say anything. Instead, she stepped aside and let him in.

"Come on in," she said, "May I offer you tea or water?"

"I'm okay, thank you. I just had a large tea with Mackie. I had to talk him into letting me come up here."

"Have a seat," Rainey said, moving over to sit in Mackie's big chair.

JW sat down on the couch. He looked around the room, saying, "Wow, your dad really collected a lot of memorabilia."

"Yes, he did and now I have to find a museum to donate most of it to," Rainey said.

"So, where is Katie?" JW asked.

"She's asleep, in the back bedroom."

JW set his coat down on the couch beside him and leaned forward, clasping his hands and resting his elbows on his knees. Rainey could tell he was trying to find the right words.

Finally, he said, "You've been a really good friend to Katie. I appreciate how you've taken care of her and I need to say thank you for saving her life."

"So, you don't blame me anymore, for what happened?" Rainey asked.

"No, I realize now how twisted John Taylor was and how he used us all. I'm sorry I didn't see it before," JW said, adding, "I even talked to him about the stalking. When I told him you were in town, he's the one who suggested I see you, instead of the police."

Rainey knew how he must feel, now that he knew the truth. "He fooled a lot of people, JW. From what I know about this guy, he spent a great deal of time planning this out, right down to his most recent escape."

JW sat back against the couch. "Would you say he's one of the smartest criminals you've ever dealt with?"

What an odd question, Rainey thought, but answered, "One of the luckiest, I'd have to admit."

"So, still not ready to concede he outsmarted the FBI, not once, but three times?" JW asked.

Rainey felt a bit defensive and said, "He made mistakes. He just got away with them, until now. Not real smart to use property that could be traced back to him."

"Yet, he got away," JW countered.

Rainey really didn't want to debate the efforts of the FBI with JW. She would prefer he say what he had to say and leave. His cologne was making her sick. JW must go through a gallon of that stuff a month.

JW continued his thoughts about the case. "Isn't it amazing that you could know someone almost your whole life and not really know them?"

Rainey thought that was true of how she felt about JW, now that she knew what Katie told her. She agreed, "Yes, that is remarkable."

Rainey's attention was drawn to Freddie, who leapt down from the windowsill, hissed at JW, and disappeared into the kitchen. Rainey had never seen him act like that. He must smell how nervous Rainey was around JW. She was nervous. Her palms were beginning to sweat. It felt weird, but she was sleeping with his wife and that could make anybody apprehensive.

She said, "I'm sorry, he isn't used to strangers."

JW smiled. "It's okay, maybe he's a democrat."

Rainey laughed. "Most folks around here are."

There was an awkward silence between them. JW stood up and crossed to the bookshelf. He picked up a round from an AK47, examined it, replaced it, and moved on to another piece of weaponry. His back was turned to Rainey, as he quietly studied the items on the bookshelves.

He stopped and asked, "What's this?"

Rainey stood and joined him, looking to see what he had in his hand. It was the dagger that Billy Bell had taken from his would be killer. She took the dagger from JW's hands. She studied the blood patterns on the cloth handle. Rainey felt the hair on her neck and arms stand up. The dagger never caused that reaction before, but then she hadn't known the story of how it ended up here.

Rainey answered, "It's a dagger my father took off of a guy who almost killed him."

They were standing very close together. JW's cologne was really bothering her. She needed to move away from him, or she thought she would be sick. Rainey turned to JW, handing him the dagger back. He looked at it, twirling the tip of the blade against his forefinger. He turned his eyes from the blade and looked down at Rainey.

JW asked, a peculiar smile on his face, "Are these real blood stains?"

Rainey met his gaze. His blue eyes where almost twinkling with delight. A spark of recognition sent a jolt of adrenaline through her heart and in that instant she knew she was looking into the eyes of her attacker. She blinked once to make sure, but there was no doubt in her mind, JW was Johnny. His cologne was making her sick, because it was the smell she had associated with her rapist. Her body knew JW was the man she had so desperately wanted to find. It was screaming at her to run.

Rainey could not run. Katie was in the other room. Rainey's pistol was in pieces on the kitchen table. If she could get to the bedroom there were other weapons at her disposal, but first she had to get there. Her cellphone was on the coffee table, in front of the couch. Rainey could not let JW know she had recognized him for who he really was. Rainey needed a plan and fast. "Think Rainey, think," her mind shrieked.

"Yeah, that's real blood. You should ask Mackie about that, the next time you talk to him," Rainey said, turning away, so JW couldn't see her face. She stepped over by the window and saw that Mackie's arm was still in the same place on the windowsill of the car. Her heart sank. Mackie was probably dead. The agents had probably been dealt with also.

JW put the dagger down and moved back to the couch. If he had a weapon, it was probably in his coat, Rainey was thinking. He was now between Rainey and the shotgun by the front door, but he left a clear path to the bedroom, where Katie slept. If she ran toward the back bedroom, he would be on top of her before she could get out of the room.

Rainey tried a ruse. She smiled at him and said, "You didn't come all the way out here to talk to me. Let me go wake Katie for you. Give me a minute will you?"

Rainey didn't wait for his answer. She was moving on the first word. JW did not have time to react and did not make a move to cut her off. She took normal steps, fighting the urge to break into a run. Rainey thought she might have him fooled, until she heard the familiar sound of a revolver being cocked behind her.

Rainey dove, half-skidding and crab-crawling down the eight-foot hallway to the bedroom. The sound of a shot and splintering wood above her encouraged her body to move faster. Her hand grabbed the doorknob and, as her weight smashed up against the bedroom door, she fell through it. Another shot fired, this one going through the door, above her head, just as she slammed it shut.

Rainey ran to the other side of her father's big, heavy chest of drawers and knocked it over, in front of the bedroom door. It did not fall all the way over, but wedged itself into the wall, on the other side of the door. Rainey grabbed her father's shotgun from the corner, before diving for the bed. Katie, who was now sitting up, with a wide-eyed look of shock on her face, grunted when Rainey slammed into her, pulling her off the bed and onto the floor, away from the door.

JW's body crashed against the door. The maniacal voice of the madman, screamed out, in the little boy voice, "Open the door, Rainey. It's time to play."

Katie whispered, "Who is that?"

Rainey answered, while looking around the room for her next move, "It's JW. He's the killer."

"What?" Katie said, astonished.

JW splintered the door with his shoulder. "I want to play with you girls. Let me in." He slammed into the door again; more wood cracked.

Rainey pumped the shotgun, stood up and blew a hole in the door. She squatted back down immediately.

Katie huddled beside her. She said, in disbelief, "JW is the Y-Man?"

Rainey peeked over the top of the bed, answering Katie, at the same time, "Yes and I don't have time to talk about it right now. I'm trying to keep him from killing us."

Rainey could see through the hole she had blown in the door that JW was either hunched down behind the dresser or not in the small hallway anymore. She got her answer, when she heard the back door open and close. If he made it onto the back deck, there would be nothing between JW and his prey, but the sliding glass doors on the opposite wall from where they were crouched.

Rainey almost threw Katie back across the bed, yelling, "Move, move. Get to the door."

Katie ran up to the chest and tried to lift it. Rainey did not want to put the shotgun down. She yelled, "Open the top drawer!"

Katie pulled the drawer open, scraping it down the wall.

Rainey yelled again, "Grab the forty-five in the corner and give it to me. Put it in my holster."

Rainey aimed the shotgun alternately down the hall and at the glass doors, unable to tell where JW was. She felt Katie slide the forty-five into the holster. Rainey handed the shotgun to Katie.

"If anything comes by that glass, aim and pull the trigger."

Katie said, "I've shot skeet, I can do this."

Katie took the gun and held it up in front of her now trembling body. Rainey wedged herself under the dresser and pushed up with her legs, lifting the corner out of the wall and up righting it. The chest wobbled with the force she put behind the lift and then fell over the other way. Rainey carefully looked through the hole in the door, and then opened it.

She pulled the forty-five out and took hold of Katie's arm, leading her down the hallway, with Katie walking backwards aiming the shotgun into the bedroom. Rainey could only see a small portion of the main room. She had no way of knowing exactly where JW was standing. If he stood in the archway to the kitchen, he could see the top of both sets of stairs, the only avenues of escape for Rainey and Katie. If Rainey peeked around the corner, JW could blow her head off.

Freddie startled Rainey and almost got shot, when he jumped on the corner of the bookshelf unit, closest to the hallway. He did not look at Rainey, but cowered, ears back, growling in the direction of the kitchen and Rainey's blind spot. Katie and Rainey pressed their backs against the wall between them and the kitchen, inching closer to the corner. Rainey's heart was thumping so loudly in her chest, she was sure Katie could hear it, but Rainey could not slow her breathing.

Rainey's hands began to shake, caused by the adrenaline rushing through her bloodstream. Her body knew she was in trouble and the fight or flight response had taken over her brain. Rainey stopped going forward, two feet from the end of the wall.

With hand signals, she indicated to Katie that she should stay put, careful not to make noise. Rainey knelt down, staying low, and crossed the hall. Pressing her back against the wall opposite Katie, she peeked around the corner.

From her vantage point, Rainey could see most of the main room, the front window, and the front door. If she made a break for the cover of the couch, she might be able to reach her cellphone. But if he saw her, he would be all over her. If she were alone, Rainey might take the chance, and just start blazing away at whatever was around the corner. She was a trained agent. The probability was good that she would kill him before he got her, but if he killed Rainey that would leave Katie to defend herself alone against JW.

JW had brought a revolver with him, but now that he was in the cottage, loaded weapons surrounded him. He might already have the shotgun Rainey left by the front door. At the end of the hallway, one way opened into the main room, the other led to Rainey's old bedroom. The door was open and they could be in that room in one step. With the door shut and barricaded, Rainey would have a better defensive front than the one she found herself in this moment. Rainey slid back across the floor and stood up beside Katie. She motioned with her free hand what was to happen next.

Rainey turned the corner quickly, firing twice in what had been her blind spot. Katie bolted behind her into the open doorway of Rainey's old room. Rainey fired once more, this time hitting the alarm panel by the front door. She hoped the redundant systems she had in place would realize the alarm had been rendered inoperable, alerting the alarm company. Rainey stepped in the bedroom, just as a bullet shattered the doorframe beside her. Katie slammed the door.

Rainey and Katie pushed the dresser over in front of the door. It would not stop him, but it would slow him down. Her answer, as to whether JW had found the shotgun, came when a blast slammed into the other side of the wall, where the bookshelf was. Rainey pushed Katie down behind the bed. She pulled the mattress over them, protecting them from the splintering wood

275

and shrapnel. Rainey was relieved to see that Freddie had sprinted into the bedroom behind Katie. He flashed through the room, taking shelter in the bathroom.

Jumping from the only windows in the room meant a drop of more than fifteen feet onto hard ground. Rainey put the forty-five in the holster and, crawling over Katie, grabbed her father's other shotgun, by the bathroom door. There was only one way out of this room, without going through the door. The floors were too thick to blast through, but the exterior wall was only seven and a half inches thick. The front deck continued just on the other side of that wall.

When JW ran out of shotgun shells, she heard him throw the gun down, his footsteps nearing the bedroom door. She heard him say, "Oh, Katie," in his singsong child voice, "Katie, you know I killed the baby, so I wouldn't have to share you with another little boy."

Rainey scrambled to her feet, yanked out the forty-five and fired into the wall and door, hopeful of hitting JW, or at least sending him toward the back of the house. After six rounds, Rainey put the forty-five back in the holster, picked up the shotgun, and pumped all nine shells into the exterior wall.

Rainey grabbed Katie, who was still clutching the other shotgun, leading her through the hole Rainey had just blasted in the wall. Rainey kicked the few pieces of wall left intact, pulled the forty-five again, and stepped onto the deck. She aimed the pistol at the front door, keeping her eye on the window. Nothing moved that she could see. Freddie shot out of the bedroom, through the hole and down the steps.

Rainey heard JW hit the bedroom door with two more rounds from the revolver. She screamed, "Run Katie!"

Rainey ran between Katie and the window, firing back into the house, laying down cover fire for them to make it to the stairs. Rainey heard the blast and shower of glass as JW blew out the deck doors in the master bedroom. He could be coming down the back steps or circling back through the house. Rainey had to get Katie behind cover.

When their feet hit the ground, Rainey pushed Katie toward the back of JW's car, parked in front of Mackie's Escalade. Once behind JW's car, Rainey peeked over the trunk, looking back toward the cottage. She dropped the empty magazine from the forty-five and slid a full one into the stock, racking a bullet into the chamber. She could see the two bodies of the agents, under the cottage, two large Styrofoam cups lay beside their bodies. JW had drugged everyone, with an offer of cold iced tea. It was then that she noticed Mackie was not sitting up in his vehicle anymore. Rainey had a spark of hope that he was alive.

Katie whispered behind her, "Listen."

Rainey could hear far off sirens, lots of them, coming fast, but too far away at the moment. Then Rainey heard the sounds of a struggle in the cottage above them. She knew it had to be Mackie. Rainey bolted from behind the car and charged up the steps.

Katie was screaming, "Rainey, don't! Stop!"

Rainey could not leave Mackie in the cottage, possibly fighting for his life. She took the steps two at a time. Rainey was four steps from the top, when JW's body crashed through the remains of the shattered front window, bounced off the deck railing, and collided with the ground below. Rainey turned to see JW trying to move. She ran down the steps and approached him.

JW was bleeding from his mouth and nose. He was having trouble breathing, but still attempting to crawl away. Rainey raised the pistol in her hand and aimed it at his face. She stood there trembling, staring down at the man who had brutalized and raped her, terrorized her and the woman that she loved. Now he lay dying, at her feet. The sirens were getting closer. If Rainey was going to kill him, she had to do it now.

JW sneered up at her from the ground. He said, "Do it."

Just as her finger began to squeeze the trigger of the forty-five, Rainey heard the shotgun blast pierce the air, without warning. JW's chest exploded in front of her. She jumped, turning around to see Katie had been standing behind her. She still had the smoking barrel of the shotgun aimed at JW's now dead body. A gaping hole in his chest had blown away his last breath. Rainey put her weapon in the holster and slowly took the shotgun from Katie's hands. Suddenly a revolver landed on the ground by JW's body. Rainey looked up to see Mackie, leaning over the railing, his outstretched hand having tossed the revolver.

He smiled down at Rainey and said, "That ought to take care of any question that your lives were in danger."

Rainey set the shotgun on the ground and hugged Katie to her. Katie had not said a word since firing the gun.

Katie finally whispered, "He killed my baby."

"I know, honey. I know," was all Rainey could think to say. She took Katie to the steps and sat down beside her, waiting while the sirens grew louder.

CHAPTER TWENTY-NINE

A small army, consisting of Mackie, Ernie, their families, and friends, along with Rainey and Katie descended on the cottage, as soon as the FBI and local law enforcement released the scene. Rainey, Katie, and a very angry Freddie, had only spent two nights in a safe house, to keep the press at bay and allow the crime scene techs time to do their jobs. Once Mackie's crew had cleaned up all the broken glass and splintered wood, the repairs began right away.

Rainey and Katie spent days sorting through all of Rainey's father's memorabilia. The shotgun blasts had ruined some of it, but for the most part just gave the pieces more character. She let Mackie have anything he wanted out of the collection. Rainey kept some things that held special memories for her, including the dagger with the blood stained handle. The rest she offered to the North Carolina Military History Society, which they gladly took.

Just ten days after the crime scene tape came down, Rainey and Katie were serving iced tea to the workers, who were putting the final touches on the repaired cottage. Rainey looked up to see a lone black SUV coming toward them. Rainey and Katie both dreaded this day, because what Danny was coming to talk to them about, they had tried so hard to forget. Maybe this would finally be the end of it and they could move on.

Rainey sighed and glanced at Katie, who was laughing with Thelma about something. Katie had sawdust in her hair, which was pulled up off her neck with a clip. She was wearing one of Rainey's old tee shirts, which swallowed her whole, a pair of shorts cut from sweatpants, and was covered in dirt from head to toe. While the last bits of trim were being added to the new bookcase inside, Katie had been slaving away on flower boxes. She built them herself out of scraps from the repair job and had been happily filling them with dirt for the last half hour.

Katie's bruises had almost faded away. The cuts were healing nicely and she could smile broadly again, which she did often. Katie was happy, for the most part, slipping into sadness less and less with each passing day. When those times came, Rainey did her best just to be a shoulder to lean on. Rainey did not offer advice, she simply did what she thought helped Katie the most, gave her time. Danny was coming to flip the hourglass again and they would start over, but time would heal them both, together.

Rainey looked over at Mackie. He noticed the approaching SUV, as well. Mackie had only been knocked out for a short time, from the heavy dosage of sedative given him, because he was so overweight, a fact that he reminded everyone at every meal had saved his life. Mackie put down the tomato sandwich Thelma had brought for him, a sign that he was dreading this last meeting, too.

"Katie," Rainey said, "Danny is here."

The laughter faded quickly from Katie's eyes. Thelma gave her a knowing pat on the hand, and went to say goodbye to Mackie, leaving Rainey and Katie alone. Katie looked at her hands, and made some excuse about needing to wash up. Rainey knew she was going in ahead of everyone else to gather herself for the coming storm of emotions.

Rainey grabbed Katie's hand as she passed, saying, "We'll get through this."

Katie smiled at her and said, "Yes, we will," then pecked Rainey on the cheek.

When Danny walked up to Rainey, he was carrying a thick file in one hand. Mackie dismissed the crew for the day. He explained Katie and Rainey needed some privacy with the FBI and the remaining few pieces of trim could be handled in the morning. Then Rainey, Danny, and Mackie joined Katie, who was already sitting on the new couch when they walked in. Mackie's big chair had been ruined in the firefight and replaced by two winged back chairs from Katie's former home. Mackie could not fit in them, so he stood, leaning against the wall behind the couch. Rainey joined Katie, and Danny sat opposite them in one of the chairs.

Danny began, somberly, "I wanted to meet with you one more time, before we close the investigation. I hope the information that I am about to share with you, will help explain some of the questions you may have."

Katie spoke, "Mainly, how I was married to the man for ten years and had no idea he was insane."

"He fooled a lot of people, Katie, that's what made him so dangerous," Danny replied.

"And evil," Katie added.

From an analyst's point of view, JW Wilson's criminal behavior would be something to study for years. Rainey, at one time, would have found him a fascinating research subject. Now, all she wanted was to get this meeting over with and put him out of her mind, as far as possible. Rainey decided to encourage Danny to hurry along.

"Danny, can we just get started?"

"Sure, Rainey," Danny said, "First let me explain what happened to John Taylor. As you know we still have not found his body, but we did find his blood in the trunk of JW's car. JW killed him and gave a homeless man, who just happened to look like JW and Taylor, twenty thousand dollars to fly to Philadelphia and disappear. The homeless man came forward after the news broke and he realized we were looking for him. There was a John Tyler on the flight to LA, but he really was John Tyler, not Taylor. It was just a coincidence. JW set Taylor up, because he needed an out. He knew we were getting too close. He thought, if he gave us someone else, he could get away with murder, go on with his bid for Senator, and avoid a nasty

281

divorce in the process, had he succeeded in killing Katie. I believe that was his intent. His mistake was he thought he could kill you both and then he would stop."

Rainey broke in. "He had to know the DNA would not match Taylor. He knew we would keep looking."

"Well, that is the really interesting part," Danny said. "Taylor's wife told us that JW convinced John to donate sperm in his name. The two men looked so much alike no one would have ever known. JW's sperm count was too low to get Katie pregnant. John and his wife discussed it, and since they were not going to have children, they thought it was a good thing to do. JW made John swear never to tell anyone. He did not know John had told his wife."

Katie was beyond shocked. She asked Danny, "So, John's sperm was implanted in my egg? How did JW think he could get away with that?"

"When he turned in the specimen at the doctor's office, JW must have kept some for himself. That's what he put on Katie, so we would think we had the right guy. The lab knew something was wrong with the sample and this explains it."

"He was planning this for a long time, wasn't he?" Katie said, quietly.

Danny nodded in agreement. "Yes, he planned things out far in advance. That was part of what made it hard to catch him. He was very cunning."

"But why get me involved, in the first place?" Rainey asked.

"JW found out you were back home. He needed an excuse to be around you. JW knew you didn't know he attacked you. He must have gotten such gratification from your assault, he could not resist coming after you again, and having the FBI to challenge fed his fantasy. It was the ultimate fulfillment of his need for sexual dominance at the destructive expense of the victim, in your case, the ultimate victim, that motivated his every move."

Katie said, "He didn't just start killing for no reason. He must have shown some signs of this behavior, at some point, but then I didn't see it either, until he raped me, and then I just thought he was a pervert, not a murderer."

Danny opened the file. He did not need it. He spoke from memory, telling the tale of one JW Wilson. "It appears JW had mental problems that were identified back when he was eleven years old. JW had become rebellious and assaultive to adults, abusive to his sisters, and was caught peeping into a neighbor's windows. He was found to be in possession of porn and bondage materials he claimed to have gotten from an older boy. Both boys were involved in a very unhealthy, sexual relationship with an older woman. His parents were a drunk ambivalent mother, who left the raising of the children to the nanny, and a cold uncaring father, who threw money at the situation. JW was sent to a special hospital in Europe for adolescent males, specializing in sexual dysfunction."

"No one ever told me that," Katie said.

Danny continued, "During his stay in the hospital he claimed his three older sisters terrorized him. They played doctor with him and made fun of his penis. He admitted, in therapy, that he fantasized about hurting women. He learned quickly that telling the truth about his fantasies got him into trouble. Young JW learned to hide his real feelings and became the All-American boy."

"I remember when he came back from Europe, telling us stories of snow skiing in the Alps all summer," Rainey said.

"He became an accomplished liar, at an early age," Danny said, "but the trouble he found himself in his senior year brought his sadistic fantasies back to the surface. His father shoved the "misunderstanding" under the rug with his money. The father also took JW to the morgue and showed him female autopsy victims, reminding him that he could have killed the girl and then he would be facing prison. It was his father's idea of scared straight, but it must have turned JW on. His father had no idea that he introduced his son to the image that would drive JW's fantasies, from that moment on."

"I wish you could prosecute his father," Katie said.

"I agree he's a jackass," Rainey said, "but I don't think he knew things were as bad as they were. JW was on steroids back then. He claimed the incident was a case of 'roid rage.' It's probably what made him lose the control of his sexual fantasies that he worked so hard to keep hidden."

"Maybe Daddy didn't know the whole story," Danny added. "We would not have known either, but we tracked down his victim, who now lives in another state. She told me that JW drugged her and then raped her unconscious body. When she awoke during the attack, he beat her brutally. She played dead. He raped her again and then left her, presumably knocked out, while he went back to the party. She escaped and was sure he would have killed her, if she had not. Her parents contacted JW's father while she was recovering in the hospital and money exchanged hands. No police report was ever filed. She never came forward, after JW ran for political office, because she was still afraid he might find her."

Katie quipped, "Well, there's another person who's glad he's dead."

Danny went on, as though Katie had said nothing, "His medical records indicate he began having erectile dysfunction fairly early, in his twenties, and required a drug to perform. The fact he could not produce a child highlighted this dysfunction. This must have been the breaking point, where he lost control of his fantasies. How else do we explain his coming up with the crazy idea to substitute John's sperm? He wanted no one to know he could not produce an heir, even Katie. We discovered that the timeline of the killings we know about, correspond to days JW went with Katie to the fertility doctor. The treatments must have reminded him of his sexual inadequacies."

Katie stiffened. Rainey put her arm around Katie's shoulder, for support. The hard part was coming. None of the rest mattered to Katie. She wanted to know why he killed her baby.

Danny cleared his throat, before continuing, "Rainey can tell you that sexual murderers are often times recreating the preferred adult/child pairing of the original sexual abuse. JW's abuser was a woman. In his sexual fantasies, JW was 'little Johnny.' When you finally became pregnant, JW learned it was going to be a boy. We can only guess that his psyche could not handle competition from another little boy, and a widower makes a great political candidate. We assume he unbuckled your seatbelt, opened the passenger door, and slammed into the tree, on purpose. We will never know for sure. He could have made that up to hurt you, Katie, there is no evidence to prove one way or another."

Katie whispered, "He did it. I know he did."

Rainey would have killed JW, if he had not already been dead. She wanted to know Katie was in the clear on the shooting. She asked, "Danny, what about his death? What does the state's attorney say?"

Danny smiled for the first time since he arrived. He answered, "There will be no charges. The official finding is self defense."

"There was never really any question about that. It's just nice to hear," Mackie's voice rumbled out behind them.

Danny closed the file. He looked at the two women, finishing his report with, "JW Wilson was a sick man for a very long time. His family knew it and covered it up. His oldest sister came forward with most of the information, after he was dead. She claimed they all thought the trip to Europe had cured him. No one, not a single person who knew him, suspected JW was anything other than what he portrayed himself to be."

Danny stood up to leave. Rainey and Katie stood, as well, and each of them gave him a hug and thanked him.

Mackie said, "I believe I'll just shake your hand and tell you that the next time I see you, I hope you're here to go fishing."

"That's a deal," Danny said and then Rainey walked him out to his SUV.

When Danny got in the driver's side and closed the door, Rainey waited while he started the car and rolled the window down.

"Danny, I'm done," she said.

"I'm glad we can finally close this case," Danny replied.

Rainey reached in her back pocket and took out the leather case, which held her FBI shield. She handed it through the window, saying, "No, I mean, I'm done with the Bureau. I want you to turn my shield in for me."

"Rainey, you just need some more time. All this just happened. Make the decision when you've had time to recover, not now," Danny pleaded.

"I don't need time, Danny. I know what I want to do with the rest of my life and chasing serial killers is not on the list. I'm going to spend my time being happy, with Katie."

Rainey had not talked with Danny about her relationship with Katie. He was a profiler. He could figure it out.

Danny put the SUV in reverse and then took the shield from Rainey's outstretched hand. He looked up at the cottage and then back at Rainey. "She's really special. I hope you two have some happiness now, you both deserve it."

Rainey smiled at him. "Thank you, Danny. Call me."

Danny drove away, with Rainey standing in the driveway, until she could no longer see the big SUV. Mackie was coming down the steps, when she finally turned to go back inside.

"I just became a full time bail bondsman, Mackie. I turned in my shield," she said, to the big man.

Mackie grinned from ear to ear. "I'm glad to hear that. I'm tired of chasing you around, trying to keep you safe from crazy ass killers."

"What would you do without me around to rescue? You'd be so bored, you'd get as big around as a house," Rainey teased.

"Don't forget, this girth saved my ass and yours," he said, laughing. "I'm going on home, now. I'll see you tomorrow."

"See you tomorrow," Rainey said, climbing the stairs to the cottage.

Rainey entered the main room and did not see Katie. She looked in the kitchen and then went to the master bedroom. Katie had redecorated the room. It now had a Laura Ashley floral print theme, which made it much more feminine than it had been before. Rainey found Katie lying in the bed, on top of the covers.

"You are entirely too dirty to be lying on that new comforter," Rainey said, hoping Katie would laugh. When she did not, Rainey climbed in the bed beside Katie, putting her arms around the smaller woman and spooning her into her hips, not saying anything else.

They stayed like that for a few minutes, not talking, and then Katie rolled over to face Rainey, still wrapped in her arms. "Are you happy?" she asked.

Rainey kissed her softly and said, "Yes, I am. Are you?"

"Yes," Katie answered, "I feel like I wasted so much of my life, not being with you."

"I just turned in my shield, to Danny, so you can be with me all the time," Rainey said.

"Did you?" Katie said, smiling.

"Yes, I did. We're going to be happy Katie, I promise," Rainey said, then kissed Katie on the forehead, pulling her closer.

There was a pause, before Katie asked, quietly, "Rainey, can we have children?"

Rainey pulled back and looked into Katie's eyes. She would do anything to make this woman happy, anything at all. She kissed Katie's lips, while she said, "Yes, but under one condition."

Rainey felt Katie's lips curve into a smile. Katie whispered against Rainey's lips, "What is that?"

Rainey stopped kissing Katie, and leaned back on her elbow. She looked at Katie, trying to sound very serious. "Well, two conditions actually. If we don't adopt, then you have to carry the babies," then she smiled, "and they all have to look like you."

Katie pulled Rainey down on top of her, sending shock waves of electricity through Rainey. She had made no move to do anything but hold Katie through the night, since the attack. When Katie was ready, Rainey knew she would let her know. Still, she tried to fight the overwhelming desire that had taken over her mind and body, not sure of what Katie really wanted. Katie arched into Rainey and a little moan escaped her throat, which sent Rainey into orbit.

Katie grabbed at Rainey's shirt, trying to pull it over Rainey's head. Rainey did not think about the scar, nor did she hesitate. She sat up on her knees, straddling Katie, and ripped the shirt over her head in one move. Katie smiled up at her and then reached up to Rainey, pulling Rainey's lips back to hers. They kissed more deeply than ever before, any remaining walls between them melting away with each passing moment.

When they broke for air, Katie said, breathlessly, "If you were having any doubts about when I would be ready for you to make love to me, now would be a good time."

Rainey smiled and began the rest of her life that second, never looking back.

About the Author...

Lambda Literary Award Finalist, R. E. Bradshaw, a native of North Carolina and a proud Tar Heel, now makes her home in Oklahoma with her wife of 25 years. She is the proud mother of Jon, a very fine young man raised by lesbians. (Authors note: "Bite me, Family Research Council.") Holding a Master of Performing Arts degree, Bradshaw worked in professional theatre and taught University and High School classes, leaving both professions to write full-time in 2010. She continues to be one of the best selling lesbian fiction authors on Amazon.com.

Printed in Great Britain
by Amazon.co.uk, Ltd.,
Marston Gate.